Fulfilling Fate

Book Three of the Fate Unraveled Trilogy

M. A. Frick

Book cover by GetCovers.com

Scene break art by GDJ on canva.com

Rafe POV Header art by jamespaul77 on fiverr.com

To Nick.

You had faith in me when I had none. Without you, I would have never learned to soar.

Caulden

Sky Trees

Northwing

Hamsforth

Southwing

Shadowlands

The Sands

RINMOTH

STONESMEAD

LEEDS

PALACE

E'OR MOUNTAINS

KING'S WALL

REGENT

TEETH OF THE E'OR

JASIRI

GRYPHON

Prologue

Summer Year 899

I cursed and rolled down the dune as Tizmet roared. She swooped low, guarding me, knowing she put herself in danger.

'I have no fire left!'

'I know!'

In a swift motion, I caught myself and braced against the shifting sand. With a bone-chilling shriek, the creature tore over the crest, and I dropped to my knees.

A hard shell protected its massive form, and dozens of legs carried it across the gritty land with ease. The thing was huge, as long and wide as three cows. Its hundreds of shiny eyes glittered in the moonlight, reflecting everything and nothing. It screamed and tore my direction, mouth open, revealing a tunnel of teeth.

Tizmet dove. *'Move!'* she roared.

'I just need to get under it!' I said, holding my ground.

'You'll be IN it soon!' She swooped over, claws seeking purchase between its armor.

It ignored her and reared, ready to lunge. I lifted my spear and braced myself. It came down, teeth piercing my flesh. A sharp screech rent the air, and I winced at the sound. Ensnared inside its mouth, I grimaced and thrust my weapon higher, giving a twist for good measure.

Somewhere outside, Tizmet shrieked. The insect shuddered once—then died.

I roared our victory. *'It's dead!'*

'So are you!' she shouted.

With a jerk, the carcass ripped off me. I cried out as its teeth slid across my body, digging gashes into my flesh. Tizmet tossed the beast aside as I fell. She nuzzled me, concern rolling off her.

I mustered a weak assurance. *'Not dead.'*

My blood dampened the sand as she channeled magic to heal me.

'Don't pull too much.'

We were too tired. She'd been flying non-stop, trying to avoid the great predators that roamed the Sands. With empty stomachs and aching thirst, our energy drained to where even the thought of hunting for food or digging for water seemed impossible.

The familiar sting of healing struck me. Agony blossomed in my chest, blooming outwards. I gritted my teeth as a seizure took me, trying to throw my spear free with my thrashing. We fought the creature too long. My rigid grip trapped the weapon within my grasp.

When I drifted into awareness, soft crunching greeted my ears. Hissing in pain, I rolled to my side. Tizmet tore into the insect. Great globs of green murky sludge oozed past her teeth.

Her wild eyes narrowed. '*Food.*'

I swallowed a gag as my features contorted with disgust. We'd been in the Sands for a long time—too long by my account. Days melded into one another, and our sense of direction waned.

I reached out to her, hand shaking. My head pounded, protesting my existence. We reserved magic for healing, but even then, monsters trailed us like vultures, sensing our impending deaths.

We were weak. Helplessness welled inside me, and I couldn't muster the energy to shed a single tear. I would never see Rafe again, never write my friends.

I would die in this blasted place.

Tizmet ripped off a chunk of gooey flesh and tossed it to me. I retched at the reek of rotting, fetid meat.

'Eat,' she growled, tearing into the beast.

Another gag shuddered through me. *'I'd rather die.'*

Her irritation spilled across the bond, and she stood with a snarl. Her heavy footsteps shook the ground before her claws forced me onto my back. She brought her bright orange eye to my face and curled her lip, baring her teeth.

'You will not die. Eat.'

'I can't.'

'You will.'

'I can't–'

She sucked in a breath and roared, leaving my ears ringing. The foul stench brought tears to my eyes.

'EAT!'

My stomach revolted as she closed her maw inches from my face. Reaching over, I grabbed a handful of goo and shoved it past my lips, trying not to think about it. My throat refused to swallow, and I lurched to my side, spitting it out. It tasted far worse than it smelled. Even with an empty stomach, the idea of consuming it was out of the question.

I wiped my mouth, then met my dragon's livid glare.

She sighed, turning back to her meal. *'You will die.'*

She was right. My life would be forfeited if I succumbed to this desert. Rafe would arrive in Leeds, left to wonder about my fate. I refused to let that happen. A growl tore out of me, and I grabbed a handful of meaty goo. Scarfing it down, I devoured what I could, swallowing as much as possible before I registered the repulsive taste.

I would conquer this desert.

Chapter 1

Summer Year 900

Yet another remark aimed at my arse had me rolling my eyes and glancing over at Kila. She just shook her head, tossing her light brown hair with a sympathetic smile and served the men their ale. Humming to myself, I dried the earthen mugs and ignored the rest of the comments.

Iana came from around the corner with a clean apron tied over her ample bosom. Her dark hair lay in tight curls, escaping her bun. "We have lizard stew tonight!" she called out over the crowded room, resulting in a series of cheers.

I smirked and kept working. The lizards she referred to were massive creatures that prowled the murky bog. Their size and hardened green scales made them terrifying, but their meat was sweet and tender. Catching one was a challenge, but it played an integral role in the reason I had this job. Many would have given a limb to work here.

'*Good hunting then?*' I reached across the bond.

Tizmet circled high in the night sky. She'd been anxious all day, sticking close to my side, venturing out only to secure food for the tavern.

'*Good enough.*'

We had earned our place by providing protection and sustenance. The residential hunters petitioned against Tizmet bringing in meat, but their efforts failed. These people were always one meal short of starving.

Leeds was not a prosperous town. The hardworking populace relied on the sweat of their brow to make ends meet. In this place, every privilege had to be worked for. In exchange for my labor, I had a room and food. I earned no coin, but rather the good graces of Iana, who owned the inn and tavern. The Bog Frog Inn was the only inn within Leeds. Unlike most establishments I encountered during my travels, the sleeping quarters were separate from the tavern.

I leaned my hip against the bar and set myself to my task—cleaning cups. The glorious destiny I always knew waited for me.

"Looks like a calm crowd," Rothfuss rumbled.

I smiled over my shoulder. He was the lawkeeper. Marshal, judge and jury. He didn't just keep the law, he *was* the law. Leeds was fortunate enough to have someone fair-minded, unlike many other villages I passed through.

"Been quiet," I said, wiping another mug.

"Avyanna's been drawing tips in," Kila quipped. She tucked loose strands of her brown hair behind her ear as she dropped more dishes in front of me.

I rolled my eyes and nudged them toward the dirty pile.

Rothfuss chuckled. "I don't know of a man here who wouldn't pay double for you to serve their table."

I shook my head, and my short white braids danced about my shoulders. They made me look younger, but it was one of the few ways I kept my hair out of my way.

Kila sighed, sliding her eyes to Rothfuss. She dropped the comment for his benefit and sauntered off to tend tables.

"No trouble?"

"None yet," I said, keeping my back to him.

"I expect some."

"Oh? What makes you say that?"

He didn't speak, and I listened to the hubbub of the surrounding commoners. They were a happy lot, resigned to their fate out here on the edge of the bog. They lived day-to-day, embracing the simplicity of their earnings, finding contentment in them. I glanced behind to see Rothfuss studying me. With a sigh, I faced him, arching a brow.

His small smile softened his gruff face. A dusting of scruff permanently covered his chiseled jaw, as if he rarely found the time to shave. He tilted his head, a lock of dark hair falling over his forehead.

"When are you going to let me court you?"

I scoffed, straightening to reach for another mug. "What, are you going to take me for a romantic walk around the bog, only to return me here covered in welts from the giant suckers? Or perhaps we will stay after hours to enjoy the leftover meal, then you'll leave me to my job to clean up after you?"

"If a man wants to court a lady, there are ways to do it."

"I see little courting going on."

Leeds was a man's town. They outnumbered the women three to one. When a woman made her choice, there was only consummating and claiming. These people lived a rough life, one that did not permit luxuries like courting.

"You're different."

"That I am." I readied a glass with the tea he drank in place of ale. "I'm off limits."

He grumbled and accepted my offering. His eyes darted between the rowdy groups.

"Luther is getting his table riled, as always," I muttered, then returned to my task.

Luther was a troublemaker, ambitious, but at the expense of others. He spearheaded the hunters' efforts to have me and Tizmet expelled from this place. With his ownership of two small meat farms, he profited heavily from people's hunger. He was greedy, and I didn't like him one bit.

"Nothing wrong with getting riled," Rothfuss murmured. "Even when a little white-haired witch is doing the riling."

"I've done nothing," I shot back.

"Look here."

I glanced over my shoulder, and he motioned for me to face him. With a grumble under my breath, I obliged.

"I've gotten word there's a force over the mountain headed this way," he said.

My lips pulled into a frown. It was common for villages to feud and war with each other. Leeds held its own. Since I'd been here, we only faced one attack. With Rothfuss leading the men, and Tizmet's support, we drove them back.

"Are they bringing trouble?" I asked.

"Depends on you."

"Me?"

"They're from the foothills of the E'or, bordering Regent."

My nose twitched in a snarl, and I reined in my temper. I leaned on the bar and brought my face close to his.

"I swore to you once. I'm not running from anyone."

"So you say–"

"So I swear."

"A banished Rider doesn't make–"

"Sense. We've been over this," I snapped.

I returned the mugs and cloth to the counter, then pushed through the swinging door to the bar as he cursed.

"Avyanna, wait."

I ground my teeth together and made my way to the kitchen. I stormed in and took a deep breath, savoring the sweet air. At the counter, I grabbed a lone knife and sliced through the bog-fern root, dicing it into small pieces. Just like I wanted to chop Rothfuss up sometimes.

"Is he at it again?" Pachu's friendly voice asked.

My chopping grew harsh with my aggravation. "He just doesn't get it."

"Don't lose a finger," he said.

He reached around me to shove a bite of something in my face. I opened my mouth and let him feed me. The sweet bread reminded me of my mother.

"Be considerate." He shifted his heavy weight. "He has been patient."

"You say that like I'm the one at fault!" I angled the knife at him, but he knew I wouldn't harm a fly without reason.

"Dear, I'm saying that it's been a long time." Pursing his lips, he returned to his chopping.

My heart fell with the truth in his words. It *had* been a long time. I'd been in Leeds for nearly a year. Before that, I wandered the Sands and the E'or mountains for over three months. That was plenty of time for anyone to get here, especially if they knew the way and didn't have to travel around the entire border of Regent.

"What if I don't want him? Isn't that reason enough to say no?"

"In any other town, yes. However, he's not hard on the eyes. He's the lawkeeper and a good one at that. You'd be well provided for and protected." He shrugged and wiped his hands on his apron.

"So that means I should simply accept his advances and claim him because he's a *good catch?*"

He offered a sympathetic smile. "It means you should consider his offer. It's only a matter of time before his eyes move on to someone else."

"That would be the day," I muttered, glaring at the roots.

He stepped around me to stir the stew perched over the stove. For such a large man, he moved with quick efficiency in the kitchen. "I'm not saying you should give up hope on your lost love," he said. "It's just—it would do you good to have some fun now and then."

I opened my mouth to argue his point, but he cut me off.

"With someone other than Kila."

"She's my friend."

"And she has plenty of other things to do than babysit you," he sighed, dumping the vegetables into the stockpot.

"She doesn't babysit me!"

"Do I have to tell you how many times I've seen her sacrificing time to sit with you, when she could be out with the young fellows her age?"

"Maybe she doesn't want to fellowship with them."

"You might be stuck on some lost love, but she is not." He angled his ladle at me, mocking the way I'd pointed the knife earlier.

I threw my hands in the air and closed my eyes. I just couldn't win against this man. "Fine. I'll stop taking up Kila's time."

"And you will take up with Rothfuss."

"No."

Pachu sighed and continued stirring. "I had to try."

I worked in the kitchen until I was sure Rothfuss left. He came in once a night, claiming he had to check on things. Iana told me he only started that interesting habit after I arrived. He was here because he thought I was mysterious, or a pretty face, not to gauge the people's mood.

I wasn't resentful, honestly. He was a fair man, just and honorable. He hadn't crossed any lines or forced himself on me. Every so often, he'd tease me and let me know his intentions, but he never used his position to coerce me.

'*Which he would be wise not to do,*' Tizmet grumbled.

I liked to think his good nature prevented him from doing such a thing. Though it could've been that he recognized I was accustomed to a different way of life. Or, he understood I had a dragon, and she would eat him in a heartbeat the second he tried.

'*I've eaten worse,*' she agreed.

The night deepened, and the crowd thinned until it reached a point where Iana had to chase the drunk stragglers out with a broom. Kila and I wiped down tables and tidied the space, collecting dirty plates and mugs. I worked through the monotony, knowing the cozy room like the back of my hand.

"Do I keep you from spending time with men?" I asked Kila as we re-positioned a table.

Her blue eyes shot to mine, and a blush crept up her cheeks. There was my answer.

"No! I mean—I choose where to spend my time." She fussed at her skirts and chewed her lower lip.

"It's alright, you know." I righted a chair, then dipped my chin. "I'm a grown woman. You don't need to watch out for me."

She huffed, waving me off. "I know that. But I should be there for you. That's what friends do."

"I'm not a child, Kila." I scolded, my tone firm. "Tomorrow, go do something. I saw you talking with Lachlan earlier. Spend the day with him."

Her blush deepened as she tucked her hair behind her ear. "Come with me." She spoke in a small voice, peeking at me from under her lashes.

"I wouldn't enjoy it."

My sad smile wavered. They would probably sneak around, start a fire, and drink someone's home-brewed mead. Definitely not what I enjoyed.

She sighed, then bustled about the room, resigned to end the conversation.

I grunted as I shoved a table into place. "I mean it, Kila. Go. Have fun."

She smiled her thanks, and we finished up. When she headed home, I stayed behind, cleaning the dishes while Iana managed the night's profit. She was meticulous about keeping her books neat and never allowed a coin to stray from her purse. Despite the close eye she kept on us, she trusted her staff. Iana wouldn't employ someone she didn't have confidence in, she wasn't foolish.

I finished with the dishes and wrapped up with Pachu. He left with a pot of leftovers swinging at his side, and I smiled, watching him leave. He had a generous heart. Every night, he delivered any extra food to the widowers' home. The town's widows watched over the orphans, and they needed every handout they could get. Taking care of children with ravenous appetites was no simple task.

I thought back to Elenor and the refugees at Northwing. They were so far away now. I wondered how they held up, how the war fared—if the army made any progress.

"Heading to your room?" Iana asked. She secured the coins in her iron chest and locked it, sliding the key into her bosom.

I brushed my bangs from my face. "Aye, unless you need something else."

"I'd like a word."

I shrugged and sat across from her at the table. She pushed the chest aside and rested her chin on her hands.

"You're a young woman."

She let the statement hang between us, and I squinted, slowly nodding my agreement.

"You should listen to Pachu." She held out a finger, cutting off my response. "No interrupting. You have your life ahead of you. You're smart, quick on your feet. Powerful too, with that dragon of yours. I want you to consider your circumstances. Right now, you have a room lent by my charity–"

"I work–"

"By my good graces. Now, hush. I've turned away valuable paying guests because you're living in one of my rooms. Think about that. You rely on me. Yes, you barter with meat for your clothes and other needs, but in doing so, you're making an enemy of Luther."

I must have made a face because her brow lowered into a glare.

"I know how you feel about the man, but he isn't one to provoke. If you stay on his bad side, eventually he will use his position to make it so no one will want to trade with you at all. My point, dear girl, is that you might say that you live in Leeds, but you are not settled. You're not grounded here. Something is keeping you adrift."

I frowned, looking down at my hands.

"What is it? What keeps you denying Rothfuss? He's a good man. You couldn't hope for better, not here."

"I'm waiting for another." My voice cracked through my whisper.

"Dear, I hate to say it, but some men–"

"Don't," I snapped, bringing my angry gaze to hers. "You don't know who you're talking about. You're lumping my–" I choked and gripped the table so hard my nails bit into it. After a quick breath, I tried again. "You are lumping him in with the scum of society. He would never forget about me, or let me go."

"But he did. You came here alone."

"Because I had to," I growled and pushed to my feet. "I had to. He couldn't come."

"Avyanna, I understand this is hard, but–"

"I won't settle because I know what I *can* have." My hands shook as I shoved the chair back. "I beg your leave."

Without giving her a chance to respond, I stormed out. I threw open the door and sucked in a lungful of night air. Tizmet sensed my unrest and landed roughly in front of the tavern. She craned her head toward me and cooed. I fought off my tears as I descended the stairs and walked across the road to climb on her back.

She launched skyward, and we soared high where the stinging insects could not reach us. Up here, the air was cool despite it being the start of summer. Tizmet flew lazy circles as I cried against her scales. She was silent in my grief, anxious, but kept her emotions in check. She coasted over the bog as my sobs slowed, and I tried to pull myself together.

Rafe would come for me. I knew he would.

Rothfuss was a good man, but he was not the one for me. My soul desired someone else, and I was committed to him. He told me to wait for him, and I would.

I just never imagined it would be this long.

Rothfuss deserved better than a woman who pined after another. He didn't deserve any less than someone's full heart, and I could never give that to him.

It would be so much simpler if he turned his attention elsewhere. According to Iana, he'd never set his eye on a life mate before. I rationalized it as a result of my oddity. It wasn't attraction; it was fascination. I was from an unfamiliar land. A dragon trailed my every step. Scars marred my skin. I was a mystery—one he wanted to solve. That was all.

'Let's go back,' I urged.

'Sleep?'

'Aye. Rest would do me good.'

I stifled a yawn as she banked toward Leeds. A night's rest would clear my mind.

Wooden buildings loomed over me as I walked through the streets, trousers tucked into my boots to ward off the constant muddied state of the road. Mud splattered the lower half of every storefront crammed onto the main roads. Cloths and hides covered the windows to keep the swarming bugs out at night. Most store owners lived above their businesses—both for convenience and safety.

People passed me, ladies with their drab-colored dresses and men with knives on their belts. Everything was brown—brown and draped in a haze of fog that even the brightest sun couldn't burn through.

I had a basket full of eggs, headed toward the tavern. It was my morning task, and one I looked forward to. Iana sent me with two brass buttons, a common trading currency, to purchase eggs from Lady Mildred. In reality, I fetched them from her daughter, Brandi, who always brightened my day.

Today, she brought me a beautiful blue pebble to trade. We sat on our trading stones, as she called them, and I set out my offers. Her curly blonde hair bounced and her eyes twinkled as she examined the goods. Bits of bones and stones, some interesting twigs, a copper from Regent, a shell, random oddments that I stumbled upon. She surveyed them with a sharp eye, settling on a twig that looked like an arrow.

We shook hands like good traders, and I went on my way as she shot down imaginary foes from the sky.

The sun rose and glared down on Leeds. Glancing over at the bog, I blinked in awe. Even in summer, the fog settled thick and heavy. I couldn't help but wonder what force of nature bound the moisture in the air.

I frowned, noting two of Luther's goons leaning against the wall of a shop directly in my path. Izaak and Bodrin. My hand slid to my bandit breaker as I sucked in a deep breath.

"Morning, Avyanna," Bodrin said, peering from under his wide-brimmed hat.

Izaak stroked his beard, gaze roving over me.

"That's 'Lady' Avyanna. Has your mother taught you no manners?" I corrected him and kept walking.

Bodrin straightened to block my way. "Oi, *Lady* Avyanna, a word."

"I apologize for the inconvenience, however, Lady Iana needs these eggs." I shifted to pass them, and he grabbed my arm.

"Luther wants–"

"Get your hand off me."

I froze, staring straight ahead. Anger surged through my veins. Tizmet roused from her slumber in a nearby clearing and took to the air.

"You can't trade with whoever," he spat. "If you want something, you go through–"

I yanked my weapon free and slashed across his arm. The curved blade bit deep, gouging his flesh. He cried out and lurched back, cradling his wound.

Izaak whipped out his knife. "You'll pay for that!"

"I gave dear Bodrin fair warning. Good day, Izaak. I'll be on my way." I made to leave, rushing my steps. "Give Luther my regards."

Izaak yanked on my tunic, pulling it tight. I spun, dodging a naked blade, and hooked my bandit breaker along his flank. He growled, clutching the wound as he came at me again. My heart raced as I danced back, giving his brain time to catch up with his body. He faltered and frowned, looking at his side.

My blade might not be long, but it was wicked sharp. When it grabbed flesh, it sliced it like butter.

"As I said, give Luther my regards."

I put some distance between us before I spun on my heel to face them. They held their dripping cuts, scowling at each other.

"Some friendly advice," I crooned, "seek a Healer."

My heart took off as they turned on me, murder in their glares. Several had stopped to watch, but none offered any aid.

A roar announced Tizmet's arrival, and people scattered off the street as she landed. She spun on me, eyes flashing, and I had a moment to wonder why she was angry with me.

My heart faltered and froze in my chest.

I gritted my teeth and took two more steps before my legs gave out. Tizmet snarled and crowded over me, pushing me to my back before I fell on my face. My head clacked against the ground, and I clenched my jaw against the agony blossoming in my chest.

I managed a small plea before the seizure set in full force. '*Take... take me away.*'

I shook and trembled, unable to cry out at the invisible pain tearing through me. It swelled with each struggling breath and receded when I didn't breathe. I fought to maintain consciousness throughout the waves of torment, riding each one.

Some time passed before I came back to myself. I worked my jaw, wincing in pain. Coppery warmth filled my mouth. I'd bitten my tongue. I rolled over, spitting out blood as I pushed myself upright.

Tizmet barricaded me from view—a wall of muscles and gray scales.

'*I haven't had one in a while,*' I mused as I looked around. The basket of eggs lay shattered and crushed, utterly useless.

'*Now would be the time,*' she replied, '*away from me, and in the presence of enemies.*'

I rolled my stiff shoulders. I was always light-headed after a seizure. They happened often while we traveled to Leeds. Perhaps the stability of rest and good meals kept them at bay. Whatever the case, I was thankful for it. Though this outburst disturbed me. Until now, my weakness remained hidden. To my knowledge, Pachu and Iana were the only two aware of my condition, thanks to an outburst weeks after my arrival.

Now Luther and his men did, too.

I brushed myself off and stood, keeping control of my movements. I found my weapon lying nearby and cursed. If I had rolled onto it, it would have cut deep. I would have bled out in the mud. Grumbling, I wiped the blade clean on my trousers before I shoved it into the sheath. I retrieved the basket dripping with raw eggs.

When Tizmet didn't move, I offered her reassurance. *'I'm good.'*

'I don't believe you.'

With a laugh, I patted her scaled side. *'Are they still there?'*

'No. Two traded places with them. They're watching from a distance.'

I sighed and shoved against her. She begrudgingly craned her head, and her tongue flicked out to taste the air. Content with what she found, she picked her large body up and walked along the street with me.

'You're awfully big,' I said, noting how people crowded together to clear space for her.

'You've been eating a lot as well,' she fired back, eyeing me.

I chuckled and patted my belly. That wasn't where I gained weight, but that wasn't the topic of conversation.

While working for Iana, I had less time to practice and exercise. And having no one to spar with didn't help things, either. I thought about asking Rothfuss, but how would he take it if I did?

'I'm just saying I think you would be better off in the sky.'

'And you would be better off with someone to watch your back before you go all fluttery like a leaf.'

'I didn't know.'

'If I were there, you would know.'

'You can't always be there for me.'

'Why not?'

'What if I'm inside a building?'

'I have these.' She flashed her claws and snapped her teeth in my face. *'I can get to you.'*

I ducked away from her and pressed toward the tavern. She was determined to walk with me, then. I smiled apologetically at those who were forced to scatter out of her way. Children trailed her, giggling and mocking the sway of her tail. She looked back and snorted, flicking her tongue. They mirrored her, snorting and showing their tongues.

'Pesky little ones.'

'You're a rare beast. You can't blame them.'

'Beast?!'

'Creature.'

'Dragon!'

I snickered and climbed the steps to the tavern, holding the basket well away from me. It stopped dripping, and I hoped that there'd be a salvageable egg or two. Tizmet coughed a tiny plume of flame and the children cheered. She snorted and narrowed her eyes.

'*Have fun, Auntie Tizmet,*' I teased, then stepped inside.

She grumbled her own curses, but I smiled, feeling her amusement.

These children didn't know she was a man-eater. Back in Regent, she was an outcast for eating a man's arm. And for devouring her kills, which happened to be humanoid in nature. There, people feared her, which suited her fine. Still, she was a curious creature, as were the little ones.

In a way, she watched over them, and they did so in return.

'Dragons do not get 'watched over.''

'You do.'

'I might eat one.'

'Tell me how it tastes.'

She gave up, and her attention focused on a child who tried to climb her tail.

"Avyanna?" Iana's gaze went from the basket to the blood on my trousers, then to my face. "Sun above, what happened?"

"I fell. I can pay for the eggs."

Her shock disappeared, replaced by skepticism. "Fell?"

"I'm terribly sorry."

I tipped the basket, showing the contents, and she let out a disappointed groan.

"See if there's anything under all that goo. I won't serve my guests broken eggs."

I nodded and pushed open the kitchen door. Pachu held out a hand without turning away from his pan of sizzling bacon. I cringed and placed it in his palm. He reached in, his mind not catching up with his actions until his fingers met the raw eggs.

"Sun above and moon beneath!" He cursed, snatching his hand back.

I laughed and took the basket back as he gawked.

"What is that?!"

"I fell and dropped the eggs." I shrugged, setting them beside the washbasin.

"Fell and dropped the... Avyanna, how am I supposed to cook a breakfast without eggs?!"

I plunged my hand inside and cringed as I felt around the contents. Letting out a victorious cry, I held up a whole egg, dripping with goo.

Pachu gave me a horrified look.

"Egg, dear cook?"

Chapter 2

I was distracted, wondering why Tizmet's nerves were flooding over the bond. Caught up in my worry, I didn't hear the chair move behind me, nor the man take his seat.

Tizmet flew circles in the night sky. She kept a tight leash on her emotions, shutting me out. I could only feel her anxiety and it made me nervous. The only other time I recalled her acting this way was when the Shadows invaded Northwing.

"Lady Avyanna, I need to ask you a few questions."

I inhaled sharply at Rothfuss' voice behind me, priding myself for not jumping. I glanced over my shoulder as I cleaned the mugs, eyes darting to where Kila wove between the crowded tables. More people than usual came for a hot meal and good company tonight.

"What is it?" I asked, turning to my mug.

"Afraid it's lawkeeper business."

"If you're here to accuse me again–"

"Avyanna."

Heaving a dramatic sigh, I turned to him. He studied me as I leaned on the bar toward him. His face inches from mine he sighed, eyes flicking down to my lips and back up.

I frowned, feeling guilty that I knew what went through his mind.

"Tell me about this morning," he said.

I pulled away and arched a brow. "Luther actually told you?"

"Saudric did. I want to hear your side."

"I guess it would seem more legitimate if the Healer reported, not Luther himself."

"Don't make this difficult. I'm not blaming anyone."

He ran a hand through his dark hair, and I felt a little bad for shirking him.

"There's not much to tell." I propped a hip against the bar and stared at the mug I dried as I spoke. "The two blocked me. I tried to get past, and they laid hands on me. I did what any self-respecting lady would do."

"They were warned?"

"Well enough."

"Verbally, Avyanna."

"Aye." My teeth ground together. "I warned them verbally. What did they say?"

"Nothing yet. I came to check on you."

I frowned. "How thoughtful."

"Witnesses mentioned you were... ill afterwards. Tell me what happened."

"Is that part of your lawkeeping?"

"It's part of me caring about my citizens."

"Iana would be pleased to hear you consider me a citizen," I muttered under my breath. I returned the mug and picked up another.

"Are you well?"

"I am," I snapped.

He let out a quiet curse.

I sighed and prepared his tea, then set it in front of him before returning to my task. "I'm fine. And those goons got what was coming to them."

"I expected they would." The chair creaked under his weight as he shifted in his seat. "You know how to use a blade."

"You should see me with a crossbow."

I froze, biting my tongue. I tried to keep as much from these people as I could. It wasn't that I was being dishonest—it was as Iana said. I wasn't ready to settle.

"I'd like to see that. You use a sword as well?"

"Perhaps."

"I saw you with a spear once..."

He trailed off as the door opened and closed. Tizmet's anxiety hit an all-time high, and she landed outside the tavern. I pursed my lips as the place went silent. I was lost in my mind, pushing over the bond to figure out what riled her.

The hairs on the nape of my neck stood on end. Heavy footsteps started my direction, and I tilted my head, refusing to make any sudden movements in the tense room.

"Can I help you?" Rothfuss' voice deepened with authority.

"No."

I *knew* that voice. I scrambled to get a grip on my racing heart. There was a scuffle of sound, and Rothfuss cursed.

"Easy there, man." Another familiar voice.

My pulse pounded a chaotic rhythm, and I squeezed my eyes shut, terrified this wasn't real.

Heavy boots landed on my side of the bar as someone jumped it. Patrons murmured throughout the tavern, their voices rasping above the silence.

"I'm the lawkeeper here and I demand you step away from her." Rothfuss was irate as the sound of steel sang, being drawn from a scabbard.

A large presence moved in front of me, and thick callused fingers tilted my chin up.

"You don't want me to leave, do you?"

The deep voice murmured against my ear, and I shivered. I clutched the mug between us so tightly I thought it might shatter.

"Open your eyes."

"I can't."

"Why not?"

"What if it's a dream?"

He chuckled in answer, and strong hands removed the cup from my white-knuckled grip. I shook as he gently placed my arms around his neck. His solid, corded muscles rolled with his movements.

"Avyanna, you know this man?" Rothfuss demanded.

I knew him. I knew him in my very bones.

Beneath my hold, his laughter shook him as he ducked low. The warmth of his breath caressed my cheek.

"Does this feel like a dream?"

He pressed his lips to mine, and I trembled, tugging him to me. He was warm and solid—and *real*. A fire ignited within me. His body was hard as he crushed me against the counter. His buckle bit into my belly, and I resisted the urge to wrap my legs around him. He smelled of woods, leather and man. He smelled like freedom.

Like love.

Whistles erupted throughout the room, followed by a few cheers. I laughed breathlessly, and he smiled against my lips before he pulled back.

"Look at me, Vy."

My eyes fluttered open, tears blurring my vision. I swiped at them and grinned when I took in the man before me.

"You shaved."

"Blasted beards are itchy."

"Your hair!"

"Better to shave it than have people see how much gray I have."

"It was silvered—dignified."

"Like Willhelm?"

"Like Willhelm." I laughed.

His right eye crinkled at the corner with his smile. A metal patch concealed the left side, held in place with a leather thong. I took all of him in, from his vest to his boots.

"All black in summer?"

"Not my wisest choice." His gaze traveled across my face to my hair, and he tugged on the braids. The warmth of his palm cupped my cheek as his thumb rubbed an old scar there. "What's this from?"

"Long story. Giant bug. Tasted how dragon dung smells."

"Avyanna," Rothfuss seethed, "do you know these men?"

I beamed and spun, pressing my back against Rafe's chest. He looped an arm around my middle and tucked me close.

Rothfuss held Jamlin at sword's length, tip pointed at his neck. Jam's smile was bright in his dark face, his long braids tossed over his shoulder. His brown eyes sparkled with mischief as he raised a brow.

"Oi. Hail, little one."

Tegan, with his freckled skin and stark red hair, leaned against the bar, calm and relaxed, watching the crowd with an easy grin.

"Aye," smiling so big my cheeks ached, I nodded to Rothfuss, "I know them."

I sat next to Rafe, tucked into a secluded corner of the common room with the others across from us. I grinned like a fool as my gaze bounced between them all. Tegan leaned his back against the table, facing the crowd. Jamlin straddled the chair, his sword ready to draw.

And Rothfuss remained at the bar, studying us with guarded eyes.

"You waited for me?"

Rafe's question had me scrunching my nose.

He smirked, tipping his head toward Rothfuss. "Seems like he's got a thing for you."

"You've been here not ten minutes and you think I've been sleeping around with someone else?" I asked in disbelief.

"Asking if you waited for me, is all. I know that look." He brought his lips to my ear, and Rothfuss' face grew darker. "It's how I'd look at a man who took my girl."

I had a stupid dreamy smile on my cheeks, but I couldn't help it. "Oh?"

"Aye. Still my girl?"

I arched an eyebrow. "Do you think I'd let you kiss me if I wasn't?"

He grinned and sat back, leveling a taunting smirk at Rothfuss. The lawkeeper chugged the last of his tea and jerked to his feet. He gave Rafe a curt nod before storming out.

Oh, this wasn't good.

I took in Rafe's rugged features. He had gained weight and muscle since I last saw him. "What happened?"

A dark expression clouded his face as his smile fell. He shut down, and I could almost feel his wall blocking me out.

"Rafe." I did not wait here for over a year—I did not deal with braving the Sands and the perilous villages to the south just for him to shut me out.

"It wasn't his doing," Tegan said. He glanced in my direction, then returned his attention to the crowd. "The Generals fought him on it."

My frown moved to Rafe. He glared across the room, refusing to meet my gaze.

"How did they keep you?"

"He swore an–"

"I asked Rafe."

As much as I missed Tegan and Jamlin, I didn't like how Rafe locked me out. I deserved better than that after what I'd been through.

"I'm here," he growled. His gaze was sharp with hurt, but tender at the same time. "I told you I would come."

Dread filled me, wondering if he still struggled mentally. He suffered far more than physical abuse at the hands of the Shadow Men. After I rescued him, he said things that gave me glimpses of his trauma. I wondered just how bad it had gotten in the months that lapsed.

"You did." I pushed out a sigh. "We have some catching up to do."

I would test the waters some other time. Right now, I was content to have him near.

The sharpness in his gaze faded, and he crushed me against his shoulder, which I objected to, squirming.

He pressed his mouth to my ear. "Mine," he breathed.

I giggled, resigning myself to him. If he needed to be close to me, so be it. As long as he was here, I couldn't be bothered to care what others thought.

Jam watched us with a smile.

"Why are you here?" I asked.

His eyebrows raised at my question. "Oi, didn't you miss me too?" He slapped a hand over his chest, feigning offense. "I'm not going to pull you in my lap and make a scene, but I thought we were close."

Laughter bubbled up at his antics, and I wrapped my arms around Rafe.

"We were freed from our oaths." Jamlin's tone softened, though he tried hard to maintain his mirth. "I decided to follow you two and see what adventures might ensue."

"I'm afraid life here is quite boring." My lip lifted at the corner. "No adventures to be had."

"No? You just need to know where to look." He dipped his chin, giving Rafe a pointed stare.

Iana approached, her gaze wary and guarded. "Avyanna, are you going to leave Kila with all the work?"

"Iana, this is Gen–"

"Rafe," he interrupted, deep voice vibrating against my back.

I nodded to the others. "That's Jamlin and Tegan. My friends."

"'Tis a pleasure, men." She propped her hands on her hips. "I asked you a question, girl."

Friends or not, I was her employee, and I had a job to do. "I'm coming."

"See that you do." She eyed the group once more, then left.

"I've work to be doing."

I turned to Rafe, our faces a breath apart. His gaze darted to my smile, then up to my eyes.

"Save it," I whispered.

I pressed a finger to his lips. He snapped and held it in his teeth, eye twinkling with mischief.

I pulled myself from him, straightening my clothes as I stood.

"Can I get you anything to drink?" I asked, propping my hand on my hip.

"Ale." Jam and Tegan spoke in unison.

Rafe nodded once. "Water."

I started for the bar and poured their drinks.

Kila sidled up next to me. "Who in all of Rinmoth is that?! You've got the whole place in a tizzy!"

"Rafe," I said, unable to keep the smile off my face.

"Which one? The big bald monster?"

I snorted and hefted the mugs. "Aye, he's mine."

"*Oh.*" Mirth gleamed within her features as she looked me over with new eyes. "What about Rothfuss?"

"What about him?"

With a shrug, I headed to the corner table. I set the drinks down with a wink, then returned to my station to clean cups. Tizmet's mood made sense now.

'You knew.'

'I suspected.'

'How?'

'I felt it. I wasn't sure at first, but today—I knew.'

For the rest of my shift, I worked in far better spirits than I had been in a long while. People came and took up seats at the bar behind me, which normally remained empty. They fished for details about the newcomers, but I offered them nothing more than their drinks and a smile.

Time stretched on with the tantalizing knowledge that Rafe was near, tempting me, but I had to remain focused on my task. His gaze held such warmth and intensity that I couldn't help but feel a surge of excitement, as if I glowed from within.

People filtered out, braving the night. Iana chased out the last stragglers before heading to my friends. I followed her, straightening chairs as I went.

"I'll be needing you to leave." She spoke in the same tone she used on drunks.

"Do ye have any rooms available, innkeeper?" Tegan asked with a bright smile.

I shook my head. He could charm a snake.

"I might, depending if you're bringing trouble."

Rafe's dark eye settled on me. He leaned back, content to take me in. My cheeks warmed as the two talked.

"We're peaceful, I promise," Tegan said, clamping a hand over his heart. "Wouldn't harm a bog frog."

Iana frowned, looking between them. "Peaceful? The amount of blades you carry says otherwise."

"Aw, this old thing?" He patted the ax hanging from his belt. "How else would we deter those nasty frogs?"

"How long will you be staying?" She crossed her arms.

"For a while, I'd think. Let's say a fortnight to start."

"And how many rooms do you need?"

"How many do ye have?"

"Brought a small army, eh?"

I snickered and caught Iana's glare. I arched a brow, then scooted a chair closer to a table, as if I was working.

"We'll take five rooms, providing there's a single bed in each."

"So five of you, then."

"Can ye keep a secret, milady?" Tegan stood and dropped his voice to a mock whisper. "There's six of us, but I don't expect we'll need a room for one." He jerked his head toward Rafe.

Only six? Who was missing?

Her eyes darted between Rafe and me before settling on Tegan. "I'll give you three rooms and provide extra cots for a fee." Her chin lifted with her curt tone. "Six beds in all, and I expect them to be used."

I shook my head and cleaned up the common room with Kila. She snuck glances at my friends, curious as a cat. Tegan handed Iana some coin, and I returned to take their mugs.

"Kila, show the men to their rooms."

"I can do that," I offered.

She leveled me with a hard stare. "I asked Kila."

I had no doubt there would be a motherly lecture coming about how their type wasn't exactly friend material.

With a shrug, I continued cleaning. Tegan and Jamlin followed Kila out, but Rafe hung back, gaze fixed on me.

Iana shooed him. "You, too."

"No."

Her shoulders squared as she worked her jaw. "You don't get to tell me no in my tavern."

Rafe gave her a dismissive glance. Secretly, I preened under his gaze, pleased he couldn't take his eyes off me or be bothered with anything else.

"Go." I offered a smile. "I won't be long."

I whisked some mugs off another table and set them aside to be cleaned. Rafe stood, pushing his chair back with his knees. I caught the line that worked its way between his brow. He masked his pain well, but I saw past it. The hunger in his gaze sent static dancing across my skin. He prowled over like some mountain cat, stalking its prey.

We stood toe to toe, forcing me to crane back. His hands found my waist, and he picked me up, setting me on the bar. Wedging my legs apart, he pressed up against me, then gripped my chin for a kiss.

"Enough, you two!" Iana screeched.

I barely pulled away before a broom whisked over my head. Rafe caught it and held fast as Iana struggled to yank it back. He scowled at her glare, then slowly lowered the broom.

He turned his eye on me and smirked. "Later," he rumbled.

"Later."

He released his hold and marched out the door. As it slammed shut, I hugged myself and squealed like a child.

"Is he gone?" Pachu inquired from the kitchen.

"For now." Iana crossed her arms over her chest. "I don't like him."

"I didn't ask you to." My legs swung, and I leapt down. I hummed and danced about the room.

Pachu sidled his big frame toward the bar. "He's yours?"

"Aye, he's mine."

"Rothfuss won't like him."

"And why do I care what Rothfuss thinks?"

"Because he's the lawkeeper."

"And Rafe is a–"

I twisted my lips to the side. He stopped me from mentioning his title earlier.

"Is a what?" Iana pressed. "As innkeeper, I have a right to know."

"You'll have to ask him."

"Is he wanted?" she snapped. "A criminal? A mercenary?"

I shrugged, then started on the dishes. "I'm not sure what he is anymore."

Pachu and Iana studied my every move. I hummed with delight as I worked, ignoring their studious scrutiny.

"I expected someone younger," Pachu murmured.

My cheeks lifted in a smirk. If only Rafe had heard that.

"I expected someone more peaceable," Iana countered.

Pachu rubbed at his jaw. "You think he will be trouble?"

"His kind always is."

"Rothfuss will be sore about it."

"It will do us no good to have the lawkeeper on our bad side."

I ignored the rest of their conversation and did my job. I was eager to get out, and once Kila returned, we hurried through our chores. Pachu watched us rushing about with disapproval. We finished in record time.

"Goodnight!" I called as I headed toward the door.

"Avyanna."

Iana's stern tone stopped me short. My palm froze on the handle before I turned with an impatient sigh.

She held my gaze a moment longer than necessary. "If you get with child, you can be replaced."

Internally, I groaned, but gave her a nod of understanding, then rushed into the fresh night air.

"Took you long enough."

Rafe leaned against the door frame, one boot propped on the wall.

My eyes traveled his body in the weak moonlight, noting how he filled in his clothes. "You look good."

"You look better."

I scoffed, then traced the growing welts on his arms. "Come on, you're getting eaten up."

"Blasted bugs," he growled.

He joined my side as we made our way to the next building over.

The main floor held the first two rooms. The one on the left was shut, occupied by a family passing through town. And the space on the right was ajar. I peeked inside. Dane spotted me from his cot and gave me a salute. I smiled, returning the gesture.

"Hey there, kitten." Blain looked up from unpacking his bag.

"It's been a while," I said.

"Aye, that it has."

"What's your reason for coming?" I asked, leaning against the frame with a smile.

"Oh, seeing more of the world. You know how we are. Never been to this town, figured we would find out what it's all about."

"Nothing at all to do with Rafe?" I pressed.

He chuckled. "Not at all."

Dane rolled his eyes at his brother's playful tone, and Rafe grumbled, pulling me against him.

"Perhaps we'll catch up later," Blain said, eyeing Rafe with a taunting smile.

"Later, then." I started toward the next floor.

"Are you going to visit everyone?" Rafe asked.

"It's only polite."

I smirked in the darkness. With no lamplight in the cramped corridor, I ascended the steps by feel and memory.

At the landing, I glanced through the doorway on the right. Inside, Tegan and Zephath were washing up.

"Zeph."

He leveled a glare, as if it was rude of me to greet him.

"It's good to see you," I said.

He made a sound in his throat and continued washing his face as Tegan winked at me.

"Why did he come?" I asked, thinking Zeph wouldn't answer me.

"Not like there's anything left for me in Regent," Zephath huffed.

His voice deepened since the last time I'd seen him, and he filled out. The past year shed his boyishness. Now, he embodied the strength and stature of a grown man.

"Well, I'm happy you're here."

"No you're not. But I don't care," he shot back.

I chuckled, and Tegan gave me a helpless shrug as he stripped his tunic off.

"Night," I said, then left before he disrobed even more.

In the room across the hall, I found Jamlin resting on the bed, with the cot abandoned on the floor.

"Where's Xzanth?" I asked, noting the lack of a second pack.

Jam's eyes were guarded as he stared past me. I followed his line of sight and frowned at Rafe's clenched jaw. With his lips pressed tight, he shook his head.

"He didn't come," Jamlin offered.

He knew as well as I that Rafe was closed off and wouldn't respond to my question.

"So you get the bed?"

"He gets his own room," Rafe said.

"And why's that?"

"Seniority," Jamlin stretched out along the threadbare sheets, "highest ranking. Call it what you will—I get first choice. The others know I can best any of them. Better to give me what I want."

"Where do you sleep?" Rafe asked, changing the subject.

"There."

I pointed to a tall, slender door tucked at the end of the hall. When we neared, I opened it and laughed at Rafe's frown.

"It's going to be a tight fit," I teased.

The entrance was, at most, a pace and a half wide, leading to a small staircase. I could fit, but Rafe's bulk? He cast a longing stare back at Jamlin's room, and I scoffed, heading up the stairs. He grumbled, then squeezed through sideways to follow.

"Lock it," I said.

"Are you expecting someone?" He struggled to twist his massive frame to secure the bolt.

I shrugged. "Habit."

He grunted in approval, then shooed me up the stairs.

At the top, the room opened up. I squinted at the low ceiling, wondering if Rafe was too tall. The room was easily the biggest, but instead of being something I enjoyed, it was almost oppressive. I took up the corner closest to the stairs. My bed was pushed against the wall. My well-worn pack rested against the small dresser that held a washbasin and lantern. A thin rug decorated the floor, and my spear was propped on the foot of the bed. The vast space made my belongings seem even more paltry.

Rafe came up behind me and placed his hand over the top of his head as he stood upright. He glared at the ceiling as his hand got crushed. I laughed and opened the window to let in some cool air. The thin sheet fastened to the frame kept the bugs out.

Tizmet rumbled from the other side. *'I'm going hunting.'*

'Have fun.'

'You as well,' she teased, then took flight.

She always waited until I was in my room with the lock secured before she left. She had to hunt every evening to provide enough for both herself and the tavern.

It was a tedious job, but one she enjoyed. She was free here, able to explore at will. She thrived in Leeds.

Rafe sat on the edge of the bed. He studied the room, and I swallowed past a lump in my throat. It was the first time we were alone in well over a year. I dropped my gaze and tapped my toes, suddenly not knowing what to do or say.

I anticipated this day for so long, dreading it would never come. And here I was, with him, and all I could do was stare at the floor.

Rafe shifted, drawing my eyes back to him. He bent to loosen his boots, then kicked them off. As he unbuttoned his tunic, I started, noting his arms. I moved to the drawer and pulled out a salve.

"Here," I said. "Saudric, the Healer, showed me how to make this when I arrived."

I settled in beside him. The bed seemed so much smaller with him there.

"My first week here, I was covered head to toe in bites." I dabbed the salve over his raised welts. "It would do you good to wear a long-sleeve tunic. Even though it's summer, it protects against the swarms.

"That's why women here rarely wear dresses. A few might, but most just wear trousers. Otherwise, we'll have bites and stings in all sorts of uncomfortable places."

I moved to his other arm, avoiding his dark gaze. His fingers were frozen on his buttons, head tracking my movements.

"When I first got here, they called me Dot. The swarms devoured me. I learned to mix mint weed and vibrant leaf in my washbasin. It keeps the pests at bay and smells nice, too. With no springs like in Regent, it's either the bog, or the filtration pits. It's a hard toss up.

"There's a well to the far south side, but that's a terribly long walk for water. The town is more populated down there, but I like it up here. There's a good amount of people, and I have work, and Tizmet–"

"Vy."

I snapped my mouth shut. He studied me with a frown, his dark eye unreadable in the dim moonlight, but the wrinkle between his brows showed his irritation.

"Oh, I forgot. I should light the lantern. I rarely do." Pushing up from the bed, I replaced the salve on the dresser and grabbed the lantern. "I only come up here to sleep. There's almost no books in Leeds, and Iana works her people hard. I simply don't–"

"Vy." His voice was rough and firm.

I bit my lip to keep from going on and faced him.

"I don't need a light. Be calm," he said, reaching out for me. "Come here."

My breath rushed out with a sigh, and I replaced the lantern to take his hand. As I sat on the bed, he knelt on the wood floor, looking up at me. My heart raced as he trailed his palm down my thigh, past my knee, to my calf. He pulled off a boot and set it aside.

"Relax," he murmured, then removed the other.

His gaze in the weak light sent butterflies swarming in my belly. An eye patch didn't take away from his appearance, but rather added to the roguish appeal.

"Do you want me to bunk with Jam?" Concern lined his features.

"No!"

The corner of his mouth twitched as if he wanted to smile, but he held his somber demeanor. "You want me to sleep here?"

"Aye."

"With you?"

I bit my lip and nodded. My gaze darted to the floor, the window, the ceiling, anywhere but him.

"Vy," he urged, "say it."

"I—well. I want you to sleep with me... in my bed. But I'm just not–"

"Then I'll sleep with you," he spoke as if he declared the moon was out, "in your bed."

He stood and resumed unbuttoning his tunic. I rubbed my cheeks, trying to cool them from the red stain of embarrassment plastered there.

He shrugged out of his shirt, and I looked up at him in wonder. When I last saw him, he was so thin, skin and bones, abused and tortured—covered in half-healed wounds. Now, his scars replaced the countless injuries, but his body made miraculous improvements. Sharp lines defined his chest and abdomen. Although he lost some mass, he retained the same muscular physique.

He stilled as I traced a large raised scar. It zig-zagged down his middle and disappeared below his trousers. He grabbed my hand when my fingertips brushed his waistband.

"That's one scar I'll never regret," he murmured. He brought my touch up to his heart where it pulsed a strong steady beat. "I owe you everything for that. My only regret is this is all I have to give."

I smiled. "It's all I could ever want."

Chapter 3

"The big woman is yelling for you."

Tizmet's rough voice jerked me awake, and I blinked at the bright room.

"No, no, no, no, no!"

Rafe trapped my arms and legs from every angle. Frantically, I yanked myself free from his constricting embrace. His groggy curse followed me as I tore from the bed. I threw on last night's tunic and pulled my trousers up, hopping from foot to foot as I stepped into my boots.

"Late?"

His husky tone was almost enough to lure me into his arms.

"Very!"

I took the stairs two at a time before I careened to a stop. With a curse, I spun, then ran back.

"I'll see you later!" I yelled, then rushed down again. After flipping the lock, I growled at myself and stomped up a few steps. "Rafe!"

"Hmm?"

"I love you!" I shouted a bit more forcefully than was necessary.

"Go, Vy."

There. I spoke the words, knowing he could hear them.

With a lopsided grin, I tripped on a step. I cried out and caught myself on the wall. After righting myself, I sped off, slamming the door shut behind me. Jamlin's laughter mocked me, chasing me down the next flight. I ran to the tavern as fast as I could, bursting through the entrance.

"Avyanna! What in all of Rinmoth!" Iana yelled, locking angry eyes on me. "If you can't be bothered to be on time–"

"I'm going!" I snatched the basket from her grasp, then rushed for Lady Mildred's.

The sun was high, far too high for my liking. I was always up long before it rose, but Rafe blew that trend. Something about being wrapped in his arms, him holding me tight, keeping me safe...

I shook the thoughts free from my mind. Propping the handle on my arm, I plaited my hair as I walked. Tizmet circled in the clear sky.

'Why didn't you wake me sooner?'

She scoffed. *'It's been too long since you slept that deep. I had no intention of disturbing you, so you might fetch eggs.'*

'Iana will have my head!'

'The big woman can find other help.'

'I need this job! I don't have anywhere else to stay!'

Across the bond, I could almost feel her rolling her eyes.

'Find another.'

It wasn't as if there were a lot of options. Without a life mate's home to live in, there were no places for women. Besides the widowers' house, but that was already packed beyond capacity. There were a few secluded shacks deeper into the bog, but the idea of living under the permanent oppressive fog didn't resonate with me.

Staying at the inn was convenient. I worked there, and it was safe. Out on the bog, the risk of attacks was always looming, with Luther and his crew being the biggest concern. A smile lifted my lips as I tied my braid off. He had another thing coming if he thought he could push me around with my friends here.

I hurried along the path that broke from the road and found Brandi sitting on our trading rocks. Her bottom lip stuck out as she glared into the distance.

I jogged over. "Hail!"

"Lady 'Anna!" She leapt to her feet. Her blonde curls bounced with her movements as she wrapped her little arms around my legs.

I bent over to return the embrace and glanced at the basket of eggs she set in the thick grass. "I'm sorry I'm so late."

"Mommy says being late means the other person isn't important." She sniffed against my leg.

I dropped to a crouch, my lips twisting to the side. "That's not true! Well, what your mommy said *is*—but without the eggs, people at the tavern would go hungry! Pachu wouldn't know what to cook!"

"So the *eggs* are important." She wiped her wet cheeks on her sleeve.

"*You* are important!" I tapped her nose for emphasis. "If you weren't here, I wouldn't have anyone to trade pretty bits with."

"Oh!" She reached into her apron pocket. "I have a frog today!"

I eyed the red and blue creature she drew out. Those colors weren't natural on an animal.

"You'll have to give me something good for it." A smile tugged on the corner of her tiny lips.

"Ah, I forgot all my trinkets in my room." I rushed my next words when her grin faltered. "How about I tell you something for it?"

"In-for-mation?" Her nose scrunched as she broke up the word into pieces.

"Aye, information."

She perched on her trading rock, frog in hand. "It's got to be good."

"Hmm." I settled into my place, tapping my chin. "What about a secret?"

"Mommy says secrets are bad. She said if I keep them, she'll find them and whip me." She squinted, looking me over. "Where do you keep your secrets? Do you have pockets?"

"No." I laughed and shook my head. "Alright, well, not a secret, then. Just something no one else knows—not even the other children."

Brandi gasped and leaned forward. "Is it about your dragon?!"

I nodded along, trying to think of something she didn't know about dragons. "Aye."

Tizmet's annoyance filtered across the bond. '*Telling my secrets to the little ones?*'

'*Got any ideas?*'

"She's going to have babies, isn't she?" Brandi's eyes sparkled with wonder. "All the other kids say she's just a fat, lazy dragon–"

'*They say what?!*'

"But when my mommy gets her secrets and hides with Daddy, she gets really fat, too! That's how I got my brothers!"

I hid my cringe with a smile as I shifted uncomfortably. That was far more information than I ever wanted to know about Lady Mildred.

"Well, they don't have babies like mommies do," I hedged.

"They don't? How do they make babies?"

'*I'm not answering that one.*'

Tizmet circled lower. '*You shouldn't be answering anything about dragons!*'

"Erm, I'm sure you'll learn about that when you're older. I'll trade you information about dragon babies for your frog."

Her eyes narrowed like a true trader. "He's a *pretty* frog."

"Knowledge of dragon babies is really rare," I replied.

'*Is it, really?*' Tizmet drawled.

'*No, but don't tell her that.*'

"It has to be special," she countered. "Something that will make the other kids go, 'Oh Brandi! That's so neat! How do you know that!' If they already know it, I want my frog back."

"Deal."

We shook on it, and she handed over the wet creature. It squirmed in my hands, both tickling and horrifying me.

"Dragons lay eggs," I said as she transferred eggs from her basket to mine.

"I knew it! Your dragon is going to have a *lot* of eggs, isn't she?!"

"I think so. They come in all sorts of shapes, with the most beautiful patterns."

Brandi nodded her understanding. "Babies need their mommies. I have to go play when my brothers need our mommy."

Her newest brother was only a few months old, still very reliant on her mother.

"When they hatch, they can take care of themselves. They don't need their mommies—fully independent." I straightened, hefting my basket.

"When she lays them, will you let me see?" She clasped her hands under her chin, giving me the biggest, saddest eyes. "Please? Please, please, please!"

'No.'

"Perhaps. We'll have to wait and find out."

I glanced up at Tizmet. She banked, watching me with a bright orange eye that reflected the sunlight, reminding me how late I was.

'You can tell her no,' I said, flashing Brandi a smile. "I've got to be off. I'm late."

"Alright! Wait till I tell the others!" She ran off, her basket swinging at her side.

'Now I'll have all the little ones looking for my nest,' Tizmet whined.

'You're a dragon, for love of the sun.' I laughed, starting my brisk walk back. *'You should be able to hide a nest from human children.'*

I avoided Iana's wrath as I went about my day. The family in the lower room continued their journey, and I was tasked with tidying their space. I swept and cleaned, catching up with Blain while I worked.

He filled me in on what happened over the time that passed, though it was obvious he left out some crucial information. Rafe took longer to recover than anyone predicted. Months went by before he regained his strength. As soon as he was able, he sought release from his position, but the Generals objected, denying his resignation.

They ordered the Tennan across enemy lines, which infuriated me to no end. I hadn't rescued Rafe just for them to send him back in harm's way.

After an incident between Rafe and General Faulkin, the King dismissed the Tennan from service and imprisoned Rafe at the palace. Apparently, he spent quite some time there. Blain glossed over the details but explained that between Darrak and Ruveel, Rafe was freed and took off for the E'or mountains like an arrow, with his Tennan racing to catch up.

I changed the sheets and blew a few stray hairs out of my face as Blain finished the tale. I huffed, shoving the mattress in place, then straightened, placing my hands on my hips.

"So domesticated."

The familiar rumble pulled my attention behind me. I snorted and looked over my shoulder at the most handsome man I knew.

"One day soon, I'll show you just how domesticated I am." I grabbed the broom, sweeping the dust freed from the straw mattress.

"Oh?"

A shiver ran up my spine as Rafe came to stand behind me, not touching me... just present.

"And when will that be?" he asked.

"I'm not sure."

"But you said soon."

Those shacks in the bog seemed mighty appealing right about now.

"Rafe, I–" I faced him, then snapped my mouth shut when I noticed who took up the doorway. I dipped my chin in greeting. "Rothfuss."

He tilted his head and nodded.

Rafe regarded me, raising an eyebrow. "You were saying?"

I ignored him. "Can I help you?" I asked Rothfuss.

He gestured toward Rafe. "I'm here to talk to the big man."

Rafe hummed to himself, then turned, blocking my line of sight. I stepped around him and watched the two as if they were bulls facing off. Tegan lumbered down the stairs and leaned against the wall. Blain joined his side, both just as invested in watching the scene unfold.

"Talk," Rafe said.

"Let the woman work."

"I don't do what people tell me to," he growled, then arched a daring brow.

"People do what I tell them."

"I don't."

"Don't like it?" Rothfuss jerked a thumb over his shoulder. "Find another settlement to join. And take your small army with you."

"If I don't like it, me and this small army will remove you from the settlement."

"Is that a threat?"

"Does it threaten you?"

The amount of masculine pride in the room was beyond my tolerance.

"Shoo! Both of you!" I spat.

I swiped the broom at Rafe. He reached out to catch it, but I sidestepped, then slapped it against his rear. His eye widened in shock, and a grin split his face.

"Shoo!" I waved the makeshift weapon, my warning clear.

Rothfuss watched with hooded eyes, taking a step back as Rafe crowded through the doorway. When they stepped over the threshold, I slammed the door behind them, not at all sorry if it hit them on their way out.

I frowned, glaring at the wooden planks.

This was so not good.

Once I finished cleaning, I was free till evening. Kila and I normally passed the time together, but today was different.

Rafe walked beside me through the market. It wasn't as large as those near Northwing, but it had a decent selection. Many of the small villages scattered across the E'or foothills didn't have a market at all.

He looked at the various goods, tilting his head at some and handing others over to me to purchase. He left the bartering for me, as he would overpay these people by far. Not that I was against the citizens earning a living. I simply wanted him to save as much for us as possible.

We were going to start a life together.

Or so I hoped.

Earlier, Zephath took off with Jamlin and Blain to explore Leeds. Being the bookworm he was, Zeph knew quite a bit about other lands. Dane drifted here and there, in and out of sight. With his knack for picking up mannerisms and his practical choice of clothes, he blended into the crowd far better than the others.

Tegan stayed close, and I smiled as I caught him observing everyone who passed by. He wasn't completely at ease here. I didn't blame him. Leeds differed from Regent in more ways than one. The people here were kind, but they had a hunger in their eyes, as if no matter how much they ate, they were anxious about where their next meal would come from.

I picked up some foraged fruits and fresh bread. Cheese was a tempting option, but I couldn't bring myself to splurge. Luther had complete control over the only dairy farm, and I really didn't want to contribute any more coin to his pockets.

Rafe watched me with careful eyes, studying my interactions. I wasn't terribly friendly with many of them, but they had grown accustomed to me. Only a handful knew me by name, but for the most part, all of them were familiar with the white-haired woman.

Rafe reached past me to examine some fruit. "Three men seem to be quite interested in our purchases," he murmured.

"Those are Luther's men. He has them tail me everywhere."

"Who's Luther?"

"The man who owns half the town."

"Does he own the lawkeeper?"

"Rothfuss is one of the few keeping him in check." I paid for my fruit and set off toward my favorite clearing on the outskirts of town. "What did you two talk about, by the way?"

Tegan trailed behind, and when Rafe was slow to answer, I glanced at him for an explanation.

He offered a crooked smile. "Just wanted to be sure we aren't trouble."

"So Rafe clarified you *are* trouble?"

"Something like that," Rafe mumbled.

I snorted and shook my head. "Nothing happened between us." I sighed. "You don't have to puff up like a rooster every time he comes around."

"I don't like the way he looks at you."

I scoffed. "There's no law saying men can't look at me."

"I said, I don't like the *way* he looks at you." He narrowed his glare.

"And just how does he look at me?"

"Like he wants you."

I pursed my lips. He was right. I didn't like it either. It was flattering at first, but I expected once I dismissed him, he would move on. I was wrong.

"I've told him I'm yours," I said as we cleared the edge of town.

"Some men need it beaten out of them."

"Rafe!"

My steps slid to a stop. He faced me with a smirk, and I gave his arm a playful slap.

"You are not *beating* the lawkeeper!"

"I'll try not to."

"No, you can't!"

"Why not?"

I took a deep breath and turned to Tegan. "Would you be so kind as to have a word with our tails?"

He looked between me and Rafe and nodded, grateful that I gave him an out. He left, heading back the way we came.

"You can't start trouble here. I get that you're the biggest and the strongest–"

"I am."

"And quite full of yourself," I blurted.

He chuckled, and I couldn't help but smile.

"This is where we're supposed to settle." I gestured toward town. "We're supposed to make a home here."

His grin died, and my hopeful little heart stuttered. He glanced around, suddenly somber.

I worked my jaw and tried again. "Are we? Making a home here?"

"Perhaps."

"Rafe of Deomein, you better not tell me that I waited all this time in this fog-cursed place for you to admit you're not committed to me."

His dark eye flicked to mine, and a crease worked between his brow. "I never said that."

I crossed my arms over my chest and glared. "Perhaps you should clarify your intent," I snapped.

His chin dipped in confusion, and the crease deepened. He studied me, and I could almost see his mind working to process why I was upset. When realization dawned, he shook his head as his frown disappeared.

"I intend to have you."

"And?"

He formed his next words with care. "You want more?"

"Of course I want more, Rafe! I'm tired. I want a place to be safe. A place to settle."

He sighed and wrapped his arms around me, crushing the food between us. He rested his chin against my hair and rubbed my back.

"Home. You want a home."

My throat tightened. "Aye."

"No more adventures?"

"Adventures are fine. I just want to go home when they're over."

"You speak to this old man's heart."

I scoffed and pulled away.

Holding my arms, his smile widened. "I can get you a home."

"Here?"

His nose crinkled. "It smells."

"That's the bog."

"It's gloomy."

"Also, the bog."

"Terrible place to make a home."

"Agreed," I laughed, "but I haven't seen any better, and I've been to almost every village south of here, all the way to the Teeth of E'or."

"If you want to settle here," he heaved a sigh, then shrugged before letting me go, "we will settle here."

Taking the crook of his arm, I smiled, and we continued to the clearing

I would finally have my own home.

Our home.

Chapter 4

As we ate, Tegan kept his distance after somehow chasing off Luther's men. The small clearing was a stone's throw away from the nearest building. The location was just the right distance from the swamp, providing a sense of privacy without being too close to the dense fog.

I leaned against Rafe, his arms snug around me as the birds flitted here and there. Tizmet flew overhead, her thoughts muddled. She was content to leave me with him, trusting him to protect me.

"Will you tell me what happened?" I asked quietly, glancing up to judge his face.

His eye twitched, as if he fought a flinch. His peaceful demeanor broke when he worked the muscles in his jaw.

"Don't lock me out," I whispered.

I pressed my cheek against his chest as silence lapsed. It was not a friendly stillness as it had been before, but rather a heavy, tension-filled quiet.

"I came as soon as I could. I wouldn't leave you here alone."

Relief sagged my shoulders. "I believe you."

I paused, testing the static between us. Could I push him? Perhaps he wasn't ready. I chewed my lip.

"What happened?" I asked.

He rested back on his palms, tilting his head to the sun. Closing his eye, he loosed a few steadying breaths before he spoke. "I was weak—so plague-cursed weak!" he bit out. "I could barely walk."

His features tightened as he fought the memory of humiliation, gritting his teeth together. His lips pulled downward in a deep frown.

"It took ages for me to gather enough strength to spar again, to move without fear of tripping over my own blasted feet. I felt like an old man, terrified of falling or dropping my sword. I hated it—hated being weak, unable to do my job. When I could finally fight, I petitioned for my release. The blasted Generals wouldn't give it."

"I thought the King would be the one to release you."

"He wouldn't have to. The Generals had every power to declare I was unfit to lead," he growled and peered over at me.

"But they didn't."

Baring his teeth, he took another deep breath before tipping his face to the sun once more. "No, they found they could use me as bait."

A bitter smile quirked the corners of his lips. "When I fought on the front, it became a hotbed for action. The Shadows knew who I was, and what I'd been capable of." He tapped the metal patch. "I was the one who got away. General Faulkin did his job. He used me strategically, drew them out. But I was done fighting."

I tilted my head as confusion pulled at my frown. My Rafe? Done fighting?

"I wasn't *rescued*," he choked on the word like it pained him, "just to abandon the woman who risked everything to save me." His steady gaze lowered to mine. "You didn't give me a second chance just so I could throw it away and die."

I grinned up at him, then settled into his chest.

"I was a General, not a soldier to be used like a pawn." He hissed through his teeth, keeping his anger in check. "I went over their heads and petitioned the King for release. He denied me. So, I caused an incident."

"What kind of incident?"

"One that called my sanity into question." He laughed under his breath, as if the memory amused him. "I was summoned to the palace, and when the King told me I would never be released from service... Well, let's just say he'll remember that day every time he looks in the mirror."

"You struck him?!" I pulled away, horrified.

"I wanted to, but no. I threw a plate at his face."

My jaw dropped as he smiled into the sun's warm rays.

"Broke his nose."

"That's why they threw you in the dungeon," I said with shocked realization.

"Aye. They kept me there for months."

"How did you get out?"

He sighed and rubbed the nape of his neck. Pulling his mouth to the side, he worked through his reluctance. "Ruveel."

My brows rose in disbelief.

He continued, "The pile of dung spoke for me. Apparently Darrak found out a secret of his. The plan was to either break me out, or use the Dragon Lord as leverage."

"Darrak blackmailed the Dragon Lord?"

"He's a sharp man." Rafe smirked. "Glad he's on my side. As soon as they released me, I came for you."

I braced my palm against his jaw. "I missed you."

"Missed you, too." He traced the scar on my cheek with a frown. "Tell me how you got this."

"That's one of the smaller ones." I scoffed, facing the bog. "Turns out the Sands are a dangerous place."

"You kept to the border?"

"Couldn't. My escorts left us deep in the Sands. I tried to keep track of where we were headed, but it was hard."

"Plague take them. What about your dragon? Couldn't she fly straight?"

"We fought off monsters all day and flew as long as we could at night. She was exhausted. I was exhausted. We got lost more than once."

The memory knotted my stomach. His arms tightened around me, chasing the sensation away.

"That scar is from a giant *bug* of some kind." I laughed bitterly. "It's funny thinking about it now, but at that moment it was terrifying."

His anguished breath blew the hair at my temples.

"I'm sorry," he whispered.

"It wasn't all bad. Some sights I encountered were nothing short of extraordinary. Did you know just north of the Teeth, there's a great waterfall?"

"I did not."

"It's beautiful. Flows right out of the mountain. Me and Tizmet took a couple days to explore it. Maybe someday we will head that way again to see it."

"I'd like that."

"But then return home."

"Aye, home."

He rubbed his hands up and down my arms, pulling my back tight against his chest. I sighed happily and settled against him.

"Do you have a place in mind?" he asked.

I smiled. "There are some abandoned homes within the bog itself, but nothing in town."

"Can't say I want to be penned up like cattle anyway," he grumbled.

"But the bog is always gloomy."

"Have another place in mind?"

"Luther owns all the outlying farmland." I sighed. "If there's another option, I don't know about it."

"Why don't we build?"

I frowned at him, expecting that to have been some sort of jest. No trace of mirth showed on his features.

"That would take a long time," I said slowly.

"I'm in no rush to go anywhere," he studied me, tilting his head, "not without you."

"I'm not going anywhere without you."

"Well then, I'd say we have time."

"Do you know how to build a house?"

"I'm sure someone around here could show me."

His determination had me shaking my head. I wanted a home, and he was willing to give me one—build me one with no prior knowledge.

Warmth flowed through my soul, and I pulled him in for a kiss. "I love you."

"I know," he murmured against my lips.

He held me tight, kissing me gently. His hand slipped to my waist, and a long-lost, but increasingly familiar heat spread beneath his touch. He nibbled at my lips before pulling back.

"Careful."

His voice was thick and husky—and I loved it. As desire darkened his gaze, a wicked grin spread across my face, fully aware of the power I possessed.

"Why should I be?" My fingers trailed down his chest to his abs.

"Do the kind people of Leeds often mate in public?" he ground out, snatching my hand.

"Who said things will get that far?" I teased, raising an eyebrow.

"Remember who you're pushing."

"I remember *that* all too well."

I smiled, but pulled away. He was right—it wasn't appropriate. We hadn't claimed each other. To show such affection in public would only hurt my standing with the townsfolk.

I glanced at the sun. I had a few moments to freshen up before my shift. "It's about time for me to go."

He pushed to his feet, extending his hand. "You earn coin for your work?"

"No. I earn a room," I said as he helped me stand. "When I came here, I had nothing. My coin was spent, my resources depleted. I was fortunate enough to barter for odd jobs. Now, Tizmet hunts for the tavern, and I work for Iana."

He grunted and gathered the remaining fruit. Together, we walked to where Tegan leaned against the wall.

"What will you do?" I asked.

Rafe blinked, lost in thought. "Hmm?"

"What work will you choose?"

"I'm only good at one thing." He smirked.

"Please don't pick a fight with Rothfuss."

"We'll see."

I let out an exasperated sigh and started for the tavern. Along the way, Rafe and Tegan watched the townsfolk bustle here and there. When we turned onto the next path, Rafe slowed, holding my arm.

"We have another tail."

I glanced behind us and made eye contact with a slender, bearded man. Osciene. He tilted his head in silent question. He never gave me any trouble. I smiled and waved before continuing on.

"One of Rothfuss' men," I said, unbothered.

Rafe muttered under his breath, "You have an awful lot of men tailing you."

"Remember, I'm still an outsider here. I've made an enemy of Luther, and now the lawkeeper is unsure of me because *someone* likes to push him."

I leveled an accusing glare at him. He raised his eyebrows and gave a shrug.

At the inn, he followed me up the stairs as Tegan disappeared into his room. He glanced at the closed doors that flanked us, and I headed up the stairs to my space, laughing as he cursed and snapped the lock in place. Inside, he ducked his head, glaring at the low ceiling. I turned away from him to wash my face, then slid the washcloth over the nape of my neck. Pulling my tunic free of my trousers, I faced him as he sat on the bed. His eye lingered on my fingers as I plucked at the hem.

"I didn't have time to fetch clean water this morning." My voice came out higher than I intended.

"I'll take care of it."

"The filtration pits are south of the clearing we were just at," I explained, biting my lip.

"Where I saw people pulling water from?" he drawled.

"Oh, aye."

He was observant enough to have seen that. I tugged at the hem of my tunic again, and he squinted.

"I have to change."

"You wore that last night," he said.

"I threw my clothes over my night shift this morning. I have to... well..." My lips pressed together as I pulled my chest binding from my drawer. "To avoid lewd comments, I mean–"

"Aye." His tone took on a rough edge.

He laid back with a groan, folding his hands behind his head, careful to keep his boots off the blankets. With a sigh, he closed his eye.

I worried my lip and turned away. I changed quickly, stripping my night shift, then binding my chest. As I tucked my tunic in, I peered his way. He hadn't moved a muscle.

"Did you peek?" I asked quietly, leaning over him.

He kept his eye closed but the corner of his lips quirked up. "I'll never tell."

"Oaf." I laughed, slapping at his shoulder.

"Tease," he shot back.

My eyes traveled over his rugged face, down to his thick scarred arms and muscular chest. As my gaze darted to his full lips, I frowned.

"I think we should talk," I started.

He made an encouraging sound, but didn't open his eye. I cleared my throat. It seemed easier to discuss this when he wasn't looking at me.

"We should discuss claiming."

His eye shot open and narrowed on me.

"If you still want to," I blurted.

His lazy smile sent a heated blush to warm my cheeks. I bit my lip again and waited.

"Mm-hmm."

I wrapped my arms around myself. "Well... you're sleeping in my bed."

"If you don't want me to, I won't." His voice softened with understanding.

That's not what I meant. I looked away and sighed, not knowing what to say or how to say it. It was a messy situation, not as clean cut as it should have been. We promised ourselves to each other, but never went over any details.

"Vy." He drew my gaze to him, then propped himself on his elbows, forming his words with care. "I'm a man–"

"I know. And I just–"

"Let me finish."

He scowled, and I clamped my mouth shut, pressing my lips together.

"Sun above, Vy. You make things complicated. I'm a man sleeping in your bed. People are going to assume things. That said, I won't press you if you're not comfortable."

"I'm *too* comfortable with you," I muttered.

He pushed himself upright. "If you need time, I'll bunk with Jam."

"No! I just don't want to—well, I miss you. I want you to be close. But without another place to stay, if my moon cycle returns and I end up with child, Iana will kick me out."

He hummed in understanding. "Do you trust me?"

"Aye."

"Then, for love of the sun, trust that I'd care for my woman and child." His tone sharpened as if I offended him, and a frown worried his brow.

"I didn't mean to imply that I don't trust you. I just worry about how we're going to make this work."

"If you don't want me to claim you until we have a home, then we'll wait." He heaved a sigh, then took my jaw, turning me to face him directly. "I'm not some animal, Vy. Have a little confidence in my self-control."

"What if I don't have control?" I breathed.

His eye flared with heat, and a smirk lit his features. "I'm not responsible then," he teased. "Sun and moon, I want you, but I respect your desires. We've waited for how long to get to this point? What's a little longer?"

"I expected a comment about your old age."

He snorted. "Aye, well, *you're* young. I won't rush you."

My heart thrummed through my chest. "Thank you."

He shook his head with a rueful smile. "I wonder how fast I can get that house built."

I worked hard that night, bustling between the kitchen and the bar. Tizmet brought in a bog deer, a great hairy thing. Pachu and I butchered it, preparing it for the evening meal. After that, I kept as many mugs clean as possible and smiled politely at everyone.

Rafe sat in the corner nursing an ale, never taking his eye from me. The thought of his unwavering observation motivated me to push myself further, determined to prove that I would go the extra mile in pursuit of our shared dreams. I wasn't afraid of work.

As time passed, I contemplated the ideal spot to construct our home. I pondered the herbs and flowers I could grow and anticipated the challenges of tending a garden in this location.

The tavern's door opened, and I glanced up as Rothfuss entered. He scanned the crowd, settling on me. I arched a brow, then busied myself, dropping off the dirty mugs at the bar. Out of the corner of my eye, I caught his movements as he took a seat across from Rafe.

That was puzzling.

Too far away to hear their exchange, I frowned, watching their lips move. Rafe made a comment and Rothfuss' mouth twitched in what could almost be a smile. He replied and Rafe gave a begrudging nod.

"Stop eyeing the goods and get to work."

Iana's sharp voice cut from behind, and I resumed my cleaning.

Some time passed before Rothfuss finally got up. He nodded my way as he left. His eyes were not as warm and welcoming as before, but they weren't cold or resentful, either. His gaze told me I was simply one of his people, nothing more.

I smiled to myself, watching him go.

Chapter 5

I hummed a tune and snatched the tunic out of Rafe's hand. He frowned, reaching for it.

"I can do it." I pushed it into the soapy water.

He squinted. "Who do you think did my washing before you?"

"You probably hired someone." I was gentle with the fabric. Sun above knew the man wasn't tender with anything.

"I did it myself," he said, defensive. "I'm practical."

"Well, so am I, and I can do it for you." I pulled it up for inspection.

He made a thoughtful sound, then reached into my pile of soiled garments. I yelped and scrambled to snag my night shift as he held it out, eyeing it before plunging it into the lukewarm water.

"Give that back!" I bit out.

"Give my tunic back," he countered, scrubbing the thin, delicate fabric.

"Remember the days when Rafe took what he wanted?" Tegan shook his head, smiling as he washed his trousers.

"Aye, the days no one teased our dear Rafe." Jamlin feigned a sad sigh. "He was much too foreboding."

"Now he barters for his laundry." Tegan snickered. "He's been reduced to–"

Rafe moved without warning. He snared Tegan by the collar and belt, then hurled him into the pool.

Bystanders cried out in protest as Tegan spluttered and stood, flinging water out of his face. Rafe glowered at my night shift as he knelt. Jamlin laughed outright, and I caught Blain grinning. I offered him his clean tunic, fearing for my gown. By his expression, I thought he might tear it.

Rafe snatched it back and raised an eyebrow at Tegan, who made his way out of the pool.

"Well, at least all of my clothes are clean!" He flashed a bright smile.

I laughed, and the sun peeked from behind the clouds. I closed my eyes to revel in its warmth.

"Take me to see the builder later," Rafe said.

I dipped my chin. "There's actually a glorified guild of three men and two apprentices." I pulled out my dripping clothes and wrapped my bar of soap.

"Take me to them."

"There's our bossy Rafe!" Tegan quipped.

With Rafe's glare, he chuckled and stepped behind Jamlin. Jam shoved him off, and he stumbled back into the pool.

I pushed myself to my feet with my wet laundry gathered in my arms. "I'll take you to them, but I can't stay."

"Well enough." He wrung out his under-breeches.

With a nod to the men, we headed to the inn to hang our clothes to dry.

"I can't believe this is happening," I murmured, pinning my tunic up on the line out back.

Rafe grunted, and I found him scrutinizing me.

My lips pressed into a smile. "We're really doing this?"

"That's what I thought..." His brow arched high with his amusement. He shook out his clothes, then asked, "Where's your dragon?"

"Nesting," I whispered.

He stilled, pausing a moment before he faced me. "There are dragons here?"

"No, she's the only one, but there's soon to be many. She carries Flinor's clutch."

"King Aldred won't like that."

"He's the one who banished us."

"I'd be willing to wager he didn't know she was gravid."

"Well, he *did* banish us, and now Regent won't be the only kingdom with dragons."

I reached across the bond. Tizmet drifted along a high current, looking for the best place to build a nest. She perked up, suddenly interested in our conversation.

"You plan to let the townsfolk at the hatchlings?"

"That's not my call." I shrugged. "Tizmet is their mother. If she wants them wild raised, that's her business."

'*Humans do not get the final say in the ways of dragons,*' Tizmet added in agreement.

I shook off my wet sleeve and watched Rafe hang his last pair of trousers.

"I'd feel better if they had no Riders," he said. "Not that Regent can face a front on two sides, but he might try to reach out and lay claim to the eggs. Do the people of Leeds know?"

I clenched my jaw, now regretting that I told Brandi. "Aye."

He looked up as Jamlin and Zephath rounded the corner, ready to hang their clothes. He jerked his head, motioning for me to join him as he started away from the inn. I frowned as I followed, wondering if the King would strong-arm us into giving him the eggs.

Tizmet snarled at my thoughts. '*Mine.*'

'*Aye, they're yours.*'

I just hoped they would stay that way.

We walked in companionable silence, both of us lost in our thoughts. I frowned at the hazy sun, knowing well that my shift started soon. He could handle the bartering on his own, but I still wanted to be there. After all, it would be my home too.

Among all the structures in the town, the builders' guild was the most well-constructed. They never permitted it to show signs of wear. It wasn't as gaudy or engraved as the shop the jeweler shared with the cobbler, but it was still one of the nicest buildings in Leeds. It spoke of their pride.

Pride was a dangerous thing. It implied one of two outcomes: that the builders would execute their job with precision, eliminating any concerns we may have, or they would exploit the situation by imposing exorbitant fees.

I'd never dealt with them directly, but I overheard plenty of conversations at the tavern. They seemed like a group of easy-going men.

A young boy looked up from the plans scattered atop the desk as we opened the door. He blew strands of black hair out of his eyes, then arched a brow, taking us in.

"Greetings," he called. "Can I—can we—can the builders' guild be of assistance?"

The corner of my mouth quirked up, knowing he saw something daunting in Rafe. With his twin blades secured to his back, peeking over his shoulders, and his thick, muscular arms, bearing endless scars... He was quite intimidating, and not one to be ignored.

The boy straightened and cast a nervous glance toward the rear of the building, where loud banging resonated.

"That's why I'm here, boy." Rafe gave the boy a frown and crossed his arms. "Bring me your Master."

"Yes, sir!" He practically fell over himself, rushing to the other room.

I elbowed him in the ribs. "Be nice."

"I was."

"Be nicer."

"No need."

I scoffed as Master Val stepped through the doorway, eyeing us. The boy stood near, acting as though he wasn't peering from behind his Master's back. Val was an older man, his hair gray but thick. Muscles corded his lean frame, and his sharp eyes sat deep in his wrinkled face. He always struck me as the cunning one of the guild.

"Master Builder?" Rafe rumbled.

"Greetings, soldier."

Tension thickened, and I frowned between the two as they stared each other down, daring the other to speak first. Rafe went still, not even blinking. I didn't sense animosity from Master Val, but how did he know Rafe had been in the army? Clearly, it bothered Rafe as well. Was this man from Regent?

"If you do not wish to be pegged as a soldier, don't stand like one." Master Val coughed, then looked over the plans on the desk. "What is it you need?"

"A house."

Val hummed to himself, then pointed at a calculation. "You forgot your allowances. Can't make a wall eight paces tall when a whole pace of wood is in the ground, lad."

The boy's face went crimson. His shoulders slumped, collapsing in on himself, humiliated. "Begging your pardon, Master Val."

"I'm not giving you my pardon. I'm giving you another chance. Correct it and try again." Val walked around the desk and met Rafe's gaze. "I'd tell anyone two years."

"What will you tell me?"

"Depends on your coin."

"My coin depends on your skill... and speed."

Val's eyes crinkled at the corners with his grin. "You won't see better."

"I haven't seen any," Rafe growled.

Val leaned on the desk. "You came in with that group of soldiers," he mused. "I want to know what you're doing with her." He tipped his head to me but kept his eyes on Rafe.

"That's none of your business, old man."

"Avyanna?"

I chuckled. "This is between you two."

"Tell me you're friends."

"Why?" Rafe demanded, shifting his stance.

"Because if you're here to claim her and strong-arm her into being your wife, I'm going to say no."

I liked Val.

"I'm not forcing her to do anything," Rafe bit out. He dropped his arms and clenched his fists, irritated. "Are you interested in building or not?"

"Avyanna, am I?"

I scoffed at the old man's antics. "Aye, you are."

"Then yes, I *am* interested in building your house." His bright gaze twinkled. "Let's discuss it at my desk."

As he started back the way he entered, I touched Rafe's arm, drawing his attention. By the distant look on his features, his guard was up, shutting out the world.

"I have to get to the tavern," I said.

He blinked, and his wall lowered as he nodded with a frown.

"Please don't put down coin without me," I added.

He arched a mocking brow. "I'm not foolhardy. Go."

"I just know how eager you are," I teased, then peered at him from under my lashes.

"Go, woman," he groaned with the smallest smile.

I grinned, then dragged my hand down his arm. As I wiggled my fingers in a goodbye, I spun on my heel to leave.

I loved that man.

I hurried through my work, smiling when Zephath came in. He glared around with his nose crinkled in distaste and took a seat next to Rafe. The townsfolk commented on my high spirits, and more than one asked about Rafe, fishing for details of our connection. I avoided their questions, keeping my responses vague.

Rothfuss entered. This time, he ignored Rafe, heading straight for the bar. Without a word, I poured him a lukewarm tea. He studied me for a moment before he dipped his head in thanks and accepted the drink. He turned his back on me, facing the crowd. I scrunched my nose, curious about what Rafe said to deter his advances.

Kila and Iana slipped easily between the tables, delivering food and drink, collecting coin and dirty dishes. They did their dance, putting up with crass comments from single men, and avoided the lingering glances from those who had a woman at home.

Pachu called for me through the cracked kitchen door. I finished with the cup and bustled in, waving my hand to clear the steam.

"Avyanna, what am I supposed to do with this?" he cried in dismay.

I squinted through the haze, seeing a ridiculously large fish plopped on the counter. It was longer than I was tall, and thick as a sheep in full wool.

It also had a bite missing out of it.

"Chowder?" I offered.

"There's a common room full of guests! I need more than a fish that's already been snacked on!"

I shrugged with an apologetic smile. "She must have been hungry."

"Hungry or not, she can't bring me half-eaten animals! She took the head! Their gills make the best dishes!"

'Tizmet?'

She flew above the bog, circling low through the fog. She was hunting and would be distracted.

'Food.'

She pushed her hunger at me. It was getting harder for her to lift off the ground with her weight. She would lay her clutch soon. I couldn't wait to see the eggs.

"If anyone knows how to make use of this, it's you." I plucked up a knife, angling the blade at the scaled thing. "Like an anchor fish?" I ventured.

Pachu pressed his wrist to his forehead and let out an anguished cry. "Like an anchor fish," he conceded.

We set to work, chopping and prepping. Once he was settled, I headed back out to the common room. Rafe and Rothfuss were gone. I detoured to Zephath, who glared at the crowd as if they killed his best friend.

"Where did Rafe go?"

"That is none of my business. Or yours," he snapped, refusing to meet my gaze.

I smiled and sidled next to him. "How's your night going?"

"Terrible now that you're here."

"Fancy that, you didn't look as though you were enjoying it to begin with. I surely couldn't have made it worse."

"You make everything worse."

"I swear, Zeph. If one day you were ever nice to me, I'd know you were ill."

Kila spun out of reach of a man and darted to us, flashing a sweet smile. "Would you like an ale?"

I braced myself for Zeph to tell her off.

"Yes, please."

My mouth fell open.

"I'll be right back with it." Kila beamed, then made her way to the bar.

Slowly, I faced him, giving him plenty of time to slink away or think of a defense for his actions.

"Yes... *please?*" I repeated, shocked.

His jaw worked as a blush crept over his face. "Look, you're not the only one who can find a mate."

"I've never heard you be nice to anyone! Is this a new habit of yours?" I mused.

"Don't count on it. At least not to you."

"To Kila?"

"Anyone but you."

I shook my head and stood. She returned with his drink, and I spotted Iana's glare as I stepped from the table.

"Take good care of him, Kila. He's special." I grinned at her puzzled look.

I hummed to myself as I cleaned. Zephath was a prickly character, but he was loyal to Rafe, and that was enough for me. An incident at the palace indicated Zeph had a rough history, and I was willing to wager he followed Rafe to escape whoever he was running from.

As the tavern closed, Kila and I frowned at the scene playing out in the far corner.

Iana was ordering the last stragglers out. Three of Luther's men. They were drunk, paying her no heed. She raised her voice, pointing at the door, but they laughed, brushing her off.

When I first arrived, I found it absurd that a woman ran the tavern—for this very reason. How was a plump older lady supposed to fend off unruly men? Pachu was no help. Being soft and timid, he avoided any and all confrontations.

"Should we do something?" Kila whispered.

She was thin, delicate. She wouldn't stand a chance against them. I pressed my lips together, stealing another glance at the scene.

I learned early on how Iana ran this place on her own.

Rothfuss.

He kept a tight leash on the citizens of Leeds, keeping trouble to a minimum. The majority were peaceable, with only a handful of incidents during my time here. The inn was protected by reputation, as well as the honor of its guests. When someone drank too much for their own good, others removed them before things escalated.

But tonight, the common room was empty save for Bodrin, Izaak and Dirk. Belligerent fools.

I straightened and glowered as Bodrin pressed into Iana's space. She might've been overbearing, but she was my boss. I wouldn't let anyone push her around, especially in her own establishment.

My hand slipped to my bandit breaker as I eyed the angry red stitches across Bodrin's forearm—the remnants of our last encounter. I marched over. Gleeful rage burned over his slackened features as his attention shifted to me.

"Get Rothfuss," Iana ordered.

My heart stuttered as her gaze met mine. Her tone held unwavering anger and determination, but her eyes were fearful. A protective need swelled within me, an urge to protect my people.

"Kila, get Rothfuss," I called out, glaring at the drunkards.

"Rothfuss, Rothfuss! Always that lawkeeper," Dirk spat. He ran a hand through his dark beard, then pushed to his feet, kicking the chair out behind him.

The door slammed as Kila rushed off. I hoped she found him quickly.

"Want to know a secret, little girl?" Dirk hissed, stalking toward me.

Iana bristled. "Just leave! All of you!"

I had to keep my cool. In my experience, getting riled only led to drunks becoming more volatile. "I don't need to know any of your secrets."

He sneered. "You should have taken that man when you had the chance."

I eyed Izaak, who still sat at the table, hand on the pommel of the sword at his waist. He didn't speak, but watched with cold amusement. I couldn't imagine the cut on his side healed much since our last visit.

"Not like she would have had him for long," Bodrin scoffed.

Their unfiltered focus on me sickened my stomach, but at least Iana wasn't their target anymore.

"That's what I mean, you fool!" Dirk spoke through his maniacal laughter. "She should have enjoyed him while she could!"

"Poor bastard never caught her," Bodrin agreed. Malice burned through his glare as it lingered on my body.

I gritted my teeth, fighting a shiver.

'Avyanna?'

'Tizmet–'

He stepped closer. I held my ground, but had to lift my chin to meet his gaze.

"Someone should catch her and enjoy her before she goes, too." His slurred tone lowered.

Terror gripped me like a vise, squeezing my throat. Were they planning to overthrow Rothfuss?

I could handle these lowlifes—I faced worse. Compared to the Shadow Men and giant horrifying bugs, these three drunks were nothing.

Still, my frantic pulse warned me that the odds were not in my favor.

'Where is Rafe?!' Tizmet roared.

"Back up," I said.

Part of me hoped they hadn't caught the tremor in my voice. I wasn't afraid of them. I'd kill them before I let them hurt me. Yet memories flooded me, unbidden.

Cold snow against my skin. Unbridled terror, unable to move. Men laughing as they cut through my clothes.

"You don't order us around," Dirk snarled. "We get enough of that from Luther."

"You think boss man will give me extra coin if I take the white-haired witch?" Bodrin laughed.

"Get out! All of you!" Iana yelled, her voice pitched high and hectic.

Dirk wiped his mouth, rushing toward her the same moment Bodrin lunged for me. He moved fast for a drunk, and I drew my bandit breaker a second too late.

He snatched my elbow, his grip hard and unrelenting. I twisted, putting my back to him in hopes to free myself. The motion snapped my arm the wrong way, and I ground my teeth at the pain. I dragged the curved blade across his cut, tearing the stitches, then threw a kick backwards, striking hard against his knee.

He fell with a curse, pulling me with him. As I struggled to regain balance, he snagged my ankle, ripping my foot out from beneath me. My head slammed against the corner of a table, and lights danced in my vision.

Tizmet raged across the bond, too far away to help. '*Brace yourself!*'

I blinked, desperate to clear the haze of glittering stars. A weight dropped along my body, and Iana wailed in outrage.

Blind and frenzied, I slashed to maim, to kill, anything to free myself.

Then I felt it.

A moment of dread and horror slowed the seconds before pain burst through my chest, burning and tearing. My back arched as a scream tore from my throat.

I hoped Kila had found Rothfuss.

Chapter 6

Air rushed into my lungs as I took a gasping breath. I thrashed, fighting instinctively. The ringing in my ears deafened me from any other sound. Strong arms like bands of iron tightened, and I threw my head back. It smarted, colliding against something hard.

The pain faded, leaving me drained and weak. Shapes and colors materialized with the slow return of my vision, and I tried to make sense of my surroundings. Iana sat in a chair nearby, hands folded, with a worried frown marring her features. I sucked in another deep breath, trying to steady myself. If she was here and calm, I was fine.

I was fine.

My heart spasmed and my head fell forward to hide my grimace.

"She should see Saudric," Rothfuss said.

His voice was steady as he leaned against the table. The lanterns burned low, but I still caught the determined look on his face.

"I don't care what you say," Rafe rumbled from behind, his arms locked protectively around me.

Just like that, my body relaxed of its own accord, my pulse slowing to a natural tempo.

"I'm still the lawkeeper here, and what I say is law."

"I d-don't–" A cough took over my words, wreaking havoc on my dry throat.

Rafe moved his hands up and down my arms, bringing me more security. He was here. I was safe.

'I'm going to kill him.'

Tizmet hissed through our bond as she neared the tavern, and I grimaced.

"I don't need... Saudric," I rasped, pushing against Rafe. "Get me... out."

He moved with me, pulling me upright. "I'll be back to see those men."

My mind tried to figure out what he was doing as he bent his head close. His arm looped under my knees, and I whimpered as he stood. He tucked me against his chest, then headed for the door.

"They're mine, Rafe, not yours," Rothfuss called after us.

"They attacked her," Rafe growled, "they're mine."

I curled against him, hiding my face in his neck, breathing in deeply. I gripped his tunic and held on tight, even though his arms were strong and sure.

"She's going to eat you," I whispered as he pushed outside.

"She can go swim in the swamp for all I care." His steps thudded against the dirt-packed road.

"No, she's–"

Tizmet's roar was loud enough to wake every soul in Leeds. She barreled from the sky, crashing to the ground with her wings spread wide. She opened her maw and threw sparks, but didn't set us ablaze. Rafe ignored her, heading toward the inn.

Tizmet snaked her head into our path and snapped her teeth in Rafe's face.

'I trusted him to watch you!' she screamed.

I flinched away from her fury, and Rafe stopped to glare at her.

"Move."

She snarled and spat. Ire ignited her eyes, almost glowing in the dark night. With a devastating growl, she snapped her maw over Rafe's head, his shaven scalp disappearing from view.

I remained silent, knowing she wouldn't actually eat him. The fine points of her teeth pressed against his neck, drawing blood. His tightening grip was his only reaction.

"Are you done?" he asked, his deep voice muffled.

With a hiss, she pulled off, teeth scraping his skin. I knew better than to scold her, even if I wanted to. Not only was she my bonded, she was gravid—heavy with eggs and the maternal instincts that came with them. She would not respond well to me defending him, so I kept my mouth shut.

She flicked her forked tongue along her teeth, glaring down at him. Rafe ignored her and started for our room, blood trickling down his back. I curled against his chest as he kicked the door open and stormed up the stairs. Dane leaned against the wall, watching silently as we passed, yet none of the others came out—if they were there at all.

He cursed at my doorway. The stairwell was too small for him to pass through straight on, let alone with me lying against him.

"Let me walk."

"No." He glared as if the space would widen under his angry gaze.

"Rafe, put me down."

"No."

With a scant breath, I reached for my magic. Outside, Tizmet roared, worried I was healing him. I ignored her, clearing my mind to focus. Keeping tight control, I gave it a simple purpose and locked it away.

Rafe set me down, cursing. He shook his hand as if it burned. I staggered against the wall, pressing my weight on it for support as I moved toward the stairs. His touch slipped to my waist, bracing me as I climbed.

"I'm not as helpless as you think," I muttered.

I crawled up and collapsed when I reached the top. Everything was so exhausting. I just needed a moment to catch my breath.

"Not helpless," he ground out as he scooped me from the floor. "Careless." He placed me on the bed and set to remove my boots.

"I was very careful." The room was too dark, and I really wanted to see his face.

"Not careful enough," he growled, reaching up to unfasten my belt.

"Easy there, big guy."

"Vy," he stopped, going deathly still, "do you know how I found you? No? Too engulfed in your spasm to remember? Let me tell you."

He braced his arms on either side of me. His chest pressed close, and his heart pulsed a steady beat against mine.

"I found another man on top of you. And if that's not enough, you were thrashing around like a fish out of water, eyes rolled back. And guess what—that dungheap didn't care. He and his friends would've taken you and that pathetic innkeeper without a thought. Do you know what that felt like?"

He paused, but I couldn't bring myself to speak.

"I think you might," he said. "Remember how you felt when you found me?" His words were thick, drenched in rage.

Something warm dripped against my face. It had to be blood. Rafe never cried.

"Tizmet was on her way," I whispered.

"That blasted dragon is gravid. She only has one thing on her mind."

Tizmet's eye illuminated my room as it filled the window. Crimson streamed from his wounds. It slid from his cheeks, dripping on my face.

"Rafe, it's alright. I'm–"

"No, it's not!" he bit out, then jerked from me.

When he attempted to straighten to his full height, he collided with the low ceiling. He snarled and slammed his fist against it, then palmed his head. He tore it away to eye the blood and, with another curse, stalked over to the washbasin.

I waited as he cleaned his wounds, letting him have his moment of rage. Nothing I could say would be calming. The last thing either of us needed was for me to further enrage that beast inside him.

He kicked off his boots and jerked his tunic over his head, not bothering with the fastens. After he removed his belt, he tossed it aside, then stalked to the bed. He snagged my belt, and I lifted my hips, allowing him to slide it out of my trousers and throw it.

"Off," he said, then stomped to the small dresser.

Tizmet's eye left the window, and I felt her curl up behind the inn. I hoped she wasn't lying on the clothesline.

My tunic fought with me, and I sat up, trying to pull it off. There was a quiet hiss, and the glow of my lantern flared to life through the fabric. Strong, callused hands slid up my waist and tugged it over my shoulders and head. Rafe tossed it to the side and crouched in front of me. He motioned to my trousers, and a nervous thrill ran through me.

"Off."

His eye glittered in anger as I hesitated.

"Vy, if you don't take them off, I'm going to tear them off."

"Yes, sir," I murmured, then shimmied out of my trousers, kicking them off my feet and to the side.

"Blasted headstrong woman," he muttered under his breath.

My small smile widened a fraction. "I heard that."

He walked back to the dresser and faced me. His gaze darted over my body. "Come here."

I checked my chest binding to be sure it was still tight, and stood, tugging on the hem of my under-breeches. They were hardly modest as far as garments go, reaching the tops of my knees. I took hesitant steps toward him, bare feet against the warm wood floor.

He reached for the lantern and held it close. His eye tracked every inch of me. His attention snagged on the largest of my scars, but moved on quickly. With gentle hands, he spun me, inspecting my body. I obliged, knowing he had to see me to gain some peace of mind. A weary sigh slipped through his lips, and he returned the lantern to its place.

"You didn't hurt yourself?" His tone softened, the sharp anger from before gone.

My fingers searched the back of my head for lumps or dried blood. His eye flashed to mine as I winced, finding the tender spot.

"I hit my head on the way down." I shrugged. "Just a tap."

He tucked me in close, and I smiled, resting my forehead against his firm chest. I stared at the large scar that ran down his middle as he prodded the back of my head, searching for any other wounds.

"You're well?" He pulled away, looking down at me as he cupped my cheek.

I pressed my palm over his touch, holding him there. "Aye."

Still, his lips formed a hard line, and he broke our embrace. "You should rest. Go lie down."

When he turned, I frowned at the blood trailing down his back. I took a step to close the small distance he put between us, and he spun, glaring at me again.

"Lie down."

"No."

"Vy."

"No." I reached past him to grab a clean cloth, then dipped it in the basin. "You're going to bleed all over my bed."

"I'll bunk with Jam."

"After tonight? I don't think so." I returned his look with my best glare.

The muscles in his jaw clenched as he studied me. "No magic."

"As long as you behave."

Not like Tizmet would let me heal wounds she dealt.

He grunted, then turned away so I could clean his injuries. Three vertical lines ran from the nape of his neck to the top of his skull. They were shallow, but bled as head wounds do, which was a lot.

More scars to add to his collection.

'He's lucky he has his head.'

She wouldn't have eaten him, but was angry at herself for not being there. After the night I had, knowing they cared enough to worry about me was everything.

I cleaned him, wiping the streaks of blood as he braced himself against the dresser. Scars littered every muscle, and I wondered if he even remembered what caused half of them. When I finished, I set the bloodied cloth down, then leaned against his warm back. I wrapped my arms around him and squeezed.

"Come to bed," I breathed.

His muscles rippled as he tensed. "I have to take care of those men."

"You can't kill them."

"I *can*."

"You shouldn't."

"Are you defending them?" He peered over his shoulder, but made no effort to move.

"Rothfuss should deal with them."

"When I am wronged, I take revenge."

"Actually, *I* was wronged." I planted a kiss along his spine.

"And *you* are *mine*."

"What happened to me being an independent woman?"

"Finding you straddled by another man while you writhed on the floor happened," he groaned, then turned to pull me to his chest.

The sensation of my bare skin against his caused an intense yearning to surge through my core.

"I want you to remember how you felt when you found me. Describe it," he ordered.

I frowned. I didn't want to think about that. "Like a failure. Terrified. Helpless—hollow."

"What did you do about it?"

"I did the only thing I could. I–"

"Exactly. Vy, there's so little I can do." He held me at arm's length, his voice sharp with anguish as he pointed at my chest. "I cannot fix this! I caused it and I can't make it better. How am I supposed to protect you from something that already happened? Let me do what I *can!*"

My heart ached with empathy. I would have hunted down the Shaman that tortured him if it was the last thing I ever did. I would have made him suffer, reveling in his screams of pain.

"You can come to bed with me."

"Vy–"

"They will be there in the morning."

I shrugged off his hands, then ventured to my bed. With the blanket tucked to my chin, I watched the lantern's amber glow dance across his features.

"Hold me, Rafe."

He stood there staring at me for a moment. When he slammed his fist against his thigh in frustration, I knew I won. He tore off his patch and threw it on the dresser. As he made to put out the lantern, I frowned, taking in what was left of his eye. All that remained was a gaping hole, surrounded by a starburst scar. Unease thrummed through me before he blew out the flame. The wound itself didn't disturb me, rather the memories that came with it.

The bed dipped with his weight as he climbed in behind me. He pulled me tight against his chest and pressed his palm over my heart.

"I love you."

The words tore out of him, both a promise and a plea.

The next morning I woke with Rafe against my back, warm and solid. I stretched out my legs, wiggling my toes.

I could get used to this.

Rafe groaned, throwing a leg over mine to hold me still.

"I have to get up." I snuggled into him, completely undermining my statement.

"Not yet." His voice was low and husky with sleep, turning my insides to mush. He pressed warm kisses to the nape of my neck.

"I have to."

My breathy words were weak even to my ears. His lips tickled me as he hummed, content to ignore me. My skin pebbled despite the blanket trapping in his warmth.

"Right this very moment?"

"I should."

"Should. You don't have to." He brushed my hair aside and propped himself up, trailing kisses across my shoulder. "You should rest today."

I grinned, then rolled onto my back to meet his gaze. The sun was just making its way toward the sky, letting a pitiful amount of light into the room.

"My old General would have never given me a day off," I teased.

"I object." He frowned and trapped my hips with his legs. "I distinctly remember a time when I gave you days off."

"After I was *poisoned*."

My hands found his broad shoulders, and I kneaded the tight muscles there.

He nipped at my wrist, not taking his eye off me. "Tell me you're well."

I smiled at his order. "I'm well."

"No more spasms."

"I'll try not to."

He sighed and rested his forehead against mine. I giggled and stole a quick kiss. He looked so serious.

"It still happens when your heart picks up?"

"Sometimes. I've kept it secret till recently."

"Now they know your weakness," he growled, biting at my fingers.

"I've got Tizmet." I laughed, tapping his mouth.

He started to speak, but I held his lips together.

"She'll hear you."

"What your dragon thinks of me doesn't keep me up at night."

He pushed himself to sit on the edge of the bed. I ran my hand up his arm, curling around his biceps.

"Take today off," he said. "The innkeeper can find another worker."

"If she does, I lose my room."

"I'll pay for it."

"Just how much coin did you make off with, General?" I laughed, pushing against him.

"Enough."

Shaking my head, I wrapped my arms around him and pressed my chest to his back. He sighed and braced his elbows on his knees as he rubbed at his eye.

"I need to keep busy," I murmured. "It's my job for now, and I should keep it. I'm proving my value to the townsfolk. It will help us get settled here."

I massaged his shoulders, and he groaned, relaxing into me.

"If you need something to keep you busy..."

A laugh bubbled out, and I pressed harder, working out the knots. In the weak light, I spotted the three scores along his scalp and kissed each one.

"I have to get going."

I stepped off the bed, and he snagged my arm, spinning me toward him.

"Rafe, I have to–"

"Tell me once more."

He pulled me between his legs. His big hands settled on my waist, sending flutters through my stomach. My heart raced as I studied the scarred, gaping hole where his eye had been. It reminded me of the damaged soul inside.

He slid his arms up my back, crushing me against him in an embrace. This was the side of Rafe no one else saw—wounded and vulnerable.

"You're getting sappy," I mused, my voice breathless.

"Seems being tortured, watching your woman get banished, then getting thrown into a dungeon makes a man sentimental." He clenched his jaw in a tight grin.

"I am well," I whispered in his ear.

He took a deep breath and gave a crushing squeeze before he released me. With a shy smile, I turned to the basin to wash up. After that, I pulled on my trousers as he walked around the room, picking up pieces of clothing littered about. I reached for my belt, and he handed it to me before shrugging on his tunic.

"You're going out?" I asked.

"Lawkeeper."

I glanced out my window at the sun barely rising over the horizon. "This early?"

"The law should never sleep."

I scoffed, then pulled on my tunic before tucking it in and fastening my belt.

"He's still a man. He needs his sleep as much as any other." I threw an elbow at him when he pressed close to pick up his boot.

"Then he needs to find a new job."

"I quite like him."

I waited until Rafe's gaze slid to mine, daring me to finish that statement.

"As the lawkeeper." I giggled as I braided my hair.

His jealousy did something to me. The possessiveness of the man I loved brought me a strange sense of joy.

"I've yet to be impressed by his ability," Rafe grumbled. He sat on the edge of the bed to yank his boots on.

"You're used to the army." I shrugged. "There, everyone obeys, and no one has a will of their own. It's hard to rule people who can think for themselves. You have to balance freedom with justice. That's not always an easy line to walk."

He fastened his weapons to his back. "I remember a certain girl who didn't always obey."

I grinned and set my boots next to the bed. Rafe watched as I leaned in slow—my intent obvious as I brought my lips to his. Just as my breath hitched, and he deepened our kiss, I pulled away, plopping beside him.

"You don't seem to regret it," I teased, pulling my boots on.

He grumbled something under his breath, then shuffled over to the dresser. When he slipped on his patch, he grimaced as the leather thongs scraped against the fresh wounds. After securing it into a comfortable position, he lifted it briefly to rub at the socket vigorously.

"Does it still bother you?" I asked.

"Sometimes I forget it's not there." He turned on me with a rueful grin. "I'll think I saw something out of it, then remember there's no eye to be seeing anything."

I pushed to my feet and joined his side, grabbing his arms to wrap around my waist. "Well, it lends you a certain air of... danger."

His dark gaze flitted over my face. "I would think you like danger the way you play with it."

"I definitely like you."

He leaned in closer. "I like you, too," he murmured.

"That's a good foundation," my words faded as his warm lips pressed against mine, "for life mates."

"I agree." A deep chuckle shook his shoulders as he placed a kiss on my forehead. "Let's go."

I sighed, and we descended the stairs. On the second floor, I watched wide-eyed as he threw Jam's door open with a bang.

He bellowed loud enough to wake the whole inn. "Jamlin!"

Inside, something crashed, and Rafe twisted, narrowly avoiding a knife that flew past. It sank into the wood along the far wall with a thunk.

"Send Zephath to change out the water in the room. Have Blain meet me at the tavern."

Muttered curses reached my ears as another crash sounded. Rafe ignored it and offered me the crook of his arm. I chuckled and took it, heading down the rest of the stairs.

We made our way through the mist-covered street. It was a gloomy morning, promising to be overcast. Rafe walked at my side, silent and stalwart.

When we entered, I blinked at the lantern light. Iana stood at the bar, setting out mugs for the morning guests.

"Avyanna?" she called.

"Good morn." I went for the basket that awaited me.

"Kila can fetch the eggs."

Her words gave me pause, and I regarded her, confused.

"If you need a rest," she added.

"I'm fine."

She studied me as if she could scour my mind for anything amiss.

The door opened behind us, and Rothfuss stepped inside. Dark circles lingered under his eyes. Apparently, the law didn't sleep.

"Rafe." His voice was heavy and thick with fatigue. "A word?"

Rafe nodded and headed away from me and Iana, with Rothfuss following behind. I watched the two, wondering what made Luther believe he stood a chance. Rafe was big, bulky and scarred—intimidation incarnate.

Rothfuss emanated strength. He was slightly shorter and thinner than Rafe, but he had a muscular bulk of his own. He wore his sword at his hip with confidence and his sharp eyes caught everything—always three steps ahead of everyone else.

"You should have gone," Iana muttered.

"And leave you and Kila with them?" I snorted. "She couldn't fend off a bog lizard, much less defend herself against a drunk."

Iana gave me a flat look. "*She's* not sickly."

"I'm not either." I frowned. "It only happens now and then."

"At terribly inconvenient times."

"Usually." I agreed.

That much was the truth. I had my spasms, or seizures, when my heart raced. It happened when I pushed myself too hard while sparring, or when I was threatened.

I was, however, far more equipped to handle any threats. Besides, Kila ran faster than me. She had a better chance of fetching Rothfuss in time.

"Next time I give you an order, you listen." She slammed a mug down.

My brows raised as I met her glare. "Yes, ma'am."

Dane and Tegan walked in. Tegan pushed a hand through his wild red hair and took a seat at the bar. Dane's dark eyes took in everything at once, jerking his chin at me in greeting.

"Morn," I called.

Tegan flashed his brightest smile. "And what a good morn it is! I wake up and the first thing I see are two beautiful ladies?! I'm a lucky man!" He winked at Iana.

Dane approached Rafe. He stepped close enough to take part in the conversation, which drew Rothfuss' glare. Dane paid him no heed, but rather said a few short words to Rafe. Rafe replied with a glower, and Dane simply lifted his shoulder in reply. When Rafe reached up to rub the nape of his neck, his hand jerked away from the angry scabs and I winced for him.

I waited to fetch the eggs while they finished their conversation. After last night, if I set off without Rafe, I would never hear the end of it.

Tegan flattered Iana, and she scolded him. Listening to their banter was music to my ears. I could get used to being surrounded by friends and their day-to-day lives. Leeds would make a good home.

Rothfuss nodded to Rafe and left the tavern while Dane stood, listening to something Rafe was saying. I pushed off the bar and headed toward the two men, curious as to what they were discussing.

"–off on his own," Rafe muttered.

Dane gave another shrug. He wasn't being rude. It was simply how the man spoke. Without words.

"Let me know when he's headed back," Rafe said with a sigh.

I took his arm and smiled up at him.

He dipped his chin at Dane. "Go with her."

"You're not coming?" I hated how needy that sounded.

"Lawkeeper asked for me."

"Are you in trouble?" I mock-whispered.

"The men from last night are," he growled. He gave my hand a squeeze before pulling away. "We'll meet up later."

I frowned as he left. In my year here, Rothfuss never needed help with anything. He had a crew of loyal men who were vigilant in upholding his laws.

What would he need a General for?

Chapter 7

The sun was breaking up the mist as I sat on my trading stone with Brandi. She held out a small orange lizard, and I swallowed, wondering how long I would have to hold it before I could release it.

"No more in-for-mation." She stuck out her bottom lip. "My friends knew dragons laid eggs. They're like the bog lizards."

I sincerely hoped the children forgot Tizmet was gravid and wouldn't pester her. Currently, she flew low circles overhead. She'd been seething since last night and hadn't let me out of her sight since I left the inn this morning. Across the bond, her fatigue nagged at me. She'd need to rest soon, but for the moment, she didn't trust Dane to keep me safe.

He leaned against a thick tree, watching us with sharp eyes. His bow hung over his shoulder, and his quiver dangled at his hip. Dressed in brown from head to toe, the man seemed to fade into the scenery, barely noticeable in his stillness.

"I forgot my treasures in my room," I said, wincing my apology.

"You're forgetting a lot lately." She squinted and tugged on her short braid. "When you get old, your hair turns gray. How old are you?"

I laughed and poked at her hand. "Not that old."

"So, you have nothing to trade?" Her sad gaze dropped to the lizard. It squirmed in her grasp and her nose crinkled as if she really didn't want to hold it anymore.

"Trade."

We startled when Dane towered over us. He crouched low, putting himself at Brandi's level as he opened his hand. In the center of his palm, a small purple crystal glittered in the morning light, twinkling like glass. Brandi's big eyes went wide and she licked her lips, looking up at him.

"Is it a good trade?" she asked carefully.

He tilted his head. "A gem for a lizard?"

I grinned between them. She was afraid he was overpaying. I didn't know how he kept from smiling at the small child.

"It's a *pretty* lizard." She grasped the wriggling thing by its tail.

I swallowed my laugh. Clearly I was wrong—she thought the lizard was more valuable.

Dane's lips formed a line as he motioned for it. Brandi reluctantly handed him the tiny beast, and he trailed a finger from its spine to its tail, where it was slightly crimped. Arching a daring brow, he looked back at her.

"It was like that when I found it!" She pushed her bottom lip out again.

Dane shrugged and held out his offering. "Trade."

"Fine." She snatched the crystal and turned her little scowl on me. "Your friend drives a hard bargain."

I laughed as Dane and I pushed to our feet. He pulled the collar of his tunic out, and to my horror, dropped the lizard inside. He adjusted the strap to his quiver and went back to watching the surroundings as if he were bored.

Brandi helped me place the eggs in my basket, and I traded her the brass buttons for her mother. As we set off, I watched Dane carefully. He walked with an air of calm confidence—as if he didn't have a lizard squirming beneath his shirt.

"A crystal?" I asked.

It was a valuable treasure here in Leeds. He would have made good coin if he had traded it with the jeweler.

He shrugged in reply, and I shook my head.

"I wasn't aware you liked lizards so much."

He scoffed and offered me a tiny smirk before returning to his stoic self.

Dane accompanied me all day as I ran errands and started my shift. He was quiet, more a shadow than anything else, but I enjoyed his company, nonetheless.

I walked out of the steaming kitchen, wiping the moisture off my face with the hem of my apron. Tizmet had taken off in the afternoon, unable to resist the urge to find a place suitable for her nest. She had not returned from hunting, and Pachu was punishing me in his own way by making me peel a mountain of potatoes for the vegetable soup.

I breathed the somewhat cooler, less humid air of the common room, scanning the crowd. Dane was missing, but I soon found the reason for his absence. I smiled and trotted over to the table, taking a seat and scooting close enough to press my thigh against his.

Rafe glanced my way, his face sober and angry. His scowl deepened before he turned back to Rothfuss.

The lawkeeper wrapped his hands around his mug of tea, giving Rafe a weary look. "No. Even if she asked—no."

"You'll regret it."

"I won't," Rothfuss replied. "My men are watching them. If they choose to repeat their actions, then they will regret it, not I."

Rafe pressed his elbows into the table and growled, "I know their type."

"You know soldiers—military. When was the last time you were around common folk, when you couldn't simply whip out your sword and take someone's head if they offended you?" Rothfuss leaned forward to meet Rafe's gaze. "You have the strength of a leader, but you have no compassion."

"Men like that don't deserve compassion."

"Everyone deserves it. Do you know why they were here?" Rothfuss dipped his chin my way. "To watch her for Luther. Those men don't know a trade. They take what work they can get. So, they sat here and did their job. They drank their coin away and waited. They made a mistake. I would wager Luther wouldn't have sent them to hurt her."

My eyes bounced between the two, my smile dropping into a frown.

Rothfuss shook his head. "I won't have them killed for making a mistake."

"They attacked a woman."

"And they've been punished."

"They *attacked* her," Rafe snarled, pushing to his feet and looming over the table.

I glanced around, noting the looks people cast our way. I caught Iana's glare, and she bustled toward us.

"She can hold her own. Sit down—for love of the sun." Rothfuss leaned back, putting distance between them, but kept his eyes leveled on the seething giant in front of him.

"What if it had been another woman? What if they had attacked the girl there?" Rafe threw his hand in Kila's direction.

"Sit down!" Iana hissed as she approached. "You're causing a scene in my tavern!" She cast me an accusing glower, and I held up my hands in mock surrender.

"Better than last night's," Rafe quipped, glare set on Rothfuss.

"Keep it up and I'll have your hide out on the road with your belongings tossed on your head." She reached out to push him into his seat.

Rafe moved like a snake, snatching her wrist in a firm grip. His gaze snapped to hers as he eased her hand back, his movement slow and deliberate. I touched his forearm, and he glanced my way, anger and hatred swirling in his dark eye.

"Enough," I whispered, holding that heated gaze.

After a steadying breath, he let go of Iana, then slammed down beside me. Raising his eyebrows, he dared her to object. With a huff, she nodded her approval and spun away to wait on tables.

"What is this all about?" I asked.

"Your man doesn't like my ruling."

"It's cowardly," Rafe spat.

"Luther's men?" I prompted.

"Aye. Sentenced them to a moon's cycle with the waste wagon."

I grimaced and nodded my understanding.

Rafe lived most of his life in the army where they followed the King's laws and the consequences of breaking them were harsh. When Victyr and the others attacked me all those years ago, they were dead by morning.

Here, things were different. Luther's men made threats and roughed me up a bit, yes, but hadn't followed through with their intentions. Rothfuss ruled with an iron first, but he was compassionate. If he sentenced them to a month dealing with the town's waste, then he found the threats harmless.

In Leeds, people were not killed for disobeying. In this harsh country, there were always underlying motives behind people's actions. Rothfuss made it seem like the men were hard up—in the wrong place at the wrong time. Had the attack been thought out and planned, he would have been more severe in his judgment... but Rafe didn't know that.

"Like it or not, I outrank you, soldier." Rothfuss lifted his mug in a silent toast. "If you want to settle here with Avyanna, you best realize that."

With that, he drained the rest of his tea. He gave me a pleasant nod before he stood, then headed for the door.

"That was intense," I murmured.

Rafe relaxed a fraction now that Rothfuss was gone. "Blasted fool thinks he's wise," he grumbled, surveying the crowd. He threw his arm over my shoulders, pressing me close.

"I trust him."

He tensed and squinted down at me. I met his perplexed gaze with a smile.

"I trust his judgment. He's a decent man," I said. "There's far less crime here than in any villages I passed through. There's a reason Leeds is as big and powerful as it is. Having a disciplined and principled lawkeeper has been a boon to its people."

"He's a good lawkeeper," he relented.

I scrunched up my face at his words, then grinned up at him, amused.

"Don't give me that look. Just because I want them dead doesn't mean I don't understand his principles."

"Good. I'm glad you like him."

He deadpanned. "I don't like him."

I snickered. Kila and Iana darted between tables, working hard. I needed to get up and do my share.

"I just wanted a moment or two alone with them," he muttered. "That's all. Not too much to ask."

"They wouldn't have lasted *a moment or two*." I laughed, pushing to my feet.

"That's not my problem."

"Correct, it's the lawkeeper's," I agreed. "I've got to work or Iana will kick us both out on the road."

He snorted, but dropped his arm and let me go.

I worked my shift, catching Jamlin and Zeph popping in to speak with Rafe. Jam gave me a friendly nod, but Zephath didn't bother. Though I noticed whenever his eyes lifted from the table, they found Kila.

"I think you have another admirer," I whispered when we met at the bar to fill mugs.

She had more than her share of men wanting to court her. With a new option every week, no one held romantic interest for long before she moved on.

"What? Who?" She glanced around before her eyes caught Zeph's. She smiled, and a blush lit her cheeks as she averted her gaze. "He's a friend of yours?"

I smirked and shook my head. "Something like that."

She leaned against the bar, waiting for me to elaborate.

"He's earned my respect," I said. "He's been a tough shell to crack, but I owe him."

Zeph frowned and turned his glare on Jam before saying something, then stared at his hands. When I was injured after Tizmet and I first bonded, he offered his aid. And he helped me rescue Rafe from the Shadows. His unwavering support throughout my journey made me realize I owed him my loyalty.

"So... he's..." She glanced over her shoulder to smile at his table.

"As far as I know, he's free." I shrugged, hefting my mugs. "He could do with a friend, Kila."

She tilted her head. "You're his friend."

"He deserves a friend he *likes*." I laughed.

I hummed to myself as I worked through the tables, collecting coin and serving food and drink. Zeph was my friend, not because he accepted me as such, but because I made him so. If he ever needed anything, I'd be there for him—I'd always be there to watch his back. He didn't have to like it. He was stuck with me, regardless.

I woke with a start, jerking out of my dream. I blinked at the shadows, varying shades of black, trying to comprehend what startled me awake. Rafe lay beside me, half covered by the blankets, but drenched in sweat. Propping myself upright, I slid my hand over his chest to his shoulder. His muscles strained, pulled taut.

"Rafe?"

His muffled moan greeted me, and I scrambled off the bed. Something wasn't right.

"Rafe, talk to me."

I rushed to my dresser. Feeling for the lantern, I opened myself to my magic. Tizmet roused, noticing me tug on it, giving it purpose. The flame flickered to life, and I padded to the bedside, lifting the lamp high.

Rafe was tense and damp against the sheets, his fists clenched tight. His right eye was shut, his left a gaping hole. He twitched, and his lips moved a fraction as another moan fell into the night.

"Rafe?"

I set the light down and climbed beside him, gently shaking his shoulders. My heart ached at what he might be suffering through. Was he reliving injuries suffered from battle—or the weeks of torture behind enemy lines? I couldn't fathom what he must have endured, and I couldn't leave him to face that terror alone.

Not anymore.

"Rafe." I shook his shoulders again.

His body strung tight as a bowstring, back arching off the bed, ready to snap. Muscles in his jaw worked, as if he wanted to say something.

I bit my lip and placed my palm on his cheek. "Rafe, I'm here."

He jerked as if he'd been struck. A low groan slipped past his lips as his body trembled like one of my seizures. I threw my leg over his hips and laid my chest against his, holding his hands. Pressing my lips against his ear, I ignored the sweat dampening my night shift.

"Rafe! I'm here!"

Rough hands crashed into my arms, his grip tight. He tossed me aside with the ease of a pillow. My head crashed against the floor, and I blinked as Rafe launched himself like some wild cat. He slammed into me, crushing me with his weight. His hands whipped to my neck, and I gasped when he squeezed.

With my experience of night terrors, I had expected *something*—for him to wake or lash out. Not this.

Tizmet's awareness dove into me, but I brushed her aside.

Rafe's gaze was wild with terror, his eye wide, but unseeing—still in the clutches of his dream. My lungs struggled for air as his grip crushed my throat. His chest heaved with panting breaths, hissing past his bared teeth.

Reining in my panic, I rubbed my hands up his arms, coaxing him back to me. Tizmet's roar rent the night. I cupped his jaw, trailing my thumb across his cheek, and his eye twitched, snapping to my face. I offered him a shaky smile.

Tizmet screamed, the force of it shaking the walls as the door to my room crashed open. Rafe's grip on my neck faltered as he faced whoever stomped up the stairs. I sucked in a gasping breath with the small reprieve.

"What in—Avyanna! Rafe? You with me?"

Rafe's hold loosened, and he frowned, looking back down at me. His eye didn't see my face, my assuring smile. He saw his fingers against my throat.

We all looked up as the roof creaked. Tizmet's rage was palpable.

'I'm well!'

'He's trying to kill you!'

'Tizmet, stop!'

The creaking halted, and Tizmet roared, bringing her eye to the window.

"Rafe, you with us?" Jamlin asked again. Wearing only his under-breeches, he lingered at the top of the stairs, his sword drawn and gleaming in the lamplight.

"We're fine," I rasped.

Rafe leaned back on my hips with a scowl, looking between me and Jam as his mind struggled to process what happened.

"Jam, we're well," I whispered. "Please go."

He paused, then pushed out a slow breath. "If you're good–"

"Aye, we're good."

Rafe stared at his hands as if they belonged to someone else. His weight crushed my legs, but for once, this strong mountain of a man needed me to be his strength.

There was a skeptical grunt before Jam's feet retreated down my stairs, and murmurs sounded below.

Rafe blinked, turning his gaze on me. His jaw clenched as he frowned, trying to make sense of the situation.

"You had a night terror."

I tugged his thick forearms down so that he was braced over me. His face contorted, flinching as I reached up to hold his jaw.

"You're with me now, in Leeds. Remember?"

His dark eye settled on mine and I rubbed my thumb over the crease in his brow.

"Talk to me."

His nose flared, and a tremor ran through his big body. His eye welled with a tear, and my smile faltered in response. He reached a shaking hand out to brush unsteady fingers against my neck, where I was sure bruises stained my skin. He blinked, trying to fight something inside himself, and the tear fell free, splashing against my cheek.

That broke me.

My Rafe was strong—far stronger than any man I'd ever met. He knew what he wanted and how to get it. Bull-headed and stubborn, he never took no for an answer. He could handle anything—strong-willed to a fault.

He was my solid mountain, never to be shaken.

Yet, here he was, broken and hurting.

"I—I *hurt* you." He breathed the words, voice trembling.

I wiped at another tear that fell. He tried to sit back, but I moved faster, lacing my fingers behind his head, holding him above me.

"Tell me I'm beautiful."

"You're beautiful."

He pressed his lips together, and I caught a glimmer of hope spark in his eye.

"Tell me you love me."

"I love you," he replied without hesitation.

"Tell me you love Tizmet."

"I don't."

He shook his head, and I giggled. The tiniest smile lifted the corner of his mouth. I slid my touch to his face and drew my thumb across his lips. His gaze was still miles away, lost in torment.

"Rafe, you can't hurt me unless you push me away."

He glanced at the bed, then at me, raising a brow. "Pretty sure I tossed you away."

"Rafe–"

"I could have hurt you." His eye clouded over with some memory and he frowned, looking into the distance above me. "I *did* hurt you."

"Rafe." When he ignored me again, I tugged his face to mine. "Do you trust me?"

His brows met as he studied me. "Aye."

"With your life?"

"Aye."

"With mine?"

He took a deep breath, his gaze darting to my neck.

I forced my next words to come out steady, conveying their truth. "Trust me—if you tried to hurt me, I wouldn't let you. Have a little faith in me."

He scoffed. "So you were *letting* me hurt you a moment ago?"

"I wasn't fighting back, now was I?" I smirked. "Rafe, Tizmet was ready to tear the roof off and eat you. Trust me to take care of myself."

I tugged him closer, ignoring his brief resistance. Our lips crashed together, and I tried to assure him with my kisses in a way that my words never could.

Chapter 8

I hummed to myself as I hung the laundry. It had been days since Rafe's night terror. While Tizmet still didn't trust my judgment, she was too busy nesting to be bothered to do much about it.

To my puzzlement, Rafe took a job with Rothfuss as one of his enforcers. Apparently, they resolved their differences—the most obnoxious ones, at least. I no longer felt like a bone between two snarling dogs.

Enforcers were the minor lawkeepers of the town. They kept the peace and helped maintain order. It surprised me that Rothfuss would offer such a position to a newcomer, and Rafe's acceptance was just as shocking. He seemed far too independent to take a job working under another man's authority.

The Tennan joined him, except for Dane, who was my constant companion. Both Rafe and I knew I didn't need a bodyguard, but it put him at ease to have someone else looking out for me.

I had no complaints, as Dane was good company. Brandi was smitten by his quiet charm and brought him all sorts of creatures in trade for whatever he might have that day. It would be nothing for him to walk around with a toad or lizard in his shirt, much to my horror.

I pinned my last pair of trousers up and nodded to Dane, who was hanging his own laundry. I reached out to Tizmet while he finished and found her pawing at an immense boulder deep in the forest north of here. It was nearly a day's ride away, which meant she would be there till nightfall.

'Look promising?' I asked, pushing my contentment toward her.

Her awareness flickered at my question, but she didn't grace me with an answer, focused on her task. I'd never heard of a dragon laying eggs on a rock.

Dane straightened, and we set off to the main street. I walked, excitement making my steps skip through the crowd. He snorted and lengthened his strides to keep up with me. The townsfolk finally adjusted to the Tennan's presence. Though most realized they were tied to me, I hadn't given them any answers to their pressing questions. Rafe held off divulging who he was, and I would respect that. I understood his reluctance. He planned to settle in Leeds, but even I didn't trust everyone here. They knew he was my promised, and that was enough for me.

When I first came, I kept to myself and was wary of using my name. At the time, it seemed safer to just be a traveler—with a dragon. I thought out here, a dragon might be seen as a badge of honor, or a symbol of power. Yet these people knew the Dragon Riders of Regent protected their realm, and didn't concern themselves with the hardships of others. I was outside the borders of Regent. With a dragon. That bode ill for my reputation.

Inside the guild hall, Rafe watched Master Val speak with his young apprentice. I made my way over, and Dane lingered near the door.

The old man pointed to something on the plans and shook his head. "Build it like that, and you'll bring the roof down about their heads. You need more support, boy," he scolded.

I stepped close enough to Rafe that our sides touched. His arms were crossed over his chest in his guarded, but relaxed, manner. He looked down and arched his brow, then grunted a greeting. Still, he couldn't hide the faint smile that teased his lips.

"How has your morning been?" I asked.

"I was told to fetch a chicken thief."

"And, did you?" I snickered, knowing the answer.

"No."

"What did Rothfuss say?"

"Don't know. Didn't catch his words when I left."

I smiled and shook my head. Why Rothfuss even wanted someone as bull-headed as Rafe, I had no idea. Plenty of the Tennan would make great enforcers. But Rafe? He wasn't exactly employee material.

A hard glint came to his eye. "You know the baker's old woman?" he asked.

I squinted. "His wife?"

"No. Older."

"White hair with an odd streak of black?"

"Aye."

"Emilia. She's his mother. He supports her. She lives with him and his wife above the bakery. Why?"

"I found some of Luther's men cornering her."

I frowned and crossed my arms over my chest. "Their bakery is the best in Leeds. Luther owns the other two, but they can't compete. I can't say I'm surprised he set his dogs on them." I huffed a sigh, then a sympathetic smile lifted my lips. "Emilia can hold her own. Did you get to see?"

"Not till after I told the men off." He rubbed at his arm. "Old women and their canes."

I let out a laugh, noticing the red welts on his forearm, then settled against him. Emilia wielded her cane as a staff. Rumors claimed that with a twist of her hand, the wooden casing shed away to reveal a wicked-thin blade.

"I don't like it," Rafe murmured.

I glanced up and noted the firm line of his lips. "No one likes it. Rothfuss does what he can to keep Luther in check."

"Not enough."

His statement got under my skin. I knew Luther's actions were wrong, but Rothfuss held him accountable. Unfortunately, painful repercussions weren't always the best deterrent. There wasn't anything anyone could do about it. Leeds was one of the calmer settlements along the E'or, due to both Rothfuss' law and Luther's business.

To be honest, I didn't want to talk about why Leed's wasn't the best place, or how it lacked the same orderliness as Regent. I wanted to settle here. I wanted a home—and I wanted Rafe.

"This isn't Regent," I fired back.

His eye glittered. He didn't reply, but the stiff set of his jaw proved he wouldn't leave it alone.

Master Val interrupted our little conversation. "My apologies. Are we ready to head out?"

I held my tongue and glanced at Rafe. He asked me to meet him here, but hadn't told me why. I assumed it was to go over some plans for our house. Clearly not.

Rafe pushed off the wall with a curt nod. "Aye."

"Good. It's a bit of a ride."

Master Val started for the door. He held it open for me, and I cast a curious glance between the two. Was this some kind of meeting concerning materials? To inspect different trees or stones? Rafe smirked, offering nothing. My eyes narrowed, but I didn't question him.

Outside, I noted Rafe's stallion beside another sturdy horse. Strong hands lifted me, and a small yelp spilled from my mouth before I could press my lips together. Rafe chuckled as I straddled his stallion. The great beast snorted and pricked his ears back, as if offended by my paltry weight. I gripped the mane as Rafe mounted, sharing the saddle with me. The horse snorted a sigh of relief at his weight and his ears pricked forward.

When he pulled me tight against his chest, I couldn't help but smile at his proximity. I felt safe, cherished—loved. He wrapped an arm around my waist and held the reins in his right hand. Even Master Val's judgmental frown couldn't damper my high spirits. He made a thoughtful sound and gave a one-armed shrug before directing his horse down the road. I beamed as Rafe's stallion set off after him in a ground-eating walk, forcing myself not to wave and giggle at Dane, who watched us leave with bored eyes.

We rode in comfortable silence. I enjoyed the moment, simply *being* with Rafe. This was all I wanted in life—a series of content moments like this where we both felt safe and loved.

Who needed adventures?

Not me.

Master Val led us north, through the small wooden wall that surrounded Leeds. A chime passed, and the horses took their time picking over the path that was more mud than solid ground. The roads near the bog were in a constant state of muck.

We passed through clearings and dense copses of low-hanging willows, ducking to avoid the dangling branches. By the state of the road, it was obviously less-traveled than most.

Master Val steered his horse onto a game trail that wound its way between the trees. Rafe's stallion snorted and huffed at the tight squeeze. A bog was no place for a warhorse.

"Ah, here we are."

Master Val's comment drew my attention ahead. We broke through the treeline, and my heart skipped a beat as I took in the scene. A large clearing spread out in front of us, blocked in on three sides by dense forest and underbrush. To our right lay a body of water. I doubted it was connected to the bog, because the heavy fog was absent. The sun shone bright, sparkling over the glassy surface. Lillies and water flowers bobbed with the slight ripples jostled by the breeze. A few ducks eyed us warily and called their alarm, rushing their little ones away from the bank.

I smiled and drew my eyes back to the main attraction. A small, vine-covered shack leaned askew at a precarious angle, its door hanging open to the elements. Decay and wood rot were evident beneath the tangled foliage. As the breeze picked up again, I wondered if it would topple, or if the vines kept it upright.

"It's beautiful," I breathed.

Rafe grunted in a disapproving tone and urged his stallion beside Master Val's horse. "It needs to be torn down," he stated with disgust.

"Aye, it would seem that way," Master Val gave him a sharp glare, "to the untrained eye. Come, have a look."

Rafe dismounted and shook out his legs as if they were tired after the ride. He looked up at me expectantly, and I grinned like a fool, letting him see my open excitement. He rolled his eye, then supported me as I climbed down. This place was a little haven longing for someone to claim it as home—a hidden gem tucked away.

"See the pond? 'Tis freshwater," Master Val said. "Hard to come by in these parts."

"I didn't know there was any in Leeds," I mused.

"There isn't." He led us toward the shack as he nodded to Rafe. "Having a pond is a luxury. Still, I'd recommend you dig a well."

"A pond doesn't make up for *that*." Rafe jerked his head toward the shack.

Val gave him another sharp glower. "See her up close before you make any assumptions. I'm a Master of my trade, soldier."

I offered a placating smile before he continued on. The tall grass around the decrepit structure was untamed. Small game trails trampled tiny paths from the water's edge to the forest. I smiled as a butterfly flew from a flower, taking to the air with vibrant orange wings. Tizmet reached across the bond, curious, then started our way.

Rafe's heavy hand rested on my shoulder, drawing my gaze as he squeezed. I grinned as amusement pulled at the corner of his mouth.

"You own this, Master Val?" I asked as we neared the shack.

"Aye. Old Trodor lives about two chimes west of here. That'd be your closest neighbor." He paused at the threshold before stepping inside. "Most folks wouldn't like to live this far from civilized country. Risk of unseemly rogues might be too high."

"Rogues." Rafe scoffed under his breath, then followed and peered in.

"Stone foundation," he murmured.

"Aye, it's not just what meets the eye that counts." Master Val's tone grew smug with Rafe's appraisal. "We strip all the rotted wood, and build her from the ground up—good as new."

I held my breath as I entered behind Rafe, the cramped space moving my heart. It was smaller than my room at the inn, perhaps twenty paces long, ten wide. The solid stone floor was relatively flat. I knelt, brushing the dirt away to feel its rough security. A small creature skittered in the corner, and I smiled as a pile of leaves shifted with its panicked breaths.

"It will need some cleaning." Nerves heightened my tone.

Rafe grunted, walking about the space, checking the floor. "Needs a bit more than cleaning."

"Aye, she needs new wood, but won't find a stone foundation and freshwater anywhere else within riding distance of Leeds."

Master Val returned to his horse to give us privacy, and Rafe joined my side. We stepped out to view the clearing again.

Orange and red wildflowers grew among the tall golden grass, swaying with the same breeze that teased the willow branches at the edge of the forest. Chicory, a lovely blush pink flower, bloomed in the shady sections. It made a wonderful tea. Brambles grew along the treeline, and I was sure they'd be lush with ripe berries by fall—perfect for picking and preserving.

The simple sounds of nature sang in my ears as I took in the beauty of this little place. Ducks called to each other. Birds whistled in the trees. Small squirrels hopped from branch to branch, clicking their interest at us.

This felt—*right.*

"Don't look at the field that way," Rafe groaned. "I'm no farmer."

My laughter was airy and breathless as I wrapped my arms around him. He draped an arm over my shoulders, pressing me close.

"No farming for you," I agreed. "I could have a garden, though. Just a small one. And I bet there are fish in that pond. The woods will be teeming with game this far out."

"The house will need work."

"Yes, but–"

"The builder says he can have it done by spring."

I pulled away with a frown. "At what cost?"

A project like this took time. Between materials and labor—it wouldn't be cheap to rush things along.

"Vy," Rafe lifted my chin to meet my eyes, "I would pay all the gold in the world for a place to settle with you."

Tizmet flew into my line of sight, pulling my attention from him as she landed in the clearing. Master Val's horse snorted and danced to the side as she drew in a deep breath, taking in the sights. I stood there, filled with anticipation, though I didn't understand why I was so concerned about her response.

She turned her large flaming gaze on me, then reached across the bond, testing my emotions. *'Home?'*

I looked at Rafe, then around the property, tears pricking at my eyes.

'Yes. Home.'

Chapter 9

Back at the guildhall, Rafe and Master Val discussed various details, windows being the current topic. I already clarified that I didn't require any, but Rafe was adamant. Glass was something I overrode though. It was an expensive, fragile barrier that broke far too quickly for it to be worth its cost. A tanned hide would block drafts in the winter and a thin sheet could keep bugs out in the summer.

I kept one ear on their conversation and my eyes on the street. Dane leaned on the wall just outside, standing at the mercy of the vile stinging insects. I tilted my head when he frowned and straightened to his full height. Something in the distance caught his attention, and I stood, peering into the crowd. People jostled about, running last-minute errands, or hurrying home before sunset. Nothing seemed amiss.

Dane whirled, rushing inside. "Blain."

The rasped word was enough to pull Rafe from the conversation and out the door. I started after them, but Master Val called my name, giving me pause. Graphite smudged his hands and forearms from drawing up plans. Beneath his fingers was a small, rough sketch of my future home.

My home.

"He's a good man," he said.

I clenched my jaw as my eyes burned with tears—sudden and unexpected. Not everyone bothered to see beyond Rafe's rough exterior. Master Val saw past the warrior to the man who cared about me, who cared about *our* future.

"I know." I offered him an apologetic smile. "We'll be back."

I slipped out and followed Dane and Rafe toward the stables. I noted in passing the two men who pushed off their post nearby to trail me. Luther's goons never gave me a moment's peace.

Tizmet reached over the bond, content. She was close to laying her clutch—tired and swollen, but at ease. The new plot of land we planned to purchase was only a half a day's ride from her nest. She was pleased we would be close when her young hatched.

That I wasn't nervous for her had guilt gnawing at the edges of my mind. Some dragons, especially younger ones, experienced complications. The Dragon Masters often intervened, but I had no way of knowing what to do if something went wrong.

'I have laid before, little one.' Tizmet pushed amusement, unconcerned. *'I am a Wild Dragon. Unlike your tame beasts of burden, I know how to handle my clutch.'*

A smile tugged at my lips. She was confident in her abilities, as was I. She was strong and could handle laying on her own.

Blain latched the stable gate when his eyes settled on me. "Hail, Avyanna." His tone was tired, his clothes filthy. His beard grew out during his travels, but his eyes lost none of their sharpness.

"Tell me next time," Rafe snarled. His look of disapproval masked his worry.

Soon after the Tennan arrived in Leeds, Blain set off on his own, telling no one other than Dane. He headed over the E'or, back to Regent. Dane wouldn't say why, which irritated Rafe to no end.

"Hail, Blain. You look a little worse for wear," I teased.

His smile faltered, and he cast a sidelong glance at Rafe before jerking his chin toward the inn. "There's something we should discuss."

Rafe's glower darkened, and he nodded to me, then fell into step behind Blain. I frowned as we followed the twins out of the stables.

We entered the bustling inn, seeking out the little table in the corner near the kitchen door. Iana squinted at me from the bar, as if my presence on a night off was offensive.

Rafe and I sat across from Blain and Dane as Kila approached with a friendly smile.

"Three ales and a water," I called before she could ask.

She winked and spun on her heel, skipping off while humming some tune.

Blain took a deep breath, as if collecting himself, and sat tall. Eyeing Rafe, he pursed his lips and shrugged. "I returned to Regent."

"Why?" Rafe asked, his tone low—not menacing or angry, just flat.

"I go where I will."

"When you will," Rafe added.

"Aye," he agreed. "Still, I thought you'd like to hear what I saw."

Rafe held up a hand as Kila brought our drinks. I thanked her and as she scurried off, Blain took a long pull from his mug before moving on.

"It's not good," he said, smacking his lips.

"It wasn't good when we left," Rafe scoffed.

Worry thrummed beneath my skin. The War of Shadows started long before I was born. It had obviously never gone well. To have one of Rafe's Tennan say it wasn't good, sounded ominous.

"It's worse," Blain said. "There are multiple reports of raids throughout the plains. More winding north and east."

"Northwing?" I cut in. I had friends there, loved ones. Surely they were not targeted again.

Blain sighed and looked into his mug as if it had the answers. "They know there are dragons there, and that Regent hides them in the south. I'm getting the feeling they're looking for them elsewhere."

Not this side of the E'or—they wouldn't cross the mountains. Would they?

Tizmet was riled by my anxiety. *'If they do, I will kill them all.'*

"How often?"

Rafe's inquiry roused me from my thoughts.

"Often enough that King's Wall feels the pinch now that farmers are sending less. They're too fearful to be on the road carrying goods. Trade routes are slowing. People are going hungry."

I thought back to my final weeks at Northwing. They barely survived with the rations they had. The refugees spilled over into nearby villages, as the school itself was no longer capable of meeting their needs.

"It appears they have the advantage," Blain murmured, swirling his ale.

"Raids that far must spread them thin," I pressed.

"How many dragons?" Rafe interrupted.

Blain winced. "How many are left, or how many have they taken?"

My heart stuttered at his reply.

"Both."

He shook his head and glanced at me before looking back into his mug. "They've taken four. I'm not sure how many remain."

Four? The Shadows claimed *four* dragons?

"The Dragon Lord?" Rafe asked, shifting in his seat.

He didn't see eye to eye with Ruveel, but he never denied his abilities on the front. Tizmet and I witnessed Ge'org in action when the Shadows attacked Northwing. He was a sight to behold.

'He wasn't that impressive,' Tizmet commented dryly. She headed toward Leeds, awake and aware of my thoughts.

I pushed back at her teasingly. She detested Ge'org, who didn't give her the respect she demanded. She fought with him on several occasions and despite him being larger than her, she often sent him running.

"Safe. His nightmare of a dragon has protected the flank, though they're pulling the Fleets back."

"They'll be sitting ducks." Rafe hissed a curse under his breath.

Blain's sober nod showed his agreement. "Tightens the target."

"What chance do we have?" I asked.

Between the two of them, I was bound to get a blunt response.

"*We?*" Blain scrunched up his nose, tilting his head.

"Vy."

I looked up at Rafe with a frown.

"It's not our fight," he said.

My heart dropped like a stone. I couldn't help the people if I returned. I was no longer a citizen or a protector of Regent. It wasn't my home to be fighting for anymore. I was an outsider, a nobody who lived on the outskirts of Rinmoth.

Rafe reached under the table and gripped my thigh. He knew those words stung.

"I'm heading back in a month," Blain said, clearing his throat.

Rafe gave him a stern look. "I'd like to have a report then as well."

"Ever the General." He laughed.

Blain and his brother retired, and I stared after them as they left. I heaved a sigh and let myself fall against Rafe. He didn't embrace me, but turned so I could rest on his side.

"My friends are still there." I bit my lip and glared at the table.

How could I have been so happy earlier? I'd been so content planning my home while those I loved were in danger.

"My mother is there—in Stonesmead." My heart twisted thinking of her and Ragnath, the blacksmith she'd taken as her life mate after my father died.

"The Shadows wouldn't venture so far from their homeland."

I closed my eyes, taking comfort from his words. I wanted to believe him. "You sound so sure."

"For them to reach Stonesmead with force, they would need trade routes of their own." He nursed the last of his ale. "They're a long way off from that."

"But it's not impossible," I pressed.

"Neither is it impossible for Regent to rally and stave them off."

"It doesn't make sense. How can there be so many of them? Why are they so hard to defeat?"

He spoke in a low tone, surveying the room and its occupants. "They're not like us. They're different. Driven. They are greedy and know where to sniff out power." He looked down at me with a frown. "You're special, Vy. Not only because you have that dragon, but because you can use magic. If everyone in Regent could access magic, do you think they would be struggling to win this war?"

"Surely not all of them–"

"No, but far more of them have magic than Regent has Riders," he said. "I've met few Shadows that couldn't tap into magic. Shamen aren't common, but they aren't rare either. Regent is outmatched."

When he finished his drink, we retired to our room. Throughout the night and well into the next morning, I tried to ignore the guilt that came with living my life so far from the war. I was living my 'happily ever after' with Rafe while my friends struggled to fill their bellies or get a good night's rest.

"Peace, Vy," he murmured, his chest vibrating with his words.

"Our people are fighting for their lives and we're lying here in a nice soft bed." I sighed and sat up, studying him in the weak morning light. "Don't you feel bad?"

"No," he grumbled.

"How? I feel–"

"Like you owe them." He knitted his fingers behind his head as his dark gaze met mine. His empty socket twitched as he did so, as if it wanted to see me as well. "You owe no one. I owe no one."

"They provided for me. I was fed, I was–"

"And you came for me," he said. "Do you think I owe Regent?"

I thought about that for a moment, staring at the wall. He hadn't exactly been kept safe. He fought his entire life. It's not like he ever lived off the charity of the crown.

I formed my response with care. "No."

"You'd be right. I gave my best years to King and Country, and served them well."

I scoffed at his arrogance.

He arched a daring brow. "Didn't I?"

"Aye, the mighty General, who fought off the droves of Shadows," I teased, poking his chest.

"Vy, I more than returned any good I received. If anything, Regent owes *me.*"

I frowned. He was right. He sacrificed so much. Regent as a kingdom at least owed him a little.

"When I was taken–" He clenched his jaw and glared at the wall with his lip curled in a snarl. "No one sent aid. Not that I expected anyone would. It was a suicide mission."

"But it wasn't." I flashed a small smile.

He cupped my jaw. "No one came for me, but *you* did. So, no. I don't owe Regent, and neither do you."

I sighed and sought comfort in his touch, turning my face to his palm. "What about my friends?" I asked, voice muffled by his hand.

He tugged my chin and brought my gaze to his. "Darrak? His red-haired companion? Will-something–"

"Willhelm." I scoffed, knowing he knew his name, but forever teased me about him.

"Aye, him." He smirked. "Can you do more than any of them?"

"Well, not exactly."

"Then let them do their jobs."

"Rafe–"

"Vy, they are wanted. They are welcome." His lips dropped into a serious frown as he continued, "Let them protect the land that sees *them* as assets, and not you."

With a shuddering breath, I closed my eyes. I did this—put myself in this situation. If given the chance, I'd do it all again, no question. I had to suffer the consequences of *how* I went about rescuing him. This was my punishment to bear.

"Go on, now." Rafe nudged me off the bed. "I'm sure that little girl is eager to trade pebbles with you."

I rose and washed my face, trying to shake off the weight of the conversation. "Ah, so you know about Brandi?"

"Dane's been sneaking creatures into Tegan's bed."

I laughed outright. "So that's where all the creatures are going?"

"Aye."

Rafe let out a long groan, then swung his bare feet to the floor. He winced and rubbed at the wound on his face.

"Will you ever tell me how it happened?" I whispered.

He stilled and clasped his hands in front of him, elbows on his knees. He peered up at me with a dark frown. "Which part? When it turned, or when they ripped the blasted thing out?"

My lips pressed together. It felt as though I crossed some personal boundary. I was asking a lot of him to share this, and rushing it before I had to go collect some petty eggs was not the time. He watched me warily as I closed the space between us. I cupped his left cheek, running my thumb over his empty socket, across his scars.

"Both."

He flinched, and I pulled my hand back, wondering if I pushed too far.

"Either." I rushed my words. "Or none, if it's too–"

He snatched my wrist and returned my touch to his cheek, holding it there. His brows sank into a self-loathing glare, and anguish swirled in his gaze. He wasn't ready to relive that.

"Vy, I'm trying." His voice cracked. He bit out a curse and turned away, as if fighting his shame and humiliation.

I dropped to my knees, still holding his face. "I know."

All he'd ever known was war. He was trying to make this life away from the barracks work—for me.

For *us*.

"You're doing so well," I teased, attempting to draw him out of his torment. "No men to order about, and you're doing grandly."

He scoffed and nipped at my hand. I rose, laughing as I grabbed my trousers and tunic.

"Find me after your shift, and we'll head to the guildhall," he said.

I smiled as I dressed.

That's right. We were building our house.

Chapter 10

Tegan recounted the story of how he found a beetle in his boot as we walked through the crowded streets. It had been Brandi's morning find, one I wasn't willing to trade for. Dane, of course, gave her a tiny blue-speckled egg for the insect. I watched in horror as he reached in his pocket, pulled out a drawstring bag and slipped the giant iridescent bug inside. Drawing it tight, he stuffed it down his shirt as if there was no chance it would come undone and skitter across his skin. "So, I not only had the half-alive thing crawling up my leg, but I had blasted guts sliming my boot." He lifted his foot, giving it a shake.

My nose wrinkled. "Disgusting."

'Remember that bug in the Sands?' I reached through the bond to Tizmet.

She paused digging her nest. '*Which one?*' she asked, mildly amused.

There *had* been plenty.

'Tegan would have enjoyed them.'

'Those he could fight, perhaps.' She resumed her task. *'It's the little ones that send them running.'*

"I'd like to know where they're coming from." Tegan's mouth pulled into a grimace.

I eyed him, pressing my lips together to keep my laughter from spilling out.

"You know something!" He jumped into my path, pointing an accusing finger.

Rafe pushed the riled man out of my way, and I giggled.

Tegan's eyes widened. "Who? Surely it's not ye!"

"I would never!" I gasped and held a hand over my heart in mock horror.

"If it's Jam I'm going to–"

"Tegan, shut it," Rafe snarled.

I grinned at Rafe, thinking he had enough of the man's theatrics, but my smile fell as I noted the deep creases of irritation on his face. I followed his gaze to three of Luther's men, lounging in front of the guildhall. Two of them I recognized, though the third wore a leather hat, shrouding his features in shadow.

"Look at that. It's the lovebirds," Bodrin jeered before Izaak threw an elbow at him.

They looked rough. Shortswords hung from their hips and they watched us with wary, dangerous eyes.

Tegan's mirth fell away. He stepped closer to my side, his hand braced and ready to draw his short sword.

"Avyanna." The one with the hat spoke first. Dirk. Though I should have known. He leaned against the wall, smoking a pipe. "Luther's been expecting you."

"He gets me instead," Rafe growled. He stormed ahead and threw the door open.

'This won't end well.' I complained to Tizmet, following after.

'Your mate better keep you safe,' she snarled, then took wing, heading our way. *'Or I* will *eat him this time.'*

I stepped inside, taking in the sight before me. Master Val stood behind a desk stacked high with papers and drawings. Frustration drew out his weathered features. Rafe stood with arms crossed, looking as if he could kill Luther with his glare alone.

Rafe and Luther's stature was where their similarities ended. He was dressed in a fine embroidered tunic and overcoat. His boots shone from their glossy tops down to where mud inevitably coated the toe.

"Avyanna, dear. How good of you to join us." Luther's tone dripped with condescending sweetness.

His sharp eyes caught mine, and he tossed his cane to his left hand before swiping his wool cap off in a mocking bow. His dark hair was combed to perfection. He tilted his chin upward, giving me a wicked smile.

This was *so* not good. Things could get out of hand very quickly.

"Rafe, I think we should–"

"No, no, dear. I'm pleased you're both here," Luther assured, straightening to meet Rafe's glare and tug on the lapels of his overcoat.

Rafe crowded into his space, but he refused to back down.

"I believe Master Val has some unfortunate news he would like to share with you," he mused.

My heart raced and my fingers tingled as I glanced at the Builder, who dropped his gaze to his papers with a severe frown. Rafe didn't move a muscle, choosing to glare Luther down.

"Master Val?" I choked out.

Surely this wasn't going where I thought it was.

"Avyanna, I'm sorry."

I held my breath in check at his words. I would not lose my head. Despite the panic creeping beneath my skin, I was an adult and could respond with dignity.

"You see," Luther drawled with a smile, adjusting his sleeves, "I was recently made aware of a lovely plot of land."

A muscle in Rafe's jaw twitched.

"When it was brought to my attention, I thought, 'Oh, now Luther, *that's* a valuable asset.' And I simply had to inquire after it."

I stood there, horrified, trying to understand how Master Val had been swayed by this man.

"Yet, when I did so, he claimed it was spoken for." Luther turned a condescending smile on Master Val, who stared at his papers with fists clenched tight. "I just had to procure the plot, which again, was quite lovely—simply perfect for a humble home. A dainty cottage with a garden to raise little ones."

Luther's brown eyes found mine, and my vision burned red with hate. "Anyway," he continued, "I offered our Val here a bit more than the previous buyers."

"I'll double." Rafe's voice dropped dangerously low.

"Oh, not so fast, you sly dog." Luther pushed out an airy laugh, leaning heavily on his cane. "I presented an offer that Val here couldn't resist. Rafe, chap, you're new in these parts. Let me explain. I own the woods the Builders log from, and the mill used to make lumber. I own the quarry where the stone is mined, and the equipment used to bring the stone from the mountains. So, you see? I owned the little cottage before even paying for it."

Surely there was another place for him to build. I straightened my shoulders, ready to plead my case. "But–"

"Oh, no dear. The contract has already been signed." Luther turned his wretched smile my way. His gaze sparkled at my misery and the power he held over us. "Our kind Master here is going to build me a pigsty."

His grin got a margin larger, and I couldn't help the step I took back from the vile sight of it, from the hatred in the depths of his eyes.

"A lovely little pigsty," he mused, "right where the cottage would have been. Now, I'm not an unjust man." He angled his body toward me, following my retreat, and gave Rafe his shoulder, clearly dismissing him. "I'd let you live there."

Rafe snatched the front of his overcoat and threw him onto the desk. Val scrambled back, shouting for Rothfuss as papers scattered across the floor. Rafe ripped Luther's cane from his grasp and slammed it down across his knee. A terrible scream tore out of his throat as his goons stormed past me, ready for blood.

'I'm coming, little one.'

Tizmet snapped me out of my haze. I gripped my bandit breaker and snatched the back of the man nearest me. I hauled on Izaak's tunic, pulling him off Rafe, and pressed my blade to his throat. Tegan rushed in, grabbing Dirk as Rafe kicked Bodrin's thigh. A sharp snap sounded and I winced as the man howled, holding his leg, going down hard. Luther thrashed and flailed as Rafe slammed his fist into his face, drawing blood.

"Rafe! No!" I screamed, but he tossed the cane aside and hit him again.

"Rafe of Deomein!"

I spun with Izaak, pivoting as Rothfuss stepped up with three of his enforcers. He strode inside with his hand on his sword. His men lingered on the wooden deck instead of crowding the space.

Rafe smashed his fist into Luther's face one last time, and the bloodied man went limp.

"Rafe Shadowslayer!" Rothfuss bellowed.

I hauled Izaak back as the lawkeeper drew his weapon.

A dragon's roar sounded in the distance.

Rothfuss braced the tip of his sword along Rafe's bowed neck. My heart crashed against my ribcage and I reached for magic without thinking. Rafe looked over his shoulder, gaze locked on mine as Tizmet shrieked again.

Then the pain in my chest blossomed.

I came-to slowly and painfully. Groaning, I lifted my weak hands to rub at my temples. The last of the seizure trembled through me, and I bit my lip against crying out at the ache beneath my ribs.

'I will eat them all!'

My eyes snapped open. The dark sky loomed above me, stars hidden by the ever-present haze. I sat up, scanning the area. A crowd gathered, nervously taking in the scene. The lawkeeper and his men had their weapons drawn, pointed at Rafe and the Tennan. Tizmet crouched behind me, lips curled in a snarl.

'Don't eat anyone!' I pleaded.

"There. The level-headed one is awake," Rothfuss called.

"What–" I broke off with a cough.

Rafe stood with his twin blades pointed toward the ground, but looking no less dangerous.

'They tried to take you from me!' Tizmet roared, baring rows of terrible teeth. Saliva sprayed with her shriek, and my ears rang.

"Avyanna, call your dragon off." Rothfuss kept calm, keeping his eyes on Rafe.

Dane had his bow drawn, aimed at an enforcer. Jam and Zeph stood in a perfect battle stance, their weapons at the ready. Blain simply picked his nails with a dagger, eyeing the crowd with a bored look. There was no sign of Tegan.

'Tizmet, please. I'm not going anywhere.'

'You were!'

She roared her anguish and pushed an image of two men carrying me between them. In the memory, Rafe walked close by, focused on me as Rothfuss prodded him with his sword.

'I wouldn't leave you!'

Tizmet rushed them, stepping over me. Her gravid belly hung low to my head. She skidded, throwing up clods of mud as she hissed.

"Avyanna?" Rothfuss called out again.

I was sure I wasn't the only one who heard the nervous tremor in his tone.

"They were taking me to Saudric!" I shouted, hoping they'd catch on. They needed to verify that for both Rafe and Tizmet's sake.

I struggled to get my legs under me to stand and winced in pain as my head throbbed with the effort of raising my voice. There was a moment of tense silence, and I clutched her foreleg to haul myself up. My chest screamed in complaint and I gritted my teeth, heaving myself upright.

"Aye, taking you to the Healer," Rothfuss agreed.

'See?' I leaned my forehead against her scales and took a ragged breath. My limbs were so weak. *'It's alright.'*

I pushed calm, relief and comfort her way, then thought of warm compresses and gentle salves.

'They lie.'

I smiled at her flaming eye as she crowded my face. *'They would have taken me to Saudric,'* I repeated, assuring her.

'After they locked you in a cage.'

I took a deep breath and gave a weak shrug. *'I was a danger. Rothfuss has to care for the people. He has to protect them from dangers.'*

'Like me.' She lifted her head to snarl at Rothfuss.

'You're scaring the little ones.'

To be honest, I couldn't see any children. Their parents probably whisked them off at the sight of an enraged dragon.

'They should be scared! I am a dragon!' Tizmet braced her forelegs and lifted her maw to the sky, letting loose a stream of fire.

Bystanders gasped and stumbled a few steps, but they didn't run—as they should have. Tizmet screamed and whipped her maw toward the crowd. I fell from beneath her, drawing her attention back to me as I lurched forward. Rafe shifted his stance so he could see me from the corner of his eye, without leaving himself open to Rothfuss.

'You're gravid. This is a people matter, Tizmet.'

'You,' she hissed, snapping her teeth near my face, *'are my people!'*

'I am.' I stroked her scaled lips, then pressed my forehead close. *'I am yours and I am safe. No one is taking me anywhere now.'*

'Now! Now that I'm here!'

Across the bond, I glimpsed her thoughts—a vision of her snatching me away to her nest.

'They wouldn't dare try to take me from you. Stay. Let me see the Healer.'

She huffed and pulled her head up, looming above me. *'I'm not leaving you.'*

I offered her a small smile, then turned to Rothfuss. "Now would be a good time to send for Saudric."

We were all seated in the muddy street in front of the law house. Tizmet hovered over me like an anxious mother. Rothfuss' men had cleared the crowd, though I was sure several watched from nearby windows and cracked doorways. Rafe sat closest to me, both his swords sheathed and on the ground. Jam, Zeph, Blain and Dane were all unarmed, sitting in our group as well. Apparently, Tegan was dragged into a cell before Tizmet arrived.

Saudric shook his head, sitting back on his heels with a frown. "I don't know."

A bitter smile lifted my lips. I knew what caused the seizures. It was my price to pay for the amount of magic I pulled when I found Rafe behind enemy lines. No medicine could fix that damage.

"Is your dragon calm now?" Rothfuss crouched next to Saudric.

'No.'

"As much as possible," I replied, ignoring Tizmet's comment.

"I'd like a word with you and Rafe—in private."

'You're not leaving my sight.'

"She won't let me go into a building."

"Well, you better figure something out to appease her."

Rothfuss glanced at Rafe and shooed Saudric away. The Healer stood up and walked off with jerky steps. No one wanted to be this close to an angry dragon.

Tizmet huffed and moved slowly, her swollen belly making her look cumbersome.

'I do not look cumbersome.' She batted at the men who didn't move out of her way.

'I was just musing.'

'I shall have musings when you are with child as well.'

She sighed, settling beside me. I brushed off the familiar worry that came with her statement and sought Rafe. He scrutinized her and pushed himself to his feet. Rothfuss stood with him, glancing at the swords on the ground.

"I wouldn't need them," Rafe bit out.

Rothfuss glared at him, but his features softened when he looked down at me. I cursed and struggled to my feet, gaze darting between the two.

"This looks bad," he started.

Rafe grunted. "I could have made it worse."

"Rafe, you're not helping," I muttered.

Rothfuss dragged a hand across his jaw. "I have an irate dragon–"

Tizmet swung toward him, hissing, and he dodged her glob of spit.

He gritted his teeth and continued, "I have a small army willing to fight me in the streets after I *hired* them to help me keep the peace!. I have Luther–"

"No, you don't." Rafe sneered.

"I have him." The leather-wrapped hilt creaked in his clenched fist, as if he fought the urge to slay Rafe where he stood. "I have him now as much as I ever did, and he will *always* be trouble. If I can't control this town, who will?"

"Luther," I answered, and Rafe's hard gaze met mine for a brief moment.

"You're a soldier. You know how this works." Rothfuss gestured to our surroundings. "If I'm unable to hold the law here, Luther will. Do you believe he'll let you hang around causing trouble? No. He'll send you packing. The specifics of your dispute are of no interest or concern to me. I care that you faced *me* down in *my* streets, soldier. For that, I have to take you in."

"You don't have a chance," Rafe scoffed, arms crossed over his chest.

"Aye, that may be true. But what I can do is what Luther would do. Send you packing." Rothfuss' blue eyes danced over my face, and his tone softened. "I thought you wanted to settle here?"

Hurt and concern glittered in his gaze. He wanted me to settle with him, but he was willing to accept me settling here with another man.

"I do."

"If I can't hold the law in Leeds, or against you, I have to chase you off. So you choose. A few nights in a cell, or move on elsewhere."

A tick worked in Rafe's jaw. He avoided my gaze as I studied him. Rafe didn't get pushed around. No one scolded him or told him what to do. Helplessness welled inside, finding its place within my heart. I bowed my head, knowing we would have to leave Leeds.

"One night," he said.

With a surge of hope, my gaze fixed on Rafe. He glanced at me before staring the lawkeeper down.

"One night, and Avyanna stays at the inn," he continued.

"I hold you and your men for two nights, and Avyanna is bound to the inn."

'They speak as if they have a say where you go,' Tizmet huffed.

"Her and one man walk free," Rafe grumbled, his patience waning. "Me and the rest will take two nights in your pathetic cell."

"Which man?" Rothfuss asked.

"Dane." Rafe jerked his chin toward the man in question. "The quiet one." My gaze bounced between them as they haggled. The knowledge that Tizmet would never agree to my separation filled me with a deep sense of helplessness. I couldn't escape the fact that my own involvement would cause suffering for the rest of the Tennan.

"Done. At least he wasn't there when it started." Rothfuss settled with a quick nod.

Rafe grunted in agreement. He walked past us and slapped a hand on Tizmet's side, causing her to jerk away and snap her teeth.

"Rafe, wait."

I rushed to his side, ignoring his harsh frown. His stare was hard as granite, having set his mind to his task.

"Thank you," I whispered, bracing my palm on his chest.

He glared at my touch, then brought his tortured gaze to mine. "We can't all be the General now, can we?"

My hand fell to my side, and I bit my cheek, wondering which was harder—seeing Rafe bow under another's authority or the possibility of leaving Leeds. I wasn't the only one making sacrifices for our life here. And yet, as Tizmet rose, I stared at the Tennan. My friends readied to spend the next two nights in a cell while Luther would rest at home in a soft bed attended by Saudric, no doubt.

I wondered if I really wanted to call Leeds home.

Chapter 11

Pachu took the basket of eggs, eying me with a glower that said I crushed his heart into a thousand pieces.

"I knew it," he muttered.

I threw a cautious glance at Dane. He lingered in the kitchen's doorway. He hadn't left my side all night. Since Tizmet refused to let me out of her sight, even to enter the inn, we slept outside in the elements. The raised welts on his arms matched mine.

"Knew what?" I asked.

"This man."

He pointed his knife at Dane, who blinked inquisitively.

My chin dipped as I struggled to connect the dots. "Dane?"

"No!" Pachu sighed, angling the blade at me as if it were an extension of his hand. "Well, yes, but the glowering one. That big, bald, buffoon!"

My lips wavered with my attempt to hide my smile. "Buffoon?"

"Don't give me that look, young lady." He waved the blade at me. "You know who I'm talking about."

Dane came near, then gently tipped the knife away from me and stepped back. Pachu glared at him as if he overcooked a slab of steak.

"I know who you're talking about," I said. "I don't know *what* you're talking about."

"Iana and I, we knew he was bad news." He set the knife down and pointed a thick finger at me instead. "Bad news for our Avyanna! And here he is! Spending his nights in a cell."

"Willingly."

He rolled his eyes. "Right. Now that you're aware he's no good, will you let him go? Find yourself a nice young lad to spend your days with!"

My shoulders stiffened. What was it about older people that made them think they could tell me how to live my life?

"Pachu–"

"No, don't *'Pachu'* me. We care about you!" he huffed, inspecting the eggs. His gaze darted to me with a frown. "I'd hate for you to end up in the charity house one day."

"I have a job."

"Do you? Have you seen Iana this morn?"

As his words sank in, I frowned and moved closer to the door. This position wasn't just a job to me, It gave me footing in a place where I could belong, where I could be valued and contribute to my community.

"Oh, and Avyanna?"

I hesitated, glancing over my shoulder at the heavyset cook.

"One day, that man's gold will run out."

I brushed him off and left the kitchen, scanning the tavern. Iana stood at the bar, inspecting mugs. She had been absent when I brought Pachu the eggs, but I could tell she was aware of my presence by the way she stiffened at the sound of the door.

"Iana." My tone was cold and flat as I approached.

Dane leaned a hip against a table as I bent over the bar, forcing her to meet my gaze.

"Avyanna." Her eyes darted to mine before refocusing on the mugs. "I assume Pachu told you."

I wanted to tell her not to assume, but correcting my employer seemed like a poor move, considering the circumstances.

"He told me to see you," I said, twisting the truth.

If Iana had something to tell me, she would have to do it herself.

"Did he now?" She glanced at the kitchen as if Pachu would come out to support her, then sighed and settled herself against the bar. "Two nights. Two nights you have not worked–"

"I had the first night–"

"Yes, yes. You begged for it off and I *let* you." She shook her head. "Two nights you have not worked, and your dragon has brought us no meat."

Tizmet's awareness skittered across the bond and dismissed the idea that she *had* to hunt for the tavern.

"There are too many who would gladly have your position," she added.

"You're firing me." I dared her to object.

"No," fire sparked in her gaze, "but I should! Sun above knows I should, but I'm giving you one more chance."

She turned her ire on Dane, whose brows rose above bored eyes.

"I'm giving you *all* one more chance," she said. "Any further incidents, and I'm tossing you all out on your ears."

"Is it because of Luther?" I accused.

Surely Iana, strong, independent Iana, wouldn't bow to the will of the biggest bully in Leeds.

"Luther? Valleys beneath, girl. He makes life hard enough without you antagonizing him, but no. It's not that your big, bad shadow mussed up his face, either. I've been waiting *years* for someone to put him in his place."

She shook her head and went on, frowning fiercely. "No matter how much Luther would like to think he's above the law, he isn't. But neither are you nor the small army you have trailing you. I'll not employ criminals, nor have them sleeping under my roof. Am I clear?"

"I didn't disobey Rothfuss," I muttered, glancing away.

"From what I hear, Rothfuss had you carried out, and that hulking ogre turned on him when your dragon came. That lumps you in with their lot. Troublemakers are not welcome under my roof." She paused, raising a stern brow. "That goes for you, too."

With a curt nod, I pushed off the bar. "I understand," I bit out. "Am I free till this evening?"

"I should find some work for you," she murmured, then waved me off. "Go. Be back before tonight's rush. Be sure that your oversized guard dog actually brings in some meat tonight."

A snarl sounded from outside.

"That's right! I'm talking about you!" Iana shouted. "Take your anger issues out on something tasty!"

I shook my head and headed for the exit. I held the door open for Dane, who trailed behind me, then took a breath of fresh, muggy air. Tizmet's nose was in my face the moment I stepped outside. She inhaled deeply, as if she could smell any potential danger.

'You heard her.'

She huffed at my comment and flashed her flaming eye my way. *'I'm not leaving you. You're too weak,'* she said. *'Tell her to find her own meat.'*

'Your hunting is why they let me work here.'

I sidestepped around her massive head and walked along her flank. Her belly was so swollen her scales were lifting.

She followed me, eyes flicking over our surroundings. *'You don't need to work.'*

'You're mothering me simply because you haven't laid.' I stroked her scales. I could almost see the outline of the eggs inside her.

'Soon.' She lifted her great head, facing north. *'Deter the snake from settling in that clearing.'*

I pressed my lips together and dropped my gaze. I understood her apprehension. If he made good on his claims to make the shack a pigsty, it would be far too close to Tizmet's nest for comfort. Her raised scales were rough under my palm. She didn't have time to make another somewhere else.

'I could eat him.'

'Stop threatening to eat people!' I glanced back at Dane. "I'm going to pay the Master Builder a visit."

He shrugged.

"I'm just asking why he wants it."

Apprentices moved around us, quietly working on their tasks. I kept my voice as soft as possible, folding my hands in my lap, trying to make myself smaller and less intimidating. Master Val wasn't afraid of me in the slightest, though he didn't want to be in the middle of Rafe and Luther.

"I'm telling you, he won't let you have it."

"It was *your* land."

"Now it's his."

"Did he even tell you?" I pleaded, frustrated that Luther's hands were buried in the Builders' pockets, too.

"He simply doesn't want you here." Val loosed a heavy sigh. "That man doesn't control you, and he can't control that dragon. If he can't get you under his thumb, he will use everyone in Leeds to push you out." His arms crossed over his chest. "He set your soldier up, and he fell for it."

My eyes dropped to the floor. Of course Luther did all this to antagonize Rafe. His first meeting with the man and he challenged his dominance, causing a rift between the lawkeeper and us. Knowing Luther, that was only the beginning.

"I'll talk to him," I murmured under my breath.

It would take every ounce of strength I had, but it needed to be done. Master Val rose as I pushed to my feet.

"Getting your soldier riled will only complicate things," he said. "My advice is to put the strapping lads in your group to work. Build your own house."

I scoffed, looking back at Dane, who watched an apprentice with disinterest.

"Does it look like we have a Builder in our lot?"

"Something is better than nothing. Living at the inn will drain your coin, eventually."

I sighed, then dipped my chin in dismissal. "Good day, Master Val."

Dane pushed off the wall and followed me as I left the guildhall. Outside, I put one foot in front of the other. If I wanted to settle in Leeds, I had to do this.

"Not a word of this to Rafe," I muttered.

A bored look is all I got in response.

We made our way to the center of town, with Tizmet plodding behind. People crowded against buildings as she passed, careful not to get too close, cursing when she couldn't help but press into their space. They were anxious after the previous night, and I couldn't blame them.

Tizmet's pain trickled over the bond as she walked, and a pang of guilt wreaked havoc in my gut. She should be resting, not trudging down muddy roads, or flying and hunting for the tavern's benefit. She was a dragon. Had she been at Northwing, she would have been doted on, fed to her heart's desire, soaking in the warm springs, cared for by Dragon Masters. She would have her clutch in near luxury. Even in the wild, she would have gorged, nested and relaxed until she laid. She wouldn't have gone about on foot, mud seeping between her talons as the eggs jostled inside of her.

A man rose from his chair, bringing my attention to the most lavish building in the town square. He stood on the wooden deck, heels clacking against the planks as he shifted to lean against a decorative pillar to watch me. Four others crowded around him. As impressive as the establishment was, with its ornate wood engravings and detailed stone carvings, the roguish men stuck out like a sore thumb. The trio of goons I was used to weren't among them, likely nursing their wounds from the other night.

"I'm here to see Luther."

The first man jerked his head at one of his companions. They turned with a sneer and entered the building, closing the bright crimson door behind him.

Dane pressed close to my shoulder, lending his silent support.

'I'm not committing to his demands.'

'I can always eat him.'

Tizmet lowered her head to sniff at the men. They straightened and placed their hands on their shortswords, ready to draw at the slightest show of menace. She bared her teeth and gave a quiet growl.

'Easy.' I pursed my lips. *'I'm trying to get him on our good side.'*

She snorted, blowing a gust of sulfuric air at them. She craned her head to her full height and towered over them with a glare. A few moments passed, and then, to my shock, Luther limped out of the building. A girl shadowed him, just a slip of a thing, with a tray of tea and pastries. Her eyes flitted to mine, then down in fear. I had thought he would summon me inside. Either he understood Tizmet would pull the roof off, or he was playing at some game. His face was clean, though his jaw and right cheekbone were swollen. His skin was a touch darker, as if he used cosmetics to hide the bruising.

"So good to see you again, dear Avyanna." Luther greeted, his voice as smooth as silk—and grating on my every nerve. He walked to the edge of the deck, then peered up at the overcast sky. "Care for some tea? It's a lovely day."

He waved behind him and leaned on his cane. With the gesture, his men scrambled to pull two chairs to him, then backed against the far wall.

"I'd have a word," I called, refusing to get closer than the fifteen paces I was. This all seemed so wrong.

He flashed me a bright smile. "Over a cup of tea, then."

"In private."

"Here."

He lowered himself into a chair, sitting primly. He stretched out the leg Rafe had bashed with the cane. Aside from his swollen face, he looked for all the world as if he hadn't taken a beating the previous night.

I glanced over the crowd who made themselves appear busy, but they listened to our every word, ready to gossip about it for the next fortnight.

"Luther, I'd rather–"

"My dear, you sought *me* out," he cut in, then nodded toward Tizmet. "I've braved the elements for your sake, not mine."

Tizmet lowered her head directly above him and hissed. Her breath tousled his perfect black hair. He didn't even flinch, his predatorial smile never faltering.

I clenched my fists and forced myself to take a step forward, then another. I had to do this—for me, for Rafe, and for Tizmet.

Luther's men hovered close as I approached the deck. "Just her," one bit out, glaring at Dane.

I lifted my chin, my heart pounding against my ribs. "A dragon towers over your boss, and you're worried about *him*?"

Luther laughed, as if this was all some big joke for his benefit. "Let him up. She has a point."

They parted, and we stepped up on the deck, marching to where Luther sat. He waved at the spare seat, and I frowned at the amount of people crowding us. Tizmet swung her tail, shoving bystanders out of the way. They cursed and cried out, rushing to avoid her thrashing.

"Please, sit." Luther gestured to the chair again.

"I want the shack."

"Straight to the point, as always."

He grinned as if indulging a child, then glanced at the girl with the tray. On quick steps, she settled at his side and bent low to offer him a cup, which he took with care.

"You have no use for it," I continued, squeezing my hands at my sides to hide my anger.

"True." He nodded before taking a sip. "Oh, it's positively divine. Please, help yourself."

"Luther–"

"Have a cup."

His smile disappeared, his mask of pleasantness dropping away. Here was the real man behind the scenes—the ruthless bully who would have his way.

I took a deep breath and, drawing strength from Dane's presence, snatched a teacup from the tray. Tea sloshed over the brim, spilling onto the deck.

"See, that wasn't so hard." His mock-praise pulled at his grin. "I have no use for that land, but I *can* find one."

"What do you want?" I growled. This lowlife was greed and evil embodied.

"Oh, I want a lot of things, dear," he murmured, tracking my body.

I bit my tongue to keep from lashing out at the wretched man.

"Yet, I would settle for a favor or two," he said.

Dane shifted behind me. I refused to look back. I could do this.

"What?"

"First, I would have you and that General of yours stop harming my men. After all, they're just doing their jobs."

I stilled. It wasn't common knowledge, yet him knowing Rafe used to be a General was far more information than I ever wanted him to have. To avoid showing my nerves, I straightened my shoulders and thought back on all the times his men got a little too friendly with me.

"Roughing people up? You call that doing their jobs?" I demanded.

"Oh, I would respect your boundaries. After all, I have noted that your General has taken to sleeping with you. Truth be told, there are wagers you'll be with child by the next moon."

Dane bumped into my shoulder, reminding me I wasn't alone. This wasn't about me or my pride. This was for all of us. I'd take his ridicule, suffer this humiliation.

"Hands off me and my friends," I snarled through gritted teeth.

"Ah, but you must let my men do *their* jobs." He leaned back again. "There are scoundrels out there who would borrow my coin and forget to pay what is owed. A businessman has an obligation to collect outstanding debts. You cannot stand in the way of a simple man earning a living."

I rubbed the bridge of my nose, frustrated. Could I stand by and let his men harass others? When I first arrived, I had. Only when I learned I had a minor power as an independent woman bonded to a dragon did I begin to fight against Luther's injustices.

"What else?" I ground out.

"Just a small favor." Dread filled me as he looked at Tizmet, hungry eyes on her swollen belly.

"No."

My refusal came fast and without thought. There was no way I was letting him near her or her clutch.

"Are you certain?" A daring glower burned deep in his gaze.

Tizmet prodded at our bond, and realization struck me. I smiled. He desired an egg—that much was obvious. But they were not mine to give. It was clear now. He didn't care about the shack or the land. He wanted a hatchling to raise and rival whatever power he thought I had.

"A small favor." I agreed.

"Ah, see? I'm not so unreasonable!"

"A favor from me, and we leave your men alone—as long as we don't see them roughing people up."

"Now, dear. Sometimes people need a little," his lip curled in a terrible smile, "*encouragement.*"

Just like he *encouraged* me to come talk to him. I set the cup on the tray with care. The girl's eyes darted to mine, then dropped again.

"No. I won't sit by while your goons terrorize the town. If Rafe or I see *anyone* attacking *anyone*, they will be dealt with. He's an enforcer now. Keeping the peace comes with the job."

Luther reclined in his chair, ignoring Tizmet's looming maw as he openly studied her belly. "Deal."

I refused to shake on it. Instead, I demanded a contract be drawn up. He laughed at my request, but obliged. He made it seem as though this was simply a trade between friends. I wanted it in ink—every detail of what he was asking of *me,* and his promise to not interfere with the building of our home. He would find out soon enough that he got the worse end of this bargain.

As we walked away, Dane kept close to my side with a deep frown pulling his face.

I pushed out a breath. "Just trust me."

When he met my eye, his usual bored expression shifted across his features. "Rafe isn't happy."

I snorted, making my way to the law house.

Of course he wasn't.

Chapter 12

"Vy." Rafe sounded as if he choked back the urge to rip through the bars.

The law house only had four holding cells. He shared the cramped space with Blain, while the others lounged in another. The third was occupied by Brunor, a beggar who, while sober, was as cheerful as the morning sun, but while drunk, was volatile and dangerous. The cells themselves were simple wooden rooms constructed from sturdy oak, but the doors were fashioned out of iron bars.

I had no doubt he remained in his cage of his own accord. Between the lot of them, the prison was hardly restrictive. He glowered, arms crossed over his chest while Blain sprawled on the lower bunk, eyes closed as if he was dozing. No doubt he was to blame for Rafe finding out what I was up to, thanks to his and Dane's strange connection.

I offered Rafe a tight smile. "I took care of it."

"And is he going to take care of you?" he growled.

"Rafe, I know these people."

"I know his type."

"As do I," I hissed.

I experienced his type too often during my travels. While I met unsavory folk in my bounty hunting days through Regent with Darrak, there were far more in the Sands and on this side of the E'or. These people had no King or true government to enforce their laws. More often than not, misfits and criminals banded together to form colonies. Because of that, I had seen more than my fair share of oppressors and rulers that were nothing short of cruel.

"Rafe, Tizmet needs this." I reached through the bars and placed a hand on his arm. "We need this."

"Ahem."

We both glared at Rothfuss, who leaned against the wall. He offered a shrug and an unapologetic smile.

"Can't be fraternizing with the prisoners," he said, reasoning away his interruption.

I pulled back with a scoff. He was right there. It's not like I was going to try to break the Tennan free with the lawkeeper at my side.

"I don't like it," Rafe grumbled, still seething.

"Neither do I."

"What deal did you make with that snake?"

"You meet him once and think him a snake," I huffed.

He gave me a droll look in response, his eye rolling with impatience. He wasn't wrong. Luther was the scummiest vermin in the pond.

I craned past his hulking form to peer at Blain. "You didn't tell him?"

He peeked under his lashes with a sly smile pulling his cheeks. "This is more fun."

"I'll kill him later," Rafe muttered, glancing at Rothfuss.

"I had to step in and break them up," Rothfuss said. "Kill anyone, even one of your men, and we're gonna have trouble."

I shook my head. "He's jesting."

"I'm not."

I shot Rafe a stern look. He just glared at me without moving a muscle.

"I agreed we wouldn't interfere with his business," I said, finally answering his question. "He wants us to stay out of his affairs."

"I imagine so," Rothfuss mused, not surprised in the slightest.

"Me and my friends are to leave Luther's men alone, as long as they're not laying hands on people." I gritted my teeth as I spoke, angry that I even had to concede that much. "That doesn't apply to you, Rothfuss," I added with a pointed look.

"Luther understands you can't speak for me or my men." He nodded, then ran his hand through his hair as he stared at Rafe. "Speaking of which, you're not my man now."

"Never was," he scoffed with bored amusement.

"We'll work out the details later. I could still use your men."

"Depends on the details," Rafe muttered, then faced me. "There's more to it."

"Aye, there was another deal. I agreed to a small favor."

"What?"

I crossed my arms defensively and glared, challenging him. Jam and Tegan leaned forward on their bunks, watching with eager smiles.

"Vy," he growled through gritted teeth, "what *favor?*"

"I don't know."

Blain choked on a laugh at the same time Rafe cursed and slammed an open palm on the bars, rattling the door. Rothfuss straightened, but didn't come closer.

"Rafe, trust me."

"Trust you?!"

He tilted his head, strangling the iron with his white-knuckled grip. The tendons in his neck stood out as he seethed. I assumed he was struggling not to rip the door off its hinges.

"Trust me," I repeated so quietly it was almost a whisper.

I gripped the cold iron and pressed my forehead to the bars, looking up at him. Anger and torment distorted his features.

This was hard for him.

He sat in a cell while I traipsed around, making deals with a scumbag of a man. He trusted me to wait for him while he fought his way through Regent to Leeds, and I was asking him to trust me again.

After a deep breath, he let it out with a groan and stooped low, bringing his face close. "It's not you I don't trust."

I wished I could calm the turmoil in his dark gaze, but if we were going to make a life here, we had to silence the doubts and fears that threatened to tear us apart.

A string of curses spilled past his lips, venting his frustration. He was making himself weak for me. He had never been in a position where he, my mighty and strong General Rafe Shadowslayer, had to humble himself.

"I know what I'm doing, Rafe."

He rubbed his jaw, his eye dark and glittering. "I hope you do," he bit out.

I hoped I did too.

Life settled back to some sense of normalcy, with the sole exception of Tizmet. She was cranky, and even after Rafe was released, she wouldn't let me out of her sight. She became more and more lethargic, and I no longer asked her to hunt for the tavern. Dane and I scavenged what we could while she slumbered nearby—meager rations compared to what she brought in.

She lapsed into a sleep so deep I struggled to rouse her, and I wondered if this was normal for a dragon so close to laying. From my time at Northwing, I learned lethargy was expected, but I'd only been around dragons who had a healthy brumation period, who were well fed and cared for with staff on hand to monitor their progress.

I doubted my ability to care for her.

The full moon shone bright, the sky clear, lending its meager light through the thin hide covering my window. When I snuck out of bed, Rafe knew exactly where I was headed.

"She can care for herself," he said, voice groggy with fatigue.

My teeth sank into my lip as I paused at the stairs. "I'm just—I'm worried."

He groaned and rolled his feet to the floor.

"No," I shook my head, "you don't have to come."

He squinted, an expression that conveyed the foolishness of my statement, then grunted as he grabbed his boots.

We slipped down the stairs, then outside, and rounded the building to find Tizmet's sleeping form. Rafe braved the stinging insects as he stood guard without a tunic. I crept to her head, touching her scales as I reached across the bond. She seemed so distant and exhausted. Her awareness slowly drifted to me and she rolled her eyelid back, taking me in.

'Are you well?' I asked softly.

'Tired,' she murmured, then shifted, trying to adjust the weight of her belly off her legs.

'I worry.'

She huffed. *'I have laid before.'*

Even so, I sensed her pain and discomfort across the bond.

'Is this clutch different?'

'No, little one.' She sighed and drifted again.

I pressed my lips together and stepped back, eyeing her nervously. Her temperament was so different from the dragon I had grown to love. Where was the beast who was always aware and ready to devour the slightest threat? Where was the beast who roused herself with any trivial worry in my mind?

Rafe draped an arm over my shoulders. "You act as though you've never seen a mother nearing her time."

"And you're an expert on that." Sarcasm dripped from my tone. "I'm sure the frontlines had masses of pregnant women."

He went silent, and I looked up at him, expecting a response. He stared at Tizmet with his mouth set in a firm line. Anger and hurt stiffened his features.

"Rafe?"

He worked his jaw and threw up his wall, shrugging. "You're right," he replied, voice thick.

He cleared his throat and turned toward the inn. I watched after him, wondering if I should press. It was a toss up if he would answer me or shut me out. Sometimes things I said triggered events from his past, and those of which he shared with me weren't pretty.

He stopped and glanced over his shoulder. "Coming?"

I frowned and looked back at Tizmet one last time, assuring myself all was well. Nothing out here would hurt her. I sighed, then followed Rafe to our room.

As I stripped, he sat on the bed and removed his boots, then tossed them aside. He pulled off his eye patch and chucked it near the rest of his things. As he settled, he scooted to make space for me, but sensed my hesitation and looked up. I stepped out of my trousers and curled against his side.

"I apologize," I murmured. His warm chest muffled my words.

"Hmm?"

"I snapped at you. I didn't mean it."

"You're worried. It happens."

I sighed. "I'm used to her being aware. She seems so far away."

"She's about ten paces through a wall."

I gave his shoulder a playful smack. "You know what I mean." Silence lingered for a beat, and I stilled, worrying my lip. "Rafe?"

"Hmm?"

"So it's normal? For mothers to act this way when their time is near?" I formed my words with care, broaching the topic that set him off.

I'd seen pregnant refugees come to Northwing, but had little experience with gravid dragons.

He tensed, as if holding his breath, and I silently pleaded he wouldn't shut me out.

"You don't want to know, Vy."

He recognized what I was doing, that it wasn't necessarily the topic that piqued my interest, but his reaction to it.

"I want to know about you."

He refused to meet my gaze, but he resumed breathing, though his body was still taut, as if ready to fight someone off.

"Some things are better left unknown." A bitter chuckle chased his words.

"Do you think it will change how I feel about us?"

He opened his eye and studied me, as if searching for an answer.

When he didn't speak, I tried again. "Nothing you say could change how I feel about you."

"Vy," he broke our gaze and stared at the ceiling, "I'm learning there are things better left unspoken."

"What do you mean?"

Where was the man that wasn't afraid to tell anyone and everyone off?

"I care." His laugh was cold and distant as he looked back at me. "I feel like some whipped dog."

I sat up and leaned over him, placing my hand on his chest. "You believe that makes you weak?"

"Aye. If you *really* knew me girl–"

I placed a finger over his lips. We'd been down this road before. He would lecture and rant about how I couldn't possibly comprehend his true self in an attempt to distance us even more.

"Stop," I whispered.

He frowned, clenching his jaw as I pressed a kiss to his cheek.

"I love you, and always will. No matter what."

He tucked my hand over his heart, and I held his gaze as it pulsed beneath my palm. I wasn't afraid of him, or his past, or what he had done. I feared losing him, of him building a barrier between us, convinced that he wasn't worthy of being seen as a whole.

He sighed, then nestled my head on his shoulder as he stared into the dark room. "I've told you the Shadow's seed takes?" he asked, voice gruff.

"You've alluded as much." I spoke softly as if he was a wild colt I didn't want to spook.

"It does. If the victims survive the attack, there's a chance they will carry their young to term." He swallowed and took a deep breath. "There are those that would be rid of any trace of the Shadow, terrified to give birth. Then there are those who hide their pregnancy and bring that cursed life into this world."

He paused and the muscles in his jaw twitched as he gazed off into the distance, as if a scene from his past replayed itself.

"Are there half breeds?"

I kept my face schooled in case he turned my way, aware that any reaction from me might end the conversation.

"No," The single word was choked with emotion, "not anymore."

I forced myself to keep my breathing normal, recalling the moment I learned the true nature of the tea provided for refugees, how it prevented pregnancy from taking.

"You've seen what the Shadows are capable of. What they do–" He broke off with a curse and rubbed at his eye socket angrily.

I didn't speak for a moment, granting him the stillness he needed to gather his thoughts. After a handful of breaths, I asked, "The women who carry to term, you believe those children take after the Shadows?"

"I know it."

Pure rage consumed his features, and I swallowed past the lump in my throat, not fully understanding. The anger in his gaze faded to pain, as if his soul pleaded for something he wouldn't say. I would give it to him. I would give him all of me and more.

"Tell me," he rasped, the demand naked with need. "Vy, tell me again."

"I love you."

I attempted to push myself upright, but he pinned me to the bed. His mouth slammed into mine, rough and insistent, almost painful. His hurt spilled over, breaking through the dam that forced it back for so long. I let him take what he needed from me, surrendering to him. He crushed me, holding on as if I'd disappear. When his lips parted, his tongue brushed mine, hot with need.

Then he pulled away, breaking the kiss just as abruptly as it started. He whipped his head to the side, clutching me to his chest.

"I can't lose you," he choked out. "Curse it all, I can't!"

Torment laced his every word. Though it wasn't fear that had him trembling. It was anger—a rage so pure it chilled my bones. He was vulnerable, and he fought the urge to shut it down, avoid it all together. I didn't want to lose him now, not when he was so close to the edge.

"Rafe," I breathed, "tell me."

He stilled as if he'd been struck, his body taut and rigid. With pain and a quiet terror, he spoke the words that would forever be burned into my soul.

"I'm a Shadow bastard."

CHAPTER 13

My chest stilled, leaving me breathless as my brain momentarily forgot how to inhale. "Your mother–"

"Was raped by a Shadow."

"But your surname–"

"She passed giving birth. I was taken in."

"Then how do you know?" I asked, shocked.

For the first time, I was thankful Tizmet was in such an exhausted, distant state. She overcame much of her fear of the Shadows, but a strong hatred remained. I wasn't sure how she would respond to Rafe's revelation.

"I was born nine months after a raid." He chuckled darkly. "You saw what I could do. Do you doubt it?"

"But there was no one there to witness–"

"What, the woman who bore me being raped? As sick as the flaming bastards are, they don't leave witnesses."

"Then maybe you aren't–"

"Is the idea so repulsive that you have to find a way out of it?" he snapped.

His arm fell away as I sat up. I glared down at him, frowning. He studied me with an expectant face, soul laid bare and bitter. He expected me to run, to voice my disgust and toss him out as if his lineage was something he was to be blamed for. His scowl was brutal and defiant, his wall up, protecting his wounded heart.

"Rafe Shadowslayer," my palm pressed to his cheek, "your past molded you into the man you are now, the man I love. Don't doubt my feelings for you."

My lips met his with a fierce kiss of my own. He matched my intensity and gripped my hips. He rolled, pinning me beneath him, and settled between my legs.

Breaking away, he pressed his forehead against mine and cursed. "You would still have me?"

The disbelief in his expression told me he was sure I'd lost my mind.

"I wouldn't have you any other way," I murmured, bringing his lips back to mine.

A good while later, we held each other as the sun rose. It took time for him to relax—the remnants of his fear of rejection clung to him. His trust was humbling. He could have kept it from me, but he didn't. He shared with me his most vulnerable pieces. Just like he did when I first saw his shadow-touched eye up close.

The memory of sparring in the sand, the first time he truly played with me, brought a smile to my face. I curled up against his side, draping my leg over his hips. My teeth bit into my lip as he hissed, pulling my thigh higher on his stomach.

"Curse you, woman," he growled.

I smirked against his shoulder, nipping his skin. "Tell me how your eye changed."

I reveled in how relaxed he felt beneath me. The question didn't rile him or cause him to tense up. He was letting me in.

"It was a long time ago."

"Oh, so I'm sure you don't remember." I snorted.

He chuckled, and I traced the scars at the corner of his empty socket. A brutal wound that spoke of the true horrors of war.

"Just like when I lost Gareth, I was too cocky." He sighed. "Scouting behind enemy lines, ran into a pocket of Shadow Men—and thought I could take them. I didn't know half their party was on their own reconnaissance mission."

He rubbed his jaw. "Looking back, it was obvious. They had far too many supplies."

I opened my mouth to tell him he couldn't have known, but he raised a brow, cutting me off. He placed a finger on my lips, and I smiled against it.

"We engaged, and beat them back. I would have taken them, but just when we thought we won, their other half arrived—and they had a Shaman. My men never stood a chance." His voice was rough with regret, but not guilt. "I fought until my last man, Nival, fell. He was my best—like Jamlin in more ways than I'd care to admit. I was alone. Cornered and weaponless, I did the most reckless thing I could. I met his gaze."

A shudder ran through me, remembering Tizmet's memories of Shamen stripping her of her will. To be a puppet, unable to move your body as it ignored every command it obeyed since birth—the thought was terrifying.

"I'd never seen *true* evil until that day, Vy."

Pain laced each word as he relived the moment, and I placed my hand on his chest, reminding him we were tucked safe in bed, far from the front.

"They plunge inside. It's like breaking through a frozen lake. It's shocking and *wrong.*" He swallowed thickly. "It sifted through my head, and I did what I always have. I said to myself, 'Flame the bastard, if he wants to rifle through my mind, I'll tear his apart.'"

"You didn't!"

"Aye." He gave a bitter chuckle. "I earned the soldiers' respect for having the guts they didn't. But I thought that was my last breath, and I wasn't about to have a blasted Shadow bring me to my knees without taking him with me. I'm not sure who was more surprised when I managed to wrangle him back. Fighting the *thing* inside my head felt like an eternity, but it couldn't have been more than a few breaths. I bested him—put a knife through his eye and faced the others. They ran, Hunters and all."

"Yet, now they flock to you."

He scoffed. "They've had time to adjust to their surprise."

"You have the strength of a Shaman."

He accomplished a feat no one else had. Rafe was not just strong in body—his will was made of steel.

"Vy, facing him woke something inside me." He shifted to meet my gaze, uncertainty edging his features. "Something dark and greedy–"

"You've led armies on the front, faced and survived Shamen, controlled dragons, and you're telling me you're afraid of some Shadow power?"

My magic called to me when I needed it. It flowed under me like a surging stream, begging to be used. He was stronger than me. If he had access to magic, even a twisted vile kind, he could keep it in check. I had every bit of faith in him.

He snorted, and the crease between his brows eased a fraction. "Still not scared of me?"

"Not in the slightest." I gave him a quick peck on the lips, then flashed a bright smile.

"You're braver than I was. On my way back to camp, I caught my reflection in a pool. I almost ended it that day. For years I fought against those eyes, avoiding them, fearing them—and they were mirrored in my face."

He shook his head and stared at the ceiling. "But if I could take down that Shaman, who's to say I couldn't take another? So, I covered it up and told everyone I lost my eye. I never let the Healers examine it. They always tried, but

I kept it hidden. I used it more than once to keep a Shadow-controlled dragon grounded. When I grew too reckless, General Faulkin turned the others on me and they sent me back to Northwing for a respite. Like I needed it."

"Well, I'm glad they did. If they hadn't, I would be out on my ear after trying to force the bond with that hatchling. Controlling a dragon can't be easy."

"No." His lip curled in a small smirk. "Yours has a will to be reckoned with."

I smiled to myself, glancing at my window. He used his shadow-touched eye on her when we made the frantic run back to Northwing after she found me. It took a toll on him, drained him more than I'd ever seen.

"Today is going to be tiring," he murmured against my neck.

I laughed and rolled to face him. "I know—and I have to get going."

"Right," he groaned, "fetching eggs and all that."

"Some of us have jobs to do."

After a quick kiss, I pushed off the bed. He stretched, and I cringed at the amount of pops in his joints. He sat up and swung his legs to the floor, rubbing at the nape of his neck. I turned away and pulled off my night shift, then slipped into my tunic before facing him again. His gaze was dark and hungry as it traveled over my features. A wicked smile lifted his lip.

"She loves me," he muttered, low voice cracking.

With a shake of his head, he approached as I fumbled with my trousers.

He cupped my cheek and ran his thumb over the scar there. "How come I can't scare you off?"

"I don't scare easy, General."

He scoffed, pulling me against his chest, and I beamed, melting into his embrace. I would gladly suffer through any details of his past, any walls we worked through, any fights we had, just for small moments like this. Moments when he was *my* Rafe—not the glowering, ominous soldier everyone else saw. He was mine.

"You should've been afraid of me," he murmured.

"Good thing I wasn't," I pulled back, smiling up at him, "or we'd both be cantankerous old soldiers. Now, I *really* have to go!"

He released me with a snort, and I fastened the bandit breaker onto my hip.

"The builder wants to discuss rafters later," he said.

"I think they'd be good." I stepped into my boots. "It would give me a place to hang herbs for drying. We'll head there after I finish my chores for the day."

Rafe grunted as he fastened the draw strings on his tunic.

"I'll see you then," I called, braiding my hair as I bounced down the steps. Stopping with a frown, I jogged back up, meeting his curious gaze. "I love you."

"Still?"

"Always."

He scoffed and focused on his boots as I headed down the stairs, beaming like a schoolgirl with her first crush.

"Mommy says you're a bad man." Brandi waved a small kitchen knife at Dane.

To his credit, he stood there with a bland look on his face, blinking at her tiny weapon.

Her wild curls bounced around her as she took a few steps back. "She says I can't trade with you no more."

"What about me?" I asked.

She spun to me, stumbling as she attempted to balance the basketful of eggs and her grip on the knife. I reached out to steady her, and she smiled, lowering her weapon.

"Mommy says you're just confused."

Her little hand beckoned me lower, as if to keep it secret from Dane. I leaned in, and she pressed her lips so close, her whisper tickled my ear.

"I heard you're in *love.*"

A dreamy sigh chased her words, and I straightened with an amused grin.

"With a *bad man,*" she added.

I choked on a laugh, but she wasn't done yet.

"Daddy says you should commit to mister 'Fuss." She nodded soberly, her smile gone from her face. "But Mommy says that she doesn't love Daddy like you love your *bad man,* and you should have babies with him."

I pressed my lips tight as she studied me with a critical eye. It was true enough that most married for convenience. Here in Leeds, what I had was special. Our love reached deeper than any simple attraction or young lust.

"How about we count the eggs together?" I asked, steering the girl back toward the task at hand.

Her smile returned, and we counted each one as we moved them from her basket to mine. She kept a sharp eye on Dane and held her knife ready. He leaned against a tree, watching us with hooded eyes.

When we finished, Brandi hurried home. Pachu would be pleased there were so many.

As we headed to the tavern, my mind wandered to Tizmet's clutch. What color would her eggs be? Would they take after her mottled earth tones, or Flinor's bright emerald?

"Babies?" Dane interrupted my musings.

I frowned. "What about babies?"

"You?"

My steps slowed to a halt. He stopped too, but didn't face me. He wasn't good at conversation. Getting more than a few words out was no easy feat. It was like pulling teeth to get him to talk about anything. But *babies?* He thought that would be a decent topic?

"I say, Dane, you're positively becoming an old woman." I laughed before continuing on my way to the inn.

"Forty-two." I beamed as I held out the basket.

Pachu waved me off, and I set it on the counter, watching him glare at the slab of meat before him, still wrapped in wax paper from the butcher. It puzzled me what he found so upsetting. Then the smell hit me.

"This," he said, pointing his blade at the meat, "this is what they give Iana's tavern?"

"Is it bad?"

I already knew the answer. No amount of seasoning could hide it, and consuming it would likely turn stomachs for days.

"Is it?!" He curled his lip, disgusted. "I would never feed this to anyone. It's not even fit for the dogs!"

"Is there something else that–"

"No! You and your hunting friend barely bring in enough for the evening meal. Iana ordered from Luther's shop." He poked at the meat with the blade before he huffed, then tossed it into the waste bucket.

"I'm sorry. We will try to get more."

"For all our sake, I hope you do." He eyed the eggs and sighed. "These shall be the highlight of the morning."

A bog deer was the biggest we could bring down with any hope of carrying back to town. My lips pressed tight as I recalled the many times I went hungry in the Sands. A simple egg would have gone far when my diet consisted of insect guts.

"I'll be back tonight," I assured, then rejoined Dane in the common room.

A wave of pain trickled over the bond, and I stumbled. It was faint, but enough to make me reach out to Tizmet.

She fought another surge before she spoke, *'Avyanna–'*

Worry soured my stomach. *'Now?'*

'Now.' Determination sharpened her tone.

I ran for the exit, passing Iana. "I'll try to return before nightfall!"

"*Try?!*" she screeched.

I shoved the way open as Dane jumped to his feet, rushing after me. The morning sun warmed my cheeks as I took the stairs two at a time. It was a clear day—as clear as Leeds had—perfect for laying.

I glanced at Dane, who jogged to my side.

"Rafe. I need Rafe!"

"Smithy," he rasped. He caught on that something was happening, but hadn't put the pieces together yet.

Behind the inn, Tizmet took to the air. She struggled under her weight, wings beating hard. At Northwing, most dragons stayed grounded in the weeks before they laid, but she had to get to her nest.

High above, her head craned toward me as she headed north. *'Hurry,'* she urged.

I picked up my pace, heading for the blacksmith, but tried to keep my wits about me. I didn't need to draw unwanted attention and broadcast she was laying. People would find out soon enough, and so would Luther. I could only hope no one went searching for her nest.

I sped along down the muddy streets and rounded a corner, spotting the smoke from the forge. The smithy pounded away, and Rafe stood off to the side, speaking with two of Rothfuss' men. As I approached, his gaze caught mine, and he broke off mid-sentence with a frown.

He turned and stepped toward me. "What is it?"

I eyed the others, then gave him a pointed look. "We need to go for a ride."

He paused for a moment, blinking once before he nodded. "Stay here, Dane. We'll meet up later."

Dane shrugged and wandered off as Rafe headed for the stables across the road—with me on his heels.

Inside, he grabbed the tack to ready his stallion. The beast snorted at us with interest, lowering his gray head. I took the opportunity to slip the bridle on as he did so.

Rafe grunted, securing the pad and saddle in place, then reached under to fasten the girth. The horse lowered his muzzle to snort at my trousers as if I had treats for him. I smiled and pushed him away. Rafe took a knee, then knitted his fingers to give me a leg up. I reveled in the fact that he dropped everything to help me without question.

"It's Tizmet." I kept my voice low in case any unwanted ears were listening, then stepped into his cupped hands.

His chin dipped in a brisk nod and his gaze darted to the aisle as he lifted me up to his stallion's back. I settled in the saddle as Rafe led the beast out of the stables.

Clearing the door, he mounted, then wrapped his arms around me, letting me have the reins.

'I'm coming.'

I urged the giant steed through Leeds to the edge of town at a brisk trot.

Across the bond, Tizmet's pain rippled into a deep ache, and I gritted my teeth. I battled with the urge to block her out, but I wanted her to feel my presence and know I was there for her. Rafe must have sensed my distress, because his hold on me tightened, and as we turned onto the northern path, he prodded the stallion into a canter.

I wouldn't allow my absence to cause her more stress than she was already in. I was limited in my ability to assist her—the least I could do was make sure I was close by, so she didn't worry about me.

The stallion's stride ate up the muddy ground, cutting through the forest. Chimes passed, and the day wore on, drawing my anxiety. Before long, we reached a point where the horse couldn't continue. The brambles and trees grew too thick—no place for a great warhorse. I felt for Tizmet to let her know we were close.

She closed me off, working through her pain. Still, it trickled over to me. It was only a fraction of what she experienced. Even so, it was enough to make my stomach clench.

"She's east of here."

I scrambled to dismount, but Rafe held my shoulders, forcing me to let him down first. I swung my leg over and pushed off, not waiting for his assistance. My feet slid out from under me, and I landed hard on my rear. Stars danced in my vision as I blinked up at the horse's white belly.

"Curse it all, Vy. She's done this before," Rafe growled, hauling me upright.

"But she wasn't mine back then."

"She's a grown dragon." He gave me a sharp once-over before tying his stallion to a tree. "Let her be one."

"What if something goes wrong?" I shoved at low-hanging branches and stomped through the brambles. "I won't know how to help her."

"She's not had issues before."

"Aside from Shadows stealing her eggs? No."

I really was overreacting, but what was I supposed to do? I'd never sensed her in so much pain before, never felt her so distracted. She shut me out to focus on herself, but having her so closed off brought on painful memories of when we first bonded.

Rafe quieted and stayed close, steadying me when I tripped on a vine or slipped in the mud. When I let a branch fling back, it struck his arm, splitting his skin. He cursed, but urged me on, ignoring it as it bled.

Tizmet's presence loomed ahead, and a hard grinding sound met my ears. I frowned, pushing through the last bit of thicket, and sighed my relief when my eyes landed on her.

She perched on a rock three times my height, alternating between standing and lying. Her talons dug into the stone, and small pebbles skittered down the sides. She whipped her head in our direction, pupils narrowed in pain, then flicked her tongue out, tasting the air.

"I'm here," I murmured, backing into Rafe.

I had never been so close to a laying dragon, not even while training to be First Chosen. It was a private matter that Riders and their dragons worked through together. I knew a bit of the process from my studies, but any real details would have come from Riders' classes at Northwing.

Pain was normal, and she would be hungry after, but I didn't know what to expect. Would she want me up there to comfort her, or down on the ground for privacy?

I hissed as another wave of pain passed through her—to me. I doubled-over at the ferocity of it and sensed her pull further from our bond. Rafe held my shoulders as I gasped up at my dragon.

"She's not holding it back?" he asked, bracing my weight.

I shook my head. "Not all of it. She's not entirely with me."

Rafe guided me to a small grassy clearing nearby, then pulled me into his lap. He held me close as we watched her. She paced, then settled at the center of her boulder. After a breath or two, another wave crashed through her. She growled with the strain, then paced again, crumbling the boulder's edge under her mighty claws.

We worked through the pain together.

I clenched my jaw and whimpered, curling into Rafe. His arms were comforting steel bands as her first eggs emerged. Her wall between us steadily fell as she laid one after another. It was as if her agony and fatigue left her too drained to block me out. My stomach roiled, angry at the constant spasms. I panted against Rafe as she took a break, too exhausted to keep going.

Sweat beaded along my skin as time passed. Gnats and stinging insects started to show themselves, heralding the oncoming night.

Tizmet panted, nostrils flaring with each breath as she slung her head over the edge of the boulder in my direction.

'Tired.'

Her voice was weak and my nerves were frayed.

'How many more?'

She blinked and huffed, rolling her muzzle to her side. *'I know not.'*

Was taking a break normal? Did dragons often rest in the middle of laying?

"She done?" Rafe asked.

I peeked at him over my shoulder. Discomfort edged his features, his lips pressed into a thin line. We'd been sitting like that for several chimes. He had to be in pain.

"I don't know." My mouth pulled into a grimace, and I eased my weight off him. "I'm sorry."

He stopped my retreat, holding me tighter. "She'll let you up?"

I gazed up at her. From this angle, I only saw the top of her neck. Her exhaustion left her calmer, not as high-strung as earlier.

"Maybe. I want to check on her."

He shuffled back, then stood and stretched. Several bones along his spine cracked before he offered me his hand.

"Can you stand?"

"I think so."

My legs shook as he pulled me up. A deep ache settled into my bones. If this was a taste of childbirth, I was glad my womb was closed.

Rafe helped me stagger over, and didn't hesitate when Tizmet snarled, throwing her head over the ledge at us. Her glare flared with warning, but he ignored her, supporting me as I climbed the smooth surface. When I reached the top, he stepped away, maintaining a safe distance.

My eyes slid to the center of the boulder, and the sight stole my breath.

Eggs crowded the hollow she clawed out—a cascade of colors clumped together, glittering in the setting sun.

Tizmet dropped her head on the stone with a weary thud. She huffed, and her pride swelled across the bond as she urged me closer. I crept forward on my hands and knees. She wouldn't lash out at me, but rushing this didn't feel right.

They shimmered in hues of green and silver, with a few blue and red-tinted ones tucked amongst the rest. I paused at the hollow's edge and ran my fingertips across the surface of a dark blue. The raised veins decorating the shell suggested this hatchling would fly like lightning.

My attention shifted to the others, admiring them in passing as I counted. It was a large clutch, by any standards, but compared to the recent clutches at Northwing, it was enormous.

"–thirty-nine, forty, forty-one."

The forty-first was a deep forest-green. It lay closest to Tizmet's swollen vent. With her tail stretched out, I saw a bulge inside her, as if an egg was waiting its turn to be pushed into the world.

"There's more?"

I breathed in wonder, glancing at her giant head. Her eyes were closed, and she huffed, scattering loose dirt.

'Tired.'

I frowned. This didn't seem right. How long could they stay inside like that? Was it safe for them—or for her?

'I don't know what I'm doing.'

I spoke more to myself than to her as I crept toward her belly. She didn't even open her eyes as I ran my hands down her scales, shuffling my way to her vent. The bulge was larger than any of the eggs she previously laid. Perhaps there were two trying to come out together.

'Is this normal?'

She didn't respond. She was focused on recouping her strength, breathing through the pain.

I waited patiently for any sign from her that this had happened before—for her assurance that this was dragon business and to stop my human meddling.

None came.

'Tizmet?'

I scrambled over to her head. Every muscle and joint in my body screamed for me to rest. Her eyelid took ages to open, and when it did, her pupil barely tracked me before she closed her eye and drifted off again.

I rushed to the edge. "Rafe?!"

He straightened from his position propped against a tree, and his frown deepened at my call.

"I think something's wrong. I mean, I'm not sure, but," I glanced at her anxiously, "something isn't right."

He stormed through the brush and brambles like they were simply weeds in a clearing. My teeth sank into my lip as I watched his broad back disappear, hoping he'd return with someone who knew about dragons—anyone with an inkling more knowledge than my own.

I clenched my jaw, fighting off worried tears as I crawled back to Tizmet's head, then leaned against her neck. I stroked the horned ridges above her eye and opened the bond completely. Exhaustion flooded me. I shared her pain as we settled in to wait.

Chapter 14

"Avyanna?"

Sluggishly, I detached myself from the bond with Tizmet, and as I opened my eyes, I squinted at the bright light ahead. Tizmet rumbled a quiet growl deep in her throat, but she didn't have the strength to rouse herself, let alone ward off any threats.

"Blain?" I called, peering at the shadowy figure.

His smile split his beard in a slash of white. When he lifted the lantern to his eyes, I caught the worry etched in his gaze.

"Aye." He glanced at Tizmet's resting head and all mirth fell from his face. "Dane's out hunting for her. Think she'll let us take a look?"

A shadowed figure shifted behind him. I pushed myself upright, squinting through the dark.

"Zeph?"

"Apparently your dragon isn't so tough after all," he sneered.

Irritation spiked under my skin. How dare he ridicule our strength while she suffered! If he challenged us any other day, she would crush him beneath her–

"Peace."

Blain's calm gaze met mine, and my anger sputtered out.

"He's the only one that might be able to shed light on the situation," he explained, voice soft. "Dane knows animals, but dragons are a beast of their own. Zephath had a bit more liberty to study the creatures."

I glanced back at Zeph and took a deep breath. If he could help Tizmet, I could humble myself.

"She laid forty-one, and she has–"

"Forty-one?"

The shock in Zeph's tone spoke volumes of her accomplishment. Northwing averaged ten to twenty. Usually, larger clutches had a greater amount of unfertilized eggs. Out of those I counted, all were seeded.

"Aye, but she's struggling." I pushed myself off her neck, then dipped my chin toward her belly. "I think two got stuck, but she's too tired to push them out."

"Come on, then."

Zeph reached for the lantern. I made to move, but pain tore through my body, opposing my effort. With teeth bared, I forced myself to slow, breathing through the worst of it until it subsided. When my vision cleared, concern bled over Blain's features. Zeph, on the other hand, whisked off, taking the light with him.

I limped to where he stopped at her belly, letting the lantern's glow illuminate the bulge. Her vent was swollen and angry, and she still hadn't roused, which deepened my worry. I reached over the bond where she drifted in and out, struggling to stay aware, but too worn out to manage it.

Zeph muttered under his breath, then shifted the light over the clutch. "These are large eggs, but that—that's got to be two."

"How do we get them out?" I asked, chewing my lip.

"Did she try to rub on something? Force them out?"

"I don't think so." My shoulders lifted in a tired shrug. "I wasn't up here when she stopped laying."

"You can't let them stop! You should have known that." He huffed, his tone edged with irritation. "They stop, and there's no hope for that egg."

Ignoring my body's complaints, I squared my shoulders and lifted my chin. This was *my* dragon. Still—how was I supposed to know I shouldn't have let her slow down? He hadn't felt her exhaustion—her *pain.*

Tizmet groaned and tried to pull herself awake. Her foreleg flailed before she stilled with a sigh.

'*Rest,*' I urged.

Blain strode over, his stern look warning me not to argue with Zeph's insufferable attitude.

"You're riling her," he mumbled. "What do you need?"

Zeph glared my way. "Can she get up?"

"I don't think so." I glowered right back at him.

"Either she can or she can't."

"She can't," I snarled.

"We need to push it out."

With a sigh, Blain stepped into the shadows while Zeph shifted the lantern to examine her vent. I flinched when he laid his hand on it, and Tizmet hissed in pain. He jerked back and glanced at her head with a frown.

I needed assurance that this was fine. That this happened with large clutches and she'd recover.

"She'll be alright?" I asked. "You've seen this before?"

"Of course I haven't," he snapped. "It's not like *I* studied to be a Rider."

Zeph's words were sharp and cut me to my heart. As First Chosen, I should have been ready to take this on. Not only was I unprepared to bond with a fully mature dragon, but I also neglected to attend any classes on how to care for her, making the task even more daunting.

"But, I've read about it." His tone softened as he met my gaze. "It happens with younger females—ones who haven't quite matured enough before they mate."

"So, she'll be well?"

"I'm not a Dragon Master, Avyanna. Don't ask for promises I can't keep." He sniffed, then studied Tizmet's underbelly. "The eggs are probably lost, but if we can get them out and there's no infection, she'll probably make it."

A heavy weight settled on my shoulders, realizing she might have lost two of her young. Still, there was hope. I just had to be patient.

"She should be at Northwing. There are Masters who help with things like this. This is your fault–"

"Zeph." Rafe cut him off.

I glanced back with a thankful heart to find him coming into view. Beside him, Jam pressed closer to the light. My smile brightened upon seeing him.

"She's happier to see me than you," he jeered.

Rafe leveled a glare at him before turning to Zeph. "Push it out?"

"Aye, we have to help it along the canal," he huffed, then gestured between me and Tizmet. "Rouse her."

'Tizmet?'

Rafe knelt beside me. He and Jam readied themselves around the bulge, hands at the ready. Both of them angled toward her vent.

She didn't respond.

'Tizmet!'

I reached over the bond and tried to jerk her awake. She drifted, barely aware that I was even by her side.

'You have to push.'

The sensation she shoved over felt like a thousand stones pressing on my back. I grunted, knowing she was exhausted, but forced all my urgency and anxiety her way. She roused a little more—enough that she groaned and rallied her strength.

"Push!"

I hissed as she moaned. Her agony flooded over, sinking into my bones. Sucking in a breath, I doubled-over, clutching my stomach as my forehead slammed against the stone. I curled my knees to my chest as Tizmet keened.

"Stop!"

"No!" Zephath shouted over our cries. "Keep going!"

The pain was intense. It felt as if a knife plunged through me, gutting me like a fresh field kill. A feverish sensation gripped me, aching deep and endless. My head pounded and my ears rang as I choked on a sob.

It was over as quickly as it started.

I gasped and panted, my shoulders heaving as I sucked in great lungfuls of air. Sweat drenched my clothes, and I lulled to the side, forehead pressed against the stone as I reached across for Tizmet. She was so weak and distant—so far from my reach that it felt like she would never come back. Tears pricked my eyes as sobs tore from my throat.

If I just listened to Ruveel and suffered through the Riders' classes, I would know better. This was all my fault. Tizmet was dying because of me.

I didn't bother to fight as Rafe hauled me close. My hazy vision blurred the disappointment I was sure graced his face. My tears broke loose, soaking my cheeks, and I closed my eyes, letting Rafe prop my head on his lap.

"This isn't over, Zeph," he snarled. "What now?"

"I have no idea! She's supposed to know!" he shouted.

"Well, she doesn't, so think of something."

"Reach in there and grab them, I guess!"

In an instant, my eyes flew open, and I blinked rapidly to clear them. My features must have conveyed my disbelief, because Zephath pinned me with an accusatory glare.

"You have a better idea?!" he sneered. "I've read that the Dragon Masters use an oil and a special tool—but it's not exactly like we have a Master at our beck and call!"

Rafe nodded. "Do it."

"It's not my dragon!" He held his hands up in a show of refusal. "I'm not reaching in there!"

"Vy," Rafe's dark eye locked on mine, flashing in the lantern's glow, "you're going to do this."

I cried, unable to speak. Couldn't he just make it better? This had to be some awful dream. Soon, I'd wake up safe and sound beside him.

"Zeph, go."

"Gladly," he bit out, and his shuffling footsteps receded.

"You did this." Rafe grabbed my hand and guided my fingers under his tunic to the raised scar beneath, then held my gaze. "You fixed this, you can fix her."

My eyes pressed shut again. "What if I hurt her?"

What if I kill her?

"Look at me."

He eased me upright, then crouched as if he had a steel beam for a back. This was my fault. I couldn't fix her anymore than I fixed Rafe. I only held him together until the Healers showed me what to do.

"*Look at me!*"

I jerked at the sharpness of his words as his firm hold gripped my chin with bruising pressure.

"If your dragon dies, she dies. But you will not sit here and cry until she is dead." He pulled my face to his, causing me to stumble forward. "You will exhaust every last option. Now get your hand in there."

He let go, and I gasped, shuffling away from him. I forgot this was the loving, caring Rafe that would never hurt me. I scrambled to obey my General's orders and scooted to Tizmet's vent.

"We don't have all night," he growled.

I dared a glance his way, and he struck me with a glare so fierce it would've sent Tizmet snarling. I shoved my sleeves to my elbow and cringed at the dirt that caked my skin from crawling around the rock.

Rafe was right, though. I had to try.

Taking a deep breath, I slid my hand into my dragon. A part of me rebelled, screaming that this was wrong. Pushing those thoughts aside, I pressed in deeper as Tizmet hissed. My teeth ground together when her searing pain slammed into me. My eyes fluttered shut, and I focused on the task before me. It felt as though I reached inside a fresh kill, slick and fleshy. I extended my reach, hoping to find something that resembled an egg, but there was nothing.

Then, elbow deep, my fingers brushed against what felt like a leather waterskin—moist and rubbery.

"Do you think they're soft at first?" I choked out, prodding at the rounded side of the sack.

"Snake eggs are like that," Rafe murmured, close beside me. "Out with it."

"How do I–" A harsh tremor cut my words short as Tizmet's pain rushed over.

His firm hand landed on my shoulder and shoved my arm in past my elbow. I gasped, my touch sliding over the egg's side. Shoulder deep, I still couldn't find the tip.

I winced. "I think it's only one."

Rafe shifted away and angled himself against her belly, ready to coax the egg out. "Have her push."

"I can't, she–"

"Vy, do it!" he bellowed.

I flinched, reached across the bond, then frantically tugged at her mind. She was too distant, too tired. There was no luring her back from where she drifted.

"Bring her back," he said.

I met his dark gaze and knew what he was telling me to do. With a slow exhale, I closed my eyes.

"Careful."

My lips lifted in the smallest smile at his muttered warning.

As I reached for our magic, it sprung up to meet me like a child ready and eager to please. I brought it to the surface—slowly, carefully, trying my best not to pull too much. I tethered it around her consciousness, drawing it to me.

She resisted, struggling to remain in the state of slumber she found peace in, but I fought her. Magic bolstered my efforts as I pulled on her with everything I had. Her body shifted, and I clenched my jaw in concentration. I could not rely on her mental strength to keep me in check. I had to do this on my own.

My hand slid around the egg. Tizmet contracted, and I attempted to soothe and relax the muscles in its path. Rafe pushed, and she bore down—but it wasn't enough.

I drew more from that endless, raging river and poured it into her, giving her strength. She hissed as the egg inched down, guided by my hand. As it passed through her vent, I released the magic and wrapped my arms around the egg. Its heavy weight settled against my lap—and my vision went red.

Agony tore through my chest, slashing at my heart as if it would rip me apart. I screamed as my sternum and ribs felt as if they shattered into a million pieces.

All I knew was white-hot searing pain before I slipped into a blessed dark abyss.

Choking, I rolled to my side, spitting foul blood. Every inch of my body throbbed in protest. I gasped, gripping the muscular leg underneath me, and cradled something large and warm to my chest.

As I spit again, I watched crimson splatter gray stone. I stared at it for a moment, realizing if I had been alone, I could have choked, drowned in the vile stuff. With a groan, I rolled to my back, my head cushioned by Rafe's lap. Looking up, I squinted against the sunlight streaming through the trees and found his frowning face.

Tizmet craned above us. Relief and pure joy consumed my soul—she was awake.

Lowering herself to my level, she blinked her fiery eye. *'I've never struggled with an egg,'* she said, indignant.

'Let's not do that again. Aye?' I winced, then looked at what I held in my arms.

Sunlight dappled the dragon egg's black surface, catching the white speckles. It was too long—too large. I'd never seen an egg like it in shape or color. It reminded me of a night sky speckled with stars. I was positive a beautiful hatchling would have dwelled inside.

'It's a shame we couldn't save it.'

'There is life,' Tizmet said, her gaze flicking to the egg.

'Can you tell if it is well?'

Dragons weren't born with deformities. There had been eggs that housed ill-formed dragonlings, but the mother often disposed of them before they fully developed. I never witnessed such things, though talk of it grew more common as the quality in Regent dropped every year.

Tizmet huffed with a tone of finality. *'It is well.'*

I frowned up at her. She differed from any dragon I studied. Perhaps she wouldn't get rid of an egg that had a poorly formed dragonling inside.

Slowly, I set it off my lap, and she nuzzled it closer to the rest. As she settled it with the others, I pulled my feet away from a bluish egg which was askew as if I had kicked it.

'Calm,' a note of amusement lingered in her tone, *'it would take more than a kick from you to harm them.'*

Jamlin's face popped over the edge. "Is she awake?"

Tizmet snarled and snaked her head in his direction, chasing him off.

I looked up at Rafe with a small smile. "It's a wonder she hasn't eaten you." My words rasped from my raw throat.

'He watches over you.' She seemed irritated, as if she only let him stay because he protected me.

He worked his jaw. "Water?"

I nodded, and he shifted, pulling his legs from under me with a grunt. I hissed in pain as he propped me against Tizmet's warm side. His frown deepened, but he left me without a word to slip off the boulder's edge.

My eyes snagged on a half-eaten deer carcass a few paces from the clutch.

'Dane?' I asked.

My stomach rumbled with hunger. I smelled smoke. The Tennan must have camped here all night.

'And the big red one.'

She pushed an image of Tegan and Dane dragging kills to the boulder. *'They were dirty,'* she huffed unhappily, *'but still warm.'*

My heart twisted, and my eyes welled with tears. I had friends who were not only there for me when I needed them, but for my dragon, too. I thought back to a time when I believed I didn't need anyone. Young and independent, I figured I could do everything on my own. As I got older and matured, I realized sometimes

I needed help, and it wasn't shameful to ask or to be thankful when someone did so.

Rafe hauled himself over the lip of the boulder, muscles bunching as he pulled himself up with one arm, the other holding a waterskin. I ogled him with open appreciation. If he hadn't been here—if he hadn't brought the Tennan, I would have lost Tizmet and myself in the process. He cared for me when I was too weak to protect myself.

Tizmet's lips curled back. *'I don't want him here.'*

She wouldn't harm him, but she put on a defensive display, placing her head directly in his path and snapping her teeth. He used an open palm to shove her maw aside, then continued my way. I almost laughed at the offended look she gave him.

'I am a great dragon,' she said in her defense. *'He should fear me.'*

I snickered an airy, tired laugh. *'So scary.'*

Rafe dropped to a crouch and lifted the waterskin to my lips. I fumbled with it, too weak to even hold it as I drank greedily.

His features warred with concern and irritation. "Easy," he murmured, so low I almost missed it.

I offered him a feeble smile. "Thank you."

"If she mates again, I'll castrate the dragon that takes her."

I laughed, cutting it off with a grimace as my muscles and joints complained with the exertion. After a calming breath, I watched Tizmet flick her tongue, amused.

'Tell him he can have a say in how I mate—after he mates you.'

My cheeks warmed, and Rafe glared at her. She bared her teeth at him in response.

"I want you off this cursed rock," he growled.

That was Rafe-speech for, 'Avyanna. I'm worried about you. Can you move? Because I would like to make you more comfortable.' But that wasn't his way.

"I can try."

I attempted to sit up on my own. My chest flared with pain and my limbs trembled. Rafe looped an arm under my knees and another around my back, hauling me against him. I couldn't help but cry out as my broken body screamed in agony.

Tizmet snapped her teeth. *'Stay here, with my eggs.'*

"Move it, lizard," he grumbled, stepping around her. "You might be made to rest on rocks, but us mere humans would rather have a blanket or two."

She lipped at the back of his tunic. *'Make a bed here.'*

"One tear and you'll go hungry."

'Please, Tizmet. Let me sleep on the ground at least.' Dirt had more give than solid stone.

She snorted and pulled her head away, allowing Rafe to pass. *'Stay in sight.'*

A camp crowded the clearing, with the smallest fire and six bedrolls. Jamlin and Tegan rushed over to help me down as Blain sprawled on his bedroll, happy to watch the scene with a smile. Dane perched on a low branch. And Zephath sat on his blanket, knees pulled to his chest, nose-deep in some book. Irritation soured his features.

I clenched my teeth together as Rafe eased me to the lip of the boulder. Tegan stepped to my right, while Jamlin took up the left. They barely reached my ankles. Rafe cursed and jostled me as he lowered me a bit more. I hated being so helpless, yet I knew I didn't have enough strength to make it down alone.

After a few more painful movements and a small drop, I was carried over to the fire. They settled me onto a thick bedroll, and the blanket almost felt as good as the down-filled bed in King's Wall.

Rafe jumped off the boulder, landing with a soft thud.

"Show off," I hissed.

Rafe grunted in response and stomped to a small pot near the fire. Tegan and Jam moved aside as he sat next to me and plunked a spoon in a bowl and handed it to me.

"Eat."

"Yes, sir."

A few tense moments passed while I shoveled in bites. Blain chuckled at the awkward silence and Jamlin answered him with a grin.

"Smitten," Tegan called, watching Rafe loom over me, "just smitten."

"Ready yourself," Rafe bit out, in no mood to be teased.

However, I didn't miss the tiny lift at the corner of his mouth.

I rolled my eyes as he pushed himself to his feet and met Tegan at the center of the clearing.

"Surely, not swords." Tegan's amused grin only grew.

Jamlin laughed, taking a seat on his bedroll next to Blain. "You wouldn't stand a chance."

Tegan clutched his chest in a show of offense, but Rafe only scoffed as he removed his sheath and tossed it my way. When he pulled off his shirt, Blain whistled in mock admiration.

Tegan paused as he unfastened his sheath and gazed up at Rafe as if he had mortally wounded him. "Now, how am I supposed to compete with that?"

He tossed his weapon, then reached up to tear off his tunic the same way Rafe had, but struggled when his sleeve got caught on his wrist. Rafe took that moment to charge. Tegan cursed, dancing to the side, but Rafe struck out and snagged him by the waist, throwing him to the ground.

"That's fighting dirty!" Tegan wheezed, then pulled his tunic free. "If I ripped a seam, you're paying for it!"

He scrambled to stand as Rafe turned on him with a sneer.

"Getting slow, old man," he snarled.

"You're older—oof!" Tegan threw his arms up to block a punch to his face.

They traded jabs, neither of them besting the other for a few moments.

Tizmet straightened to her full height, watching them wrestle, then snorted in annoyance. Unamused, she curled around her clutch. *'They play.'*

'Aye, it's great entertainment.'

I admired Rafe's quick movements, without shame. These were my friends, and I had nothing to hide from them.

He sidestepped and blocked a fist aimed at his head, then twisted, landing a blow to Tegan's gut. The man doubled-over and held up his hand. Rafe shuffled back, then smirked as Tegan struggled to breathe.

"I—I yield!" he gasped, peering up with a mischievous grin. "But you've still—gone soft!"

He danced out of the way and lunged for the bedrolls when Rafe stepped toward him, fists clenched.

"Oi!" Jam pushed up. "Got more to give?" He wore an easy smile and removed his sword, then gave me a wink.

Rafe sighed, as if he did this only for their amusement. "Come on, then."

"Should I say a few words about your big heart, or undying love for our dear Avyanna?" Jamlin jeered. "When should we expect little white-haired devils running about?"

Breathless, Tegan collapsed on the bedroll beside me, and a tiny prick ached in my chest. My moon cycle still hadn't returned, and nearly two years passed since I last used the tinge berry tea to keep it at bay. Healer Rashel told me the stuff could result in a barren womb.

Rafe frowned, being the one who provided the tea for me in the first place. He had deemed the moon cycle a weakness, a risk that a soldier shouldn't take. What he hadn't anticipated was the long-term effects I would endure.

Fueled by genuine anger, Rafe picked up his pace, his frustration aimed inward rather than at Jam. Jamlin sensed the change and moved deftly. He not only used his fists but his legs too, trying to trip Rafe up. It was a risk I knew well, though. Once upon a time, I attempted such while sparring, which resulted in him snaring my ankle and holding me upside down like a rag doll.

Rafe blocked a kick from his right, catching Jam's leg. But before he could throw off his balance, Jam threw a punch in his blind spot, aiming for his left cheek.

The blow landed hard along his jaw. I cringed as he staggered back. His fists flew up, protecting his face as Jamlin swung a kick at his stomach. Rafe dropped his weight and swiped Jam's feet. He collapsed and Rafe was on him in less than a breath. They wrestled, getting cut by branches and sharp stones half-buried in the dirt.

"Jam has the advantage on the ground," Tegan commented dryly.

Blain yawned. "Nah, Rafe knows he's been matched. It's not a game anymore."

"Rafe has more weight, but he should have kept it upright," Tegan argued.

"Jam has a height advantage," I offered.

Tegan snorted. "Only by a breath."

"Height and weight doesn't matter." Blain set his sharp eyes on me. "Jam struck a nerve and our General is quite riled."

When we turned back, Rafe had Jamlin pinned, his thick arm wrapped around the man's neck. Jam thrashed and clawed at Rafe's hold, but he pulled back hard. It was clear Jamlin yielded and struggled for breath. Still, he didn't let go.

"Rafe?" I called.

He looked up, and worry knotted my stomach.

He wasn't here.

"Oi–" Tegan groaned.

Blain straightened. His interest ignited. "Again?"

Clearly, they weren't much help.

I pushed to stand, but my aching legs gave out, and I fell hard on my rear. Cursing, I crawled toward the two as Jam gasped, trying to worm his hand between Rafe's arm and his neck.

Tizmet's interest in the fight flared again, but my full attention was on Rafe's eye. It was cold and distant. He bared his teeth and let out a string of curses, not at me, but as if he were caught in some memory.

"Rafe?"

I settled in front of him. His gaze was wild as he tracked my every move. He clenched his jaw, and my heart twisted as he fought some inner demon.

"Little—help—Blain?" Jam gasped.

He shrugged. "If anyone can calm him, it's her."

My hand pressed against Rafe's corded arm, tight with tension. I said his name again, and he flinched, curling his lip in a snarl.

"I'm here."

My touch slid up his shoulder, and he ground his teeth, watching my face.

"Let go," I whispered, cupping his cheek.

I traced my thumb over the scars under his eye patch, and he trembled. His arm shot forward, and so did Jam, coughing and gasping for air. As his vision cleared and awareness shifted over his features, he stared at Jamlin.

"Got what you deserve," Zeph muttered.

"Well, I wanted a challenge." Jam coughed again, then rubbed at his sore throat. "All's well?"

He might've been smiling, but the concern in his tone was obvious.

Rafe grunted, stood, then surveyed the small camp. Without a word, he stormed into the thicket, brambles tearing at his skin.

Jamlin shrugged when I met his gaze.

"Just needs some time to cool off," he said. "Come along. You should be resting." He stooped down and secured me in his arms.

"You're filthy." My nose wrinkled as I pushed away from his sweaty chest.

His head tipped toward the sky as he laughed. "Look who's talking."

I peered down at myself. Crusted in dried blood and other fluids I'd rather not think about—I had to agree with him.

"Rest, then we'll wash up."

"In the bog?"

I choked on a gag. Surely they didn't mean to clean themselves in that vile water. Just being near it made me uneasy—forget bathing in it.

"Stream," Dane said, dropping from his perch.

Jamlin set me down on the bedroll, and I grimaced as my body hit the ground.

"That would be nice," I murmured.

I couldn't help but glance where Rafe disappeared into the thicket. I hoped he would return by then.

'He lingers.' Tizmet flicked her tongue. *'He is angry.'*

I sighed, letting my eyes flutter shut. *'He got lost in a memory.'*

'He will come back.'

I knew he would, but I hated that he had to walk away.

And I hated that I was too weak to follow.

Chapter 15

I drifted awake to the rumble of Rafe's voice. My head was pulled into his lap, and I remained still, listening to the conversation.

"When will you be back?" he asked.

Blain drawled, "That remains to be seen."

"And Dane?"

"He's staying behind."

There was a tense pause before Rafe let out a thoughtful grunt. "Curious?"

"Mildly. Truth be told," he sighed, "you're getting boring, General."

I couldn't help the smile that lifted my lips. I was his reason for being boring, and I was proud of it.

Rafe scoffed, the movement jostling me, and I groaned as I rolled to peer up at his face. The sun was setting, painting the sky a beautiful pink. The stinging bugs buzzed about, a telltale sign of the night's approach.

He smirked. "Go."

"Go where?" I mumbled.

"Across the E'or—addle-brained man."

"Yes, sir." Blain's droll reply was chased by a mock solute.

I tried to stretch. My muscles complained but weren't shrieking in agony as they were earlier. I took that as an improvement.

"I was told there's a stream nearby."

"Nearby?" Rafe snorted. "It's a bit of a walk."

"Well, you need it."

I sat up and twisted to face him. Dirt and dried blood littered his arms, and he smelled more rank than I did—which was saying something.

"I wasn't elbow deep in a dragon's arsehole." He stood, offering me his hand.

I smiled as he pulled me up with care. I glanced over at Tizmet's nest and could only see the ridges on her back and the tips of her wings.

"She's been sleeping—like you," he said, then slung his pack over his shoulder.

I reached across the bond and sensed nothing alarming, but I wanted to be sure. "Is she well?"

"Thus far," he muttered, heading east toward the thicket.

I crowded after him, trying to keep my feet under me, but careful of the low-hanging vines and brambles. The trampled path, worn down by the men as they took their turns washing in the stream, provided only a slight improvement to the harsh terrain. Rafe was careful not to let branches swing back and catch me, but more than once I stumbled into him. He turned to frown at me until I recovered and gave me a stern look, as if to say he'd carry me if he could.

Our journey led us to a man-made clearing where the once-thriving tall grass and thin saplings were cut away and scattered into the foliage. It was a tight squeeze, with just enough room for us to maneuver. 'Stream' was quite a generous term as the creek was only a pace deep and wide enough for me to sit. Yet the clear running water was a refreshing, inviting sight.

"She chose a good nest, at least," he muttered, yanking off his tunic.

I sighed as I sat, exhausted from the walk. "She would need running water close by. She won't travel far from her clutch now that she's laid."

Satisfied that I was resting, Rafe reached for his pack, rummaging through it. "The men can't keep feeding her."

"Dane has a soft spot for her," I replied with a smile.

He looked up and glared.

I laughed and added, "She can hunt for herself. She's laid clutches before."

"Dane stays with us," he rumbled.

He secured the soap, then tossed his pack aside. As he removed his pants, I turned away. Even after all the time we spent alone, I only saw him without trousers when I rescued him. Being flayed open at the hands of the Shadows was hardly a moment to take in his body—not that it had been worth ogling at that point.

One day—when we had a house. When we were intimate.

I rubbed at my face as a blush heated my cheeks. "This *boring* life isn't suited for Blain."

"I'd like to know what was boring about last night," Rafe scoffed. Small splashes signaled he began washing up.

"That's what I was thinking." I pulled my knees to my chest, then rested my cheek against them, gazing up at the hazy sky. "It's not every day that a dragon lays forty-two eggs."

"We need to talk about that."

I looked his way as he splashed water on his face, then ran his hands down the back of his head and neck. Clearing my throat, I studied my boots as if they were the most interesting things.

"She laid clutches in the Sky Trees?" he asked.

"Aye, at least a few. In the memories that she shared with me, they were taken by the Shadows."

"Which is why they're bolder," he mused. "One wonders if any bonded them."

"Shadow Dragon Kind?" Shock and disgust smothered my words. "The dragonlings would never. Their magic is–"

"Perverted."

I braved a glance at him as he crouched in the stream, his left side to me. I could only see his eye socket, but he seemed to be lost in thought. Surely he didn't think of himself like that—he wouldn't lump himself in with those that used their Shadow magic to control others. He was different.

He was good.

"It feels wrong," I clarified, averting my eyes as I broke his spell. "Tizmet has felt it, been under it. It was rotten and fetid. It's not normal. No dragon would willingly join with that."

"But they could be forced to."

I scoffed. "Can you force the bond? I couldn't."

I thought of my second rejection, how I sought out the little dragonling. Back then, I believed I could help it along—and I wasn't the first who attempted.

"Others have tried," I said. "It's not something you can force. The magic chooses who it will."

"And those who command magic? Who could tell it who to choose?"

I frowned thinking about that. The Shadow Men controlled magic without dragons. Dragon Kind only had minuscule access *because* of their dragons. With power like that, was it possible to force a bond?

"And what of these eggs?" Rafe asked, stepping from the water.

I kept my eyes trained on the ground as he dressed.

"They will be Wildlings."

"'Til the locals learn of them."

"They won't," I said, meeting his eye.

Tizmet reached across the bond, feeling my anger. *'They belong to themselves,'* she agreed.

He paused in fastening his trousers and studied me. "Protective of your eggs?"

"They are their own."

I frowned, shaking off the maternal protection I felt from Tizmet. I shared her pain, helped bring the last one into our world, but they were not mine. "When they hatch, they will be independent."

"Hatchlings at Northwing aren't."

'He dares to compare my young with domesticated pets?!' she snarled.

I pushed her aside. Rafe didn't mean any offense, and he had a point.

"Those Hatchlings are *raised* to be dependent." I struggled to my feet, then held my hand out for the soap. "They follow the traditions set by their sire and dam. Once they hatch, if they bond, they grow and learn together with their Riders under the Masters' guidance."

A whine slipped out as I fought with my shirt. My muscles and joints were stiff, sore from my seizure and the chimes spent laying on stone. Rafe's hands trailed along my bare sides, easing my tunic over my head. I smiled my thanks, then examined the blood staining the fabric—both Tizmet's and my own.

Rafe chuckled, then tossed it into the forest. "No saving it."

"I suppose I know the men well enough to wear this." I scoffed, gesturing to my chest binding and trousers.

Rafe's eye glittered darkly as his gaze traveled over my body, taking too long to reach my face. I cleared my throat before he could make a move.

"Right. Cleaning up."

I faced the flowing water, turning my back on him as I unraveled the binding. When I set it aside, I glared over my shoulder, then pulled it a little closer to my spot near the stream.

He chuckled and sat down on the cut grass, and pulled one knee up to his chest. He gave me the wickedest grin and arched a brow, daring me to keep going.

"I suppose you won't be modest about this."

"Me? Modest?"

I sighed, ignoring him, then pulled off my trousers. In my mad dash, my foot caught, and I went down hard on my rear. I shrieked as water splashed around me.

His snicker was answer enough to know he had witnessed that.

"Graceful."

"It's why you love me," I shot back.

I reached for the soap, trying to keep myself covered.

After a few moments of lathering myself up, Rafe spoke again. "So, you expect these dragonlings to hatch and be Wild?"

"Aye. They will have no Riders if Tizmet has anything to say about it. The people of Leeds won't even know about them."

"And when she disappears for what—a year? And returns leaner, they'll not suspect a thing."

I paused, glaring at the slow current.

"And when local game thins? When sheep go missing?"

"Wild dragons are solitary creatures." I said, pulling from Tizmet's memory. "They might spread out and populate the E'or."

"Or the townsfolk might hunt them down."

I whirled to face Rafe with pure horror and shock. "They wouldn't–"

"Wouldn't let their livelihood be threatened by a predator? No, I don't think so."

His body was deathly still as he met my gaze. I didn't want to contemplate this. I muffled the bond, thankful for Tizmet's distracted state. She would rage if she knew what he implied.

"They're dragons!"

"See any Dragon Kind about, Vy?" He held my livid stare. "Know of anyone to tell them different? To force them to listen? No. The only way they won't turn on the beasts is if they're useful—if they're bonded."

"No." The truth of his words sapped all strength from my tone. "Dragon Kind wouldn't allow it."

"The ones in Regent—that banished you? The ones barely holding their own in a war? Use your brain, Vy. No one would stop these folk from hunting down dragons or stealing eggs just like the Shadows, hoping to bond them."

"You want me to let the people of Leeds at them?" My tone was accusing, though my heart knew better.

I defended a clutch that wasn't even mine. I wanted them to live free—yet this was a world where those who had freedom were hunted as game.

Rafe sighed, pulling his gaze up to the clouds. He let the accusation hang in the air long enough for me to turn back and scrub at my skin as if I could peel off the layer of dread that slid over my heart.

"We have time."

"They're Tizmet's eggs."

"And she has a few weeks to decide what to do with them."

"It's a year before they hatch." I stood and faced him, my irritation making me bold.

His eye raked down my body, but he simply pressed his lips together as I threw the lump of soap at his pack and reached for my trousers.

"Luther will find them sooner than that."

"Luther can–"

"He's going to ask for one."

"I know, Rafe!" I yanked my trousers up, fumbling with my belt, enraged. "But it's not within my power to give him any. They're hers, not mine. I don't understand why you think I'll just pawn them off like they're some kind of commodity–"

"Vy."

My breaths came fast and heavy as he loomed above me. I expected to see irritation at my childish reaction, but instead compassion shifted through his dark gaze.

"A soldier should always know what they're up against," he murmured, then cupped my chin, pulling me close.

Tears blurred my vision as I fought to keep hold of my emotions. This isn't what a soldier would do. They wouldn't cry in despair.

"This is a mess." I choked out.

"And here, Blain thought this was boring," Rafe muttered, drawing a sad smile from me. "Vy, you and your dragon need to have a plan. That's all I ask."

He held me as I bit my lip and blinked furiously to clear my vision. I took a deep breath. We had time. We would think of something to get around this mess.

"And that you put a tunic on before I take you right *here*."

I grinned as my cheeks burned. He removed his hand, letting me avoid his heated gaze. He stepped aside, pulled a spare tunic from his bag, and tossed it my way. It was big enough for three women my size. How was I supposed to tie it?

"This?"

"Make it work."

I laughed at Rafe's pained tone and hurried to bind my chest before pulling the sleeveless tunic over my head. The hem hit my knees, and the lacing dropped to my navel. I looked up at him and spread my arms.

"Happy?"

He grimaced and pulled the lacing taut. His eye glittered in the low light as he worked his fingers over my chest, securing the tie as tight as possible before he stepped back.

I laughed, fingering the bow he made. "Well, don't I look the proper lady."

He grunted, but I caught the look of mischief in his features.

"We should probably head back," I said, tucking the tunic into my trousers as best I could.

"Right," he placed the soap in his pack, "wouldn't want them to think anything *indecent* was going on."

"What? Us? Bathing within a few paces of each other? No one would doubt your virtue, dear General." I headed toward the dimly lit path, feeling much better now that I was clean and had a chance to stretch my sore muscles.

"If only I had such faith in myself," Rafe mumbled behind me.

I had the silliest smile on my face as we returned to the nest.

It would all work out.

Chapter 16

I stayed with Tizmet for the entire day, avoiding the inevitable confrontation with Iana. How was I going to explain this? Rafe was right. I wouldn't be able to hide this from the townspeople. They would ponder her whereabouts and my unexplained absence. Given that I had already been on the brink of losing my job, I doubted she would extend any further leniency after disappearing for two more nights.

My breath rushed out in a sigh, lost in my thoughts as I looked over the dragon eggs. Under the blazing midday sun, they gleamed and shimmered, creating the illusion of a treasure trove filled with precious gems.

'Treasure.' Tizmet hummed her agreement, lifting her head to nudge an egg closer.

A smile teased my lips, then with a groan, I pushed myself off her side and stood. As tempting as it was to linger, I had to hear what Iana had to say about my disappearance.

With a command in her fiery eye, Tizmet blocked my path with her head, urging me to stay. I stroked her muzzle, feeling the warmth of her sun-soaked scales against my fingertips.

'I can't.'

She snorted, the force of the blow tousling my hair. As she pushed over the bond, her powerful desire to keep me tucked away, safe and secure, engulfed me completely.

'I'm not a hatchling.'

'No, you're more helpless than my young.'

I laughed, pushing her massive head away. *'I have Rafe.'*

She curled her tail tighter about her clutch. As I neared the stone ledge, Rafe glanced up from packing his bedroll.

The Tennan returned to Leeds shortly after Rafe and I finished washing. Guilt weighed on my shoulders when I saw the red welts that covered their skin. I instructed them to find Saudric for a salve. They endured the stinging insects all night, just in case Tizmet needed anything. My heart swelled with that knowledge. My friends were willing to suffer to make sure we were well.

I frowned as I struggled to climb down the side of the stone, thinking of Blain's return to Regent. He never shared why. The journey over the E'or was a difficult one, so whatever drove him back to that kingdom had to be important.

I had friends there. Niehm. Elenor. Willhelm. What kind of person knew their loved ones were in mortal danger, but simply wiped their hands, claiming it wasn't their problem?

My foot slipped, and I grunted as my forehead smacked against the stone. "Blasted woman."

Rafe's strong hold encircled my waist as he took my weight and helped me down. I sniffed, rubbing at the fresh lump as he examined my head. He pressed his thumbs over my temples, brushing my unruly hair aside.

His dark eye caught mine, and his mouth dipped in a harsh frown. "What is it?"

When I didn't answer, he gripped my chin in his calloused hand, inspecting my face.

"All is well?"

I tried to look anywhere to avoid his fierce gaze. "Aye."

He suffered so much for my sake. How could I tell him I wished to go back to the country that banished me?

"I'm thankful the Tennan was here, that they could come," I said.

"I think a certain woman has turned their hearts to mush." He chuckled, tugging me into a rough embrace.

I relaxed against him and closed my eyes. "I wish I could repay them."

"Peace will be enough."

Guilt spiraled through my heart, and I clenched my jaw. Willhelm would never know peace. Elenor, Niehm—the hundreds of women and children they cared for–

'Do not worry over matters you cannot change.' Tizmet lowered her head over us, sensing my unease.

'They're my friends. Of course, I'm going to worry.'

I pulled myself out of Rafe's embrace, noting the way his eye trailed me, as if he knew there was more I wasn't saying.

The saddle blanket took the brunt of my irritation as I threw it under my arm with a bit more force than necessary. Grabbing the saddle, Rafe angled himself so he could watch me, and I stomped toward the small path the men created to access their horses from the clearing. I pushed through the dense growth, making sure the brambles wouldn't whip back and hit him. He didn't deserve to be on the receiving end of my guilt.

The path to Rafe's stallion took far longer than it felt coming in. His horse snorted when we approached, pricking his ears in interest. As I neared the large gray beast, I held out my hand. He sniffed my palm, whiskers tickling my skin. I smiled, stroking the bridge of his nose.

After we had him saddled, Rafe lifted me onto his back. Settling behind, he wrapped his arm around me and I cast one last look over my shoulder. The trees and undergrowth were so thick I couldn't see the clearing, let alone the nest.

Tizmet pushed her anxiety, and I nudged all the calm I could muster back at her.

'Don't worry about things you can't change.' I echoed her words from earlier.

'I can always bring you back to my nest.'

With a soft laugh, I leaned my weight against Rafe as he guided his horse through the woods.

"She's threatening to keep me with her eggs."

We ducked low, riding beneath a thick branch.

"Like I would let her."

'He does not let *me do anything.'*

"I have to say, a straw-stuffed mattress is sounding quite appealing after a night on stone, and another on the ground."

"You're going soft."

I pressed my lips together in a bitter smile, trying to pull my thoughts away from Regent.

We rode to Leeds at a slow walk. I enjoyed this stolen moment with Rafe. There was nothing but me and him and the rocking gait of the stallion beneath us. I dozed in his arms, the warmth of his chest against my back, the sun peeking through the forest canopy, and the sounds of nature lulling me into a peaceful sleep.

My boots carried me up the tavern steps as dread wound through me. Rafe walked beside me, a silent support to the outrage I was sure to face inside.

The room was as busy as ever, the crowd in good spirits, ready to unwind after a long day of hard labor. As the door shut behind us, curious eyes turned our way. Conversation stuttered, then picked up in full force. I scanned the tables for Iana.

I didn't have to look long.

"You. Kitchen. Now."

She spoke low and quiet, barely carrying over the merry din, but I heard her loud and clear. I clenched my jaw, knowing this was the moment I would lose my job.

Rafe's bulk followed me as I squeezed through patrons. Iana smiled at a couple nursing their ales. Kila flitted about, spinning and dancing between tables. When she caught sight of me, she didn't slow as she flashed me a smile. Jam and Tegan sat in the far corner, lifting their ales in greeting. I offered them an unsteady nod as I headed for the kitchen.

If Iana let us stay, Rafe could afford our rooms, but losing this job would take away my place in the community. What else could I do? With Tizmet guarding her eggs, I wasn't likely to bring down enough game to pass as a hunter.

This was my only contribution to Leeds, and I was going to lose it.

Before I opened the door, I placed a hand on Rafe's chest. His eye sparked with silent question.

"I can handle this."

"You don't need this job, Vy."

"No, but I want it," I replied softly.

I shooed him over to Jam and Tegan as Iana made her way over. Rafe grunted, clearly not pleased, but gave a one-armed shrug before stalking off.

As soon as I passed the threshold, I cringed. Letting the door close behind me.

"You!"

Pachu brandished a ladle, wielding it like a sword. His thick lips pressed together, eyes red and bloodshot. He had a hand perched on his ample hip and glared as if I was next on the menu.

Iana pushed inside, crowding me closer to the irate cook, and my gaze darted between them.

I didn't want to end up in a soup.

"You abandoned me!" Pachu started in with a wail. "You promised me meat, and then you disappear–"

Iana's features soured as she tracked me head to toe. "You look like you've been dragged through a dungheap, girl. What *are* you wearing?"

"Do you know what I had to serve two nights ago?! Do you know?!" Pachu cried and ran his hands down his face, pulling his skin into a horrifying expression. "*Vegetable soup!* On a hot summer night!" He whipped his ladle to point at the giant pot over the stove. "And tonight?! *More soup!* If you–"

"Where have you been?!" Iana demanded, drawing my attention again.

I opened my mouth to reply, but didn't get far.

"I tell you if you miss another night, I'll find new help, then *that same night* you don't show up?" Her eyebrows nearly met her hairline in disbelief. "If you were done here, you could have at least cleared your belongings out of your room!"

I was sweating now, not just from the kitchen's humid steam, but from the heat of their questions and demands.

"You don't underst–"

"You let me down, Avyanna!" Pachu cried. He spun on his heel, gripping the counter as if he couldn't bear to see me. "My poor girl, led astray by—by that *ogre!*"

"Where were you?! And why are you so roughed up? Iana propped her fists on her hips. "I know you love that man," her statement earned another wracking sob from Pachu, "but if he hurt you, I'll not be sparing your feelings when I pass it on to Rothfuss. I told you–"

"Stop!"

Iana's open mouth snapped shut with a click, and Pachu whimpered over the pot. I closed my eyes and took a deep, calming breath before daring to open them. Iana seethed, glaring daggers while Pachu's weeping endangered the soup of being contaminated by his tears.

"Something came up," I started, my tone low and careful. "I didn't think the errand would take as long as it did—for that I am sorry."

"You couldn't warn us?" Iana bit out.

"I had little warning myself." I hedged. "It was sudden, and I had no choice but to see to it."

"Townsfolk saw you riding out with that man."

"I needed him."

"Girl, if you don't tell me what happened, what sudden, unexpected errand warranted that beast and his small army—all of you will lose those rooms." Iana stated flatly, her brown eyes unyielding as she spoke.

I pinched the bridge of my nose with a groan. "I can't."

"Did your dragon bring any meat, at least?" Pachu sniffled.

"No, and she won't be able to for quite a while."

"How long?!" he demanded.

"I'd say a year or so."

Iana's glare softened a fraction as realization dawned.

Eggs in Regent always hatched on Summer Solstice, the longest and hottest day of the year. I didn't know if that would change in Leeds, where it was hot and muggy. The constant humidity might affect the incubation period.

"Your dragon laid her clutch." Iana guessed, studying my face.

I pressed my lips together in a firm frown, giving her a jerky nod. "I'd like to keep this quiet. It was a rough laying. I don't want–"

"You don't want a certain man sending his goons out looking for her eggs," Pachu whispered. He wiped his nose on his apron and dried his teary eyes.

"Aye."

"He'll know soon enough." Iana leaned against the door, drained by her anger. "That dragon is never far from you. She's gone and so is our source of meat. I can't afford to pay another barmaid and purchase cuts from Luther's butcher."

I swallowed past the lump in my throat.

Her weary gaze met mine. "And I can't afford Luther selling me spoiled goods because of you."

"He and I have an agreement."

Since we signed our contract, he had kept his tails a safe distance away and had been fair to Iana.

"I'm reminding you, girl. If you bring his wrath about my ears, I'll be tossing you out on yours." She sighed, brushing her hair back. "Clean yourself up as best you can, then get out there."

Hope blossomed in my chest, and I couldn't help the smile that split my face. "Thank–"

"I expect no more running off, and a warning before you go and visit that dragon of yours. I also expect you to make up for the work you missed the last two nights!"

"Yes, milady–"

"Call me that again, and I'll let Pachu at you with that spoon!"

"It's a *ladle!*" he called as the door slammed behind her.

I turned to Pachu with the biggest grin. He studied me for a moment, then gave a bark of laughter. He wrapped his beefy arms around me and pulled me in close.

"Survived, yet again!"

The following weeks brought high summer, and with it, Summer Solstice. A busy time for Leeds, but especially for Iana and the Bog Frog Inn.

The Tennan had to bunk up. Zeph moved in with Jam, and with Blain gone, Dane roomed with Tegan to free up space on the first floor. Even so, the two rooms filled up quickly, and she had to turn travelers away.

It was a curious thing how cultures spread. For example, while dragons were prevalent in Regent, they were nonexistent this far east. Through the many villages I passed, Tizmet had been quite the shock, a creature of myth and legend. Yet, the people along the E'or celebrated the Summer Solstice, and without knowing it, Hatching Day. I puzzled at the vendors who prepped egg-shaped goods, treats and trinkets. Regent's dragon culture wound its way through the E'or and down toward the Wild Marshes.

"Avyanna, more ale!"

I grunted in response to Iana's demand, three mugs in each hand and a plate laden with meat pie balanced on my elbow. I offered pained smiles at the men who I bumped into as I maneuvered through the crowd. Dropping the plate off with a hurried nod, I darted for the bar to place the dirty mugs into the stack that grew at an alarming rate.

Sucking in a deep breath, I knew I would have to clean those after closing, and probably still have some left to deal with in the morning. I passed the space that the Tennan commandeered. Unable to procure a chair with the dense crowd, Dane sat on the floor cross-legged, eyes shut and head tipped against the wall as if he could sleep through the loud festivities. Zeph perched on the table, swinging his legs back and forth, keeping a shy eye on Kila as she weaved through the patrons.

My quick glance snagged on Rafe, and I flashed him a bright but tired smile. He gave me a drawn out blink in response, unimpressed by my choice to work on the Solstice. I refused to shirk the busy night, knowing Iana would be thankful for my aid. It made me feel *useful.*

It was sweltering outside and positively boiling in the kitchen. I bustled through, dodging Pachu as he crimped the edges on more meat pies, prepping them for the stove. The premade ones sold out faster than we anticipated, and he was frantic, prepping more.

I jogged out the back door, down the stairs, then rounded the corner to the tavern's storage shed. Fishing the key out of my shirt, I unlocked the iron padlock.

It was odd, enjoying this exhaustion, but without it, life was almost... *boring.* I scoffed at my thoughts and hauled the door open. I went by feel, knowing the space by heart, having done inventory far more times than I'd care to count. After a deep breath, I hauled the cask of ale to my chest. Grunting, I fumbled it onto my shoulder, letting out a wheeze under the weight. I *could* lift the thing, but that didn't mean it was easy.

A shadow blocked the weak moonlight that drifted in from the door, and I turned to meet a man's gaze.

Luther.

He leaned on his cane, dressed primly in an embroidered tunic and overcoat, even in this suppressing heat.

Panic flooded me, even as my brain fought to keep calm. I knew he wouldn't hurt me. We had a contract.

"Avyanna, dear. How nice to see you." He stepped aside, motioning for me to pass.

I gritted my teeth and shuffled past, grimly noting the four men at his back. Luther gestured to me, and a strapping man moved to relieve me of the cask.

I appreciated the freedom of movement, so I relinquished it with a warning. "Iana expects that whole cask, not a drop missing."

With my hands free, my left found my bandit breaker. Not as a threat—instead, a reminder of who they were dealing with.

"Yes, ever the careful worker ant, aren't we?" He huffed a quiet laugh.

With a flick of his wrist, the man with the cask walked off, heading toward the front entrance. Pachu would've diced him up and slipped him into a meat pie if he dared enter through the kitchen.

"What is it?" I sniffed, looking back at Luther.

"So eloquent."

His lips thinned into a smile that never reached his eyes, baring his teeth like some kind of weasel. I felt the strongest urge to recoil from the sight.

"I just wanted to pay a visit," he said. "Check in on my investment, if you will."

"I'm well enough."

"Ah, that is music to my ears. I have to say, with your dear General paying out so much coin, I'm surprised to see you still working in such a state."

Familiar fear thrummed through me, realizing he referred to our deposit to the guildhall. Our future house was paid for, with the condition that Rafe and some of his men assisted in the construction.

"I was unaware my physical state would render me unable to work." I formed my words with care.

"Well, one would have to assume that after three moon cycles, the virulent General's seed would take."

He eased toward me, leaning heavily on his cane, and I allowed myself to retreat a step.

"Pardon a man for asking," he said, "but are you not yet with child?"

I couldn't help the snarl that lifted my lip, baring my teeth at the snake. My hands trembled as I fought the urge to throw myself at him and teach him a lesson on appropriate conversation.

"No? Oh, well, that's good to hear. At least for Iana, I would assume. Though so long and no child? Will the little cottage on the pond only have two lovers grow old in its walls? No cheerful laughs, no shrieks of joy? No–"

"Luther."

My fingers ached as I clenched them into fists at Rafe's voice, hating that he had to come to my rescue—hating how Luther's words were like hooks in my heart.

His tone was not one of greeting, but of warning. I wasn't sure how much he heard. Regardless, my reaction alone told him something was amiss.

"Ah, there you are, General." Luther grinned, dipping his chin.

Rafe stalked to my side, bumping his arm against mine in a show of support.

"I was simply asking after Avyanna's health. After all, a certain dragon has been missing of late."

Panic seized my heart in its iron grasp. Of course he noticed—everyone had. Tizmet's absence was the talk of town.

"I admit, I am more curious as to the great beast's health. I am not well-versed in the workings of Dragon Kind, so I ventured to ask after Avyanna." He turned to me with a vile smile. "If you are well, she is as well?"

I had a moment to be thankful Tizmet was slipping into an early brumation-like state and was so distant she didn't have an ear on the conversation.

"It's none of your concern."

Rafe swung a heavy arm over my shoulder, and I stepped into his embrace. He tucked me against his side, facing down Luther with his chin raised.

"It is, though. Isn't it?" Luther crooned, adjusting his sleeve. He watched with hooded eyes, his gaze dancing between us. "Contracts and all that, the fine details no one bothers to read," he muttered with an easy laugh.

I read those fine details. I knew our contract, and his favor was from me, not Tizmet.

"Go." Rafe gave me a gentle shove toward the kitchen.

My touch trailed along his arm, and I grabbed his hand, giving him a tug. He resisted for a moment, then let me pull a step away from Luther. I couldn't trust him alone with that snake.

"Ah, yes. Go on, dear General. Follow your Dragon Rider. I'm sure she takes the lead in the bed as well."

Rafe's hand jerked out of mine, and I whirled, grasping at thin air as he threw his bulk. Horror filled me as Luther snapped his cane up just in time to hit him squarely in the chest with the end, giving him a breath of hesitation. Every inch of him trembled with rage.

"A cottage?" Luther quipped, eyes flashing. "A little cottage on the edge of a pond? Lovely clearing. I remember seeing the most charming wildflowers. It would be a pity for them to be trampled by pigs. You know the dastardly creatures have no appreciation for beauty."

Rafe let out a choked growl and gripped the end of Luther's cane in his fist. He was breaths away from killing him. I shook in my own restrained anger and came up behind, gently pulling on his arm. He didn't take his eye off Luther as the cane creaked under his grip.

"Go on, now." A cruel smile lit Luther's face. His dark eyes danced with mirth as he grinned, making him appear all the madder.

Rafe snarled, thrusting the cane away from him with such force that Luther couldn't stop it from smacking into one of his goons.

Rafe turned on me with such a murderous look that I forced myself to keep from breaking into a run back to the kitchen door. Angry tears welled in my eyes as hopelessness spread through me.

If we stayed in Leeds, we would never be free of him. Rothfuss was wrong.

Luther already owned Leeds.

Chapter 17

Rafe brooded in silence, nursing his wounded pride. There were no comforting words I could offer, no assurance that this would get better. Our only hope was for Luther to either lose interest in us, which was unlikely, or cross Rothfuss and get kicked out of town.

After the kitchen was back in order, Pachu staggered out with his tray of leftover pies for the widows' house. I stayed late, cleaning the tavern with Iana and Kila. Well into the wee hours of the morning, I headed to the inn, sore and exhausted.

Rafe wasn't there.

I sighed and drudged up the motivation to change into my night shift and collapse on the bed. I couldn't stay up for him even if I wanted to. Between Luther's dramatics and the bustle of Summer Solstice, the last few chimes had been far too trying.

Rafe climbed in beside me as birds chirped outside our window, heralding the new day. I groaned and wrapped my arms around him, feeling his damp skin and the many welts along his arm.

"Were you out all night?" I murmured.

He grunted and pulled me to his chest. I sighed, giving in as I cuddled against him.

Perhaps all was well.

A smile teased my lips as I watched Rafe wake. He moved slowly, allowing his body to catch up with his mind. It had to be quite the change for him compared to the front, where he had to lurch into battle the moment he opened his eyes. My grin melted away when I noticed the state of his arms and chest. I pushed myself upright, leaning in to examine his skin in the weak light. Scratches and gouges marred the surface, most of them scabbed over. A brutal bruise stained his right side, promising to darken.

"Sun above and moon beneath, Rafe. Did you fight a bog lizard?" I hissed.

He groaned in reply and tried to stretch, wincing with the movement as he reached over his head. "One could almost pretend it was that son of a whore."

I scoffed in disbelief. Of course, when presented with an opponent he could not battle with his swords, he found *something* to fight. I had nothing to say about his coping techniques.

I dipped my chin toward the purple splotch. "That's going to hurt."

"Already does." He grimaced as he lowered his arms.

"Did you break a rib?"

He froze, giving me a droll look, as if the mere suggestion of him breaking a bone was absurd.

"I'm not that old yet, Vy."

I laughed, then gave him a quick kiss on the cheek, careful not to jostle his side. Mindful of my movement, I slid over his hips, then let my feet find the floor. The water from the basin was warm on my face as I washed. When he groaned again, I shook my head, grabbing my trousers.

I watched him below my lashes as I pulled them on. "About last night–"

"Don't."

He growled, cutting off in a strangled sound as he threw his feet over the bedside. I glanced at his right foot, missing two toes. Guilt slammed into me, making me hesitate as I reached for my tunic.

Here I was, expecting him to just come along and make his home under the rule of another. Rafe was always his own man. He never let himself get pushed around before. It took a toll on him, far more than the warfront ever did. He was shoving himself into a mold that wasn't made for him.

Not for the first time, something whispered in the back of my mind.

This isn't for him.

I bottled up that fear and shoved it away. Leeds was our home, the only place left for us. Tizmet laid her eggs here. It was supposed to be where we'd settle and grow old.

"Give me time, Vy," Rafe said with a grunt.

His words brought me back to the present, and I pressed my lips together, throwing my tunic over my head. He washed up in the basin as I finished getting ready. When he moved to grab his shirt, I slipped in his way, stopping him with my palms on his chest. Something angry lurked in his dark gaze, something he held at bay.

"I understand this is hard for you. I just–"

His finger found my lips, and he sighed, flinching when his breath tugged on the injury. "Don't. You don't apologize for anything. This is our lot. We'll figure it out."

I deflated, pressing my cheek against his chest.

"I'm still going to kill him," Rafe rumbled. "Just have to find a way."

I scoffed, dancing aside, knowing he wouldn't risk our future by sating his need for revenge.

We headed down the stairs, with Dane and Tegan trailing behind. Jam and Zeph took their time rising, their door still closed as we passed. On the main floor, I offered a smile to the family that trickled out of their room. The mother had a toddler on each hip. The father and a young boy shared the burden of the packs. I raced to hold the door open for them as they struggled with their loads.

"Good morn!" I called, and they smiled their thanks. "Will you be taking first meal at the tavern? The cook makes delicious eggs."

The father gave me a longing stare as if I held the secrets to his heart, but his wife laughed and shook her head.

"Best to get the little ones on their way before too long," she said. "Sit them in a quiet room and they won't know what to do with themselves. I fear the room would be covered in eggs by the time we left."

We walked together, exchanging pleasantries, and when the path split, they took their leave while the rest of us trudged up the tavern steps. At the door, my gaze snagged on Rafe. His brow was furrowed as he studied my face, but when he noticed me watching, he looked away.

"There he is. The man of the house," Iana called as we entered.

Tegan pulled the door shut and preened under Iana's words, puffing out his chest as if he'd done some great deed.

"No, not you," she scoffed from her place at the bar, "big, bad and scary."

I cast an apologetic grin back at Dane. "Guessing that's not me or you."

He cracked a small smile and started toward the bar.

Pachu's muffled voice came from the kitchen. "Is he here?"

As I crossed the room, my steps faltered as the man rushed out, bloody knife in hand. His features brightened with elation as his arms spread wide and welcoming.

"You're here!" he proclaimed. "Bless you! May the sun look upon your path for winters to come!"

I stared at Rafe with a single brow raised, wondering just what he did to earn Pachu's good graces. The cook despised him. He shrugged in reply, a smile lifting the corner of his mouth.

"A whole bog lizard! *Whole!* No chunks missing. No teeth marks. I have meat for two, if not three, nights!" Pachu cried, waving his knife about as he sang Rafe's praises.

"You brought back the bog lizard?" I asked.

He grunted. "Didn't seem right to waste it."

I laughed outright. If I'd known game meat would win the man over, I would've had him hunt forever ago.

My heart warmed at the scene, chasing away some of the fear that had chilled my spirit earlier. I took a step toward the bar, reaching for the basket to collect eggs.

A gut wrenching cry rent the air, and Dane hit the floor.

I froze as he crumpled, his mouth open in pain, back arched off the ground. He clutched his right hip as Rafe dropped to his knees, pinning his shoulders to keep him steady.

"What happened?!" Tegan shouted, crouching beside them.

Worry pinched Iana's features as she leaned over the bar to watch, and Pachu rushed to my side, his mirth gone. My hands twitched, begging for me to help, as Dane went still. His cries died off with a scant breath, and he clacked his teeth together, his eyes a million miles away.

Rafe helped him sit up. "Blain?"

Dane worked his jaw for a moment, meeting his glare. "The E'or."

I glanced between the two. Then Dane was on his feet, sprinting outside. I stared after him, shaken by his reaction. He was as steady as they came. Nothing fazed the man. He never ran.

Rafe turned in his crouch, facing me, and my heart splintered. He clenched his jaw and pushed to stand, stalking over. I gazed up at him, knowing what was about to happen—and hating it.

"I'll be back."

He pulled me in for a rough kiss—which I returned with passion, clinging to his neck. He broke away, giving me a chaste peck on the temple before turning to Tegan.

"Ready our horses. Be quick about it. I'll rally Zeph and Jam."

Tegan gave a curt nod and ran off, Rafe following at a brisk walk. He didn't even glance back as he stormed out the door.

Tears filled my eyes as it slammed shut. They'd move faster without me, and without Tizmet, I wouldn't be much help.

"You're not leaving with them?" Iana muttered.

I faced her, forcing myself to smile, though the rebel tear that trailed my cheek gave me away. I swiped at it before letting out a shaky breath. "Those eggs won't fetch themselves."

Pachu looked between me and the door. Iana pressed her lips together, then offered a curt nod.

Once again, one of my friends was in danger and there was nothing I could do about it.

After the morning chores, I borrowed a mare from the stable, using the single silver I earned on Summer Solstice. Iana never paid me, but claimed Kila and I worked so hard, we deserved a bit extra.

The dark horse plodded through the thick forest and down old roads. A sad smile tugged at my lips as I stared at the wagon ruts in the mud, knowing exactly where those wagons had been headed.

For the first time in forever, I was truly alone.

There was no mother to keep me company, no schoolgirls to torment me. There were no Masters to look after me or soldiers to mock me. No Kila to comment on the populace or Iana to judge my actions. Rafe and his men were off to find Blain and my dragon was shut away in sleep.

I adjusted my seat, and the mare snorted in response. I wasn't worried about Tizmet's slumber. Wounded dragons returned to Northwing to rest and heal. Even at the height of summer, they gorged themselves, then lapsed into brumation, converting their energy into healing their broken bodies.

It was rare that a dragon made it back to Northwing with such severe injuries. Most died on the front, but I *had* seen it happen. Those memories assured me that Tizmet was at least doing something relatively normal.

I reached through the bond, testing her awareness. She felt my touch and curled around my consciousness, embracing me. I smiled to myself and pulled back as she drifted away. She was aware of her surroundings and could rouse herself if she needed.

My hands steered the mare onto a road that had been freshly cleared, with strips of bright red fabric tied in the trees. My face tilted to the warm sun that fell through the canopy as she plodded along.

I wasn't ignoring Blain's peril, but I *was* trying to make myself feel better about staying behind.

I didn't know how long they'd be gone. That the Tennan *chose* to follow Rafe resonated with him. They supported him. If any of them were in danger, he was going to help them.

The smile fell from my face as I remembered Collins. I was closer to him than the others. Both he and Zephath were around my age, but Collins was actually kind to me. He taught me how to climb and scale walls. We played games and pulled pranks on the others. He was the first *real* friend my age.

A shiver ran through me as I remembered finding him in the shack with Rafe. He had been dead for quite some time. I bit my tongue, recalling the way flesh fell from his face when I touched him.

I forced my thoughts elsewhere, though despite my efforts, they didn't lighten. Garion and Korzak were killed as well, and Xzanth and Rafe had some falling out.

That saddened me. Xzanth had been the one who introduced me to the crossbow. He tailed me for days on end, teaching me in his quiet, calm way. I hated to think that there was something amiss between them.

The forest broke, and I lifted my eyes as the mare pulled into the clearing. It was just after midday and the sun was still high in the sky, brightly illuminating the scene before me.

Master Val and his builders worked on a pair of wooden beams near the pond. The shack had been completely removed. I clicked to my mare and urged her closer to the wagon at the forest edge. I tied her, then approached.

"Hail, Avyanna," Master Val greeted.

"Good day to you."

"Coming to check on the progress?" he asked, searching behind me. "No soldier with you today?"

"Not today." I kept my tone cheerful as I shrugged. "I just wanted to come out and take a look."

"Feel free to peek around. We're building the frame for the walls now." He studied me from under his straw hat. "Here to get away for a bit, eh?"

Was I that obvious? I offered a feeble nod, and he dipped his chin toward the stone foundation.

"Have a seat. Nap if you need it, though I can't promise you'll get much rest with these lot nearby." He snapped a mock-glare at his men, then continued with a smile, "We'll be here till dark. Take your time."

I nodded my thanks, then crossed the field of wild oats and flowers to the foundation. The smooth stone surface seemed bigger now that it wasn't framed with wood.

Several chimes passed as I sat, content to just *be*. I kept my mind off painful topics and gazed around my future homestead. This was ours. This would be where Rafe and I built a life together.

I chuckled to myself, looking at the field, wondering if Rafe really would let it be as is. Knowing him, he would get restless at some point and attempt to grow something. I twisted in my seat, facing the pond. There was a perfect amount of space for a little garden. I had about as much experience growing things as Rafe did. I could learn, though.

Once the house was built and this was finally, truly, *our* land, I would spend my life here. Through long, cold winters, I'd sew clothes by candlelight, sharing the evenings with Rafe. Spring and summer would be filled with gardening, hunting, preserving foods and flying with Tizmet.

The idea of little dragonlings running about my feet while I worked made me smile. Would they hang around our home or Tizmet's nest? Or would they immediately run off to their own adventures?

Gazing out over the pond, I wondered if I would ever have a babe of my own. I was still barren. That both worried and liberated me. Not having to deal with a moon cycle was freeing in its own right, but I wasn't sure if I was content to be barren.

As if there was anything I could do about it.

I wasn't ready for the responsibility of a child. I frowned. Why was that? Was it because I didn't like the idea of being grounded, forced to stay in one place? Yet, isn't that why we were building a home? So I could settle?

Why was the more I thought about it, the more something in my gut told me I didn't want to settle?

I sniffed, lying back on the stone with my face up to the sun. I was so used to running now—so accustomed to moving and having adventures that my mind rebelled against a slow-paced life.

That was it.

My thoughts wandered to Rafe. He had made the argument he was too old to have a child. That was absurd. He was a parental figure to Zeph, and even to Blain and Dane in a way. He would make a fantastic father.

I slowly drifted off to sleep, dozing in the summer warmth.

Master Val came to wake me as the sun started toward the horizon. I hurried to the mare, urging her back to Leeds at a mad gallop. It wouldn't do to have Iana angry at me again.

Two days passed with no news. I kept a tight leash on my emotions, telling myself there was nothing to worry about. They encountered far worse things than I could imagine—aside from giant bugs in the Sands. I doubted any of them faced those particular monsters.

After a deep breath, I shrugged off the uselessness that wormed its way through my heart. I pushed in the chairs behind Kila as she swept under the tables. This used to be my routine, my safe place. Yet, since Rafe had come, the simple action of doing my job didn't give me the same satisfaction.

Rafe made everything better—more worthwhile. With him, life was exciting. I had grown to look forward to talking and cuddling with him after a long day, taking security in his warmth. Now, he was somewhere in the E'or and Tizmet in an early brumation. I pressed my lips together and sighed, pushing another chair in, lost in my thoughts.

"Avyanna. Really?"

I glanced up at Iana as she counted the coin at the bar. She watched me with tired eyes and snapped the money chest shut with a click.

"Having you disappear for a few days might have been worth it to spare me from your sighs and silence," she mused.

"I didn't know my silence offended you so," I scoffed. "Perhaps you would have rather enjoyed my comments on the wine served tonight? I saw more than one pair of lips pucker at the–"

"Oh, you're worse than your dragon with that forked tongue," she snapped.

She knew as well as I did the wine was spoiled, something she hadn't realized until she served it to multiple tables.

"Tomorrow, gather the eggs, then go off and find your dragon."

I frowned, staring at the floor. "I wouldn't be able to return by nightfall."

"That far, is she?"

My head snapped up, and I gave her a sharp glare. I didn't need anyone guessing at her whereabouts. The less who knew the distance, the less chance of those seeking out her nest.

"Don't give me that look." She walked to my side, hands propped on her hips. "Go. Take a night away." She slapped a silver down by my hand.

"Here I thought you hated it when I ran off and avoided work. Now, you're *paying* me to do so?" I laughed, crossing my arms.

"I'm already reconsidering," she muttered. "Bring back game if you can. Consider it a hunting trip."

My heart warmed at her gesture, and I pocketed the coin, knowing well that I would take her up on her offer.

Perhaps if I spent time with Tizmet and her eggs, I would feel more grounded. Riders lived and breathed their dragons, especially when they laid a clutch. There were occasions when a Rider might leave their dragon in brumation, but never longer than a few hours.

Here I was, nearly a day's ride from Tizmet. Were she flying, she could reach me in a few chimes, but by horseback through the thick forest, it would take me a full day. If I camped in the clearing with her among the blood-sucking, stinging insects, I would be gone two working days.

I hurried through my chores, noting Kila's amused smile. I helped Iana close up the tavern, then ducked out the door. On my way to the inn, my steps slowed when I spotted the figure leaning up against the entrance.

"Rothfuss," I greeted.

"Avyanna." He nodded, then dipped his chin across the road.

I followed the gesture, seeing a few of Luther's men. I gave them a friendly wave and bared my teeth in a vicious smile.

"Rafe's been gone two days," he said.

As if I hadn't been counting.

"Aye."

When I entered, Rothfuss put his hand on the door to keep it from closing in his face, then ducked inside behind me. The lantern's weak light cast him in sharp angles and shadows. He looked dangerous.

"You know how long he's planning to be gone?" he asked, putting his boot in front of the door so we wouldn't be interrupted.

"No," I huffed.

Rothfuss grunted, eyes dancing over my face. He caught my gaze and offered a small smile. "I have Gaer watching you."

"He should be tailing Luther's men, not me," I said. "Luther and I have a deal."

"One Rafe isn't here to see through."

"I didn't need Rafe when I made it," I snapped.

He let out an amused snort and tilted his head. "Fired up, are we?"

I sucked in a calming breath. I wanted nothing more than to borrow a horse and ride out to sleep with Tizmet tonight. She would understand my irritation. Were she not in brumation, she would probably offer some dragon-like advice. Like, 'Find Rafe yourself if it bothers you so.' She would probably fly me if she didn't have her clutch to guard.

"I won't be here tomorrow. Give Gaer another task."

"Off to join your friends?"

"My–" I stopped short. I trusted Rothfuss, but once again I reminded myself that I didn't want anyone knowing how far out Tizmet was. "I'll just be gone."

He grunted. "Should I send Saudric after you?"

I rolled my eyes and sighed. "This isn't a rescue mission."

"I imagine you'd say something of the sort if it was."

"I'm not headed to the E'or."

"East then?"

"Rothfuss!" I groaned, dragging my hands down my face.

He let out a dark chuckle, and I peeked through my fingers as he rested a heavy hand on my shoulder. He grinned at me, lighting his handsome features.

"Alright. No tails, no Healers. But if you're not back by nightfall–"

"I won't be," I muttered.

"Out in the open while your dragon is absent?" He tilted his head with a teasing smile.

He knew—guessed well enough that she had laid.

"One night then?" he asked.

"Why do you need to know?" I placed my fists on my hips.

I attempted to shrug off his grip on my shoulder, but he held firm.

"Because Rafe isn't the only person who cares for you." He gave my shoulder a squeeze before dropping his hand.

I squinted. I wouldn't let him get away with that statement when he knew Rafe was my promised.

"Iana, Kila, Saudric, Pachu all care for you," he said. "Val, Brandi, old widow Rheann–"

"Yes, yes. I'll be back in two nights," I huffed, waving him off as I started up the stairs.

"You better be," he muttered.

I stopped and turned on the fourth step, glaring down at him. "What did you say?"

Mischief sparked in his gaze. "I said, 'Try not to return as one big welt.'" He laughed, then took his leave.

I glared at the door as it closed behind him. When the latch clicked in place, I smiled to myself and shook my head.

The following day, I secured the horse past the worst of the thicket where it could shuffle its feet without being tangled by brambles. I brushed it down and gave it grain, then grabbed my pack and tore off.

The path Rafe and I had used was already overgrown and virtually invisible in the fading light. I would have gotten turned around if it weren't for my bond with Tizmet. I followed the pull to her, shoving past saplings, bushes, brambles and over fallen trees.

Finally, I emerged in the clearing, also overgrown. I waded through the thigh-high grass, slapping at the bugs that swarmed my face and hands. Tizmet's gray scales blended in well with the boulder. Under the dim moonlight, she seemed to be a part of it. From my place on the ground, I could only see her spine against the night sky. The rest of her bulk was hidden by the sheer size of the boulder.

I adjusted the pack on my shoulders and eyed the sheer stone. I had Rafe's help last time. At my pitiful five paces in height, this would be rough.

I wrapped my fingers in the nearest handhold and slowly climbed to the middle. Realizing I was out of footholds, I cursed. The shadowed surface to my left could have been another hold. I reached for it, knowing I was overextending myself, but having no other choice.

I regretted it.

My pack shifted along my back, throwing off my center of gravity. My right hand slipped, and I yelped, grabbing blindly with my left.

And missed.

Curse that shadow.

I fell, already tensing against the blow, when something caught my pack.

A gasp tore through me as I lifted into the air, hands and legs dangling until I reached the top. I got my feet under me and trembled with the rush of my brief fall.

Tizmet studied me with a fiery eye, pupil wide and dilated in the low light. She pushed open our bond, reaching for my emotions. She swept her sleepy thoughts around my worry, fear and loneliness, then smothered me with love, comfort and safety.

My heart swelled as peace overwhelmed me, and she used her head to herd me against her side. I smiled, crowding in amongst her eggs, admiring how they sparkled in the moonlight. A shadow dropped over them as she spread her wing, shielding us. Huffing, she nuzzled close, tucking her tail about the clutch and pressing me against them. She rested her nose near my shins, and I pulled my knees to my chest with the movement.

Was I comfortable? No.

But was I happy? Never happier.

Chapter 18

I hummed to myself as I helped Pachu prep the stew, swaying my hips in a little dance as I plopped potatoes into the pot. He eyed me with a sly grin as Kila darted in and took two full bowls from him.

"I told Iana it would do you good," he mused.

With a beaming smile, I spun the knife like he had taught me, and chopped into another potato.

I spent the night and morning with Tizmet. She roused herself enough to hunt, entrusting me to watch over her eggs. There was no greater honor.

Once she had her fill, she settled over her clutch, trying to tuck me into her side. I gently reminded her I was not made for brumation and stepped away. While I was there, she sensed the unease in my heart and kept me supplied with a steady stream of comfort and love through our bond.

The few days I had been back in Leeds, I was content. Yes, Rafe was still gone and Tizmet sleeping, but I was loved. She was safe, and I had to believe Rafe was as well.

I smiled, slipping through the door in my mind once again, peering into the magic that ran like a river beneath the surfaces of everything. A thin, glowing strand flowed from my chest, disappearing through the wall to the west.

I gently closed it off, as always, feeling the slight chill that came with turning away from its pull.

Yes, Rafe was safe. I would know if he wasn't. Whatever I had done when I rescued him, when I wrapped us together in magic refusing to let him die, those ties entangled our life forces. They still held fast.

"That's all now. I'm sure the crowd is growing. Check on Kila," Pachu said, shooing me from the chopping board.

I hummed and danced to the side, hanging my apron on a hook by the door.

"Spread some of that joy to the patrons," he added with a laugh. "Maybe they will loosen their purse strings."

I dropped into a mock curtsy on my way out. "As you wish!"

The crowd was sparse, but the evening was still young. More would trickle in as darkness fell. I joined Iana at the bar, where she busied herself filling drink orders. Kila was speaking with a table of younger folks. I reached for the mugs, eager to cover for her so she might finish her conversation.

"Let Kila take them."

My smile fell a fraction, noticing Iana's pursed lips. She threw her eyes at the corner, and I followed the gesture. Luther sat in a chair, watching me with a nauseating smirk. Two of his men flanked him, glares alternating between the crowd and me.

"I've got it," I said, snatching the mugs.

"Avyanna." Iana seized my wrist in a firm grip. "Don't start anything."

I raised a brow in silent challenge. "Me? Never."

"Don't let *him* start anything."

Offering an unfazed smile, I pulled my arm away and approached. I slid the ales in front of Timor and Paddy, the two men at his side, and the wine to Luther.

"Will you be dining tonight? Bush Tail stew is on the menu," I said with a friendly smile. My toe tapped in silent rhythm with the song in my head.

"And you?" he purred.

"Me?"

Ignore him. I just had to treat him like everyone else.

"Are you on the menu?" He leaned over the table. "After all, I hear the lawkeeper got a taste of the goods."

My easy smile faltered.

"Oh, darling. You waved at my men. Did you not think they would report your little rendezvous to me?"

"Luther, dear!" Kila sidled up next to me, crushing her hip against mine, and leaned low over the table.

He brought his stomach-turning smile to her and though he was strong enough to resist the view she gave him, both of his men were not. Their eyes found Kila's generous cleavage and lingered.

"Are you dining with us tonight? Please tell me you will—you never do anymore." She twirled strands of her hair around her finger. "Avyanna, Iana is asking after you," she said over her shoulder.

I took a quick breath and turned on my heel. Could I have handled that? Yes. But in doing so, Luther would've learned he had gotten to me.

I thought nothing of waving at his men, other than to let them know I saw them. I also didn't think a thing of Rothfuss following me inside. It was a public building—which is why I kept my door locked.

From the bar, Iana glared at me as if to say, 'I told you so.'

I started her way and glanced over my shoulder as the entrance pushed open. I slowed, seeing Zephath cross the threshold. He was worse for wear, clothes tattered and worn, face smudged with dirt and scratches. The door slammed shut, and he dragged himself to the far corner near the kitchen. He collapsed into a chair and dropped his forehead to the table, wrapping his arms over the back of his head.

He looked like he needed an ale.

I rushed to the bar and reached for a mug. Iana grabbed it first, then threw a dishtowel over her shoulder.

"I told you not to start anything."

"I didn't," I said, eyes still on Zeph.

She smacked her lips and filled the mug. "Thanks to Kila."

"Nothing would have come of it." I assured her, meeting her gaze as I reached for the drink.

She held it fast, waiting for me to register her anger.

"Luther just said something that made me pause." I shrugged. "It was nothing."

She let go, clicking her tongue. "We all know it's a rumor, dear."

"Oh? And what rumor do you all know?"

She huffed, rolling her eyes before resuming her task, washing the dishes. "We all know you wouldn't have put Rothfuss off for so long, only to take him to bed when your *true love* came marching over those mountains."

"The whole town thinks Rothfuss warmed my bed?" I groaned, slapping my forehead.

"The *whole town* knows you didn't." She pushed out a sigh, as if placating a child. "Now, get the ale to that lad. He looks like he needs it."

I turned toward Zeph again, who still sat curled over himself against the table.

"Aye, he does," I muttered, then made my way over.

I slipped into the seat across from him and nudged the mug over. Wearily, he peeked up and blinked. With a glare, he pulled it closer. His gaze darted over to Kila before he dropped his head to the table with a thunk.

"How is Blain?" I whispered.

His reply was muffled—I couldn't make it out.

"How far did you have to go? Was he over the mountains?" I asked, resting my chin on my arms to peer at him.

He lifted himself only to take three long healthy gulps, then dropped again. "Near the peak," he growled.

"And Blain is well now?"

"He's–" His arms muffled the last of his words.

"He's what? Is he still set on Regent?" I pressed. I was happy to see him, but curse it all, Zeph was prickly.

He jerked upright. "He's *dying!*" he shouted. His eyes flashed and tears glimmered in their depths.

He wasn't hiding because he was tired—he was crying. His outburst silenced the crowd, and dozens of eyes stared our way. Horror chilled my soul as I eased back in my seat.

Dying

Blain was not dead.

Not yet.

"Where is he?" I asked.

Zeph resettled against the table, remaining quiet.

I shot to my feet and hurled my palm down. "Where *is* he, Zephath?!"

He stared at me through teary eyes and gave me a condescending smile. "The Healer, you fool."

I took off, toppling the chair in the process. The tavern door slammed behind me and I sped down the dark, familiar streets, cursing the burn in my lungs.

My boots slid as I skidded around the corner to the Healer's quarters. Tegan leaned over the hitching post, staring off into the darkness. He looked up, hearing my approach, but I didn't stop. I darted past him toward Saudric's office, where warm light glowed through the glass-paned windows.

I stopped at the door, catching my breath with my palm pressed to my chest. Tegan rushed to my side.

"Oi, lass–"

"Don't."

I panted, and he frowned at me, shaking his head.

"It's not pretty," he muttered.

His face was caked with sweat and dirt, his hair matted. Blood stained his clothes and his trousers were ripped at the knees. Every surface of him was covered in bloody grime.

"It never is." I yanked the door open.

Dane crowded the doorway, blocking my path, and I met his fierce gaze. The man who always kept his emotions in check stared down at me with pain and anger roiling in the depths of his features.

"Let me help." I breathed.

His eyes were sunken against his thin face, his beard wild and overgrown. Blood covered his tunic, and I knew in my heart that it wasn't his.

Without a word, he stepped aside, letting me pass. I held my emotions in check as I surveyed the scene. Saudric glanced up from washing Blain's naked body. He opened his mouth to object to my feminine presence, but Rafe's growl cut him off.

"Leave her."

Rafe was at his shins, and Jamlin near his shoulders, pressing their weight on him to hold him steady. Their expressions were cold masks, hiding away their hurt. I stepped closer as Saudric returned to his work with a blush.

Zeph was right. Blain was dying.

His side was a giant, mottled bruise. Blotches of crimson blossomed here and there along its mass, and I knew without asking that he had broken several ribs. But that wasn't the worst of it.

His hip and thigh were at a terrible, unnatural angle, bulging in the wrong place. Dislocated. Saudric dripped water over Blain's stiff leg where a jagged, bloody bone protruded from his shredded skin. I sucked in a breath, forcing my stomach not to revolt.

He was so pale—as if we already lost him. I studied his swollen face. His nose was broken, possibly his left cheekbone, as well.

Dane leaned against a dresser along the wall, his gaze distant and unseeing. Saudric sat back, looking over Blain's body as a whimper tore out of the man. He would have already drugged him with dream flower. I searched the Healer's pinched face, his stare locked on his patient. He was trained in both Regent and east of the E'or. He wouldn't give up.

"Fix him," Rafe snarled.

"I *can't*. His leg is beyond saving."

"We didn't bring him this far just to see him die." Jam tried a bit more gently, but with no less urgency.

"I'm sorry, there's nothing I can do. I wish there was, I really do." Saudric's shoulders slumped in defeat.

"What do you need?" I choked past the lump in my throat.

He looked up, and he pressed his lips together, another blush brightening his cheeks at my presence.

"What has to be done to fix him?" I asked again, a bit more confidence in my voice.

Rafe turned my way and he studied me with a dark eye.

"He has four, if not five, shattered ribs. His jaw, cheekbone and nose are crushed as well. I don't know if his brain is addled or intact. But this, *this*–" His hands hovered over Blain's thigh. "His hip is dislocated. The bone is broken and misaligned. I can't fix that without cutting him open and bracing it. No one has survived such a procedure, and in his state–" He stopped short, swallowing hard. "Infection has already set in. At this point, we can only keep him comfortable until–"

I held out my hand, cutting him off. "Rafe–"

"No."

"I have to." I couldn't pry my eyes off Blain's leg.

"No, you don't."

"I've done it before."

"At what price this time, Vy?" Rafe snarled. He straightened and stormed over.

I took a sharp breath, really *looking* at him. His eye patch had been torn off—the socket bared to the world. A gash marred the left side of his face, as if something struck him from his blind spot. His tunic was torn and smears of blood stained the filthy, faded white of the fabric.

"You still suffer from the last time you tried this trick."

"I know what I'm doing now," I shot back.

"You don't know any more than you did before. The only difference is, in this backside arsecrack of the E'or, we have a nursemaid who claims to be a Healer." He towered over me, forcing me back a step. "You want me to trust him?"

"No. I want you to trust *me*, Rafe." My palm braced against his uninjured cheek. "I crossed the Sands and traveled the entire length of the E'or on my own with naught but Tizmet and my magic. I *know* I can do it."

The muscles in his jaw worked against my hand, his dark eye angry... and frightened.

"Your dragon's not here to pull you back," he grumbled.

I felt his will giving in, bit by bit, and trailed my finger down his cheek next to the gash. "I know my limits."

"You'll seize."

"And you'll be there to hold me."

"Vy–"

I didn't let him finish. I pulled him down, pressing in for a kiss. He froze, unmoving and unyielding. I softened my grip on him, and he sighed, drawing me to his chest. He moved his bloodied lips against mine in acceptance and a silent plea.

Pulling back, he looked down at me with fear in his gaze. "Be careful."

I nodded and took a steadying breath, then faced Saudric. "I want you to operate."

"No, just because you–"

Rafe ripped off the remnant of his tunic. Saudric let out a quiet gasp before snapping his mouth shut. He staggered around the table, his wide eyes tracking the brutal scar.

"I did that with Dragon Kind magic," I whispered, not wanting to distract him from his study. "I did it wrong the first time. When I got him to the Healers, they had to open him up, and I healed him bit by bit as they readjusted his insides and dug out pieces of debris."

"You *healed* him?"

"Aye. But if I can't see it, I can't fix it."

Saudric looked back to Blain's body as he let out a moan, and his right leg twitched.

"He still might not make it."

"We have to try."

"Is what I've heard about Dragon Kind magic true?" he asked. "That it's a chaotic, wild thing."

"When you let it go, yes," I replied softly.

He faced me, his piercing gaze finding mine. "Then don't let it go."

Rafe pushed another table up against Blain's, then sat atop it with me in his lap. Saudric readied his tools, tiny sharp knives and gleaming silver hooks that had Rafe flinching beneath me. He held me tight, as if he believed his hold alone would be enough to protect me.

"She's going to seize after this," he warned in a low growl.

"Then I will see to her once I am done here." Saudric's voice was calm as he brought another lantern to hang above the table. "Go get more water from the well. We'll need it," he said, waving a hand at Dane.

Dane opened the door and passed the command on to Tegan.

A small smile tugged at my lips as he took up his perch on the dresser. I stared at him over Rafe's shoulder, but he didn't acknowledge me. He crossed his arms and leaned back against the wall, closing his eyes.

He must have felt his brother's pain the day he collapsed in the tavern. Could he feel it now?

"Ready?" Saudric asked.

I settled against Rafe with a firm nod. "Ready."

After a deep breath, he brought a wicked-looking blade down to Blain's thigh. I let my eyes flutter shut as I extended past that door that kept the magic at bay.

It was an odd sensation, reaching for something that wasn't there, but knowing it would answer.

It swelled and raced toward me like a lost puppy to its child. I grabbed it with an iron grip and slowed the flow. It thrashed and fought against me, wanting to surge loose. I couldn't lose focus now. I had one task.

Heal Blain.

Time passed, but I was too focused to note how long. My head throbbed, but I kept a firm hold on the magic, guiding it where it was needed. The throb intensified, evolving into a persistent ache that felt as though my skull would split in two.

I only lost control once, and it was the smallest bit. Tegan had returned with the water, and I thought how nice a drink would be. The magic slipped through my negligent grasp and I heard gasps in the room as the flame in the lantern danced blue, green, then purple. The colors died as quickly as they came, and I didn't say a word—instead focused on not letting it happen again.

A wave of dizziness swept over me as Saudric shoved the top of the bone back into Blain's hip. Bile slipped up my throat, burning as he cut deep into his thigh, prying the flesh apart with tiny hooks to keep the wound open and exposed as he realigned the fracture. He had to search for any fragments that might have splintered into the wound. Jam kept Blain's face covered with a cloth soaked in a dream flower. Even so, he thrashed in his sleep. Dane had to brace his feet as I fused the bits of bone together.

My ignorance of Healer knowledge was like a spear to my heart. If I had a broader understanding, perhaps I could be of more help. I didn't know what I was healing half the time.

As it was, I mended bones and joined veins. I reattached muscle and sealed flesh. Saudric moved to Blain's chest, and I made a strangled sound.

"Enough." Rafe's voice seemed so far away.

"It will only take a moment."

"She's spent."

A huge scar mottled Blain's thigh. The worst was fixed. That would have to be enough.

I took what little I had left and looked at Blain's jaw. Closing my eyes, I set my intent, molding it along the unseen bone, hoping it wasn't doing more damage than good. Slowly, I cut off the magic, shutting the door in my mind. A chill settled in my bones with the loss. I sighed, collapsing in Rafe's arms as my heart faltered.

"I've got you."

Agony burst, shredding me apart. Endless—a terrible thing that shattered my sternum and ribs. I screamed and slammed my hands to my chest, positive that I would find my bones sticking out. The pain radiated a hot, aching trail up to my skull. A shriek tore out of me again and my body jerked once before everything went blissfully dark.

Chapter 19

The first thing I noticed when I awoke was the awful taste in my mouth. I spit, fumbling around the slab of wood someone braced between my teeth. Opening my eyes, I hissed against the painful onslaught that came with the high sun glaring through the windows.

"There she is." Exhaustion dripped from Saudric's voice, and he let out a sigh.

I groaned, trying to roll to my back, but something warm and solid pressed against me.

"Be still," Rafe rumbled in my ear.

Every single muscle ached and burned as if I fell from the cliffs of the E'or. A small whimper slid out as I relaxed into him. Blain's face was angled my way, but his eyes were closed. The slow rise and fall of his chest suggested he was alive, and Jam was no longer drugging him, so he must have been asleep under his own will.

"What time is it?" I moaned.

"Midday."

"Midday?!"

I attempted to sit up at Saudric's response, but Rafe held me fast.

"The innkeeper knows," he said. "That was a long seizure."

The longest yet, but I wasn't about to tell him that.

"It hurts." I let myself go limp against the table.

"I tried what I know to pull you out of it, Avyanna." Saudric retrieved the flat piece of wood that I spat out. "The best we could do was keep you from hurting yourself."

I winced, craning my head back against Rafe as the Healer collapsed into a chair in the corner. His exhaustion was evidence enough that he hadn't slept.

Tizmet gave a sluggish tug on the bond. She had felt something, but I kept the door between us shut to shield her from my pain. I met her across the bond, greeting her with warmth and love. She pushed a silent question, and I responded with peace and rest. I smiled as she receded into herself, assured I was well enough.

"Thank you, Saudric," I muttered.

"Thank *you*, Avyanna."

I understood his gratitude. Healers, even this side of the E'or, cared for the welfare of others. Being helpless to fix someone, to admit defeat, was torturous. To be a Healer, one had to forgo any hope of making a profit. Unlike other trades, they lived off the generosity of the public, and in turn, invested in their wellbeing. With what coin they received, they bought cloth for bandages. And any herbs they were given, they made into tinctures. Only a selfless person would submit themselves to such a trade. As a result, Healers gained a trustworthy reputation.

"Think of the things we could do–"

"Stop right there," Rafe growled, tucking me closer. "She's not a tool."

"I've never seen—never heard of such a thing." Saudric's voice was full of weary wonder.

"They're exploring it in Regent," I murmured, feeling sleep tugging at me once more.

"Perhaps I should send a letter, then. See if they will disclose what they've learned."

He went on, but I was far too tired to listen, and instead gave into a restful sleep. A sleep that actually healed my body, not wracked it with pain.

When I woke next, I found myself in my own bed. My muscles were still sore, but a far cry from the agonizing ache that lingered before. I stretched, feeling a comforting warmth behind me, and glanced at the window. It was nearing dusk. The light coming through was too bright to be dawn.

A groan greeted me as a muscled arm slung over my ribs and pulled me close. I smiled and wiggled against Rafe before rolling to face him. With a breathless laugh, I ran my thumb over the gash in his cheek. It was clean, but scabbed over. Combined with his patch, he would look fearsome.

"Dangerous."

A smirk teased the corner of his lips, and I smiled to myself, wondering how I ended up with such a roguishly handsome man.

"It would have taken my eye if I hadn't already lost it." His voice was rough with sleep and he rested his hand on the dip of my waist.

"What was it?"

He let out a harsh bark of laughter. "There are monsters out there, Vy. Monsters that don't have a name."

I frowned, pulling away in thought. I heard of giants that lived in the mountains, of bears and wildcats the size of a pony. Yet, something that could take Blain by surprise and give the Tennan a good battle? I couldn't picture such a beast.

"Blain was thrown from his horse. Fell off a cliff. Honestly, the fall probably saved him."

"And almost killed him."

"Aye. Would have, if not for you." His hand slipped under my tunic, branding my bare skin. "The twins owe you a great deal."

"They owe me nothing. They're my friends, Rafe." I frowned as the now familiar feeling of uselessness wound around my heart. "At least I can do *something* for them."

I rolled away and threw my feet over the bedside. I staggered when my head spun, and he huffed a heavy sigh. He knew I was hurting, and thankfully didn't press. I yanked my boots on and washed my face, my hand snagging over the scar high on my cheek.

"We match now," I said with forced cheer, turning to show him.

He laced his boots up and stared at me with a deadpan expression. "Aye. Glorious."

I chuckled and waited for him to finish dressing before we walked to the tavern.

It was relatively deserted. The working crowd usually came later in the evening when they had a chance to wash up after their labor. Iana looked up from the bar as I entered, worry engraved on her face.

"If not for Saudric, I would have your hide for running off last night," she called across the room.

I offered a polite smile to the two older men sitting at a table when they glanced my way with interest. Rafe shut the door and towered behind me.

"Every time." She shook her head, thrusting the mug down against the bar so hard I thought it might shatter. "He's involved every time." She dried her hands on a towel and glared at Rafe.

Pachu peeked out, having overheard our exchange, and beamed at Rafe. "You glorious man, have you brought me meat?"

"No," he rumbled as he made his way to the corner table.

Unfazed by the dismissal, Pachu turned his gaze on me. "Avyanna! Pleased to see you're doing better. Care to help with the roast?"

I eagerly stepped away from Iana's glare. The kitchen was stifling, and I shut the door behind me. With the savory scents filling the space, my stomach growled, reminding me I hadn't eaten.

"Here," Pachu said, shoving a roll in my face. With a false sense of repulsion, he looked me up and down as I took it. "You're as thin as a corpse."

"At least I'm not dead," I shot back, nibbling at the warm bread.

"No, and neither is your friend." He sliced into the hog's side, cutting portions to roast. "A fact which all of Leeds is whispering about."

The bread turned to ash in my mouth, and I stared at him as he cut away, hoping he wasn't insinuating what I thought he was.

"Now, Saudric is tight-lipped. However, it remains that old Nanor saw your friends when they arrived. Swears he saw a bone popping out of the one they carried. Little Joel validates this." Pachu glanced up at me, moving his bulk around the kitchen with ease.

"With a wound like that, he shouldn't have made it through the night." He shoved a pile of onions with his forearm, making room for his roasts. "Then Gwyneth, the dear lass that you *know* has her eye on Saudric—she brought him some fresh bread right after midday, when his office was a wee quieter. To her amazement, your friend's leg was perfect." His serious gaze met mine. "Only a suspicious scar."

"Blain let her see?" I was shocked. He would've been a bit more reserved, knowing what it could start.

"Oh, your friend was asleep, or so she says."

"Dane wouldn't have allowed it," I snapped, my appetite gone.

"When a woman wants to discover something, they always manage to do so," he said, peeking at me under hooded eyes. "There *is* a scar."

"Who's to say he didn't have it before?" I set the half-eaten roll aside and grabbed a knife.

The last thing I needed was more gossip, but based on Pachu's words, I was going to have to deal with this.

"Look at it this way, at least the rumors about you and Rothfuss will dwindle now."

"Pachu!" I whirled on him, mouth hanging open. "You're worse than the women in the widows' home!"

"Where do you think I get these juicy bits of gossip?" He laughed to himself. "No one comes to talk to me back here. Those old coots are my only company."

"You need better company," I groaned, chopping the onions.

I didn't *want* to hide my ability, but in a town like Leeds, it's easy to be manipulated. My title of Dragon Rider meant nothing to them. Here, there were no rules about magic. Regent had the King's rule and the Dragon Corps to keep things in check. There were laws in place concerning their treatment and when and if they could use magic. Improper use was handled with an iron fist.

If the people of Leeds knew I could heal, they would come to me instead of Saudric, expecting me to fix their aches and pain, to reattach limbs and cure winter plagues. I would have to turn them away, and they would hate me for it.

I growled and chopped the onion, taking out all my frustration on it.

The next morning, Rafe and I walked arm in arm to retrieve the eggs from Brandi. On the way, he told me about the time General Teak tried to convince him to charge into battle in naught but his skin.

"Believe me, it was tempting." Amusement colored his tone.

"That would have been hilarious! You should have done it!"

"Wouldn't have gotten me released."

"No? Surely, the Generals would have let you go for madness then." I laughed, wiping at the tears on my face.

"Hardly. Faulkin would've had me flogged, then put back out there."

"That's terrible," I said, still giggling. I wished I could meet this General Teak. He sounded like a fun character.

"You brought him."

I froze at the small voice, then searched the road and tall grass, wondering where Brandi was. She wasn't on her trading stone, though her basket of eggs was there. I glanced to the sides, then behind me. Rafe nudged my shoulder and jerked his chin toward the tree.

Pressing my lips together, I tried to keep from laughing. Brandi crouched in the lowest branch, a good seven paces off the ground, wielding a dull dinner knife. She glared at Rafe for all she was worth, her blonde curls blowing in the breeze.

"Oi, Brandi. Why are you up there?" I asked, holding out my basket. "Someone could just run off with your eggs."

"Mama says you're gonna run off with the bad man." She held her hand up in a mock whisper. "*Him!*"

"I think your eggs are in more danger."

"He's not that scary."

She straightened, wrinkling her nose. The movement caused her to wobble, and she gripped the tree trunk, her knuckles turning white with effort. Worry pulsed through me. I set the basket aside and crossed my hands over my chest.

"How about you come down?" I offered.

"I could take him."

Rafe made a quiet choking sound and rubbed the nape of his neck.

"I don't doubt it," I mused. "Now come on, Brandi. Down with you."

"He was just going to walk on past. Daddy says he fought scary monsters where you come from. Well, I'm not a scary monster and I could have got him. That means he's not very good at fighting."

I gave Rafe a sidelong glance, thoroughly amused that such a little girl was putting him in his place.

"Maybe he knew you were there." I shrugged.

She wobbled some more, and I flinched, reaching for her, then tucked my hands against my sides.

She waved her knife at him. "Did you?"

Rafe squinted up at her, crossing his arms over his chest.

"Daddy said you don't talk, but you were talking to Miss Avyanna, so I *know* you do."

He arched a brow in challenge, and the two stared each other down.

"Come now, Brandi. We have eggs to trade."

"I wanna know," she whined, not taking her eyes from Rafe as if they were in some kind of duel. "Did you know I was here, or could I have taken your other eye, scoundrel?"

"Brandi!" I called, shocked to hear such language from her.

Rafe snorted and shook his head, a small smile playing over his lips.

"What?" Her cheeks flushed pink as she pointed her knife at Rafe. "Daddy says *he* uses bad words all the time."

"What about me?!" I asked, holding my hand over my chest.

Realization slipped over her features, and her gaze went wide. "Oh, I'm sorry Miss Avyanna. I didn't mean to hurt your heart."

"It has suffered worse," I sighed. "Please come down. I don't want you to fall."

Brandi chewed her lower lip, crestfallen. I frowned as she gripped the tree with her free hand, balancing on the large branch and muttered something I didn't catch.

"What was that?" I asked.

She sniffed, peering down with watery blue eyes. "I can't!" The dam broke, and huge tears streaked her cheeks as she sobbed. "I climbed up when I heard the bad man coming, but I can't climb down trees. It's too scary!"

I opened my mouth, taking in the height again. There was no way I'd reach her. I turned to Rafe.

All mirth died from his face. "You want me to get her?"

I gestured at the sobbing child, as if it were obvious.

"I'm the 'bad man,' remember?" he grunted.

"She'll let you help her. She's desperate."

As if to punctuate my words, she wailed again. Her footing shifted—and she fell.

Horrified, I froze on the spot, knowing I wouldn't catch her in time. Strong arms snatched her out of the air and tucked her up against a solid chest. I snapped my mouth closed as Rafe straightened. He stared down at her, and she peeked up at him... and I knew that look in her eyes.

She was in love.

"You're not a bad man," she sighed dreamily.

"I'm a *very* bad man."

She smiled and clutched her knife to her chest, snuggling into his arms. When his gaze met mine, I choked on a laugh at the confusion, and slight panic, all over his features.He didn't know what to do with the little girl.

I cleared my throat in an attempt to rescue him. "Put her down. She's a trading woman, don't you know?"

Rafe gently set her on her feet, and she stumbled back a few steps, never taking her eyes off him.

"Brandi? The eggs?"

"Oh, yes." She nodded and straightened her shoulders, as if to make herself seem bigger. "A woman has to do her job."

Rafe studied her as if she was some new creature he had never seen before. I chuckled to myself, then sat on my trading stone.

We took the eggs back to the tavern, then set out for Saudric's. It was a hot summer day. The sun was high in the sky, burning off most of the fog that drifted in from the bog.

Dread hit me when we rounded the corner. It seemed the Healer was busy today. There was a line ten deep that wound outside his office, the townsfolk lingering and chatting among themselves. I hesitated, and Rafe bumped me with his shoulder, encouraging me on. With a steadying breath, I lifted my chin and strode down the road.

The crowd's din quieted as we approached, watching us with eager eyes. Pachu's words echoed and bounced around my head, worrying me. Rafe took the lead, heading straight for the door. He reached for the handle, pausing when old widow Faune cleared her throat.

"There *is* a line!" she said, lifting her nose in the air.

Rafe frowned, a confused wrinkle working between his brows. He straightened to his full height, well over a pace above her. As he crowded her space, she let out an exasperated cry. He turned this way and that, scanning the air above her head.

"Don't see no line," he growled, then flung the door open.

I hid my smile as I followed him into Saudric's office.

The Healer had his ear to an elderly woman's back, listening to her breathing. His eyes darted our way as we walked in. Blain laid on a table pushed to the corner, and Dane sat beside him, shielding his twin's thigh from view.

I grinned. Blain was awake. His blue eyes were glossed over from the tonic Saudric had given him for pain. His nose was still swollen and cheekbone bruised, though the swelling had gone down. I wished I could've done more to heal him, but it wasn't worth the risk. We had been lucky that the little magic that got loose only changed the color of the flame in the lantern.

Dane nodded to me as Blain made a quiet gurgling sound in way of greeting.

I dropped to my knees, bracing my arms on the table where I lowered my head. "Tell me you won't be crossing the E'or again."

"No—promises." He spoke carefully, as if it pained him.

"I'm glad to see you awake. I was worried about you."

"S—smitten."

I laughed, then plucked a strand of dark hair from his face. I was careful with my movements, not wanting to cause him more pain. "You look terrible. This scruffy beard doesn't suit you. Dane, you should give your brother a trim."

Dane turned to me, then eyed his twin. A smile split his face, as if my encouragement was all he needed to torture his brother while he was unable to fight back.

"He's doing well." Saudric's voice pulled my attention to him as he came up behind me. He nodded to Blain and flashed me a bright smile. "I'm pleased with the progress he's made."

The older woman took her time adjusting her hat. I pressed my lips together, refusing to feed the rumors. After a beat of silence, Saudric twisted to see what had my attention, and the woman huffed, clearly put-out I wasn't giving her any fodder. When I stood up, she hurried out the door, and Rafe moved to flip the lock.

"Keeping my business at bay?" Saudric laughed.

"Keeping a bit of privacy," I clarified, giving him a worried look.

He frowned, holding his hands up. "I haven't told anyone."

"No one?"

"Not a soul. Though I don't understand why it's a secret. This could help the community immensely. Just think of the things we could cure if–"

"Magic isn't a game. It isn't a toy, Healer," Rafe growled.

"True, but I had always heard it was a wild thing, uncontrollable. And here Avyanna showed incredible skill and focus."

"And I paid for that, Saudric," I hissed through gritted teeth. "I paid for it with a day of my life."

"What cost is that compared to the *rest* of his life?" Saudric asked, waving a hand at Blain.

"They will come for her," Dane interjected, voice soft.

We all turned his way, his features bland and expressionless as he shrugged over the scrutiny.

"People, warriors, rogues, lords and ladies," he said. "All who can afford to, would come and demand her healing."

"Let's get something straight. I can't *heal* people!" My fingers curled into fists at my sides. "I can only put together what I see. I can't fix someone's heart that seizes, or someone's addled brain from a fall. Plagues, diseases, internal bleeding? None of it! People will expect it, then hold it over me when I refuse. Don't you understand?"

Saudric pressed his lips together in a frown and dropped his gaze to the floor.

"I'm only one person, Saudric." I softened my tone. "This is new. It's never been done before outside of dragons healing their Riders. Magic isn't to be played with, and to the Dragon Corps, this is play. It's trivial."

"It's not–"

"When the masses come with their demands to fix a cut on their finger?" I asked, cutting him off. "I would love to help, but I can only do so much. Magic is a tool that is meant to be used sparingly, and those that reach outside its limits pay a hefty price. I paid my due."

Saudric sighed, looking up at me. "I swear I haven't told anyone."

"And Gwyneth?"

"She—oh Avyanna. She saw nothing. Please, I'm not some gullible young bull."

"She's going around saying she did."

"She's known for bartering gossip."

"Tell her to stop."

"Why would she listen to me?" he asked, taken aback.

"She's in love with you, Saudric. She'll listen."

He reeled back, a blush coloring his cheeks. For all the man claimed he wasn't gullible, he was ignorant of her attention.

"Talk to her," Rafe said, coming up behind him, "or I will."

Saudric spun on his heel to stare up at him. Sighing, his shoulders slumped as he deflated. "I will talk to her," he muttered, then busied himself organizing bottles of tinctures and herbs.

I gave the man a sad smile. He was a kind soul, but as a Healer, it was natural for him to get excited about a new and more efficient way to heal. He just didn't understand the cost.

"I owe you, Saudric," I said softly.

"I am a Healer. It is my calling and my duty. To owe me would be to offend my very soul," he called over his shoulder. "Though I did use up a fair bit of dream flower."

"Have a sketch? I'll get you more."

He flashed me an eager smile, then moved to the far shelf, rummaging through loose papers stuffed in a book.

Dane caught my gaze. "We are in your debt," he said.

"You're my friends. I would have done the same for Jam, Tegan, or even Zeph."

"Regardless, you saved my brother's life, not theirs. We *are* indebted to you." He dipped his head in respect and resumed staring at the far wall.

Saudric sauntered over with the sketch—a beautiful watercolor image with blue petals gleaming from the page.

"Oh, I know this flower."

"Perfect. It grows a bit north of the town proper."

"There are some growing on our homestead," I said with a grin.

I'd seen them all over our property. They'd make a nice boon to trade with Saudric.

We said our goodbyes, then took our leave.

When Rafe flung the door open, Faune gasped and fell back, clearly having her ear pressed against the surface. I sighed, gazing at the line of people that had only grown since we arrived.

At least Saudric had plenty of business.

Chapter 20

The seasons passed, bringing autumn rain and the chill of winter. It was cold, a wet, damping cold that chilled to the bone. Getting warm enough to stave off the bite seemed impossible. It was hard to get up in the morning and leave the warmth of Rafe in my bed.

Our little house was coming along, and though it wasn't quite finished, it would be in early spring. The northern roads were impossible to travel by wagon, either being so muddy they could suck in a whole wheel, or they were covered in several paces of snow.

Excitement practically bubbled out of me. I was settling, I really was. Tizmet was content, and though I could sense her annoyance at the frigid temperatures, especially when she was buried in slush, she was happy. She protected her eggs, and I visited her when I could.

Blain was walking around and on the mend. When he could speak, he only had more ill news for us about the Shadows' advances. I had to step away from the conversation. My happiness seemed unfair while my friends suffered so.

I buried myself into my work and foraged whatever winter herbs I could for Saudric. He was overtly grateful for what I brought him, and despite the cold, I enjoyed helping. I learned more about Healing, all about medicinal plants and what grew in the area.

I spent more time with Pachu in the kitchen, listening as he talked for chimes on end about how to preserve meat or dry fish—skills I needed to learn.

Rafe dedicated his days to working for Rothfuss. I was glad he and the lawkeeper mended their ways and found even ground. With any free time, he lent manual labor for our cottage. He had decided we needed a well, and dug it himself, lining it and building it up. I shook my head and laughed, but I assumed he did it for the same reason I learned how to dry spices.

We were settling.

We were making Leeds home.

Luther kept his distance, watching us hungrily as we went about our lives. With Tizmet safely tucked away, I wasn't worried about him. What I did worry about was when forty-two dragonlings hatched, and the changes that would bring.

One day, Tegan showed up with a lute, and amazed us with his bard skills. Iana set him up in the tavern, and he never failed to draw a crowd.

Zeph was quiet and reserved, as always. He looked less and less like a boy as each month passed, though with the resentment he held toward me, one would think he was still a child.

Jam was our constant companion. He helped Rafe at the house and worked as an enforcer for Rothfuss. He enjoyed lawkeeping and had a skill for being fair. The people slowly learned to respect him.

Dane and Blain were inseparable, always up to no good. If there was any kind of drama, they were swept up in it, if not at the center. It was mostly Blain's doing, with Dane tagging along.

There came one gloomy, overcast day when Blain told us he would head over the E'or again. That was a dark time in the Tennan's history. Rafe was angry, livid, but he kept it in check. Tegan let his thoughts be known, telling quite loudly how foolish it was for him to cross again. Blain took it with an easy grin, knowing Tegan couldn't stop him. Jam remained calm and quiet, trying to speak reason, and Zeph just watched from a corner.

The next day, Blain was gone, and Dane sported terrible bruises. He sat still while I nursed him in silence, tending to his wounds. He was seething, and that rage didn't fade.

Winter Solstice came, and I dug out the seeds I had saved from summer, then, with a candle, slipped out into the night. My cloak billowed around me in the cold winter wind as I knelt on the snow, trying to light my candle.

I hated being so far from home.

I hated that I still thought of Regent as home.

My heart ached for my mother, for Mikhala, Niehm and Elenor. I broke when I thought of Willhelm, strong and steadfast. I couldn't imagine him on the frontlines facing down the Shadows. That wasn't where he belonged.

The flint fell from my fingers, burying itself in the snow, and I cried, sobs wracking through me. Leeds wasn't Regent. It wasn't where all my friends were. It was the blasted arsecrack of the E'or. This was where I *had* to settle, not where I *wanted* to.

I doubled-over, crying for the loss of the life I once had. I mourned my losses and let my tears speak in place of the traditional words.

Rafe found me like that, crumpled in the snow. He picked me up against his chest and snatched my pouch of seeds. He opened it with one hand and threw them into the wind. The gust blew them out of sight. He met my gaze with a stern eye, as if assuring me Leeds was our home now.

Spring Year 901

Spring came, and with it, our little cottage. Excitement grew as I picked out and traded for household supplies. There was something about buying goods for our home that brought me peace.

I kept telling myself that we were settling, but seeing the cottage up and built, and buying things for our life in it assured my heart that I really was going to call Leeds home.

"And once the oil is soaked in, it will be ready for you," Master Val said.

At the guildhall, Rafe made the final payment. Butterflies fluttered low in my belly as I watched the gold change hands.

"I know you've bought some furniture," Val added. "Feel free to bring it over. The men will work around it."

Rafe grunted in agreement, then peered over at me. I grinned, thrilled that we were so close to having *our* home. He snorted in amusement and shook his head, turning for the door.

"Good day, Master Val," I called over my shoulder as I followed. "It seems so unreal," I sighed, threading my arm through Rafe's.

"It better be. I just paid real gold."

I chuckled and took a skipping step. It was as if I was living a dream. I had Rafe. Tizmet was happy and growing more aware every passing day. We had a little cottage and friends.

I waved at Luther's men, who leaned against a building. Rafe's arm tensed under mine, and I frowned up at him. His head was dipped toward me, but his glare aimed at them.

Through the passing seasons, he and Luther gave each other space. That snake and his goons were simply part of life. In a sense, Luther *was* Leeds. This was his town, and if anyone wanted something, they had to go through him. Rafe and Rothfuss were anomalies, people he couldn't control. Rothfuss was stuck between a rock and a hard place. It wasn't his job to displace Luther. And to be honest, if anything were to happen to Luther, everything would collapse. That, or someone else would have to step up—someone who could be worse.

Bottom line, we wanted our cottage, and Luther was content to let us have it, as long as he got to hang that 'favor' over my head. He preferred people under his thumb and knew how to get them there.

Yet as time went on, seeing his men about and his name on every shop became second nature. One could almost ignore the town was owned by him. Rothfuss' enforcers patrolled frequently and were quick to make sure Luther didn't overstep any ordinances. If there ever was a breach, he was there to see to it personally.

Rafe gently tugged me down a street, away from the Bog Frog Inn.

I peered over my shoulder at the main road, then up at the setting sun. "I have to get to the tavern. Someone has to work, you know?" I jested, letting myself be pulled along.

"Not much longer," he said.

I smiled down at my boots as we walked. This was something we had talked about, and I agreed with. Once we settled, my job would be the cottage. A homestead had too much work. Our home would require my full time and attention, and I was willing to give it that.

Rafe would continue working for Rothfuss as an enforcer, but my place would be growing and preserving our food, cleaning our house, looking after our land. I would hunt with Tizmet, and hopefully still earn some coin when I could by providing the tavern and butcher with game.

If there was any game left when forty-two hatchlings shared the field.

Rafe tugged me toward a shop, and I dug in my heels, pulling my hand free. "A dressmaker?"

He stopped, facing me with a raised brow. "Don't sound so disgusted."

The sign that hung above the door read, 'Talia's Dresses.' Of course, she got her fabric from Luther, but at least she owned the business.

"Why?" I asked, glancing down at my trousers. "My clothes are still in fair shape."

"Avyanna."

I jerked my eyes up to meet his dark gaze and the impatience that lay there. I sniffed and pursed my lips, but followed him as he led me up the two stairs and through the door.

As we entered, I tucked my thumbs into my belt to keep from accidentally touching anything. These were fine dresses. Not as fine as what could be seen in King's Wall, but still a step above what I was accustomed to. I felt out of place in my worn brown trousers and stained tunic.

"Greetings, Avyanna!" Talia called, coming out of the back room. She glanced at Rafe and gave him a brisk nod. "And to you, dear sir."

Talia was the type of lady that I would expect at the King's palace. She walked tall and proper, with her shoulders straight and chin held high. Her blonde hair was piled atop her head, and she wore a vibrant blue gown.

Rafe gestured around the space. "Pick one."

I stared at him as if his left eye grew back. "What?"

He crossed his arms over his chest, looking at me like I was a child throwing a tantrum.

"Are you here for a dress?" Talia asked softly.

"No."

"Yes."

We answered in unison.

I whirled to glare at him. "Rafe, I don't need one. It's silly." I cringed, giving Talia a shrug. "No offense, Talia. It's just that with the bugs–"

"There's a reason most wear breeches under their dresses. 'Tis common," she assured me, lacing her fingers together as she studied our interaction.

Rafe brushed me off. "Get one anyway."

"Why? I don't want to waste good coin on something I'm not going to wear."

"Because." He took a step forward, crowding my chest.

I swallowed through a dry throat as I gazed up at him, wondering why something so trivial set him off.

"When I take you to bed as my wife, I want you to feel like a woman, not a warrior."

I snapped my mouth shut with an audible click, and Talia gasped. A blush heated my cheeks as Rafe's mouth quirked up in amusement.

Further arguments built in my throat, but Rafe tilted his head, and the mischief in his eye made me rethink my words. The last thing I needed was Talia getting any more of an earful. Her face was as red as mine surely was, though she remained poised and composed. Her lips pressed together as her wide eyes danced between us. She was married with two little ones at home. Surely she understood how difficult men could be.

"I believe I'm getting a dress," I choked out.

Days later, I sat on my bed at the inn. It was midday, and the light was bright enough through my hide-covered window that I could make out the vibrant green fabric I held in my hands. It was soft and feminine. Its hem would hang to my ankles, and the neckline was far lower than what was considered modest at Northwing. It was impractical.

And I loved it.

Rafe was out with Rothfuss, but I had to try it on. I wanted to *feel* like a lady.

I stripped down and smiled as I unwound my chest binding. This wasn't the style for it. I used a wrap for work and fighting, so I could move freely without care. A dress, a proper lady's garment, took care.

I thought back to the split skirts the female Riders wore. Garments cut to look like a skirt, but made of two distinct legs with a flap that fell in front and behind. They had the appearance of a dress, but allowed women to ride on dragonback with ease.

I reveled in the smooth texture. It was cool and slick as water, soft as a feather. I grinned and pulled it over my head, then examined myself in the small mirror as I adjusted the lacings. My wild hair was coming free of its braid, and the neckline revealed more pale skin than my tunic allowed. I tied off the lacings, then stood on the tips of my toes to see my waist. The dress flared out at my hips, hiding the curves there, but was snug about my chest. I twirled, and the skirts spun out in green waves. I giggled like a child and jumped, watching the fabric flow with the movement.

Glee tightened my throat, and my smile hurt my cheeks. Rafe was going to take me. We would be life mates. Husband and wife, as some would call it. We had been under the same roof, in the same room, sharing the same bed for almost a year, and finally—*finally,* we would actually be mated.

I flinched, staring at the freckles over my cheeks. Would Rafe have a ceremony? I frowned, meeting my green gaze. Rafe didn't seem the sentimental type. He wasn't showy and wouldn't ask others to witness—but he had me get a dress.

He would make a big deal out of it. I worried my lip and stared at my hands. He wouldn't make a *big deal* by most people's standards, but I should be prepared.

Most couples simply shut themselves inside their house for a few days, and when they reentered society, it was known that they were life mates. By that standard, me and Rafe already were, as many assumed.

There were ceremonies. However, they differed based on culture and region. Here in Leeds, the couple made a big scene by walking the town, then settled at the tavern where people pestered them to no end. When evening fell, they ventured to the woman's parents' house. The following morning, her parents verified the consummation with horrible stories that traveled through Leeds like wildfire. After the whole town heard of the evening's activities, the man would take the woman to his home to live there.

In a city south of the E'or, a terrible and stifling place where people were cold and unkind, the mated women wore rings. I thought that was a horrible custom. Wearing jewelry so openly was just asking for an attack.

Would words be said?

Should I have words?

Even if it was only between me and Rafe, I needed to say *something.* I didn't want to seem like the immature young girl I felt. I was a woman, a proper lady. Confident and capable of caring for myself. I took a deep breath and studied my reflection. I would have words. Even if he didn't, and I was overthinking all of this, I would have vows ready.

I would be ready for anything.

The next morning, Rafe busied himself coordinating the drop off of our petty furniture, and I ventured into the tavern after collecting the eggs.

"Iana, I need to talk to you," I called.

"Speak, girl."

"I only have a few more days–"

"Don't remind me."

"Here I thought you would be eager to get rid of me."

I laughed as I handed the eggs off to Pachu through the kitchen entryway. He peered at me with curious eyes, as if he wanted to listen to the conversation, but I shut the door, regardless.

"I asked after River, but she said Luther offered her a job at his place." Iana huffed a sigh as she wiped down a table. "Serving tea to the pigs."

I propped my hip against the counter. "What about Malek? I've seen him wandering about."

The runt of a boy often wandered the town on his own. The widows didn't keep the orphans in line, they only kept them fed and sheltered.

"He's got a sharp eye and quick hands. I wouldn't trust him," she replied, eyeing me. "Now, what is it?"

"It's about the storage addition."

"Your monster of a saddle."

I cringed, glancing toward the door. I didn't want anyone looting it. It was precious and worth a great deal.

"Aye. There's no room for it on our land."

"I expected not."

"I can't leave it on Tizmet."

'It chafes,' Tizmet agreed groggily.

I smiled to myself and reached across the bond to greet her. She was waking from brumation, taking her time to come to her senses in the warm sun.

"I doubt she would like that," Iana said. "What are you getting at?"

"I would ask that you let me keep it here."

She straightened and squinted at me as if I was a puzzle to be figured out. "I expected nothing less."

I blinked in shock as a smile spread over her face.

"You're just now settling, girl. Things like barns and sheds take time to build. Getting that little cottage ready in a few seasons was miracle enough for me. You leave that saddle there. I'll make sure no harm comes to it."

I pressed my lips together in a tight smile, more grateful than she would ever know. Not just for storing the saddle, but for everything she'd done for me over the years. She welcomed me when I was nothing more than a girl off the street with a dragon at my back. She gave me a chance. A second chance. A third and fourth.

I lurched forward, grabbing her in an embrace. She cried out, then wrapped her arms around me and squeezed tight.

Pulling away, she looked me in the eye. "You'll be taking part in the traditions, aye?"

"You mean parading Rafe about like a prized pony, then bringing him back here for everyone to make terrible comments about how we will consummate the union?" I laughed, shaking my head.

"He's more of a stud than a pony, dear."

I choked on a laugh and swiped at the happy tears that fell down my cheeks. A soft chuckle drew my attention to Pachu, whose face peeked out from the kitchen doorway. He shook his head in amusement and shut the door once more.

On the night of my last shift, I weaved through the tables and realized I would miss this. Yes, I would be happy working my land. But I'd grown to know the usual crowd and anticipate their needs. I'd miss these people.

I tossed a smile at old farmer Ian. The man often drank himself into his cups, offered a few exclamations about Eliza, his dead wife, before he wandered back to his farm in the dark. Luther's men sat at their table near the door, young Dan having joined his ranks. He was barely out of boyhood, close to me in age, but had a bulk that would match Jamlin's as he matured.

I served the crowd good ale and wine, saying my silent goodbyes. I would see them, but not as frequently since I didn't know how often I would ride in with Rafe to visit. He'd make the long trek every day and could pick up anything I might need.

Rothfuss entered, and I walked to the bar to get him a mug of tea. He sat on the stool behind me and gave me a smile as I offered the beverage.

"Heard this is your last night."

"Aye, cleaning out my room in the morn. Headed to our cottage." I lingered, taking time to clean a few mugs to speak with him.

"Glad to see you're settling." He studied me over the rim of his drink.

I scrunched up my nose and tilted my head at his words. "I've been settling for over a year."

"No, you've been *in* Leeds for over a year. You didn't start settling until *he* came," he mused, nodding to where Rafe sat with the Tennan.

Jam laughed at something Zeph said as Tegan whipped out his lute. Dane leaned against the wall, his eyes closed as the crowd erupted in cheers at Tegan's actions.

"I'm happy for you."

I glanced back at Rothfuss and smiled, letting him see my thanks. He had always been there to watch out for me, even before I secured a job. I appreciated him so much.

"Let's have a lively one tonight, eh?!" Tegan roared, and the crowd responded with whistles and cheers.

"Clear the center. We'll have a dance!" He strummed the lute and gave a bow to Iana. "That is, with the good innkeeper's permission."

She laughed. "Anything that makes you lot thirstier!"

I chuckled and caught Rothfuss' gaze. He would make someone a fine mate one day, just not me.

The crowd moved at Tegan's encouragement and shuffled to clear the room. My last night at the tavern was spent surrounded by joy and love.

CHAPTER 21

The next morning, I woke alone. I yawned and stretched, patting the empty bed, wondering where Rafe was. Unconcerned, I thrashed around, excitement building low in my belly. I wouldn't sleep on this straw mattress again. Don't get me wrong, I would be sleeping on *another* straw mattress, just not this one.

Giggles threatened to bubble out, and I swung my legs over the bedside. I jumped to my feet and danced over to the basin. Rafe had washed up before me, and his belongings were gone. I smiled to myself, realizing he gifted me the morning to myself. I washed up, taking my time, then applied the bit of day blossom oil Talia gifted me for today.

As I gathered my things, I realized I had collected more than I thought. There were three ribbons that Brandi traded me. Pity I didn't have a green one. Kila gifted me the comb, and Saudric gave me a decorative jar to hold the bug bite salve he taught me to make. I folded the rags and cloths Iana had given me over the years and placed them near the basin.

With my things gathered, I braided my hair along the crown of my head, up and off my neck and shoulders. I set my full pack on the bed, then shook out my dress. It was smooth and unwrinkled, and I slipped into it. I laced it up and pulled on my boots. The skirt was long enough to brush my ankles, but not drag in the mud and dirt. Talia hemmed it up for me and saved the length to offset the cost.

'Today?' Tizmet roused slightly, reaching across the bond to test my excitement.

'Aye. We're moving into the cottage.'

We would be closer to her nest. I wanted to be there to witness the little ones hatching. I was eager to experience Hatching Day without Riders, but also couldn't wait to see what that hatchling from the night sky egg would look like.

Tizmet sighed with resignation. *'You will not get rid of him once you mate.'*

I smirked, grabbing my spear. *'I'm no dragon. Once I mate, it's for life.'*

'Pity.'

I paused and searched the room one last time. It was neat and orderly. My belt and bandit breaker were stored inside my bag, and my push dagger hung around my neck. I barked a laugh at the image I made—a lady in a fine dress with a spear at her side and a pack slung over her shoulder.

'You will have to fight your mate.'

'I am no dragon,' I repeated, humming as I shuffled down the narrow passage with my belongings.

'All mating is fighting. Have you never seen another human mate?' she asked, and I felt her genuine curiosity as she sifted through my memories.

'We aren't animals. We don't go rutting in public.'

'I am no animal,' she huffed. *'Yet, I am not afraid of my desires.'*

As I fumbled with my door, I had a moment to be thankful no one else was privy to this conversation. Shoving my weight through, I nearly collided with Tegan.

"Morn!" He took a quick step back, then made a show of eyeing me from boot to braid. "Don't we look the proper lady this morn!"

"*I* look the proper lady." I set my spear aside and reached up to fix the lacing on his tunic, chuckling at his tousled red hair and wild beard. "You look like a rogue."

He flashed me a bright smile and took my pack, then offered the crook of his elbow. "Ah, so ye're smitten with me!"

I snorted at his jest and retrieved my spear, then we walked arm in arm down the stairs.

"Blain returned early this morn, when the sun had yet to grace the sky."

A chill seized my heart.

"Oi." Tegan slowed to a stop on the landing, then spun me to face him.

My smile trembled, trying to hide the worry that came with knowing Blain would have a report from Regent.

"Today is *yer* day, lass. Rafe has given everyone orders not to relay Blain's words."

"I want to know–"

"And ye shall." He nodded. "Just not today. Let Rafe tell you later. With any luck, the two of you will be busy for a few days."

I rolled my eyes and started down the next staircase, dragging a chuckling Tegan with me.

We made our way to the tavern, drawing a few curious glances in the early morning light. I smiled to myself, but kept my attention locked on the road. The townsfolk weren't used to seeing me in a dress. I had never worn one in Leeds. The absence of trousers wrapped about my legs and tucked into my boots gave me a sense of vulnerability. But it also empowered me—in a feminine way. I felt like a proper lady that commanded respect.

Or maybe it was the weight of the spear in my hand.

Tegan opened the door to the tavern, then dipped into a royal bow. I snickered at his antics and stepped inside. From behind the bar, Iana stared at me with wide, shocked eyes. A motherly grin brightened her cheeks, accompanied by a nod of approval.

I approached the far corner table where Rafe and the others dug into their morning meal. Rafe's eye slid to mine. It traveled down my figure, taking its time trailing back up. My heart took off, heat flushing through me at his appraisal. My thumb fiddled with the braid wrapped around my spear, and I gave him a shy smile.

He wore his black military vest, in all its embroidered and braided glory. It was buttoned snug over his crisp white tunic, which was tucked into dark trousers that hugged his thighs. He even shined his boots. Back when he rescued Blain, he lost his patch and had been wearing a strip of cloth in its stead. Today, he sported a new patch. It was simple, a hardened piece of black leather that was slightly concave, giving his old scars some space. It seemed comfortable, breathable, and intimidating.

I liked it.

I bit my lip as he stepped around the table, walking to me at a painfully slow pace, my heart racing as if urging me to bolt.

He stopped in front of me, placing his hand over mine on the spear. I swallowed, grimacing as the action drew an audible gulp. He stared down at me, dark eye winking with mischief as it trailed over my face.

"Avyanna of Gareth, I intend to make you mine this day."

There was a startled cry from the direction of the kitchen. The sound shattered the dam of silence that had built from the moment we laid eyes on each other. Whoops and cheers broke out among the Tennan. Iana smiled with her hand pressed to her lips, while Pachu managed some combination of crying laughter.

"Such bold claims," I choked out past my dry throat.

He grinned at my response, and my heart swelled at the unrestrained happiness written in that smile. His eye crinkled at the corners with the force of his grin, and I couldn't help but beam back up at him. We had been waiting so long for this day—fighting and enduring endless trials all for this.

It was finally happening.

"The innkeeper tells me there is a tradition," he rumbled.

I tilted my head, wondering who this new Rafe was. "We don't need to–"

"If Leeds has traditions with claiming, we will abide by them."

I heard the words he didn't say. This was our home, and we were going to act like proper townsfolk.

"Hear now, I know of a few traditions!" Jam called out, earning Tegan's laughter.

I shook my head at Rafe as he tugged at my spear.

"Leave it with Jam. We have a walk to take," he said, fingers moving against mine.

"Oi, leave it with Zeph! I'm not missing this walkabout!" Jam laughed as he shot to his feet, abandoning his meal.

"Great idea!" Tegan echoed, rushing the few steps to drop my pack next to Zeph.

"I'm no guard dog," Zeph muttered, shoveling more food into his mouth.

"Ye're a guard goose," Tegan jeered, skipping to our side. "They're better."

"I regret that I'll have to sit this one out," Blain stated.

I craned my head past Rafe to look at him. He was thin—his cheeks gaunt and eyes shadowed. He offered me a bright smile, however, and waved me on. Dane met my searching gaze with a one-armed shrug before turning back to his meal.

Jam marched to the door and held it open. "Best you have witnesses."

"As if the whole town won't be enough." Iana wiped at her cheek before she gave me an encouraging smile.

Rafe held out his arm. "Shall we?"

I glanced up at him one last time before placing a trembling hand in the crook of his elbow. "Yes, I think we shall."

Leeds was alive in a way that it rarely was. People crowded the streets, drawn out from their homes and shops. The fathers we passed gave Rafe grim nods of approval, while teary-eyed mothers held their children's hands, lips pressed in bittersweet smiles.

I grinned at the little ones who handed me wildflowers and thanked the women who granted me their kindness. Rafe had a stalwart glare for the men who offered their blessings. Though I didn't want to admit it, this was a big deal for these people. As we walked through the packed crowds, I realized I was more than just another traveler to them. I was a symbol, a banner.

I was Dragon Kind.

By choosing to settle here, they had our protection. I was a beacon of hope. They all knew bits of our story—the long, hard road we endured. The townsfolk understood this union was one of love, not convenience. We fought for every bit of happiness we received. They respected that. We were settling. We were joining their community, solidifying our stand with them.

"True love!"

I scanned the crowd, my hand tightening on Rafe's elbow as the throng parted for Luther. Laughter and cheerful conversation died out as the people strained to hear what would pass between us. Rafe's arm flexed beneath my grip, letting me know he would handle this. Luther leaned on his cane, making his way over, followed by four of his men. My heart seized as one yanked a squealing pig along.

"The whole town is positively abuzz with it," Luther mused, blocking our path. "I wouldn't be amiss, assuming you are parading dear Avyanna around, to let it be known you intend to wed her? We know she's been in your bed, but good of you to take her as a mate. Respectable, even."

Rafe said nothing, his features set in a blank mask. To my surprise, not a trace of anger lingered in his gaze. He simply waited for the snake to finish.

"Ever the silent type." Luther sneered, then faced me. "I've brought you something!" he stated brightly, showing off his eerily white teeth. "As a reminder of my kindness and generosity—a gift for the happy couple."

He clapped his hands, and his man dragged the spotted, squealing beast over, then offered me the rope. I blinked, horrified. I didn't want to drag it along with us, but there were children about. It was a decent sized sow and could easily trample a small child. I refused to carry that kind of guilt.

The soft but sharp song of steel being bared was accompanied by the flex of Rafe's muscle. I snatched my hand away and took a quick step back before Luther or his distracted man could move. Rafe swung his sword in a vicious but quick arc.

The pig's squeals died instantly.

The crowd was so silent, I could hear a horse neigh in the distance. My gaze darted to Luther, whose smile faltered bit by bit, as if he could no longer manage to keep it plastered to his face. Rafe faced him, crowding his space, and lifted his sword hilt first. Luther's men scrambled, and Jam and Tegan drew their weapons, but stayed behind me.

Luther jerked his hand up, staying his men as Rafe reached out, tugging on Luther's overcoat. It gave him just enough slack to wipe the pig's blood off his blade.

"I accept your gift," Rafe growled. He released his hold, then stepped back, securing his blade.

Luther opened his mouth, but a deafening roar cut off his retort.

Tizmet flew low over the crowd. Relief swelled in my heart. She was here—come to spend this day with us. It was important for the people to witness her presence, to be reminded of my positive influence on them, on our town.

Her tail lashed in the air, nearly hitting a roof as bystanders gasped and murmured. She hovered above for a few wingbeats as they made their mad scramble to give her space. She landed, her weight making the ground quake.

Luther took a single step back. His men, however, chose to stand behind him, placing their leader between them and the dragon.

Tizmet lowered to my chest and flared her nostrils, taking in my scent. She clicked in pleasure as I pressed my palm to her maw.

'You are happy,' she crooned.

'You're here.'

She lifted to her full height, then bit at the air. With her face tilted toward the sun, she threw a plume of fire in the sky. I smiled up at her as Rafe crowded behind me, pressing his chest to my back. She cut off her flame and growled, eyeing the dead pig.

'Food!'

Flashing her massive teeth, she crushed it, splattering the road with blood. She lifted her head again, swallowing the creature whole. Her scales were hard and glossy with her preening. She was thick and healthy after a long brumation, and as she brought her face back down, her gaze sparkled with bright intelligence. She thrust herself between us and Luther, watching him with a fiery eye. Her slow blink narrowed her pupil as her lips rose off her fangs. With a quiet snarl, she let him know what she thought of him.

'I could still fly if I ate a human,' she mused.

'You cannot eat him.'

'One day, I will.'

Though the words themselves were a threat, it sounded more like a promise.

She pulled her head up, turning at the last moment, and snorted at Luther and his men. Dragon snot sprayed them all, and I cringed in sympathy as Luther closed his eyes. He was a picture of patience and self-control as he took slow breaths, and remained still. Opening his eyes, he flashed me a sickening smile.

"I'll be seeing you about that favor, Avyanna," he called out. "Enjoy your evening."

The taps of his cane broke the silence with occasional plops of dragon snot as he and his men took their leave.

Rafe hummed, offering me his elbow. "There goes our meat for the summer."

'He can hunt,' Tizmet huffed, offended, then lurched to the sky.

The crowd gathered once again, giving us more space, but the conversations grew to a pleasant din.

Little Brandi ran up, but instead of handing me a flower, she offered it to Rafe. He frowned at her in such a manner that sent other children hiding behind their mothers' skirts, but not Brandi. Her blonde curls bounced as she hopped from foot to foot, beaming up at him as she held out the daisy. I choked on my laughter when she realized he wouldn't take it from her, and she grabbed at his free hand.

"You're not a bad man," she said with an innocent smile, her blue eyes twinkling. She tucked the flower into his palm.

He brought it up to his face, staring at it as if someone had just given him a lizard. His frown fell, and he gave a small shrug. Brandi squealed, hugged her chest, then darted off into the crowd. When Rafe met my gaze, I dipped my head, peering at him through my lashes. A smile tugged at the corner of his mouth as he tucked the daisy into my braid.

Soon, all the children were bringing him daisies, and though he scowled at each and every one of them, they persisted. He slipped each one into the braid wrapped around my head, giving me a crown of flowers by the time we finished our walk.

We ended at the tavern as the sun neared its zenith. A small crowd trailed us, and I was both honored and horrified that they would witness our union. Rafe was determined to make a scene out of the ordeal, however. As we stopped at the steps, my heart raced and panic thrummed through me. For someone usually so reserved, he was being quite public with his claiming.

Rafe gently spun me so that I held his hands and faced him. I glanced about as the bystanders hushed and gathered closer. Nervous sweat beaded on my temple as Iana opened the door and shouted for Pachu, who came running. People crowded on the landing and encircled us. Tizmet flew low overhead, watching with a fiery eye.

"Avyanna of Gareth," Rafe began, his voice lifted, carried by the wind.

I snapped my gaze back to him, fingers trembling in his hands. He never spoke like this—always self-controlled and quiet.

"Behold my oath, that I take none but you, to hold until the end of my days."

My heart pounded in my chest, realizing he had taken the time to prepare his vows.

"I shall be the shield for your back, and the sword for your arm."

My nerves broke as a smile slipped over my lips. That was the Rafe I knew.

"I shall be the cup for your drink, and the plate for your sustenance."

His dark gaze held mine, and I shivered from the intensity burning within.

"I give you my body that we two might be one. I give you my soul till my life be done."

The crowd was silent, as if they held a collective breath.

"I pledge to you my life and my death, both equally yours. Will you accept my oath?"

I pressed my lips together, gazing up at him. He was *asking* me—not claiming me. He was giving me one last chance to run, to turn him away. Part of me shattered, wondering if even the tiniest bit of him doubted me.

"Rafe Shadowslayer," I began, then cleared my throat so that those witnessing might hear. "Rafe of Deomein. You cannot possess me, for I belong to myself.

But now and forever I give you that which is mine to give. You cannot command me, for I am a free woman. But I shall give what you ask, and it will be sweeter for my yielding. Behold, I accept your oath and give you my own, that I shall take none but you until the end of my days."

His eye sharpened on me as a full grin split his face. The crowd erupted into excited cheers. He swooped me into his arms, and I threw my head back, laughing as Tizmet roared in the sky. Rafe's hold slid under my arse, keeping me at his waist, and with his other hand, he crushed me close for a fierce claiming kiss.

The crowd went wild, Tizmet letting out a ground-shaking bugle as she flew directly above us.

I melted into him, wrapping my hands behind his head, holding him tight as I returned his kiss with equal fervency. I smiled, and he bit at my lower lip. When I pulled away to peer into his face, elation burrowed through my being. I had everything I ever wanted.

A home, a dragon, a mate.

Love.

I had love.

Rafe lowered me, letting my body drag against his as the crowd laughed and roared, their raised voices overlapping each other. I turned my beaming smile on Jam and Tegan—the latter wiping away a happy tear. I giggled as Rafe tugged me up the steps and inside.

People flooded in after us until the place was full and loud. Iana kept the drinks pouring, and the townsfolk passed them about eagerly. Rafe pulled me to the center of the room, sat me on his thigh and watched the festivities with a relaxed eye. My heart felt like it would burst.

Tegan whipped out his lute and strummed lively tunes about true love. The crowd danced and laughed as the chimes passed by. We ate and drank, surrounded by folks who were not only happy for us, but excited that we were joining their community.

It was still light out when Rafe caught Jamlin's eye and gave him a quick nod. I slowed in my dance, catching the exchange, and spun back to Rafe's lap, collapsing on him with a breathless laugh. I had tried to lure him to join me, but each time he shook his head with a smile and pushed me into the throng.

A few moments later, Jam returned. He leaned against the wall, giving Rafe a nod.

"Come," Rafe said.

I jumped up so he could stand and stretch out his legs. Tegan slowed his song to a halt, and the crowd quieted, parting for us.

"Away with you!" Iana cried from the bar.

"Aye, we expect a fat babe in two seasons' time!" someone called out.

Their comment was followed by many more concerning our night. I blushed, walking closer to Rafe to hide the pink staining my cheeks. Any other day, their remarks wouldn't have bothered me. But after the day I had, it seemed I really was a blushing bride.

Rafe tucked me firmly against his side and led me out, away from the taunts and jeers. Jam pulled the door shut behind us, and I spotted Rafe's stallion tied to the hitching post just ahead.

"Oi!" Tegan's cry was accompanied by him bursting through the door.

He had a few ales to wet his throat and was slightly unsteady on his feet. He handed Jam his lute, who took it with a playful smile.

"Oi! I has a blessing for ye!" His speech slurred as he pulled a long scarf off his neck.

He gestured for our arms. Rafe watched him with a tolerant eye, obliging him, and he fastened the fabric about our left forearms, bringing us together.

"Now ye are bound one to another, with a tie not easily broken. Now comes the final binding, where in darkness your hearts are bound. When yer bodies are joined, and two become one, it will be fastened, that which cannot be undone." Tegan spoke, his words slipping through some of the handfasting vows.

I smiled, amused at his efforts. He stood back when he was done, admiring his tight knots on our arms that would let us move only enough to get on and off the horse, and not comfortably at that.

"Ah, just in time I see," Blain said, trotting out with Dane on his heels.

The twins walked over as Rafe tugged me closer to his stallion, clearly ready to be on our way.

"A moment, Rafe."

Rafe sighed and faced the two. Happiness fluttered in my stomach, realizing they prepared a blessing for us as well.

"May the wind bear witness to this day, and carry its message to far-away lands."

As Blain spoke, the breeze kicked up, tugging at my skirts as if it answered his call. Dane lifted his hand up to my face, and I held still as he used his thumb to draw a symbol between my brow.

"May the sun warm their hearts with the passion of your love." Blain finished and drew a foreign rune between Rafe's pinched brows.

"Done?"

I laughed at Rafe's impatience, and Blain shooed him toward the horse. Dane stepped away, a rare smile on his face.

"Eager to be off, I see," Blain jeered. "Go. Burn the woods down with your passion."

My laugh ended in a shriek as Rafe picked me up by my waist and helped me climb onto the saddle. He swung up behind me at an awkward angle due to the scarf about us. He shifted, finding a comfortable seat, and spun his stallion toward the road.

"Good day, my friends!" I called over my shoulder.

Rafe kicked his stallion into a canter. The Tennan laughed, and Tegan took his lute back, belting a bawdy song as we rode into the fading light.

We made our way to our little plot of land, our home. At first, I rested against Rafe, simply content to be in his company after such a nerve-wracking day. As night deepened, however, and we got closer to the cottage, my hands grew clammy and my pulse quickened in anticipation.

I stiffened as we turned off the main northern road and rode through the newly cleared eastern trail. Rafe chuckled and pulled me tighter to his chest. A nervous giggle slipped out of my mouth, and I fiddled with the scarf that bound our arms together.

I might have known this day was coming, this *night* in particular, but it did nothing to calm my nerves. Rafe had been my friend, my constant companion—my *love.* Playing with our passion was fun, addictive and empowering, but actually consummating that love made my stomach flip-flop with worry. I was no delicate flower, nor was I naïve of how a man and woman joined.

Still, what if I did something wrong?

"Tell me what you're thinking," Rafe whispered in my ear.

When his lips pressed to my neck, kissing my bare skin, I trembled. I stared straight ahead, unable to ignore the teasing rock of his hips as the stallion walked down the path.

"Nothing," I choked out. I adjusted my hold on the horse's mane, winding my fingers through the coarse strands.

"Liar." Rafe's mouth rose to my ear and nipped it gently in reprimand. "Tell me."

Warmth spread through me, competing with my anxiety. "I—I'm nervous."

"Don't be."

"Easier said than done."

He brushed his lips to that tender spot where my neck curved to my shoulder. I shivered with his gentle touch, but found myself craning my head to the side to give him better access. He shifted and passed the reins to his left hand. When his fingers brushed the hem of my dress that had ridden up to my knee, I sucked in a soft breath.

"Close your eyes." His demand was thick and husky.

My heart beat frantically, as if it could escape my chest, but I let my eyes flutter shut, trying to lose myself in the sensation of his arms around me, his mouth searing my soul. I gasped as his warm, calloused hand found my knee. Slowly, his touch trailed up, coming to rest on my thigh.

Something wound tight in my belly as my skin grew feverish. He murmured something against my neck and nipped a trail from my ear to my shoulder. A quiet growl rolled from his throat, then he tugged at the fabric of my dress with his teeth. Another gasp escaped me as he managed to pull it away. The chill of the evening bit at my newly bared skin, but his mouth was like fire.

I arched into him, lost to the need rising through me. Curse nerves, I *needed* him. I reached back for him, desperate.

He pulled away, chuckling darkly. "No, I don't think you have a single reason to be nervous."

With a frustrated growl of my own, I twisted, drawing him close.

Nothing was gentle about that kiss. We fought for dominion, mouths slammed together. When his tongue brushed my lips, a tiny alarm went off in the depths of my mind. I threw caution to the wind, opening up to him. His mouth was hot and needy. He let out a low groan, slipping his hand higher on my thigh. I moaned as he inched higher, passion drowning out everything but him.

There was only Rafe.

He pulled back with a curse and shoved me closer to the stallion's neck. I had a moment of panic, fearing I overstepped some invisible boundary, when Rafe kicked his stallion into a wild gallop.

I giggled as the horse responded eagerly, its mane whipping at my face. Rafe's hand left my thigh to grip the saddle horn, trying not to lose his seat as the stallion tore along the path.

It wasn't long before we stormed into the clearing and onto our land. My heart thumped painfully as I took in the scene. Our cottage sat in the center, wildflowers abloom throughout. Small glowing beetles crawled and flitted among the swaying grass. The moonlight was soft and gentle, illuminating the pond, bathing our home in its peaceful light.

My soul sang in response. This was *home.*

Rafe wheeled the horse over to the lean-to connected to the backside of the cottage. He pulled the stallion up short, causing the beast to lurch on its haunches and throw its head in the air. He took that moment to slip off the saddle, dragging me with him.

I cried out, laughing as Rafe tore off Tegan's scarf. The sound of rent fabric loud in the night. He backed me against the cottage wall. A dangerous fire burned through his gaze, and my body answered with its own passionate heat. Movements rough and needy, he reached low, hands hauling me up by my thighs. He crushed me between the wall and his chest. A breathy moan tightened my throat as his hips settled exactly where I wanted them. I arched my back, holding onto his broad shoulders.

"You'll be the death of me," he groaned.

The heat of his breath tickled my neck, lips leaving a molten trail, branding me with every kiss. With a curse, he let go of my legs, and I wrapped them about his waist, his belt buckle digging into me. His hands found my face and pulled my lips to his. He kissed me with passion, wild and needy. His desperation matched my own.

He was *mine*, and this power I had over him was mine alone to wield. My nails dragged down his back, and he gasped, an airy, hungry sound.

"We're never going to make it to the bed." My words were breathless, light.

He pulled away, just enough to study me, his chest heaving in temp with mine. He hauled me in for a quick kiss, then turned his head, letting out a sharp whistle. His stallion snorted, as if offended by his call. Rafe drew in a deep breath, as if he readied himself to do something he detested, then pried himself from me. My legs were unstable as my feet hit the ground.

I tripped after him, my movements sluggish as I helped strip the tack off his stallion. Rafe threw the saddle aside and cursed when he fumbled with the bridle's buckles. I slid behind him, pressing my chest to his back. When my touch slipped under his tunic, he growled as I scored him with my nails. And when my fingers dipped beneath his waistline, he spun on me. I laughed gleefully as he tackled me to the ground, pinning my wrists above my head.

"You're playing with fire," he warned, settling between my legs.

I wrapped around his waist, arching my back. "It's a bit cold," I murmured.

When I rolled my hips hard against his, his eye darkened.

"Sun above, woman. There's a bed not ten paces away," he groaned, his eye closing as if trying to find patience.

He dropped his weight, and pleasure spiraled through me. He yanked my dress up about my thighs and then hesitated, bracing himself on his forearms. I reached between us, fumbling to reach the clasp on his belt.

"We're not making it to the bed," he choked out.

I shook my head, feeling my braid come undone, my hair tossing about me. "Take me."

Rafe needed no more encouragement. He lifted his hips, allowing me better access to his belt.

My shaking hands pulled at the strap of leather, tugging it through the loops. He lowered to my neck, using his teeth to draw the dress down further. Pulling back, his features softened with the sight of me bared to the moonlight. When his rough hand cupped my breast, I sucked in a gasping breath, writhing against his touch as he worked some magic there.

He chuckled, a low, masculine sound. "Easy now."

I whimpered and yanked at his belt, throwing it aside. He bucked his hips once, and I tore at the hem of his tunic. He wore far too many clothes.

"Rafe!" His name was both a plea and a demand.

He shed his tunic and vest, tossing them into the tall grass. His hands twitched, as if he could barely restrain his urge to *touch* me.

"Tell me what you need."

"You," I gasped. "I need you."

My fingers glided across his chest, drifting down the hills and valleys of his muscles to his trousers. He was mine, scars and all. I took my time, savoring the newfound freedom of indulging my desire. His skin was hot, almost feverish. With a demanding, searing touch, his hand slid up my thigh. The low sound that flowed from his throat almost undid me completely. I yanked at his trousers and he came crashing down.

"Then you shall have me."

It was there, in a bed of crushed wildflowers, that I first knew a man. The moon caressed our skin as we fulfilled our love. The passion that burned that night was the culmination of years spent waiting, fighting to be together. Only the animals of the night bore witness to our cries, our love a private, burning thing.

When we made it inside, our naked skin covered in dirt, grass and bug bites, we whispered words to one another. Words that we had never used before. Terms of endearment reserved for lovers and mates.

I fell asleep in Rafe's arms, my heart so full of love I thought it would burst.

Chapter 22

I drifted out of a peaceful sleep, stretching languidly, and rolled to face Rafe. He was on his side, head propped up on his hand, gazing down at me. The blanket we shared settled low on his body, draped over his hip. As the sun rose, its gentle rays flooded the room, enveloping him in soft, golden light.

He removed his patch in the night, and I looked at his bare face and smiled. His eye glittered dangerously, even as a teasing smile rode his lips. His newest scar, the one that ran from his left temple to his jaw, pulled tight at the skin around his empty socket.

"You're so handsome," I purred, arching against his body.

He smirked, then tugged a piece of grass from my hair. "More lies."

"'Tis true!" I laughed, slipping my hand beneath the blanket, searching him out.

He growled and grabbed me about the waist, rolling me on top of him. I tipped my head back as his hungry gaze danced over my bare body, bathed in morning light.

This was worth the wait.

It was several chimes later when we finally made our way to the pond to wash up. In the summer months, I'd witnessed Master Val's workers take advantage of the cool water, but I never mustered the courage to swim in it myself.

"You're sure nothing in there will bite me?"

Droplets ran off his chest as Rafe broke from the surface, and a familiar lust flitted low in my belly.

After swiping his eye, he propped his hands on his hips, dipping his chin. "There's definitely something in here that will bite you."

I paused in setting my clothes down, glaring at his wicked smile as he prowled toward me. I straightened, crossing my arms.

"Don't you dare," I huffed.

He had no intention of listening to me.

"No." I held up my hand, taking a single step back. "Rafe, no! There's all kinds of fish and bugs and–"

"You didn't mind the field last night." He came to a stop as my palm brushed against his chest.

"I'm serious–"

He grabbed at my arm, and I shrieked, spinning on my heel to make a run for it. I didn't get far.

He howled with laughter as he snared me around the waist and hauled me up like a sack of grain, throwing me over his shoulder. I wailed, slapping his naked back as he jogged into the water, eliciting screams from me. He laughed breathlessly, pulling me from his shoulder–

Then threw me into the pond.

So ensued a glorious water fight that should have been recorded throughout the kingdoms.

'Are you a fish now?' Humor drenched Tizmet's tone as she peered down at us.

We lay sprawled on the bank in naught but our skin, the sun warming our bodies. Rafe slept with his arm thrown over his face, and I curled into his side.

'Fish stay in the water,' I mused.

She sniffed at our naked bodies, curling her lip in disgust. *'So fragile.'*

She snorted, and I shivered against the draft she made.

"I can still take you, dragon," Rafe muttered.

I choked on my laughter. He pulled his arm away from his face as Tizmet blinked a large fiery eye.

'I'd like to see the little man try.'

I pushed myself to my feet, my body aching and complaining with each movement. It was a pleasant kind of soreness, one that brought fond memories.

'You have not eaten today,' she accused.

Tizmet backed away to give me space as I pulled my clothes on. I caught Rafe watching, and a smile lifted the corner of my mouth.

'Dragons go days without eating when they are in season,' I shot back, losing sight of her as I slipped my tunic over my head.

When I emerged, she had her eye in my face, looking me up and down.

'Dragons are not nearly so thin. At this rate, you will die of starvation tomorrow.'

I laughed, pushing her away.

"Tizmet insists we eat," I called over my shoulder, making my way over to the cottage.

The sun was high in the sky, warming me as I crossed the clearing. Rafe sighed, which was followed by a groan as he roused himself to get dressed.

Inside, I stared at our shelves directly across from the entryway. I worked, bartering for as much as I could in the previous months, and being late spring, I foraged and preserved what I could as well. We had jars and tins of various herbs and dried goods, and a salted and cured pig leg hanging in the far corner.

There was a table tucked against the opposite wall, beside a dresser that held a basin and mirror. The builders installed a small stove near the foot of the bed, allowing a heat source in the winter and something to cook on if we wished.

That was the extent of what we owned, and the extent of what the cottage could hold.

I snagged a loaf of bread that I had purchased two days prior, wrapped in wax paper. On my way to the table, I picked up a knife, gifted from Pachu, then cut off a portion of the ham.

It would be a simple meal. I planned to take the next few days to forage fresh foods and get a fire pit dug outside. It would allow me the ability to make bread and cook stews and meats without heating the house.

I smiled as I went about my task, wondering at the fact that my thoughts were busy with such domestic affairs. After plating the food, I spun back to the shelves to retrieve our tin cups. Them in hand, I stopped in my tracks as Rafe pushed inside.

"Midday meal?" I asked, suddenly timid, as if he knew I had no idea what I was doing by setting things out.

He raised an eyebrow and watched me with a small smile. Shaking his head, he took the cups and headed back out the door. I spun, hugging myself as my hair flung out behind me. I giggled with the joy that this was actually happening. Everything I had ever dreamed of. A home, a love, a dragon. This was my dream, and I was overwhelmed by the happiness it brought me.

In a few breaths, Rafe returned with water from the well, and I took a seat, watching as he approached. He kicked the door shut and walked the few paces to the table. Placing the cups down, he settled in across from me. He eyed our plates, and I offered him a nervous smile.

He tilted his head, studying me. "Did you poison it?"

"What?" I shrieked, clamping a hand over my heart.

"You're too invested in my reaction." He chuckled. "It's salted pork and bread, Vy."

My grin faltered a bit as I peered at the simple plate. I didn't know what else I could make. There were petty few options as we had only spent one night here.

"Vy," He reached across the small table and lifted my chin to bring my gaze to his. "I'm hungry. It's food. That's all that matters." He spread his fingers over my cheek and held me fast. "It's the company that makes it more."

I smiled at his way of apologizing and nipped at his palm. With a crooked grin, he pulled away and dug into his simple meal. I followed suit and felt Tizmet's approval across the bond. It amused me to no end the things that actually bothered her.

After we ate, we cleaned the table and dishes together.

Then, somehow or another, we found ourselves in the bed again.

'I'm just saying I hope they stay close for a bit,' I told Tizmet as I swung the hoe into the dirt.

I was busy working on our garden, or at least getting it in the ground, and she lingered at her nest. We had missed a good bit of spring, but I had to do what I could with what time we had left. I could still plant enough to preserve for winter, but next year we'd start as soon as the last frost.

'My hatchlings will do as they please,' Tizmet said with a mental shrug.

She'd never had a successful clutch that she was able to see hatch, and the only experience she had to go on was her own. She let me delve through her memories, which were a mass of hunting and base instinct. I worked as I sorted through them, trying to make sense of the blurred images and piece together a timeline. I wondered if this was what she saw when she sifted through mine.

'If they stay close, they will over hunt the land in a year,' Tizmet said.

'True.' I plucked a stone from the dirt and tossed it into the pile near the house. *'This wouldn't be a problem at Northwing.'*

I paused to lean on the hoe, wiping the sweat from my brow. Earlier, as the sun rose in the sky, I had shed my tunic, wearing only my chest binding and trousers, though I was tempted to remove those as well.

'No. In that place they would be kept as pets, ridden as beasts of burden.' Her voice dripped with disgust.

'You let me ride you,' I replied.

After a deep breath, I got back to work. Without Rafe here, I didn't want to be caught unaware if he sent one of the Tennan for me. Not that he would mind if *he* found me in naught but my skin.

I smiled at that thought.

'Only because your legs are so much smaller than my wings,' she huffed. *'You don't use me as others use their bonded. I am a dragon, not a tool to move things about, or to be a pawn in someone's game.'*

She repeated Rafe's words concerning General Faulkin moving the dragons about the war map like pieces on a board. She had been listening to me and Rafe talk of late, coming every few days to sit outside the cottage, curling her big body around it to rest her head at the window to peer inside. Her eggs were due to hatch in a few weeks, but I got the feeling she wanted to be close to me while I was happy and content. At the moment, she was conversing with me across the distance, settled atop her nest.*'I assure you, none of the Dragon Kind on the warfront think it's a game,'* I replied.

'And because they are unaware, means this is not true?'

'The King is suffering. His people are suffering. This is no game.'

'Then let the dragons do as dragons should *do. Let them be free and rain fire from the skies, and bring magic from below. They should not be controlled.'*

She distanced from the bond just a little, in a way that someone withdraws from a conversation when they were hurt. I shook my head as I swung my hoe in an arc again.

'Tizmet, without order–'

"Working hard, so I see."

I couldn't contain the thrum of terror that pulsed through me, hearing Luther's voice.

Tizmet scrambled into the sky with a roar of warning across the bond.

I straightened as Luther and two of his men rode onto our land. They were still a stone's throw away, but lost in my work and conversation, I hadn't heard their approach. My heart raced. I was a reasonable distance from the cottage, and my tunic.

But I felt far more naked without a blade.

I ignored Luther's greeting, walked calmly to the house, and laid the hoe to rest against the wall. I held an iron grip on my fear as I grabbed my tunic from the water barrel where I'd left it. Shrugging into it, I clenched my jaw in determination. As I took the step up into our cottage, the space between my shoulder blades itched, as if there was a giant target on my back.

Once inside, I didn't bother with the door, but lurched to the bed. Reaching under it, my fingers flailed, seeking my weapon.

"Oh, dear. How inviting. You even leave the door open for me?"

I threw myself to the floor, stretching my arm out. Relief flooded me as my hand wrapped around cool steel. I scrambled up, pulling it with me.

When Luther entered, he was greeted by spear point.

"Greetings, Luther," I said, proud my tone held steady.

He paused at the threshold, resting heavily on his cane. He never quite healed from the damage Rafe inflicted the first time they met. His sharp eyes twinkled, knowing he had me where he wanted. "I simply came to pay a neighborly visit. Hardly worth drawing a blade for."

I tilted my head, hearing his men walk around the cottage outside.

What were they looking for?

"It's quite *un*neighborly of you to visit when you know Rafe is away," I stated, voice even. "It could actually be considered quite improper."

"Unfortunately for you, that might be the case." He let out a mocking sigh and shrugged, glancing about the space. "I, however, needed to address matters with you that are better discussed in private. I do love what you've done with this little shack. Quite the change from what it was."

His gaze snagged on the pig leg hanging from the rafters, and he flashed a terrible smile. "See now, my claiming gift wasn't that far off."

I ground my teeth together in annoyance. "We can talk outside."

Where I had more room to maneuver my spear if needed.

"You would ask a cripple to linger in the midday sun for a friendly discussion?" He held a hand to his chest. "You wound me, Avyanna. I swear you are more and more like Rafe with each passing day."

"Luther, stop with the act. We both know you're not here for a friendly visit. Step outside, or when you finally choose to, it will be with a hole in your belly."

"Such harsh words."

He clicked his tongue, and my knuckles ached with the effort of holding back my strike.

"Such *brave* words." He took a step.

"Hold!" I snarled, both for his benefit and mine.

I was strong, but there was no reason to lash out yet. His men weren't even in the house. I'd never seen Luther fight, but I didn't doubt he could.

"Where are the eggs, Avyanna?"

'MINE!' Tizmet screamed.

Her roar tore across the sky. It echoed in the distance, still too far away to help me.

Luther's fake smile fell from his face and he took another step. That was the last he could take without limiting my ability with the spear. Any more, and I was putting myself at risk.

"Your favor is due, girl. Where are the eggs?"

All pretense at playing nice had melted away, leaving the terrible monster behind. Luther's eyes were sharp and greedy, his cheeks hollow and gaunt, as if no matter how much rich food he ate, he would never be satisfied. He wrung his ring covered fingers over his intricate cane, as if no matter the gold or jewels he had, it would never be enough to sate his greed.

A horse whinnied outside, followed by the thud of a heavy weight hitting the ground.

What were they going to do to the cottage?

"They're not mine to give," I breathed.

Evil rolled off him in waves. It was sickening.

It was frightening.

His eyes narrowed, and his mouth twisted into a horrible sneer. He lunged faster than I anticipated and snagged my spear just below the blade. My panic surged.

"I will burn it all," he snarled.

With all my strength, I pulled the shaft back to free it from his grasp, but the butt of it slammed against the wall behind me. The sudden impact sent a jolt through my arms.

"I will burn your little home to the ground."

My fearful gaze darted up as a hulking form filled the doorway.

"I will–"

"GET OUT!"

Rafe snared him by his tunic, and Luther flew back, clutching at his neck as his cane clattered to the floor. I stumbled forward, gathering my wits as Rafe dragged the snake out of our house. I allowed myself a few breaths before I ran after.

When I cleared the door, the battle had already begun. Luther's men fought Rafe as he threw Luther to the ground. Rafe spun with his shortswords, fighting like an enraged beast. I hefted my spear and took a step toward him, knowing the risk he was taking with Luther at his feet.

'Fire!'

Tizmet's worry cascaded over the bond. In a flood of color, she shared her vision with me, a disorienting act that sent me to my knees. She was still far, but with her sharp gaze, she spotted flames licking at our cottage. She released quickly, and I threw myself to my feet, retching as I went. Rafe could handle the men. The house was my duty.

I raced to the well, throwing my spear aside, and filled a bucket. Thick black smoke belched from the backside of my home. I darted around the bend, water sloshing over my clothes. Crackling flames climbed the lean-to. I ripped off my tunic, soaked it in the bucket, then slapped the fire.

Thanks to Tizmet, it hadn't taken to the fresh wood. I threw the last of the water on the smoldering embers as she screamed, launching into view.

The clash of blades had me kicking up dirt as I sped around the house. Rafe had dispatched one man. Whether he was dead or simply wounded, I couldn't tell and didn't care. Rafe staggered, his black trousers wet with blood, clinging to his leg. Luther was on the ground, trying to make it back to his feet as Rafe fought like a madman against the other man.

Tizmet crashed into the clearing, barely slowing as her massive paw dropped onto Luther, crushing him to the spot.

'Don't kill him!'

She whipped her head in my direction, eyes flaming and tail lashing in rage. I took a running step to the well to retrieve my spear when, at the edge of the woods, Rothfuss galloped through the clearing with two of his men and Jamlin on his tail.

I opened my mouth to say something, anything, but Rafe's movement caught my eye. He batted the man's shortsword, and it fell to the grass. Without a breath of hesitation, he grabbed the man's neck, thrusting his blade through his middle.

Horror welled within me as Rothfuss yanked his horse to a stop. Rafe threw the dying body away from him as if it was nothing more than a bit of refuse. The others watched in stunned silence as he stormed across the clearing, limping to where Tizmet pinned Luther. His sword swung at his side, flinging an arc of blood through the air.

"Rafe, no!" I called.

Rothfuss dismounted, and I ran, angling myself to intercept. The pounding steps in my wake suggested the lawkeeper followed, thankfully keeping his mouth shut. Rafe was lost to madness, to bloodlust. He might not know friend from foe.

I stepped into his path, holding my hands out. "Rafe, stop!"

He didn't even look at me. He rolled his massive shoulder and stepped around me. When I grabbed his arm, he halted. His whole body was tense, strung as tight as a bowstring, ready to snap. He trembled under my touch, but not from fear.

From rage.

"Rafe!"

I needed to snap him out of this. We couldn't kill Luther. *He* couldn't kill Luther.

"He dies."

"The law will–" Rothfuss started.

Rafe roared, *"HE DIES!"*

I ducked between his blades and grabbed his face. A snarl lifted his lip.

"Come back to me," I whispered.

His murderous gaze darted back to Luther, unwilling to meet mine.

"Tizmet has him," I said, voice pitching higher. "He's not going anywhere. Come back to me. *Please*, Rafe."

A dark shadow burned over his features, angry and all-consuming. I raised myself up on my toes and pressed my lips to his. He was stiff and unyielding beneath me, shaking with a fury I couldn't tame. I settled my body against his, and when he staggered, I pulled away. A frown weighed my lips when I saw the pallor of his skin.

He collapsed, knees striking the scarlet-splattered grass.

I cried out, falling with him. His eye lost none of its wrath as one sword fell from his grip, then his back hit the ground with a thud.

"Jam!"

When I pulled Rafe's injured leg straight, my hands came away covered in a sheen of red.

"Curse you!" I screamed through clenched teeth, fumbling at his belt buckle.

Just how much blood had he lost?

"Here."

Jam dropped at my side, batting me away. He ran his dagger through the thick fabric, and I helped him tear it free. My heart plummeted as I watched crimson gush from Rafe's thigh.

"Blood vein," Jam muttered.

I dug my nails into Rafe's calf. Those words felt like a blow to my stomach, robbing the breath from my lungs.

'I have to heal him.'

'No!' Tizmet snarled.

'I have to. He'll die.'

Jamlin's features paled. "We have to stop the bleeding or he'll–"

Tizmet tried to speak reason. *'You can't see inside!'*

'I know his body as if it were my own.' I placed my hand on Rafe's leg, closing my eyes.

"Oh, no. Oi, Avyanna you can't do this–"

"Jam, shut your mouth."

My voice was eerily calm as I spoke, though my throat was tight with fear. I pushed Tizmet's rage and terror aside and reached past her for the door to the magic. It welled to my call as eager as it ever was, flooding up to meet me. I pulled bit by bit, ignoring the voices of reprimand, ignoring their hands jostling my body, and slipped it into Rafe.

Healing him was different from healing Blain. Perhaps it had something to do with how I tied us together back when he stood at death's door. Somehow, by fate or by magic, I *knew* what to do.

I was mindful, only drawing as much as I could manage. Tizmet slammed into my mind, her focus as sharp as steel. As it trickled into Rafe, I focused on sealing the severed vein, taking care not to block it. Pulling away, I mended the broken, split flesh.

As if it sensed I was through, the magic thrashed at me, a wild sudden surge wanting to be loosed. I gripped it tight, hauling it back. It fought me like a slippery river eel seeking freedom, and a cascade of agony shattered through my skull. I whimpered, slamming the door shut on it.

My eyes snapped open. Seeing the gash healed, a slight breath of relief squeezed from my lungs.

Then the pain came.

Chapter 23

We might have figured out that my seizures were triggered by using a great deal of magic, or a rush of adrenaline. Though how they played out was unpredictable. The length, or how long I'd black out, seemed random. This time, I was agonizingly aware of all of it.

I screamed as pain tore through my chest, as if fire seared me straight to the bone. My muscles were tense and rigid no matter how I tried to force them to relax.

Biting down on my screams only made things worse. As if the magic sensed my attempts to fight off my punishment, it cruelly doubled down against my efforts.

When Tizmet batted Luther aside, Jamlin stepped away, giving her space. She dropped her bulk and wrapped around me and Rafe, tucking me away from the world, hiding me in my moment of vulnerability. She crooned and spread her wing overhead, sheltering us from the sun. I shook, fighting against every shudder, making it worse. My shoulders jerked so hard that my neck snapped back. My teeth sank into my tongue, drawing blood. Tears blurred my vision as liquid fire boiled in my veins. I was vaguely aware of Rafe pushing something in my mouth and rolling me onto my side.

Compared to when I healed Blain, this seizure didn't last long—though to me it felt like an eternity. Bones aching, and muscles spent, I wearily worked my jaw, releasing the leather belt Rafe had slipped between my teeth.

"You with me?"

I would have smiled at the reassurance his rough voice gave me, but it hurt too much to move.

'Foolish,' Tizmet spat.

'I had no other choice.'

She kept her tail crushed against us, pressing us into her side. She pulled her wing back and nuzzled me. *'He would not be a great loss,'* she huffed, unimpressed.

I winced as she jostled me and rasped out a response to Rafe's question. "Aye. At least it wasn't as long as last time."

"Tell your dragon to let me up." His anger was a simmering, tangible thing as he shifted against me.

"Don't kill him," I said, voice weak.

Rafe grunted, the sound resonating with frustration and indifference. My words meant nothing to him.

Tizmet's neck cast us in shadow as she peered over her back, presumably watching Rothfuss and his men with Luther. *'Can I eat him now?'*

'You cannot eat Luther.' Pressure built and throbbed behind my eyes, and I clamped them shut. "Luther has to live. If he dies, someone worse could take his place," I said aloud for Rafe's benefit.

'Then I will eat them as well,' Tizmet assured me happily. Problem solved.

"Then I'll dispose of them, too," Rafe grumbled.

I groaned as he echoed Tizmet's sentiment. "You two! Let Rothfuss handle it. That's his *job!*" I winced again as the force of my words caused the lingering pain in my chest to flare. *'The people of Leeds cannot see you as a man-eater.'*

'Why should I care what tiny humans think of me? I am a dragon.'

'He's not your kill. Don't eat him.'

She sighed, as if that argument made enough sense, and she lowered her head. One down. Now I just had to convince Rafe.

"Vy, this is our home," he snarled, bending low to my ear. "I will not stand by while people threaten it—or *you.*"

"Give him a chance–"

"He had a chance."

"You already killed one man today. Don't kill another."

"Two," Rafe corrected. "About to be three."

My pulse pounded in my ears, increasing the throbbing ache. They had been someone's son, perhaps someone's mate. Hopefully, not fathers.

"Veil beyond, Vy. You pity them." Disgust simmered in his tone as he shoved against Tizmet's tail.

"Someone has to!" I growled, forcing my muscles to obey as I brought my face to his. "This is our *home*. You can't just kill every opposition. You're not a General here, Rafe. There are laws and ordinances in place."

"And who's enforcing them, Vy? The lawkeeper? You have to stand for what is yours."

Anger devoured his gaze, but something else lingered within, carefully tucked away. Hurt. Failure. Shame. He hadn't been here to protect me.

"The same mentality rogues and bandits have, I'm sure," I murmured, collapsing against his chest. I took a shuddering breath, riding out the last of the pain wreaking havoc beneath my skin.

He went silent, keeping his thoughts to himself as we lay there, tucked against Tizmet's side. There were sounds beyond us—shuffling steps, horses neighing as if they were spooked.

Rafe stayed, holding me.

'The dark one and lawkeeper come,' Tizmet warned, and she turned her head, keeping an eye on them.

The glower in Rafe's gaze promised nothing. I swallowed past the lump in my throat before urging Tizmet to move her tail. She growled but obliged, then hissed a greeting at Jam and Rothfuss. Jam remained a respectful distance away, his hands raised in a show of peace. She appreciated the respect he gave her.

Rothfuss watched her with narrowed eyes, but stepped around her. "We're taking the bodies to be returned to their families," he began.

Rafe pushed to his feet, standing behind me. I was content to sit on the ground. There was no getting up without making a fool of myself, and I wasn't ready to try. My head complained with every blink. Moving was not an option.

"And Luther?" Rafe demanded.

I peered over my shoulder, checking his leg. The torn fabric clung to his skin, stiff with blood.

"He will be confined to his quarters and seen to by Saudric," Rothfuss said.

He gestured to where Luther sat astride a horse, sitting as tall as his bruised body allowed. Red flecks of blood splattered his face, and his right cheek was swollen and split. Rafe spat and reached for his shortsword, but his belt and empty scabbards lay on the ground beside me, the weapons removed. His hand clenched into a fist where the hilt should have been.

"Jamlin will tell you where we placed your weapons when I clear the treeline."

"Coward," Rafe snarled.

"Someone has to use their brain in this town." Rothfuss rubbed a hand down his face. "You were well within your rights to defend your land. Based on the scorch marks on the cottage, I gather you were defending home and family. You won't be tried."

Rafe let out a bitter laugh, as if the idea of being charged with a crime was comical.

Rothfuss continued, "I would advise you to stay on your own land for the next few days. Let the townsfolk calm."

"Calm?" he scoffed, glancing about, no doubt searching for his blades. "As if they were the ones attacked."

"In a way, they were, Rafe. The townsfolk rely on Luther. He holds the trade and merchant lines. Without him, Leeds would suffer. Yet, the common folk look up to you two." Rothfuss nodded at me. "They will be unsettled after this. I'd like to avoid an uprising, if you don't mind. Stay home. Help your wife with the garden. Get seed in the ground. Fish that pond and smoke some of your catch. Take a few days away."

Rafe turned from him, his dark, menacing gaze landing on Luther. "I want him confined to his quarters until I receive word."

Rothfuss agreed with a dip of his chin, and a small victorious smile lit his face. "You'll be the first to know."

"I want to be posted at his quarters until his release."

His grin faded with that. "Not a chance."

Rafe grunted, fist tensing to draw a blade that wasn't there.

"I won't have him murdered in his own home." Rothfuss took a deep breath, glancing to where his men waited. They sat atop their horses, leading two others with bodies draped over their saddles. "If you need supplies from town, organize it with your men. Mine will be spread thin the next few days."

He offered me a small bow, but kept his eye on Rafe. "My apologies, Lady Avyanna. We came as soon as we learned Luther paid you a visit."

"It's not your fault." I shook my head and grimaced at the ache it triggered.

Tizmet lowered her muzzle to my back and sniffed at me as I leaned forward to place my palms on the ground. I realized my state of undress and a small voice in my mind demanded I cover myself, but I shoved the thought away. It was hardly avoidable. My tunic was behind the cottage, scorched and soaked.

"Thank you for coming," I said.

Rafe grunted as if he wanted to add choice words to my gratitude. Rothfuss pressed his lips together in a frown and nodded once more. At the horses, he snatched Luther's reins, then swung into his saddle. Without another word, he led Luther and the others toward the treeline.

"Swords." Rafe held out his hand.

Jam shook his head. "Oi, now I was told–"

"Who's man are you? Mine or *his?*" Rafe's tone was low and cold, gaze alight with challenge.

"Rafe, help me up, would you?" I asked, drawing his attention.

He cursed and muttered under his breath, then bent to scoop me up. I sighed against his chest and wrapped my arms around his neck.

"Curse you, woman."

He walked us to the pond to wash up. Jamlin stayed at the cottage, keeping his back turned as we stripped. After scrubbing the blood from my body, I rested on the bank, feet stretched into the water. Rafe waded in, his bare legs covered with crimson grime. When he emerged, his legs were clean. Not a gash to be seen, but a pink scar ran horizontally near his groin.

"Come here," I beckoned.

When he approached, the sun shone behind him, casting his body in shadow. I traced the fresh scar. It was as long as my hand from wrist to fingertip.

"Willing to put on a show for Jam?"

"He has always been quite modest when it comes to our relationship," I mused.

It was true. Of the Tennan, Jamlin had been the first to suspect anything between us. Though Niehm and Elenor beat them all. A pang resonated in my heart, wondering what they were going through in my absence.

Rafe crouched in front of me, bringing my focus to the present. He tucked loose strands of hair behind my ear as he searched my gaze. "Many thanks," he murmured.

I smiled. "It'd take more than blood loss to steal you away from me."

He scoffed, then pulled me in for a rough kiss before he stood to dress. An amused grin lit his features. He pushed his arm into his trousers and wiggled his fingers through the giant tear. Only a few thin strands along the backside held the leg intact.

"I'll fix it," I said with more confidence than I felt. It would not be a pretty mending.

He shrugged and tossed his trousers over his shoulder before starting back.

I sighed, reaching for my wet clothes. At least they were clean. Besides, I might appreciate the coolness as I worked on the garden. I slowly dressed under Tizmet's scrutinizing attention.

'Surely you do not mean to dig your stripes again,' she huffed, bright eye flashing.

I flinched as my muscles complained against the effort of pulling up my wet trousers. *'The garden won't dig itself.'*

'Let your mate do the work. You rest.'

'I can manage.'

Keeping my movements slow and careful, I grabbed the rest of my things and followed Rafe to the cottage.

Jam glanced my way from his place atop our water barrel, and seeing me clad in only my chest binding and trousers, wagged his eyebrows. "Stunning as the sun itself, little one." He grinned, offering Rafe his swords.

Rafe watched me approach, his dark eye traveling over my body. My cheeks burned. I knew what that look meant. I offered a timid smile, and set my boots at the door, then slipped inside for a fresh tunic.

"Oh, my spear is–"

My words were cut off with a yelp as the door slammed shut. I struggled with my tunic over my head as Rafe's familiar weight crushed me against the wall. As the fabric settled around my neck, I smiled up at him even as my body ached at the pressure. His dark eye was angry—*needy.* When he gripped my waist, his hold was rough and demanding.

"I need you," he rasped.

With a breath held in anticipation, he waited. I responded with a sigh of pure bliss, my arms encircling his neck. He wasn't just taking and pillaging—he was *asking*. He sought solace in my embrace, but also craved the assurance of my wellbeing.

There was only one way I could convince him.

I pulled his lips to mine, taking his mouth in a demanding kiss.

CHAPTER 24

Dane spent the next few days with us—Rafe's way of keeping tabs on Luther. Tizmet returned to her nest, and I sensed her excitement grow each day as summer neared.

With the land tilled and stones removed, Rafe worked on a small fence for the perimeter, which I found amusing. He hadn't built one to contain his stallion on our land, but felt the need to secure one around the garden to keep out rabbits and bog deer.

As if there would be many deer left in the future with forty-two dragonlings about.

I picked some berries from the brush along the forest's edge. Rafe showed interest in my foraging, and in Saudric's list of medicinal plants. Even this far removed from the warfront, he retained his knowledge of poisons and antidotes. That bit of his personality unnerved Saudric, but I found it endearing. Those little poison books were tiny bits of Rafe.

A horse trotting down the trail drew my attention, and I smiled, hearing the man astride the beast hum a lilting tune. Blain traded places with his twin for the day.

"Hail!" I stepped from the thicket, holding my basket of red berries.

"Oh, good morn, Avyanna," he greeted. With a bright smile, he pulled his horse to a stop, searching the clearing. "I was hoping to catch you before your hulking mate could stop me."

I laughed. "Stop you from what?"

Mirth clouded his expression as he dismounted, eyeing my clothes. "I daresay you're supposed to pick the berries, not wear them."

I wiped at the apron Iana gifted me, worn for this purpose.

He reached into his overcoat and pulled out a neatly folded parchment. "This is for you."

I stared at the unbroken seal, anxiety dissolving my smile.

"I would tell you not to worry, but that's all anyone does these days," he said with a one-armed shrug.

He held it out, and my hand trembled as I took it, as if it might turn into a snake and bite me. Sun above knew it was just as dangerous.

"Now, where would you like the seed you bought? I assume by that little garden over there. Quite lovely, by the way. This place is coming together." He didn't wait for my response, instead he led his horse into the clearing.

I stared at the letter, unable to speak. He made it seem like Rafe didn't want me to have this, and I understood why. The wax seal depicted a rearing gryphon against a coat of arms—the seal of King Vasili Aldred of Regent.

I pressed my lips together and tucked the parchment inside my tunic to resume my berry picking.

Blain returned the day of mine and Rafe's joining, and I hadn't seen much of him in the weeks since. Knowing he had this letter, and Rafe warned him off, worried me. If he withheld this, it was solely because he wanted to shield me from harm. Still, I didn't appreciate it.

What if the Shadows marched on Northwing and my friends were in danger? What if a loved one was killed?

'Peace.'

Tizmet reached across the bond, soothing me as my heart worked itself into a panic. If something happened to Elenor or Niehm, Willhelm or Darrak, Mikhala, my *mother–*

'Read the blasted piece of tree!' she snapped, interrupting my spiraling thoughts.

At the other end of the clearing, Rafe greeted Blain and reached for the seed sacks. I took that moment to press into the thicket, out of sight. Thorns snagged on my clothes, and I smothered my yelps as brambles clawed at my arms. Working into a relatively clear space, I set my basket down and fished the letter out of my tunic. A thrum of fear knotted itself with the worry thickening my stomach. With Tizmet's awareness crowding my own, I broke the seal before I could think more on it.

By His Majesty King Vasili Aldred, Reigning King of Regent

Year 901 after the Treaty of Dragon Kind.

His Excellence, King of Regent in his boundless mercy, hereby extends pardon to Avyanna of Gareth, Rider of the Wild Dragon, Tizmet. Pardoning their actions of violence against the weak, unimaginable acts against the citizens of Regent, blatant disregard for Dragon Lord and fellow soldiers, risking the safety of those bravely giving their lives in the War of Shadows, and for insult to the King himself.

Grace is hereby extended, allowing the travel of the banished, Avyanna of Gareth and her dragon bound, Tizmet, to and through the borders of Regent proper. Here and henceforth, Avyanna of Gareth shall be received as a common citizen of Regent, bound by common law.

May the souls of those beyond the Veil be so forgiving as our King.

There, taking up the bottom of the page, was the scrawled, unreadable signature that I was sure belonged to the King himself.

'They pardon us*?! Pardon means to forgive, to accept apology?'* she asked, rummaging through my memories.

'Aye.'

My eyes scanned the words as unease slid its way around my heart. Why? Why now, and what changed his mind?

'When did we apologize?!' Tizmet roared, exasperated. *'Did* you *apologize?!'*

'No.'

There had never been a banished Dragon Rider. I was the first. It caused such a scene, and would go down in the records as a monumental event. Yet, there was the King, taking back his punishment. I folded the letter and fingered the seal. Something was wrong. There was more to this, and Rafe kept it from me. Regardless of his attempt to protect me, I had a right to know.

After I clawed my way out of the thicket, I didn't hesitate in crossing the clearing. Rafe shouldered a sack of oats into the house and Blain slipped the bit out of his horse's mouth, watching me with a knowing smile.

"Rafe?"

He dropped the sack inside, then faced me. He searched my features as he brushed his hands down his trousers. When his eye snagged on the letter, his relaxed expression tensed into one of irritation.

"Flaming son of a dungheap."

"Aye, that curse is befitting," Blain agreed with a smile.

"You kept this from me." I held it out, letting my accusation settle between us. "You knew, and didn't tell me."

He sighed, crossing his arms over his chest and bracing his feet as if he expected me to attack. With lips pressed tight, pulling at his scars, he stared at me, his gaze hard and unyielding.

I turned my attention to the one who *would* talk to me. "Blain, there's more to this."

"Aye."

He took that moment to glance at Rafe. Whether seeking his approval, or wondering at his reaction, I didn't care.

"He's not asking you, I am. Tell me," I demanded, gripping the basket for all I was worth.

"And have him skin my hide to hang as a banner for all that cross him?" Blain patted his horse's neck, then reached under its belly to loosen the girth.

Rafe shrugged. "She asked."

I spun on him. That he concealed this made the hurt cut deeper. Did he not trust me? "Why? Why keep this from me?"

"He came with it on the day of our joining. I'll not ask your forgiveness for telling him to wait," he bit out.

It's not like a mere pardon would have stopped me from fulfilling a dream years in the making.

"I would have still joined you."

"And worried and fretted over a blasted piece of paper worth no more than a pile of dung. Aye, clearly I should have told you," he mocked, then shook his head in disbelief. "I told him to wait on it, not keep it from you, woman. Thrice-curse it, you think so little of me?"

"I assumed you thought so little of me." I chewed on my lip, then wrapped my arms around him.

"Repulsive," Blain muttered, drawing my attention back to him. "If you would like me to share my tale, I would beg a cup of water and a seat."

I released Rafe, and he grumbled under his breath as he disappeared to grab the chairs from our table. I dipped inside to grab his drink and took my time securing the pardon in the small chest under our bed where we stored our valuable belongings. When I returned, Blain sat in a chair, face tipped to the sun. Rafe leaned against the wall with his arms crossed, determined to linger and hear the story once again.

Blain held his hand out for the cup without opening his eyes. "Luther is getting antsy," he murmured.

"Let him." I settled in the seat across from him. I eased forward, elbows on my knees, and pressed my fingertips against my lips.

Blain righted his head and took a long drink. He watched me over the lip of the cup with an amused expression. When he finished, he cleared his throat. "I think words of assurance are due first. As far as I could tell, your friends are safe. I should specify—the ones I know of. Lady Niehm and Elenor, Sergeant Willhelm, and though he is nearly impossible to track down, the King's bounty hunter–"

"And Mikhala?"

"The lass from Caulden? Aye, she's been spotted in King's Wall, last I heard."

I let out a relieved sigh, rubbing at my face. They were alright.

"They are safe for now." Blain's words echoed my thoughts. "Though for how long, is in question."

I jerked upright, meeting his sober gaze.

He took a rallying breath and shook his head. "Regent was holding its own after your banishment." He nodded toward Rafe. "When we returned to the front, it was obvious something roused them, and they *did* target Rafe as if they had a particular score to settle.

"When Rafe left, Regent lost the ability to rally the Shadows. They spread out, thin, but fierce and terrifying. They had some new power, not only motivation, but they moved deeper into Regent, taking villages they had no hope of overpowering before.

"Around the time Rafe galloped like a madman across Regent, I heard tales. Rumors, whispers of whispers, things too terrible to speak without ale loosening your tongue in the dead of night."

The hairs on the nape of my neck rose in fear, anticipating his next words. Tizmet crowded my mind, and I sensed her raise her head from her nest, flicking out her tongue, tasting the air for danger.

"Tales that the Shadow Men could fly."

"No," I breathed, horrified. A shiver slipped up my spine.

"Simple stories. Survivors were petty few, but they swore it was true. So, being the curious creature I am, I wanted to investigate. If anything happened to me, Dane would be sure to come running, and if anything happened to you, I would return just the same."

I blinked, shaking my head. "And you weren't worried about Dane?"

"The man is positively resilient. If he were attacked by a troll, weaponless and naked as the day he was born, he would still survive. No, I wasn't worried for Dane... but hearing the stories made me want to keep a close eye on a certain Rider and her dragon who faced the Shadows and came away victors.

"The Dragon Lord refuses to let his dragons get close enough to the Shamans to be controlled. Now and then, it happens regardless, but they are our best defense against the masses. We can't lose them."

"If they have dragons–"

"Ah, and there comes the next issue."

He leaned forward in his chair, bringing his face closer to mine. I nearly shrank away from the intensity in his gaze.

"Say you have a Shaman capable of taking a dragon, controlling it. How would you best fight it? With another dragon, to be sure."

"The risk would be too great."

"Correct." Blain settled back in his chair. "Now this new threat is not 'verified,' if you will, by anyone in authority, but the rumors are growing. The tales are multiplying. The whispers are rising to soft voices, soon to be full-fledged discussions."

"I was banished because I saved a *General* when everyone else gave up on him. Why would a pardon bring me back?" I scoffed. "You think King Aldred wants me to fight?"

'I will not fight in some silly war,' Tizmet snapped.

"No, abyss beyond, no." He laughed, shaking his head. "Banishing you was a moment that was recorded as a lesson to all future Dragon Kind. 'Resist the will of King and Country, and you will be thrown out of Regent's borders without a coin to your name.'

"You hold that pardon because you and your dragon are the only ones brave, or dim-witted enough to take on a Shaman and survive. If he has any chance of bringing down a Shadow that can fly and breathe fire—He doesn't want you, Avyanna. He *needs* you.

"But that's not the end of my story," Blain said, wagging a finger at me. "The Shadows are advancing on Northwing."

Cold terror seized my heart. "They will pull the women and children out." I rushed my words, as if saying them faster would make them more true.

"And put them on a road—where?" Rafe rumbled. "King's Wall is already filled to capacity. Not to mention the road east is wide open for attack. Southwing is already under siege. They are fighting with everything they have, trying to hold it."

"Southwing, too?"

"It's been the new warfront since autumn," Blain said, drawing my attention back to him. "They know where the schools are, where the dragons are, and they're closing in."

"How close are they to Northwing?"

"It depends, Avyanna. There are a lot of factors at play, some that we are guessing at. We don't know their true numbers or their supply routes. No one is brave enough or," he cast a sidelong glance at Rafe, "stupid enough to go behind enemy lines to find out. Dragons are prohibited from flying above the front unless they are stationed there. General Faulkin is the only one who can seem to predict where they will attack and with what numbers."

"Educated guessing," Rafe scoffed.

He hadn't been shy telling me how he felt about that particular General. He was the key player in forcing Rafe back to the homelands and rejecting his resignation.

"Call it what you may," Blain said. "The man is a strategist at heart."

My stomach churned as I processed all this information. "What does he think?"

Blain offered me a sympathetic smile. “Between going back and forth, there’s only so much news I can gather. I do my best, but what can I say? I miss you.”

Rafe grunted. “Or Dane calls you back.”

“Aye, he’s a terrible whiner. If you only knew,” Blain said with a wink.

“So, I was given the pardon because the King needs me and Tizmet?”

“In summary, yes.”

‘*I will not be a pawn,*’ Tizmet hissed.

“And you think I might go because my friends are in danger?”

I reached across the bond, feeling for her emotions. Would she fight me if I chose to return? Tizmet pulled back from my mental touch and pushed memories at me. Scenes of me and Rafe laying naked by the pond. Of me tilling my garden, dancing in a field of wildflowers to music only I could hear. She sent an image of her eggs, her nest.

“It’s not my place to assume what you would or wouldn’t do.” Blain formed his words with care. “I only thought that you might want to be informed of your friends. That, and the Dragon Lord himself handed me that pardon.”

Unease squeezed at my heart. Ruveel was the one who had taken my actions as a personal offense. He loathed me after I rescued Rafe. If he gave my pardon to Blain, they were truly desperate.

“Enough,” Rafe rumbled, pushing off the wall. “We have work to do.”

As the day passed by, I was lost in my thoughts, and Tizmet kept her own mental distance. With hopes of a bountiful autumn, we sowed seeds in the ground. Rafe had limited knowledge about farming, and although I had more, I wasn’t raised on a farm. We were hoping for the best. Thankfully, he was earning enough coin from Rothfuss that we wouldn’t starve, but we would need a healthy crop yield to thrive.

Blain kept us company, working alongside us in the field. He stripped his tunic as the sun burned hotter. His back was covered in raised scars from a flogging long past. He caught me staring, and faced me, striking a pose with his hand on his hip and face toward the sky. I laughed and resumed planting.

It was late that night, after Blain returned to Leeds, when I broached the subject again.

I sighed against Rafe’s chest. “I can’t believe I have a pardon.”

He hummed, stroking my hair.

"I feel bad, you know?" I chewed my lip. "Here I am, living my dream, and they're fighting to survive."

"You could have dreamt of a place with fewer bugs."

I laughed, bringing my hand up to trace circles over his bare skin. "Don't you feel bad?"

"No."

"Not even a little?" I pressed.

"We've talked about this before. I have no guilt over leaving."

"But what if you could go back?"

His heart beat a steady rhythm beneath my cheek. His hand never faltered in my hair, but I could feel him thinking about it.

"I wouldn't choose it."

A breath of silence passed, and I sighed, deflating a little. I wouldn't choose it either, so why did my heart twist hearing him admit it?

"But if you chose to, I wouldn't oppose it."

I stiffened. Pulling back, I leaned over him, my pale hair splayed across his chest in the moonlight. "You would follow me if I returned to Regent?"

"Aye, though those potatoes would go to waste."

I scoffed. "You talk of the warfront like it's a terrible memory, but if *I* chose it, you would return." I tilted my head, trying to puzzle him out.

"Vy, there's only one place I'm going to be content." He dragged his palm down his face. "It's not in the arsecrack of the E'or, and it's not in the steaming pile of dung that is Regent. It's not further north or south, it's right here."

He placed his hand between my breasts. My heart thumped eagerly against his palm, swelling with his words. I bit my lip as I held his gaze.

"*You* are where I am content," he said. "*You* are my home. So, if you decide to return to Regent to rescue your friends, I will go too. Don't get me wrong, I won't follow like some whipped puppy, but as your sword and shield. You are my mate—my partner. Your worries are my worries. And your problems are my problems. You are *mine.*"

My lip trembled, and the threat of tears blurred my vision. I could hardly believe that I ended up with a life mate like him. This was the Rafe I grew to love, the one beneath the rough exterior. When I blinked, tears slipped down my cheeks.

"Oi, now she cries," he grunted, then yanked me down to his chest.

I sniffed, curling into his side. When his lips found mine, I kissed him gently, lovingly. I took my time with him that night, letting him know how much those words meant to me.

Love was a glorious thing.

Chapter 25

My pardon was a sensitive subject, and a topic we actively ignored. Every time I let myself consider the possibility of going back, I would look around at the cottage, at our little homestead, and my heart twisted. I wasn't willing to give up this piece of happiness I carved out.

The Shadows' threat encroaching upon my friends loomed over me, but I kept myself busy as the days passed.

Rothfuss called Rafe back into Leeds, leaving me alone at the house. He fought with me, saying he was going to send Dane to keep me company every day. I won that argument with the logic that I shouldn't need a bodyguard in our home. I also might have employed some of my newfound womanly persuasion.

A smile warmed my cheeks as I kneaded bread dough against our little table. One loaf was rising, and I was busy working on another. A small roast with wild carrots was stewing in the fire pit outside. I had seen to it before I watered our garden.

Slow hoof beats drew my gaze toward the cottage door. Tizmet reached across the bond and crowded my awareness. I pushed her to the side and wiped my hands on my apron. The bandit breaker was warm in my palm as I gripped the hilt. I had taken to wearing it since Luther's visit. Apparently, I needed to be armed at all times, even on my own property.

I walked to the door and leaned against the frame, wondering who approached. The light breeze caught the woman's brown hair as she lifted her hand in greeting.

"Kila!" I broke into a run.

Tizmet huffed in relief, then focused her attention on her eggs.

Kila dismounted. When her feet hit the ground, she stumbled, catching herself on the saddle. "Could you not settle closer to the town proper?" she said with a laugh. "I can't feel my legs!"

"Aye, 'tis a long ride."

When I reached her, I wrapped my arms around her. She abandoned the horse to return the embrace, squeezing so tight I grunted in protest. Pulling away, she held me at arm's length. Her kind eyes sparkled as she beamed down at me. She might've been a bit younger than me, but she was taller by a hand.

"I've missed you!" she said.

We looped our arms and started toward the cottage, pulling the horse along. "I'm planning a trip to town the day after next. You didn't have to come all this way!"

"Oh, but I did!" she shot back. "I need to talk to you about something."

I frowned. "Me?"

"I don't trust anyone else."

"Ominous."

She laughed and waved to her saddlebags. "Pachu sent some gifts as well."

"I have a hard time believing Iana let you go for a day."

"Oh, she hired little Neena. She fetches the eggs and helps Pachu in the kitchen."

"Neena? The blacksmith's daughter?" I asked, trying to place the name.

If it's who I thought, she was a quiet slip of a thing. I had a hard time imagining her serving the rowdy patrons at night.

"Aye, Gregor and Fiona's girl." Kila nodded. "She preps with Pachu, then turns in before the crowd gets too rough. Rothfuss has been passing by as well, to keep tabs. Poor man is spread thin these days."

I pressed my lips together, keeping silent about that.

"Your Rafe has been causing quite the stir," she added.

"Oh?" I took the reins from her and led the horse to the lean-to.

"Aye, everyone is all abuzz about whether he's going to take Luther down." She spoke slowly, as if she was testing my response.

"He had a chance," I murmured.

I secured her horse to the hitching post as she untied the saddlebags. Neither of us said anything more on the topic. After showing her inside, I returned to the bread, kneading it with a bit more intensity than necessary. I wasn't sure how this would all settle, and I didn't need anything else to worry about. Such as the townsfolk looking to Rafe to lead a rebellion against Luther.

"And you're just going to leave it at that?"

I glanced over my shoulder. Her soft blue dress billowed around her as she leaned her hip against the wall with her arms crossed over her chest. She was scrutinizing me, eyebrows raised in expectation.

"It's not the first time he's had a chance to take Luther." I shrugged, then balled up the dough and set it aside.

"No, but it's the first time Rafe has killed two men."

I frowned, remembering the bodies hanging limp against the horses.

"They threatened me. Rafe took care of it," I stated and laid a cloth over the resting bread. I pulled out a chair and sat across from it, motioning her to sit. "The loss of life was unfortunate."

"No one liked those two, anyway." When she sat, she offered a small smile, resting her chin in her hands. "The townsfolk aren't angry. There's just a stir because someone is standing up to Luther."

"Rothfuss has been for years," I shot back.

"No, Rothfuss upholds the law. Luther is as sly as a swamp weasel. He finds ways to bypass the laws. No one has faced him head on and won."

"We're not taking Luther on."

"I'm not accusing you, just sharing the topic of conversation among the people."

I sighed, pushing myself back in my chair. "You didn't come here to gossip, Kila. What would you have of me?"

She dipped her chin, dropping her hand to trace the woodgrain of the table. "I think I'm ready to claim someone."

I grinned, leaning forward. "Oh, and who's the lucky man?"

She peered at me from under her lashes. "That's the problem. He isn't available."

"Girl!" I threw my hands in the air. "You have the pick of men and you choose someone already taken?! Ridiculous!"

"No, it's not like that!"

"They all say that! Who is it? Old man Tegor? How about Malil? I heard he's not happy with his wife. Or perhaps you've set your eyes on Elan. I've heard his wife complaining he doesn't give her enough attention!"

"Hardly!"

Kila burst out laughing, and I joined in, knowing it was none of those men. She was better than that and knew her worth. She took her time getting to know the young men of the village and would marry for love, not convenience.

"I'm serious, Avyanna." She stared at the table as her laughter died into a shy smile. "I'm not sure he wants me."

"Then he's a fool," I scoffed.

Who wouldn't want to claim Kila? She was beautiful and open. She was free with her laughter and love, a hard worker, and knew far more than I did about running a homestead. A man would be a fool to avoid her advances.

"I'm not sure that's it. That's why I needed to talk to you."

"Because I'm a claimed woman now?"

"Because you're his friend."

I froze as realization hit me, my jaw dropping. Kila's eyes bounced between mine, trying to read my expression.

"I knew it. He has another," she breathed, holding my gaze.

"I—Well, no–"

"Then he doesn't care for women?"

"You know, I've never asked–"

"I'm not his type? He's attracted to more buxom women. Ugh, if only Pachu made more of those berry pies!"

I leaned across the table, grabbing hold of her cheeks to force her to face me. She choked on a cry, her expression pinched with desperation.

"Zephath is different." I chuckled. "To be honest, I don't know him that well. I will say I've never seen him look at a man, or woman for that matter, until you."

Hope brightened her features. "But I've asked him to go on walks several times, and he never comes."

"Likely because he knows what you intend on those 'walks' of yours." I snorted, easing back into my seat. "He's a sharp man, wicked smart. I'd be willing to wager he knows a child could come of those strolls."

"He always has his nose in any book he can borrow."

I shrugged at that. "I have the feeling books were his only company growing up."

"Tell me about him." She grasped my hands. "Tell me what will make him ask after me."

"The first man to resist your wiles, and you're hankering after him," I jeered.

She gave my wrist a playful slap.

My lips pressed together, wishing I had more to offer her. "I think he's had a hard life. I have my suspicions about his upbringing, but I will tell you with confidence that he is a strong and wise young man. Honorable, even."

Zeph was really growing into himself. Though he was cold to me, and everyone but Kila, he would do as Rafe asked—he was loyal.

Kila groaned and curled in on herself, resting her cheek against the tabletop. "But how do I get his attention?!"

"You already have it." I laughed. "Give him time. He's not one to make rash decisions. I would wager he's noticed you 'walk' with a different lad every other moon."

She groaned again.

"Give him time to see you're interested in *him*, not the novelty of him."

"I should just tell him."

"Haven't you?"

She lifted her head to glare at me.

"You've asked him out on 'walks.'" I shrugged. "You've expressed your intentions. Now give him time to express his... or push you away."

"I came to you because I thought you'd help," she muttered.

She stayed with me for a bit before returning to Leeds. She had to be back before nightfall, and though I enjoyed her visit, I didn't want her to be caught on the road after dark.

I hummed to myself as I set aside Pachu's gifts—a pie and a small bag of sugar. It was a kind gesture, imported from the south. Luther traded for it and sold it to Leeds. I frowned and tucked it away. Wrapping my arms around myself, I gazed out the door.

That man, as much as I despised him, was important for Leeds. If something happened to him, someone would have to step up with the same connections. And everyone under Luther was just as vile as him. To most of the townsfolk, he was the leader—the man they had to go through to get anything done. Most ignored his more *unsightly* business practices. He was a means to an end. Yet, since Rafe arrived, he put a wrinkle in Luther's pretty picture of Leeds. I was content to mind my own business, and though the snake pushed me about, I was capable of being like all the other townsfolk. I could ignore him.

Rafe couldn't.

He was a thorn in Luther's side, challenging him every step of the way. He wouldn't stand aside and let him lord over the good people of Leeds. I rubbed my arms, looking over the field of wildflowers that danced in a light breeze. Luther had almost taken this from me. He came into *my* home, threatening me. I couldn't ignore that. He was bold. And now that Rafe had once again put him in his place, he would retaliate. He would come for me.

He would come for Tizmet's eggs.

'*Mine*,' she rumbled, sensing my thoughts.

The flowers swayed without a care, and I frowned. '*Aye*.'

But for how long? I would wager he already had men searching the bog for her nest. It was a wonder he hadn't discovered it yet. That he believed I would just offer an egg that wasn't mine to give was absurd. It was as if I told a mother to give up their own babe.

Obscene.

I sighed, turning back into the cottage, staring at the resting loaves, knowing I should take them out to bake soon.

The best I could do about Luther and Rafe was to keep them from killing each other. But would that be enough? Rafe despised, *loathed*, the very mention of the man. He was content to stay here because of me.

But was he happy?

I was his home. This was what I wanted, and he would endure it for my sake—but he would always be Rafe. I didn't want that to change, not even a little, but the man I knew and loved was not meant to be under a dictator's rule.

I turned to the bed, knowing what lay beneath it. Each word was engraved into my mind, memorized by heart. Even so, I still found myself reaching to retrieve the chest. Sitting atop my blanket, I pried the top off. I held the pardon in my hands, a silly piece of paper. How was it a sliver of dead tree carried so much weight?

I set the chest aside, then laid back with the paper pressed over my heart. If I returned to Regent, I could help my friends, find work. Tizmet slipped over the bond and tested my thoughts. Retreating from them, she made no comment, but I felt her curl tighter about her eggs.

Rafe would be welcomed in Regent. He knew it. He wouldn't have to be a farmer or law enforcer. If the King would have him, he could work in the ranks, train soldiers. Tizmet was wild born, so there had to be others out there. If they bonded anyone in Regent, they needed someone to show them how to navigate the connection. Someone who wouldn't cram them into some pretty mold like they tried to do with me and Tizmet. I could work at Northwing with my friends. But that would mean leaving Leeds—my home. My dream. I heaved a shuddering sigh as tears slipped from my eyes.

Rafe made it clear he wouldn't choose to go. I knew in my heart Tizmet would come, though only because our bond wouldn't tolerate great distance. Blain and Dane simply wanted to be where there was action, and Jamlin seemed content to follow Rafe. Tegan loved the long nights as a bard, and the days spent as an enforcer. He'd probably choose to stay. But Zeph? I didn't understand his loyalty to Rafe. He might follow, leave Kila behind.

I would leave Kila behind.

Pachu.

Iana.

Brandi.

All the townsfolk that I had grown to know and love. The people I interacted with and developed relationships with, knowing I wanted to settle here. Leaving Leeds would be no easier than it was when I was banished from Regent.

I rolled to my side, curling around the pardon. Nothing about this situation was easy or pretty. No one could make this choice for me. And no one could tell me how to get Luther and Rafe to tolerate each other.

A sob shook me as I closed my eyes and cried. Tizmet reached over the bond, offering no words, but embraced my mind with a blanket of peace. She let me cry, let me wail and rage at the unfairness of it all, until I drifted into a restful sleep.

I woke at sunset, wiping the crust from my eyes. The sound of boots against stone made me pick my head up and turn to the cottage door. Rafe entered with the burnt stew in hand. He scanned my body, the over-proofed dough at the table, then the pardon clutched in my fist. After a deep breath, he kicked off his boots, joining me on the bed. As he settled in, He tucked me against his strong chest without a word.

He didn't have any words to offer.

Chapter 26

Late spring melded to early summer. We buried ourselves in our work. Rafe started on a fence made of felled timbers, not for his stallion, but for a future milk cow. My garden and foraging kept me busy. I found wildflowers on my treks through the woods and brought them back to plant under the window and around my little garden.

A shadow loomed in the recesses of my mind. I might not be staying here. This might not be our forever home. But I was determined to ignore it. My thoughts would drift to the idea of returning, and every time they did, I reined them in and buried them.

Summer Solstice rapidly approached, and with Tizmet's permission, I invited the Tennan to watch her eggs hatch.

Hatching Day was a holiday of festivals in Regent. Common folk were allowed on the King's grounds in Northwing and Southwing to celebrate the new generation of Dragon Kind. Even cities like King's Wall celebrated regardless of there being no eggs in their city.

I planned my Summer Solstice with care, prepping plenty of food and baked small berry-filled hand-pies sweetened with a sprinkling of sugar.

That morning, I woke as Tizmet hummed across the bond, full of wonder and anticipation. *'They're ready.'*

"It's happening," I whispered, rolling to face Rafe.

He grumbled, pulling me tighter against him. "'Bout time."

"Come on!"

I pushed away from him and threw off the blanket. He was slow to rise, but as Tizmet urged me to hurry, I rushed him.

He helped pack the food and took care of the few chores we had on the homestead. We readied his stallion, who snorted and pranced, feeling our excitement.

Well, *my* excitement, really. Rafe simply grunted and eyed me with distaste when he caught me grinning like a fool.

By the time the sun rose, we were headed her way. I practically bounced in the saddle, and Rafe cursed, grabbing my waist. I giggled and snuggled against him, turning to peer over my shoulder to see him. He took that opportunity to seize my mouth in a kiss.

"Thrice curse you, woman," he groaned, breaking it off.

I snickered and returned my attention to the path. "You started it," I said with an innocent shrug.

"I'll end it too."

"I am *not* missing this hatching."

He chuckled in my ear and pulled me back against him.

When we arrived, we tied the stallion further out, unable to get his bulk through the thicket. It was close to midday when we broke through the overgrown clearing near Tizmet's nest.

'They will hatch soon.' She raised her head, peering at us from atop the boulder.

Rafe grunted behind me as he plowed through the intertwined bushes. I squealed with excitement and ran through the waist-high grass. Tizmet trilled in encouragement, and I threw myself at the giant stone ledge to get to her. It had been weeks since I last visited, and at the time, every egg was in good health.

'They are well,' she assured.

As I climbed, strong hands gripped my arse and shoved me. I laughed breathlessly as I scrambled to the top, hauling myself up.

Tizmet stretched toward Rafe and hissed protectively.

'It's not like he's going to interfere.' I crawled over and pressed myself against her blazing hot scales.

'This is not his affair.' She nudged me closer to her side.

I mentally shrugged, unbothered, as my eyes danced over the gleaming eggs. I was in awe once again at the sheer number that lay before me. If Northwing had this clutch, there would be a massive surge in Dragon Kind. Regent would have nothing to fear if they had these dragonlings.

Tizmet snorted, craned her head and flicked out her tongue. *'They are free.'* She clicked in the back of her throat, baring her teeth.

I smiled at her encouragement to her unborn. My gaze snagged on the abnormal one that caused all the trouble when she laid. *'The black is well?'*

'It is.' She nosed the egg in question.

The darkness of its shell hadn't dulled in the slightest throughout the seasons. It was still as dark as ever, with white speckles spread over its surface like stars in the night sky. I wrapped my arms around my legs, settling in to wait.

It wasn't long before my friends crept into the clearing. I smiled, hearing Jam and Tegan's hushed voices. Rafe rumbled at something said, and Blain commented—resulting in Tegan's laugh.

Tizmet trilled again, snaking her head over her eggs. *'They come.'*

Her excitement rolled over the bond. I placed a hand on her hide, smiling as she twitched beneath my touch. She had never seen her own hatch. She always lost them to the Shadows. The vile creatures stole every single one for their horrible magic. She flicked her tongue out, testing the air, and kneaded her claws into the stone, crumbling it to gravel.

I witnessed fresh hatchlings plenty of times, but it dawned on me that she hadn't. She never saw the small egg-tooth that helped them crack their shells, or how they emerged damp with fluid, or how their wings were thin and fragile until they hardened in the sun. She knew this because of base instinct, and scouring my memories, but in all her long dragon life, she had never *seen* it.

My awareness slipped over to hers, offering assurance and joining in her anticipation. Her bright eye flashed to mine in appreciation before turning back to the clutch.

Less than a half-chime later, the first pipped.

A small pop heralded its arrival, and Tizmet's head snapped into the air. She dipped her chin, and her eyes bounced over each egg, seeking the one that cracked. I muffled my laughter at her movements. She was often more level-headed, but right now I had more experience.

I pushed her attention to the bright green and blue that trembled. She dropped her head like a stone, putting her eye up to the egg. I couldn't hold in my giggle as she thrust herself to her feet and twisted this way and that to find the break.

When another crack sounded, she froze, still as a statue, eyes locked, as if a single blink would make her miss it.

With a loud *pop*, the shell broke free. The top wobbled and settled askew. Silence reigned, Tizmet not even daring to breathe, and my friends had quieted realizing it was finally happening.

There was a muffled coo from inside, and tears pricked my eyes as Tizmet gave a confused and nervous keen in response. The call came again, growing in intensity. The top of the egg shifted, rocking with the hatchling's movement. There was a squeal, and the tiniest blue face lifted above the rim. Vivid green irises, the color of grassy knolls in Regent. It flicked out its tongue, tasting the air, as its curious gaze landed on me.

"Oh no, little one," I whispered. "You're free."

The hatchling squealed, snapping its jaw together as if it objected to my comment. It shifted, tiny paws reaching to grip the edge of the shell. Tizmet's head blocked my view as she moved in closer to examine the newcomer. I blinked away tears as she made quiet clicks and coos, talking to the dragonling in her own way. Part of my heart twisted in pain, knowing I wouldn't share that connection, knowing my womb was still empty.

Tizmet sniffed, and without turning to face me, swept aside my sadness, flooding me with satisfaction, accomplishment and love. She brushed away my sorrow and filled me with her own joy. Pulling her head back, she nuzzled the hatchling and sent its egg rolling. I laughed as it cried out in complaint and broke free of the remaining shell. It let out an outraged cry and floundered on the ground, slapping its wet wings against the stone. I cringed, not wanting to interfere, but worried over it tearing.

Tizmet was lost to the experience as yet another cracked. She whipped her head back over the clutch, searching for the next to hatch.

The little blue with eyes like emeralds waddled over to me on unsteady legs. The green orbs danced and flashed over everything, flaring with shadows and narrowing at the light. There wasn't anything in that innocent gaze that indicated it needed—or even wanted to be bonded.

Another crack sounded and Tizmet let out an anxious keen, trying to keep her eyes on both eggs that were now hatching.

The damp dragonling finally reached my lap and collapsed against me, exhausted.

"Tearing out of an egg is hard work, eh?" I murmured.

It huffed in agreement, eyelids drifting closed. I traced my fingertips down the length of its body, marveling at how small it was. Its wings were as long as my arms, and its little legs as long as mine below the knee. Its head was a bit smaller than my own, with tiny horn buds peeking out of the crown. My fingers slid down its tail, and it gurgled in pleasure.

I couldn't help but wonder if this is what it would've felt like to have bonded with a dragonling. My life would have been so different if I had.

At its snout, I fingered the small, sharp growth that protruded from the scales. It flared its nostrils, taking in my scent, but was too tired to open its eyes.

I reveled in this moment. Tizmet's instincts crowded our bond, and I had some sense that I had something to do with this. I knew it was a lie. I had nothing to do with bringing this little one into the world, but still... I would allow myself to feel some satisfaction.

More and more dragonlings hatched, causing Tizmet to both bloom with pride, and stress with anxiety. There were too many to watch, too many to study. She wanted to soak up this moment, to learn about what she and Flinor had made.

I chuckled at her frazzled nerves. '*Independent critters, aren't they?*'

She assumed once they hatched, they would wander off and be on their own. Yet, as each one emerged, they stayed close. They either ended up with me, perhaps sensing my bond with their mother, or in a growing sleepy heap at Tizmet's feet.

She huffed and cooed in response and nuzzled the dwindling pile of eggs.

The black rolled free, a crack splitting down its length. I jerked upright, nudging a reddish-purple hatchling off my belly. This one, I wanted to see.

It trembled, and I frowned, trying to place what was off. It shook and wobbled as all the others had, but this seemed disoriented, jagged and rough. I tilted my head as unease spiraled through me. It didn't rock and sway—it jerked and pivoted with unnatural force.

Tizmet bared her teeth at me in irritation, and I gripped my emotions tight, preventing them from spilling over the bond. She assured me this egg was well, but something was wrong. It lurched one way, then without completing its rock, it rebounded and lurched in another direction.

Was the dragonling inside too long, deformed? Was it mad and unable to think properly?

I kept those thoughts tucked away from Tizmet as she flicked her tongue out. Her fiery eyes were locked on the egg as it spun, then careened over the stone surface.

Dread settled like a rock in my gut. That wasn't the movement of a dragonling trying to escape.

Fear spiked through me as it tumbled from the nest. I flailed, but the surrounding dragonlings complained about my movements. There was no way I would reach it in time.

'Tizmet!' I called, hoping to startle her out of her trance.

She watched, head tilted, as it rolled, teetering at the edge.

'Tizmet! It will die!' I shrieked, pushing dragonlings off me, struggling to stand.

A hatchling yelped, biting at my trousers when I tripped on its tail. I took a running step, frantically wondering why she hadn't stopped it.

'It will be free.'

Her words didn't register as I threw myself toward the ledge. It wobbled once, then jerked to the side–

And off the edge.

"No!" I screamed, crashing onto the stone, reaching for the egg that was no longer there. "Rafe! The egg!"

I scrambled, horror welling within as I peered below, expecting to see a shattered shell and a dead dragonling.

Instead, Blain was sprawled on the dirt, clutching the egg to his chest. Based on his position, he wouldn't have been able to catch its weight. It would have still hit at a terrible speed, but he at least broke the fall.

He groaned, muttering under his breath as he rolled to the side, staring up at me. "Drop something?"

A breathless laugh pushed past my lips as dragonlings crowded around me to peer down the stone ledge. They cooed and squealed, noticing the men who sat in the clearing, eating. They were probably more interested in the food than the men themselves.

Pop!

I gasped as the black egg cracked cleanly in half. Blain yanked his hands away and scrambled into a crouch. Two dragonlings kicked and fought free of the broken shell.

'Twins?!' I breathed in wonder.

I pulled myself further over the edge as Tizmet rested her head beside me, gazing down with satisfaction.

'They are well,' she assured me in a teasing voice, as if she had planned this all along.

The twins were small but fierce. They kicked and fought, biting and slashing their black claws at the bits of shell that dared to impede their freedom.

I frowned, squinting at the blood that trickled over their dark scales.

'They were fighting each other inside,' I mused. *'That's why it was lurching the way it was.'*

'Those two are...' Tizmet paused, searching for the right word.

"Fighters," I whispered.

She tilted her head as the hatchlings shook off the remnants of the shell. When they caught each other's eyes, they made snarling, gurgling sounds. Their undersides were iridescent and dark, showing colors of purple and green. Perhaps it was a play on the light, or were their bellies truly a different color from their black scales?

Tizmet let out a low croon, and their little heads snapped in our direction. Their snarls softened as they squinted their silver eyes, pupils narrowed to slits. The only difference between the two was their horn buds.

The one with shorter buds sneezed, then recoiled with the force of it. It yelped as it staggered, then flapped its wings as if offended by the involuntary action. I watched in wonder as it turned its head, noticing Blain for the first time.

Blain took a crouching step back from it, holding his hands up.

"Oh, no," he called as it crooned to him. "Not going to happen, little one."

He retreated from the dragonling as it tried to take wobbling steps toward him.

"No, you see, we have enough adventure between us. We don't need any more." Blain rose and offered me a quick salute.

I grinned down at him, laughing outright as he spun on his heel and marched back to the others.

"Dane, we're leaving," he said, stealing a piece of bread out of Jam's hand as he passed.

Dane stared at the little black hatchling with his mouth hanging open mid-chew. His berry pie dripped filling onto his lap. I smiled so big, my cheeks ached. Blain shouted for him again, practically running for the cover of the thicket. Dane shook himself, frowning as he looked back at his pie.

"I'll take that," Tegan said, snatching the pastry, then sank his teeth into the crust.

With a staggering breath, Dane pushed himself to his feet, glaring at his trousers, which were now covered in syrupy berries. He cast one more longing look at the black hatchling. As if sensing his reluctance, it keened, opening its mouth full of sharp, needle-like fangs.

"*Dane!*"

He heaved an irritated sigh and whirled to storm into the thicket after his brother.

'They can run, but they can't hide,' Tizmet hummed in dragon laughter.

It wasn't long before all the dragonlings hatched, leaving a mess of eggshells and bits behind. The forty-one hatchlings scrambled down the stone ledge, searching for food. Tizmet rose with instinct and took flight, causing the little ones to both scatter and huddle together. They watched her rise into the sky with wide eyes. A lovely pale red dragonling even stretched out her own wings, as if she wanted to take flight as well.

Tizmet flew low over the trees, hunting. Rafe glared at the beasts that nipped at his boots and crowded his legs as he helped me down, but I caught him smiling as two fought over a leaf. He offered me a slice of bread with a chunk of hard cheese, and I took it gratefully, watching the riot of dragonlings cavort around the clearing.

"Leeds is in trouble." Tegan laughed as a deep bronze dragonling sniffed at his hand, seeking more food. "I'm sure bread isn't part of your diet."

He scolded the little one, hiding his hands under his legs. The creature cooed, shoving its face between Tegan's thighs, drawing a yelp from the man. He scrambled back in panic, his laughter high and tight as the tiny beast laid down and happily gnawed on the bread Tegan had tried to hide.

"Either in trouble," Jam began, his attention locked on a set of sapphire eyes a breath from his face, "or setting up to be the next great kingdom."

The deep blue dragonling chirped as if it agreed with that sentiment. It tilted its reptilian head before stumbling into Jam's lap, trying to maw his chin. Jamlin laughed, pushing the beast away.

Rafe grunted and tried to shake a large red hatchling off his boot. The creature growled and attacked with renewed vigor. He kicked a little harder, and the creature hissed, making a grab at his calf, wicked sharp talons flashing in the light. He twisted in time to avoid it.

"Trouble, I'd wager," he rumbled.

A scaled head bumped my hand, rubbing its horn buds against my palm. I turned to the little blue hatchling with green eyes—the first to hatch. It chirped, nuzzling me again.

"It's amazing." I dropped into a crouch beside it. It purred in pleasure as I went on, "They're not forced into the Bond of Dragon Kind, and yet they are behaving better than the Wild Ones hatched at Northwing."

"What makes you think they're not bound by the Treaty?" Jamlin asked, looking up from wrestling with the blue. "You think only those in Regent are blood-bonded to men?"

I pressed my lips together in thought, looking back at the bright green eyes that searched my face with far more intelligence than any other animal. "They say all dragons hatched in Regent are."

"And yet it's failing," Tegan added, dancing away from the gold that hunted him like he was made of food—or was food. "I would wager that the magic was in the blood of the dragons."

"Aye," Jamlin agreed, settling to cuddle the blue, as if it was a dog. "And with each generation, it gets weaker. Say perhaps, when they first made the Treaty, not all dragons agreed–"

"Every beast hatched from that bloodline would weaken the Treaty with every generation," I murmured.

"You've seen your dragon maim men. You've thought about this before," Rafe guessed, shooing off a deep violet that joined the red in attacking his boots.

"In passing, aye." The blue in front of me pushed me off my feet and sent me sprawling. "What does that mean for the future of Dragon Kind?" I asked no one in particular.

"Fate will have her way," Tegan said.

Tizmet flew low overhead, and I squinted at the sun as her mottled stone-colored belly passed by. She dropped a giant bog lizard into the clearing, and Tegan laughed in horror. Rafe yanked me up off the ground.

Dragonlings galloped to the carcass, trampling and scoring each other's hides without thought. They squealed and snapped, tearing off chunks of flesh, hissing around their mouthfuls, sending blood splattering.

"Vicious creatures," Rafe grunted.

"They don't have a Rider to temper their urges," I said.

Tizmet wheeled, then dropped another. The hatchlings split and charged the thrashing creature with relish. I grimaced at the tenacity with which the beasts attacked it. Their needle-like teeth shredded the thick hide like butter. Blood and flesh splattered as the dragonlings quite literally *tore* into their meal.

The same dragonlings we had just been cuddling.

I glanced back at Jam, noting his sickly pallor. He stared at me, eyes wide, clearly thinking the same thing I was. He flashed me a smile that showed too many teeth, then scrambled to his feet.

Tizmet settled on her nest, sighing happily as she watched her young. She would feed them only when they needed it. She had already begun teaching them to hunt by bringing them a living bog lizard large enough to swallow a hatchling whole. Soon, they would be hunting and killing on their own, roaming the wilds of the marsh and whatever lay beyond.

It was a new dawn for Dragon Kind...

Or perhaps an end.

Chapter 27

Darkness fell, and with it came the vicious stinging bugs. Jamlin and Tegan headed back to the town proper, content with riding through the night. Rafe had to pull me loose from the mess of dragonlings that collapsed on me, gorged and sleepy. Tizmet huffed in response, reaching out to slide against the bond in parting. I sighed happily as Rafe tucked me against his chest and lulled my head to look at the pile of sleeping hatchlings she was curled around.

We returned to the cottage in the dead of night, and I tried to help him put his stallion to rest, but he shooed me into the cottage. I stumbled and fought with my clothes, barely managing to strip before falling to the bed and drifting off into a blissful sleep.

The following days, I rose early to do my chores, then walked to Tizmet's nest. After arriving scratched to bits and exhausted, Tizmet took to flying me to and from. While I was thankful, it worried me, not only because I had the hardest time keeping my seat without a saddle, but because of Luther. He still had men out searching for the eggs. If they spotted her in the sky, they could track her back.

When a fortnight passed, the dragonlings braved the thicket. To earn their next meal, Tizmet would drop injured prey outside the clearing. They had to find and dispatch it before they ate.

How she raised her brood was so different from the way hatchlings grew up at Northwing. There, they were cared for—fed and loved since hatching. Between Tizmet and me, these dragonlings were well loved, but she was a mother who pushed her young. With no one to teach her, and with no prior experience, she relied on base instincts alone. She wanted them to be independent, able to hunt on their own. She was doing her best.

They wouldn't fly for quite some time. They had to grow into wings that were comically large for their bodies, then learn to coordinate their breathing and movements. I had shared Tizmet's consciousness as she flew, and it was something I dared not repeat. So many things her body did, it did by instinct. While it looked simple, flying took so much coordination—it was baffling.

As the days passed, the dragonlings ventured further and further. Some disappeared, and didn't return. When I brought it up to Tizmet, she huffed, unconcerned, claiming they were large enough to fend for themselves. I had to rein in my emotions, feeling as though they were naught but hatchlings and needed protection. I had to let her be the judge. She was the dragon, after all. She knew best.

It had been too long since I visited Leeds, and decided to ride in with Rafe. I wore my green dress with thin breeches underneath to keep the bugs at bay. The skirts were hiked high around my thighs as I rode behind him. He grumbled that he should spend the day with me, but I had errands to run, and he had coin to earn. When we reached town, it was midday, and as we stabled his stallion, Rothfuss greeted us.

"Avyanna." He dipped his head. "It's good to see you. Visiting Iana?"

"I have a few errands. And a visit is past due." I offered him a smile, but noted the dark circles under his eyes. Apparently, he hadn't been sleeping well.

"I would ask that you take Blaer with you," he said.

When I eyed Rafe expectantly, he scowled as he pulled the saddle off his stallion. I thought that the situation with Luther had died down. The townsfolk should have settled by now.

"Could Dane accompany me?"

He rested his hand on his pommel. "I'm afraid not." His fingers pinched the bridge of his nose and he glanced at Rafe before bringing his tired gaze back to me. "Best that my man be seen with you."

"Dane's not yours?" Part of me felt guilty for pushing, but it annoyed me to no end that I needed a tail simply walking through town.

"Rafe's men are a different breed of enforcer. Please, Avyanna. I would be grateful."

With a sigh, I walked over and patted his shoulder. "I apologize for putting you in a difficult position. I know you're trying, Rothfuss," I said, hoping to put him at ease. "Blaer can meet me here."

"Have him meet her at the tavern," Rafe growled, placing his calloused hand on mine to lead me away.

I looped my arm through his. "I could have waited."

"It's a waste of time." His frown pulled his scar tight.

"Rothfuss is being a peacemaker," I whispered. "I'm sure it isn't easy—"

"He's a lawkeeper—an enforcer when he chooses."

"Luther is bound to his quarters. There's nothing to worry about."

"Aye, and he owns the town." He nodded along sarcastically. "Not a thing to worry about."

I heaved a weary breath, knowing it was a waste to convince him otherwise.

As we strode up to the tavern, Kila called out. I squinted, seeing her rushing down the path, her basket swaying at her side and her skirts hiked in her haste. As she neared, relief slackened her shoulders, and she offered Rafe a nervous smile.

"It's good to see you! Are you headed somewhere?"

"I was about to wait at the tavern. Rothfuss has a man–"

"Oh, but I could show you a new quilt I'm sewing!" she blurted, cutting me off. "I'm sure we could make it to my house and back by the time Rothfuss' man made it here."

I frowned and tilted my head at her words. Kila didn't sew. Well, she sewed about as much as any girl, but she hated it. She would do her mending, but would never willingly take on something like a quilt. That would be torture.

"Is this about what we discussed last visit?"

I formed my words with care, ignoring the way Rafe's feet shifted. He read my hesitation too well.

Kila's smile faltered for a moment before evolving into a false grin. "Oh, aye. Absolutely. Nothing your dear Rafe would be interested in." Her tone pitched high, and a blush crept up her cheeks.

Rafe's muscle clenched beneath my hands. He didn't like her warning him off. It felt wrong—*she* felt wrong.

"Let's go see a quilt." His voice lowered with caution.

"Oh, you know—it's not for men's eyes." Kila rocked back on her heel, glancing about the street. "It's just a quilt after all. Nothing anyone would be interested in. I just need Avyanna to... to look at some stitching!"

I scoffed. "You're a terrible liar."

Her features widened with panic, and she clutched her basket to her chest.

I pulled Rafe down for a chaste kiss and tugged his ear down to my lips. "It's about Zeph."

He straightened to his full height, suspicion curling his lip. When he shook his head at her womanly concerns, his hand found my waist and jostled my bandit breaker in warning.

"Eyes open."

"Aye."

He sucked in a deep breath and rolled his eye at Kila. "Be back here within a half-chime or I'll come looking for you, girl."

Blood rushed from her face as she offered a trembling smile. She reached blindly for my hand, not taking her eyes off him until he turned and stalked off.

"Sun's blessing be upon you, Avyanna!" She practically sobbed as she pulled me down the street.

I laughed, a light and hollow sound, glancing around to make sure we weren't being followed. Kila tugged me between buildings and into a shaded alley cramped with crates and baskets of waste and refuse.

"We have to go to my house!"

She panted, peering down the way before taking off at a run. Her basket flailed side to side as she dragged me along.

I had never been there. She lived with her old, bed-ridden father. Her mother passed when she was young and she cared for him as best she could. They lived on the easternmost edge of Leeds, probably one of the farthest homes out of the town proper. It would take a spell of running to get to it and back in time.

"Does it have to do with Zeph?"

"Marsh fog, no!"

She cursed, then yanked me through another busy road and down another alley. Her brown hair flew behind her like a banner as she hurried along. I fought the unease that slithered through me and cast a glance over my shoulder.

Still no tails.

She weaved between the crowds with ease. We jumped over a pile of discarded waste, and sped past a mangy cat, drawing a hiss of irritation. I skidded to a stop, yanked my hand free from hers. She gasped and stumbled forward, whirling on me in terror.

"What is this about? Is it Luther?"

I hated having to ask, but I would be foolish not to. It wouldn't be beyond him to use her to get to me.

"Avyanna, no! How could you think that?!" She doubled-over, gasping for breath.

Something crashed behind us, and I spun, narrowing my eyes on the cat that knocked over a crate of rotten vegetables. I studied the alley for a few more breaths before turning back to her.

"I need to know," I muttered.

She frowned and hurried to my side, then pressed her lips to my ear. "Dragon," she whispered.

I recoiled. "Tizmet?"

Instinctively, I reached across the bond. She was resting in her nest, watching the few hatchlings that still lingered.

"No." She shook her head and worried her lip. "Come with me?" Her warm brown eyes were pleading, as if she was afraid I would say no and leave.

My hand found hers again. If this had to do with a dragon, I needed to know about it.

When we arrived, the chime of bells signaled our time to get back to the tavern was up. Rafe would come after me.

She dragged me round to the backside of her house where a small barn leaned at a precarious angle, clearly in a need of major repairs. It sported a massive hole in the roof, and plenty of boards along the wall were broken and askew.

She stopped, holding her side as she heaved for breath. I was in a similar state, coughing and panting. A sharp trill sounded, coming from inside. Kila's wide, fearful eyes met mine.

No.

She responded with a resolved nod, then lifted the latch on the barn door.

A scaled creature half the size of a cow charged out, flapping its bronze wings. Kila shrieked, throwing her hands up to cover her face. The dragonling coiled around her legs, peering up at her with eyes that caught the sun through the clouds. Her chest heaved with panicked breaths as she trembled.

'It bonded Kila?' I asked Tizmet.

The small dragon trilled and butted its head against her leg, causing her to stumble.

"Can you make it go away?!" she cried, peeking at me from between her fingers.

Tizmet stretched her consciousness across the bond and shared my vision. *'It has* chosen *her.'* She crowded my mind, brimming with curiosity.

I dropped into a crouch and held out my hand. It crooned and approached me fearlessly, butting its head against my palm. I traced its blazing scales as it walked around me like a cat would. It rubbed against my body, nearly pushing me over with its enthusiasm.

"It appeared out of nowhere! I swear. I came out to put Bessie in for the night and—oh, sun above! Bessie was—she was–"

I frowned, and the dragonling flopped down at my feet, stretching out in the midday sun. Its long gold talons caught the light, revealing dark red crust in the crevices, and I knew exactly what happened to Kila's milk cow.

"And when it saw me—oh stars beneath, Avyanna! It had this terrible gleam in its eye—like it was going to eat me! I thought it would!"

She sobbed, pressing her hands against her mouth in an attempt to muffle her cries. She stared at the dragonling in absolute horror.

My stomach turned, this being a stark reminder that the people in Leeds were nothing like those in Regent. They had no exposure to Dragon Kind or the Treaty. To them, dragons without a Rider were monsters.

"And it charged me! I ran as fast as I could, but it wasn't enough. And now—now I can feel it." She clutched at her chest. "It was like something snapped. I felt something snap. Perhaps I should see Saudric. Maybe I've gone mad. But you—you know dragons, and–"

"Yes, I know them."

"It tried to follow me this morning. I had to get away. It kept me in the field all last night, and I was so terrified it would hurt Father, I couldn't bring it in the house. I dragged," she choked on another sob, "I dragged what was left of Bessie into the barn and somehow managed to lock it in. Oh, the cries! The cries were awful, Avyanna!"

I sighed, adjusting my dress, then settled on the ground next to the dragonling. Its ivory horns were just coming in. I rubbed the small nubs, and it purred in response. I peeked up at Kila from under my lashes.

"It's not going to hurt you," I murmured.

"It ate Bessie!" she choked out, wiping at her wet cheeks. "She was old, all bones, but the sweetest cow I've ever had."

That would be a problem. Over hunting the wild game was one thing, but if the dragonlings didn't fear people, they would kill off their livestock.

"Aye, it ate Bessie, but look at it—it's like a dog." With a light laugh, I slipped my hand under its wing to give it a gentle scratch.

"You only laugh because your dragon follows you about like an obedient pet."

'I do not,' Tizmet huffed.

"It's wild." Kila angled herself, putting me between them. "I don't know where it came from."

I rolled my eyes. "Really? You've no idea? You know as well as I that Tizmet laid last year."

I raised a challenging brow and scowled until realization finally dawned on her face. Her mouth fell open, and she looked at the dragonling with new eyes.

"It's one of Tizmet's?!"

"Aye." My thigh complained under the weight as the tiny beast shifted to rest its head in my lap. "This one has a taste for bread, of all things. About took Tegan's manhood off when he tried to hide a slice between his legs."

A tentative smile worked the edge of her lip. She braved a small step closer. It was amazing what changed a person's perception. Even when I first met Tizmet, we thought she might be a Hunter, a puppet of the enemy. Now, the men trusted her as much as they did me.

"I would wager it would be a fair bit more docile if you offered it a loaf," I added.

Tizmet scoffed with disgust. *'Bread.'*

'Oi, you made this dragonling. Don't blame me for its taste,' I shot back.

"It really won't kill me?" Kila took another step as it lifted its head to blink golden eyes at her.

I deadpanned. "If it wanted to eat you, it would have done so last night."

"I've just never seen one so little," she murmured. Her features softened as the worried crease eased from her brow. She crept to my side like it would lurch and attack any second.

"Well, considering Tizmet is the only dragon you've seen..." I laughed.

She snapped a glare my way. "This is not funny. I thought I was going to die."

"I would have paid to see it. Run down by a wee babe of a dragon!"

Kila let out a mock cry, mouth dropping open. "It's not wee! Look at it!"

Its eyes trailed her hand as she waved it through the air, dilated in curiosity.

"It can't even breathe fire yet!"

Finally, she settled on the ground beside me. "Oh, and when does it develop that joyful skill?" she huffed. "Then what?"

I trailed off, knowing it was pointless to tell her this now. She wouldn't remember any of it—and it wasn't useful to her at the moment. She carefully pressed a finger to the bridge of its nose. It sniffed at her hand, remaining still as she traced the soft scales over its nostrils.

"You're bonded to it," I whispered.

Kila's warm eyes darted up to mine. "How could you be sure?"

"Let's see, when it caught you, was there a terrible pain and ache in your chest, followed by emotions and feelings that were not your own?"

"Something like that," she murmured. "I don't want it to eat any more cows." She pointed a finger at it as if it were a child she scolded. "No more cows, hear that?"

I laughed, tugging at its horns. "It took me and Tizmet years to develop what we have. You will grow together. Don't rush it, strengthen the bond over time. Don't force it into a mold."

Sorrow tugged at my heart, wishing I had taken my own advice when I bonded Tizmet. I learned the hard way, through struggle and pain, but she didn't have to.

I sat there with the two of them as they built a fragile trust. In a hushed voice, I explained the bond as best I could, and offered her a warning about magic. I told her not to reach for it, and to ignore its pull. There was little else I could do without a school of Masters to teach her about magic. I barely understood it myself.

When we heard hoofbeats pounding the path nearby, we hurried the dragonling into the barn, urging it to be quiet and hide. Kila wasn't ready to show off her new rank in the town, and I wasn't ready for people to search the woods with pitchforks, hunting cattle killers.

The small dragon offered one last trill before it curled up beside a heap of bloody bones—all that remained of Bessie. We managed to get the barn door shut and locked as Rafe and Blaer rode into sight.

We plastered bright smiles to our cheeks and linked our arms together, striding toward them. Rafe looked me up and down, catching the dirt on my dress and my disheveled hair from the run.

"A quilt?" he barked, raising his eyebrow.

"Aye, a glorious work of art," I said with a firm nod.

Kila choked next to me, and I nudged her with my elbow in warning. I glanced her way, and she winked.

"A golden quilt," she agreed.

I returned to the main square, riding in the saddle behind Rafe. It was a much faster trek, moving at a trot on horseback. Kila walked back, and I sincerely hoped that her dragonling would be happy to sleep the day away in the barn. It would be hot, but dragons liked the heat as long as they had fresh water.

Out of everyone who could have bonded, I was secretly relieved it was Kila. She was sweet and fair. She had a fiery streak that would match her dragon, but a level head—most of the time.

What did this mean for Leeds? Rafe and I had many conversations on the matter. If the dragonlings were forming bonds, they could quickly make Leeds a force to be rivaled with. What would King Aldred do once he learned dragons roamed here? That was a worry for another time. Regent was already on the brink of losing the war. Surely, claiming Dragon Kind outside their borders wouldn't be a top priority.

Rafe released me into Blaer's care once we reached the main street. Blaer was a big man, heavyset and tall. He was imposing, and though his straw hat was practical, it took away from his air of menace. Buried under his rough exterior, he was the sweetest.

When we passed by Luther's quarters, I forced a smile to my face. Two of his men watched me, their gazes dark, before they slipped inside, shutting the red door behind them. We left Blaer's horse at the stables and set out on foot. I regretted that now. I didn't want Luther to cause a scene, especially when the townsfolk were still simmering.

"How is little Gwain?" I asked.

"Well as can be, Lady Avyanna. The lad is bound to be an enforcer just like his Da." Blaer's grin split his tan face, revealing a missing tooth. "He likes to spar. The other lads aren't giving him much of a fight."

"He'll have a fine arm on him, being yours."

"Aye, a good strong lad," he agreed.

I cast a sidelong glance at him, noting his hand on the hilt of his longsword. Blaer was competent with the weapon. I had seen him spar with Rothfuss a time or two, but would hate for him to actually have to call on that training.

My ears strained, listening for anything out of the ordinary as we passed Luther's shop. I flinched when I heard a door slam open, then bit my tongue when I peered over my shoulder to see Luther step out.

No. Please don't.

He leaned against the frame, gripping his cane. Glittering rings caught what sun filtered through the haze as he watched me with a sly smile, his eyes sparkling with malice.

Blaer bumped into me. "Now, where be your errands?"

I focused on the road, hating the shiver that ran down my spine. Luther wouldn't try anything in public.

Blaer wasn't Rothfuss' man simply because of his imposing form, he was sharp and observant. He understood what Luther just did and knew I was trying to ignore him.

"Off to the jeweler," I said, forcing myself to walk a bit slower.

I wasn't running from Luther, and I wouldn't let him think I was.

"Oh?" He rubbed his chin thoughtfully. "Has Rafe been making that much? Perhaps I need to ask Rothfuss for a raise."

He grinned down at me and offered his elbow. I took it gladly, not caring that it might seem improper to those prudish townsfolk. I refused to allow anyone to sully this moment.

We walked to the only jeweler shop, one that Luther had little sway over due to the E'or being so close. There were mines to the southwest that produced a fair amount of semi-precious stones. It still took a jeweler's touch to make them into anything presentable, which is why it cost more than the average townsfolk could afford.

But at least I didn't have to worry about Lyken, the jeweler, being under Luther's thumb.

When we entered, I couldn't help the smile that immediately spread over my face at all the glints and glimmers inside. Lyken's skill would have been better appreciated in a rich city. His talent to bend light with mirrors and glass knew no bounds. Walking into his shop was like walking into a crystal cave. Everywhere I turned, something else sparkled and glittered.

He greeted us from his place behind a tall counter, removing his glass spectacle. He was a middle-aged man with gray just starting to pepper his black hair. It was kept short and tidy, combed back from his face.

"What brings you in on this fine day?" he asked, his smile warm.

"Good day, Lyken." I unfastened the pouch from my belt. "I was wondering if you would consider a trade."

His white teeth gleamed with his bright grin. "A good jeweler is always up for a trade."

Blaer settled next to me, leaning against the wood. His eye danced over the bits of silver and gold that Lyken had set aside.

I dipped my chin. "And you're the very best."

"I'm flattered. Already off to a fantastic start with the barter!"

I laughed as I fished the items out of my pouch and placed them on the counter. Blaer made an interested grunt, even as Lyken's smile faded.

The jeweler squinted at the pieces, then at me. "Are these what I think they are?"

"If you think they are dragon egg shards, you would be correct."

Lyken replaced his seeing spectacle, then waited for my permission before he picked up a large piece of red shell. The colors had faded slightly over time, but I assumed with some sealing, they would regain their luster. Even in their tarnished state, they still had clear and distinct patterning. The one he held hatched a dragonling with a fierce crimson-gold sheen. The shell itself had a transparent imprint of gilded scales.

'He has already wrestled a bog lizard,' Tizmet hummed in pride.

"I take it they've hatched, then?" Blaer murmured.

"Aye."

A small shrug lifted my shoulders. It would be well known soon enough. There was no reason to hide it. Since one found Kila, it was only a matter of time before more townsfolk crossed paths with another.

"I don't know of a single jeweler that has handled dragon egg shards before," Lyken muttered, examining the piece. Sunlight caught the shell and revealed the shimmer of gold in the red.

"I've never seen the likes in Regent either," I replied.

To be honest, the idea never occurred to me until a traveling merchant showed off his preserved bird eggs. He'd hollowed them out, sealed them inside and out and sold them as trinkets.

"I've seen shell-work before, but never shards. And never dragons," Lyken said with a sharp look down his straight nose. He set the red piece down and looked at the varying sizes and colors I offered. "I would be limited as to what I can do—even if they respond well to the curing process."

"I would offer these," sifting through the small handful, I pushed most of them to the side, "in exchange for these cured and fashioned into necklaces."

I separated a goldish-bronze, a blue and two black pieces speckled with white.

"You understand what you would be giving me?" he asked.

I had always known that he was fair as a jeweler could be, but here he was, allowing me another chance to back out.

"If you manage to cure them, I would wager they would bring a fine price."

"And you only want to trade?"

"Aye. I just want these four."

"I would be a fool to deny you," Lyken huffed, bracing his hands on the counter.

I flashed my sweetest smile. "And we both know you're not a fool."

He let out a low whistle. "You drive a hard bargain, Avyanna." He chuckled. "Give me a few days. If I can cure them without shattering them or compromising the integrity of the jewelry, I will have them finished within a fortnight."

"Take your time," I assured him. "If I am not in town, you can send them back with Rafe."

"You ask a lot of me! To give that bear of a man anything fine and fragile–"

"He's more careful than you know." I laughed, securing my pouch. "Good day, Lyken."

"May the sun light your path, dear Avyanna."

When we left, Blaer snickered under his breath.

"What?" I asked, curious what caused his mirth.

"You're swaying the town to you without even noticing."

"I simply made a trade."

My lips pressed into a frown, noting three of Luther's men. They had been waiting for us to exit the shop.

"And in return, you gave Lyken, one of the richest men in Leeds, a priceless gift. You bought him."

"I didn't buy anyone," I growled, then shot a glare at Luther's men. Best they know I saw them. It was the ones I couldn't see that had me worried.

"So you say," Blaer drawled.

I took a deep breath, letting it out slowly as I continued down the street. It seemed as if I would never get away from the looming rivalry between us and Luther.

Chapter 28

True to his word, Lyken sent the finished pieces with Rafe. They were beautiful, simple and frivolous, but a cherished reminder of my first Hatching Day in Leeds. And, to my knowledge, the first hatching of the Wild Dragons, this side of the E'or.

I gave the blacks to the twins and the bronze to Tegan, who made a great deal over it. The blue I offered to Jamlin. He took the polished splinter of egg, removed a bone from his many ear piercings, and shoved it in. It gleamed bluish-green in the sunlight, like a precious gem. The others tucked theirs inside their tunics, Tegan's bound by leather, and the twins by slender silver chains.

The following days were busy. Between my daily chores on the homestead, and visiting what dragonlings remained at Tizmet's nest, I flew to Kila's before sunrise each morning—much to Rafe's complaint.

It was heartening to know she wasn't struggling with the bond. She was reserved, but didn't object to the connection like I had with Tizmet.

It helped that she was smitten by the little bronze. She named him Durum, after a type of wheat. When she first told me, I tried to hide my laughter, but Kila was unconcerned by my lack of respect. She said he reminded her of a field of wheat in high summer, golden and inviting. He preened at her flattery.

Durum, like all the others, grew at a rapid pace. Perhaps it had been too long since I'd been around hatchlings, but it seemed as if they were growing faster than those in Northwing. They had no cares in the world except to gorge themselves and sleep.

'It is their priority,' Tizmet said, sensing my thoughts as I mounted her. It was a miserable ride back and forth, but worth it to help Kila.

She sprawled out against her bonded, basking in the weak sunlight. I smiled at the two, knowing she would have to announce her bond soon. She made herself scarce around town. The only thing that kept the beast in the barn during the day was her pleading. A mere wooden door couldn't hold a dragonling the size of a small cow.

'Perhaps we ask too much of the hatchlings at Northwing,' I mused, settling against her scaled neck.

'We?' Tizmet craned her head to study me with one bright red-orange eye.

I frowned, realizing my choice of words, then offered her a mental shrug.

'You have considered returning,' she rumbled as she took flight.

Kila giggled and rolled into Durum's side. He lifted a wing to shelter her from the dust Tizmet kicked up. He chirped and snapped his teeth as she rose in the air.

'I would be a terrible friend if I didn't consider *it.'* Familiar guilt rose within, turning my stomach sour.

A small strand of worry wormed its way over the bond. *'You have chosen?'* she asked.

'You're concerned.'

I leaned forward, pressing my cheek against her warm scales as she coasted through the dreary skies. She pumped her wings hard, pulling above the stench of the bog, banking north so that I might see the sunrise.

'I am not worried,' she huffed, offended. *'I am... sad for you.'*

'Sad?'

'I have felt you, Avyanna. You are mine.' Her wings pumped harder. *'You have chosen Leeds, and it is choosing you. You've grown roots like a tree. They are not yet deep, but given time could grow as the oak that will never be moved.'*

I closed my eyes against the rising sun and the fires it lit in the clouds.

'You could be a queen here,' Tizmet murmured. *'They would have you. A Dragon Queen to rule the Eastern E'or. Who would stand against you?'*

'Luther,' I scoffed, brushing off her words.

I had no such aspirations, and she knew it. She was simply telling me I could, and there was unbridled power in knowing it was possible.

'I will eat him.'

'You cannot eat him!'

I smiled, even as torment twisted my heart. Turning my forehead back to her scales, I breathed in her musky scent.

'I will do what I must.' She dipped low to skim the fog's surface. *'Just as you will do what you must.'*

Her concern trickled over once more as she flowed into my mind and smothered me with her presence. She swept aside my anxiety and fear, replacing it with peace and comfort—like a mother would for her children.

Despite her efforts, I clung to that worry. Our bond couldn't handle the vast distance apart, but I didn't want that to be the reason she'd follow.

'You would leave if I chose?' I asked.

'Just as your mate said.' Her tone held mild disgust that she would ever stoop so low as to repeat his words. *'You are my home. I will go where you go. You are mine.'*

She offered one more blanket of comfort to my mind, then dove through the fog. I clenched my jaw, unable to prevent the whine that slipped out of my mouth. Wind whipped at my hair, and though it was tucked into braids, it still stung my face with the force of her gale.

My fingernails dug into her scales, and my legs squeezed her neck with everything I had. Her amused laughter bubbled through her in the form of a growling cough as she evened out to land. With a few slowing flaps of her wings, she lighted upon the ground. Rafe's stallion snorted at her antics, clearly not impressed.

'A bit of warning would've been nice,' I barked, trembling as I slid down her shoulder.

'It wouldn't be nearly as fun.'

She craned her head around to block my path. She inhaled deeply, drawing my scent in, then shoved her nose into my chest. I grabbed her face to steady myself as she gazed at me with eyes the color of a wildfire.

'Be safe, little one,' she rumbled.

"Vy." Rafe grunted a greeting as he mounted his horse a safe distance away.

Tizmet lifted her head and hissed. When his frown melted into a glower of annoyance, I flashed him an innocent smile.

"I'm shaking in my boots," he drawled as I walked toward him.

She lunged, claws sinking into the dirt, teeth bared as she let out a deafening roar. The force of her objection shook her massive body and had Rafe's stallion rearing in a panic.

'Tizmet!'

He grappled for the reins, keeping his seat, and wheeled his stallion in a tight circle. The horse neighed sharply and rolled its eyes as it pranced in place, calming down a fraction.

Tizmet huffed, snapping her jaws together as she lorded above them. *'I bet he's shaking now.'*

'And scared ten years off his horse's life!' I accused.

'Prey.' She stretched out to lie down in the field. *'When he has served his purpose, I will eat him too.'*

Rafe spoke in a calm, low tone to his horse. As I neared, I realized he was murmuring every curse I knew, and then some. I blushed at some of his words, and when the stallion finally stilled, his eye flashed to meet my gaze.

"Blasted dragon," he growled, then offered me a hand up.

I settled into the saddle in front of him. "You taunted her."

Rafe grunted in response, then clicked his tongue, urging the stallion on. He responded quickly, more than eager to get away from the terrifying beast.

I glanced over my shoulder and I swore she was smiling in her own dragon way as we rode down the path.

When we arrived, I was thankful to dismount. I loved being close to Rafe, but my backside was aching after all the morning flights on dragonback, followed by long rides on the saddle.

"Off to see the jeweler?" he asked, storing the horse's tack.

"Aye, some business there, and I have some flowers for Saudric."

"Trying to woo him?" The familiar voice had me pressing my lips together.

Rothfuss entered the stables with Luther's man, Izaak.

"Good that you're both here." Rothfuss dipped his head in greeting. "I'd like to settle things between you both and Luther."

Rafe bristled. "You can settle your–"

I touched his arm, cutting him off. "Aye, give us a minute."

"We'll wait outside for you, then." Rothfuss glanced between us, then the two took their leave.

Rafe shrugged off my hand, busying himself with the tack.

"We need to hear him out, Rafe. We can't keep this up."

"Aye, we actually can, Vy." he grunted. "Keeping the blasted whoreson locked up is working out quite well."

"You know what I mean."

He stopped so close that his chest pressed against mine. Hatred swirled in the depths of his gaze as he slipped a large hand behind my neck to cradle my head.

"I'm going to kill him." He stated those words with such deathly calm, as if they were nothing more than a passing comment on the weather.

I closed my eyes as my heart thumped angrily in my chest. It objected to the fact that my home was falling apart around me. Every time I felt like things were righting themselves, something else crumbled.

If I was putting down roots as Tizmet said, they were spindly and weak, spreading out just under the surface in Leeds, ready to be torn out with the slightest breeze or upset.

"I know."

I pressed my cheek into his palm. His thumb traced over my scar before he leaned in, giving my temple a chaste kiss.

"Then it's off to the viper's den," he muttered, then turned away.

I had a moment to mourn the loss of his warmth and security before he wrapped an arm around my waist and guided me out of the stables.

Rothfuss frowned, worrying a piece of chaff between his teeth. Izaak's lopsided grin revealed a missing front tooth—no doubt lost in a fight with an enforcer.

"Good then?" Rothfuss' sharp eyes darted between us.

Rafe glared in response. Apparently, Rothfuss adapted to his silent communication because he started off down the street. When Izaak attempted to fall in behind us, Rafe drew his sword. The man rushed his steps, learning to stay out of his blind spot.

As we neared Luther's, I held in a groan. People were already congregating, unabashedly waiting for a show. Rafe's hand tightened once against my side, letting me know he saw them too.

Jamlin and Tegan pulled themselves to the front of the crowd, hands resting easy on their blades. Jam gave us a curt nod, the familiar smile absent from his face. A quick glance revealed Blain across the road, leaning against a wall, and Dane was tucked in an alley. He fingered the fletching of an arrow before disappearing into the shadows.

A few men trickled out of Luther's shop before Luther sauntered out. Boots clicked along the wooden platform as they spread out to flank him. My heart twisted in hatred as he ignored Rothfuss and settled his gaze on me and Rafe. A small, cruel smile lifted the corners of his mouth as he walked to the edge of the platform, cane tapping as he went.

"Good of you to come, Rafe and Avyanna." His voice rang out as more people crowded the street.

We stopped paces away. Rothfuss' hold on his pommel tensed as he eyed the bystanders, as if picking out his men. If this was going to be the upsetting of Leeds, he was prepared to uphold the law.

"Thank you for bringing them, Rothfuss," Luther said in dismissal, as if that would send the lawkeeper away. "I have had time to think about my actions and have come up short."

He waved a hand, and one of his goons pulled up a chair. "You see, I feel somewhat responsible for the actions of my men, and the attempt to set fire to your little house."

Gasps peppered the crowd, as if the townsfolk hadn't already known.

"In reparations, I offer ten laying hens."

Tegan choked, and I fought the urge to glare at the man.

"However, I simply visited because Avyanna here owes me a favor. But when I called upon it, she refused." When he held out his palm, Bodrin limped forward and handed him a rolled parchment. He waved the contract in the air, as if it proved his innocence.

"Lawkeeper," he spoke in a way that one might summon their dog, "tell me. Isn't there a punishment for those who don't keep their contracts?"

"It would have to be specified in the contract." Rothfuss answered over the murmuring crowd.

Luther was trying to drag my name through the mud with the whole town here to witness.

"Why, of course. Be a dear and check this over, would you, Rothfuss?"

Luther's vile gaze settled on us as Rothfuss took reluctant steps to retrieve the parchment. He unrolled it and swept the lines, taking in each word.

I shook my head in defense. "What you asked of me isn't mine to give."

"Tsk tsk, Avyanna. It *is* within your power. What you do with your moral compass is between you and what lies beyond the Veil. The contract explicitly stated that you were obligated to fulfill any favor within your physical capabilities." Luther offered a sympathetic shrug, all the while he held my gaze with those vicious eyes.

"And if you asked me to rob Iana?" I gestured over the multitude, including them. "Would you expect me to?"

"It is not what I expect, but what you *promised*. Now, Rothfuss, did I forget to add penalties to the contract being broken?"

"The land," Rothfuss muttered under his breath. He lowered the parchment, glancing back at me and Rafe.

"Oh, is that all?" Luther pressed.

"And the cottage."

At the accusations and penalties, the crowd erupted into a full-fledged cacophony of shouts and jeers. Rafe took a menacing step forward, and I raced to block his way, facing Luther myself. I had a plan, a terrible plan, and I hated the very idea of it, but it might work.

"What is it you want?!" I shouted, silencing the rabble.

Luther tapped a ringed finger along the head of his cane. His vile stare glittered with joy, thinking he had me cornered. "You know, dear."

"You brought us here—called everyone to witness. What do you want? Tell them."

Luther's sneer faltered a fraction, and he leaned back in his chair with a shrug. A bead of sweat dripped down my temple as I begged for luck that he was as confident as I assumed he was.

"An egg."

"I can get you a chicken egg." My laughter pitched high with my nerves. "You know–"

"I'm feeling gracious today, Luther. I'll let you have another go. But your next request will be binding." I nodded to Rothfuss. "You will witness?"

As if I needed a witness with such a large crowd.

"Aye." Rothfuss rolled the parchment, then tapped it against his thigh.

"Cunning, Avyanna," Luther murmured, gripping the cane between his hands.

"Speak your favor, Luther." I demanded.

Rafe was an angry presence pressing against my back. If I failed in this, he would fight Luther and there would be an uprising even Rothfuss wouldn't be able to quell.

Luther took his time, finger tapping on his cane as he studied me. He knew I was up to something, but either he hadn't put it together, or he was trying to twist it in his favor.

Flashing a menacing smile, he spoke. "Why, a dragon egg, of course."

I lifted my chin as the crowd shifted nervously, tension hanging thick in the air. It was so silent I could hear the birds crying in the murky sky above. A victorious grin crept over my lips, and pleasure spread through me as Luther's mirth faltered.

"Within my ability, I grant your favor."

I resisted the urge to wipe at the sweat trickling down my temple. I took confident steps closer to him, reaching into the pouch at my waist. Luther tracked my movements, and his grip on his cane tightened. When I pulled out the fragments, I held them in my palm for all to see. A muscle near the corner of his eye twitched, and he peered at me with pure, unadulterated rage.

When he made no movement to take them, I turned my hand and dumped them into his lap. As I wiped my palms on my trousers, I mustered a smile of equal loathing.

I spun on my heel, facing Rothfuss. "Witnessed?" I asked.

"That wasn't the agreement." Luther's voice was hushed with silent threat.

A commotion stirred the crowd. Murmurs grew louder as bystanders parted to make way for someone. Zeph strode through, with his hand resting on the pommel of his shortsword, his overcoat buttoned snugly over his lean frame. With fine trousers tucked into polished boots, he held his chin high and looked every bit the noble's son he was. I glanced at Rafe for reassurance and received a quirk of his brow in response.

When Kila peeked out from behind him, with Durum at her heels, dread skittered through my veins. She offered me a fragile smile. The gold dragonling held his head high at her chest. His gilded eyes danced over the crowd, taking them all in. His pupils narrowed and flared as he processed the amount of humans and their varying sizes and shapes. The twitch of his wings was his only display of agitation.

She could control him, but even though I knew she could, I still worried—remembering how volatile Tizmet was at first.

And I didn't want Luther anywhere near a dragonling, bonded or not.

"The eggs have hatched." Zeph's voice was strong and steady as the common folk pressed in for a closer view.

"Within physical ability?" Rothfuss reminded Luther. His steady gaze studied Durum, and a frown pulled his lips. He likely knew this would cause more problems.

"I cannot get you a whole dragon egg, as there are none left." My arms folded across my chest. "I have brought you what remains of the clutch."

Beneath the heat of his glare, I could almost see his mind racing for a way out of this. He pushed to his feet, bringing his body close to mine. I took an involuntary step back, unable to handle his vile presence pressing into my space.

His white teeth flashed in a smile that never reached his eyes, and he held my gaze as he brushed off his fine breeches, tossing the shell fragments to the ground. He shifted his feet, crushing the colorful but fragile pieces under his fancy black boots, his smirk growing. I clenched my jaw, angry that he would destroy something so precious out of spite.

"Rothfuss," he hissed in dismissal, then turned on his heel.

Bodrin opened the door for him, but he paused at the threshold, hesitating. I couldn't keep my hand from twitching in annoyance, ready to fight.

"I can assume that we are now on good terms, Avyanna?" he called over his shoulder. "Rothfuss, have I offered satisfactory reparations?"

Without waiting to hear the affirmative, he straightened the lapels of his overcoat and stepped into his shop. I held in my relieved sigh as his men trickled in behind him and the red door finally closed.

I turned back to the crowd, realizing Rafe had moved to stand by Rothfuss, staring at the dragon. It hissed and spat as a woman touched his wing.

"Please, give us space!" Kila cried.

Zeph stepped to Durum's side, attempting to help.

I allowed myself to heave the sigh I had been holding and grabbed the chair. I brought it about, feeling petty for the pleasure I felt while stepping on Luther's chair with my muddy boots.

"Good people of Leeds!" I shouted, looking down over the crowd.

Some turned my way, squinting against the glare of the sun on the fog. Women with baskets on their hips, men with tools, and children peering between adults to glimpse the gold dragonling. Unease spread through me as I realized just how big of a crowd we had drawn. Easily over a hundred, possibly two hundred, gathered and pressed in on Kila and Durum.

My shout drew the attention of most for precious breaths and I glanced skyward as Tizmet swooped low. Bystanders gawked at her underbelly as she passed over the drab rooftops.

"You have a newly bonded in your midst. Kila has been chosen by the dragonling Durum," I called, bringing their attention back to me. "I beg of you, give space and respect to your new Dragon Rider. They are learning each other, and now Durum will learn from you. Teach him good things. Teach him love and care, and he will offer you the same.

"He will be an asset to this town as much as Tizmet is. Remember who fed the tavern. Remember who chased away two bands of rogues and bandits. Durum will be invaluable to Leeds, but he is young. Give him a chance to grow with Kila."

Murmurs of wonder sounded over the multitude as they shuffled around to give them space. Kila glanced up at me with a nervous, but thankful grin.

"You're not going anywhere are you, Kila?" I asked with a knowing smile.

"Leeds is my home, as well as Durum's," she called out.

"You will all have plenty of time to see him, to get to know him. Take a moment to extend a warm welcome to your new Rider!"

Tizmet let out a bugle high in the sky, emphasizing my words. A light cheer went up, and Zeph offered Kila a small smile. I stepped down from the chair, nudging it to the side as Rafe drew me against his chest.

"She'll be fine," he said, pulling me up for a proud kiss.

I chuckled against his lips, then leaned back to meet his dark gaze. "I think she will."

Chapter 29

The sun was hot in the sky, glaring down at me. My knees sank into the moist earth and I picked another tomato. I smiled and brushed it off, setting it in my half-full basket. It would be a long day of preserving the fruit.

A long, blissfully boring day.

Tizmet dozed in the field beside the cottage, and her awareness coiled idly about mine. She was intrigued by my sense of pride.

'I worked hard for this.'

A pale fruit caught my notice, and I left it. I would have to pick it tomorrow, as everything was ripening so quickly in this heat. My knees scuffed against the soft soil as I shuffled toward the spread of beans dangling from their vines. I plucked off some speckled pods for tonight's stew. Most of them would be dried for winter, but there was no harm in harvesting a few while they were young.

My stomach gurgled, and I snapped the ends off a few beans. I wiped the sweat from my brow and took a bite, relishing the fresh taste and sweet, juicy crunch.

Tizmet's awareness recoiled from my mind, and I blinked at the quick retreat.

'Tizmet?' I asked, rising to peer at her over the potato plants.

She lifted her head, staring toward Leeds. Her eyes were narrowed as she flicked her tongue out, testing the air.

'What is it?' I pushed to my feet, attempting to brush away the brown stains coating my knees.

She didn't turn to me, but rather ruffled her wings in unease. *'My young are independent. They are strong.'*

I frowned at the worry that trickled through the bond. *'Aye.'*

I picked up my basket and wound my way through the garden rows, eyeing her as she stomped her leg and dug her claws into the earth, pulling up clods of black soil. I set my small harvest near the cottage door before approaching her.

'You hear one?'

'The red cries,' she huffed, snapping her teeth at the air as if she could cut off the sound.

'Let's go see it.'

I didn't like the idea of a dragonling in danger. They were never in danger at Northwing—not while the Riders and army were there. What could possibly hurt a dragon? Yes, they were still cow-sized, but armed with sharp talons and lethal teeth.

'I am not a mother hen.' Tizmet kneaded the earth again.

I frowned at her anxiety and stared toward Leeds. A keen worked its way out of her throat.

'Is it the bond?' I asked.

'I know not.'

A chime passed, and I stayed with her until she settled. She laid in the long grass, but remained aware and observant—like a cat ready to pounce. It did me no good to sit there and feed into her worry.

Resuming my chores, I went back to harvesting. I pulled a large zucchini from its stalk when hoofbeats drew my attention. I straightened, then smiled as Rafe trotted down the road. Tizmet would warn me if anyone else were to come down that path. She considered him a part of me now. He was safe, even if his presence annoyed her.

I stood, brushed off my apron, and strode out to meet him. He pulled his stallion up beside me as I cleared the garden and shaded my eyes against the sun setting at his back.

"Darrak is here."

I jerked in surprise and squinted against the light to peer at his face. "Darrak?"

"Aye, and the Caul."

I shrieked. "Mikhala is here?!"

I snatched the basket and ran toward the cottage, ripping off my apron. Tizmet's eyes tracked me, curious. I practically threw my things inside, then slammed the door behind me. I sped for Tizmet as she dragged her bulk off the ground and shook out her sleepy muscles.

Rafe angled his stallion between us. I faltered and slowed my running steps, glancing up at him as he blocked my way. He dismounted, crowded me and cupped my jaw, bringing my gaze to his. "It's not good news."

"What is it?!" Joy turned to ash in my mouth and terror coiled tight in my belly. "They are well? Elenor? Niehm? Willhelm?"

His face was sober and closed off, lips set into a firm frown that pulled on his scar. "The Shadows are advancing on Northwing."

"No–" I stepped away and Tizmet snarled, feeling my terror. "They weren't supposed to get that close!"

"Vy–"

"I have to help them!"

I dodged, making a break for Tizmet. My body moved by instinct. I didn't take the time to think through my actions, and I didn't care. Something heavy crashed into me, slamming me to the ground. Tizmet's resulting growl was enough to send Rafe's stallion scurrying away. Rafe rolled me to my back and pinned my hands above my head.

Panic had me struggling against his hold. I swung my leg around him and jerked at the weak point of his grip. I managed to roll him, but he threw his weight, pinning me again.

"Rafe! Let me–"

"Stop!"

I heaved and gasped beneath him, fingers twitching in his grasp.

"Listen to me before you go flying off on that dragon of yours," he bit out.

"I need to see them!"

Tizmet bared her teeth. *'Can I eat him now?'*

"You think I don't know that?" Rafe scoffed, glaring at me.

A glob of spit fell from Tizmet's maw and landed on his back with a wet splat. He froze, fury consuming his features.

"If she doesn't move her thrice-cursed head, I'm going to remove it from her body."

'I would give my little talon to see him try.' She lowered enough for her maw to graze him. She huffed, flicking her tongue out to taste him. *'Salty. Pre-seasoned.'*

He trembled, suppressing his rage. "Vy, I swear–"

"Tizmet, back off," I snapped.

Annoyed, she growled and pulled aside. With a huff of embers, she dropped her jaw to the ground, bringing her eye to Rafe's level. Her pupil narrowed.

"Cursed dragon–"

"Rafe." I forced his name between clenched teeth.

He released my wrists, then braced his weight on his forearms. "You need to know what you're walking into. Darrak and the Caul are here for you."

"Clearly," I scoffed. "They wouldn't run from the Shadows."

"They're here to bring you back," Rafe said, slower this time.

I frowned, meeting his dark gaze. No—they weren't running. They were sent. By King Aldred. Regent was in such dire straits that the King himself risked his best bounty hunters to retrieve me.

"If you leave," his voice lowered to a harsh whisper, "you won't be coming back."

I gripped his tunic as if it would be enough to keep me grounded as the world gave out beneath me. "Leeds is my home," I breathed.

"Your friends in Regent are as much home to you as Kila or the innkeeper. Think about that before you listen to Darrak's silver tongue. If you agree, you'll be leaving Leeds," he jerked his chin toward our cottage, "leaving *this*."

I squeezed my eyes shut, thinking of the harvest I threw inside. There was a nail in the doorjamb that snagged on my dresses. I still needed to hammer it down. The damaged wood on the lean-to needed to be resealed. The fire pit had to be cleaned out before the cooler months rolled in.

It would all go undone if I left.

I *fought* for this, this semblance of peace for both me and Rafe. I didn't want to go back to war. But could I stand by as the Shadows took Northwing? Could I sit here and do nothing as they stole our dragons and murdered my friends?

When Rafe pressed his lips to mine, they were warm, gentle. Tears welled, then trickled down my cheeks as my fingers traced the rough edge of his jaw. I returned the embrace with every ounce of my frustration at the unfairness of it all. I clutched at his neck as he shifted his weight, settling between my legs. His heavy breath warmed my cheek as he broke away, trailing kisses to my ear.

"Darrak can wait," he whispered, voice husky with need.

I laughed at his reminder, as if I had forgotten. Opening my eyes, I arched under him and dragged my nails down his tunic. "Up, I have friends to meet."

He groaned in complaint, but pushed himself to his feet, then offered his hand. I took it and smiled, brushing tears from my cheeks as he tugged me against his chest. He plucked at the bits of wild rye and grass entangled in my braid.

"Afraid people might think I had a tussle in a field?"

"Wouldn't be the first," Rafe said. "Or the last." His eye darted to mine with promise, and I chuckled at his determination.

"Meet me at the tavern?" I pushed to my toes to give him a peck on the cheek.

He grunted with a nod. "We'll get a room at the inn. Can't imagine this conversation will be a quick one."

I hesitated, his words sending a thrum of panic through me. He turned from me to the cottage, glancing to where his stallion grazed a few paces away. "I'll close things up here."

The bear of a man opened the door and ducked inside. I swallowed past the lump in my throat and my heart thrashed in my chest. Something about this wasn't right. Why did this feel like goodbye?

Tizmet crooned, nosing my back, and I took a stumbling step closer to the cottage. I blinked, staring at the tiny structure. The garden was in full bloom, giving me far more than I put into it. The ducks quacked and chased each other across the pond. Rafe's stallion snorted and grazed at the lush green grass that fought for space among the wildflowers.

"Vy?"

I jerked my unfocused eyes back to Rafe.

He leaned in the doorway, his hands gripping the frame. "All will be well."

Why didn't his words assure me?

Tizmet flew low over Leeds, banking away from the tavern. I frowned, squinting at the roof as we passed over. When I reached into the bond, my concern grew, sensing Tizmet's nagging unease. She was still concerned about the red dragonling.

'Leave me with Darrak. Go look for it,' I urged.

She shook her head as if waking from a dream and flapped her massive wings to turn her back toward the tavern.

'It is not a babe. It is a dragon,' she replied tartly.

She could say all she wanted, but I felt the anxiety undermining her words. If she wouldn't go find it, I would on my own.

She let out a barking roar, scattering the few townsfolk who were headed inside. Landing roughly in the street, she craned her head to peer down the crossroads, as if that would reveal the missing creature. I slid from her back just as the door to the tavern flung open.

A mere breath passed my lips as I took in Mikhala's bright red braids and furs.

Then I was smothered.

I grunted as she wrapped herself around me. She spun us in a tight circle, squealing my name. Her vest muffled my attempt to greet her. She stopped and heaved a contented sigh, still crushing me in her embrace. My feet dangled off the ground as she held me.

Tizmet lowered, tilting her head to the side.

"Oh, and you too—you overgrown lizard!" Mikhala shrieked.

I stumbled, regaining my footing as she dropped me to charge Tizmet. She flung her arms out wide and threw herself at her muzzle. Tizmet snorted and jerked, dislodging the woman.

I laughed. "It's good to see you too, Mikhala."

She dipped her chin, staring at Tizmet with a critical eye. "She looks good. Better, even."

"A long brumation did her wonders."

Tizmet preened under her appraisal.

"She knows it, too." Mikhala laughed, then threw out her arms, letting her bright gaze travel up and down my body. "Girl, *you* look good!" She smirked, kicking out her hip. "Like a tavern wench who can't handle a blade."

"Try me and see," I dared, raising a brow in challenge.

Mikhala hadn't grown taller while I was away, but she had thinned. Her face was leaner, more gaunt, as if she had been through a lot since my banishment. She still wore her fur-trimmed sleeveless hide tunics, even in the heat of high summer. Her bright red hair was tied into intricate braids that hung down to her hips. Her vine tattoo stuck out against her pale skin, opening into a beautiful flower on her palm.

My smile fell slightly. Some of the wild, reckless abandon was gone from her gaze. I was sure the same could be said of me. Crossing the Sands would do that to a person.

"Save the sparring for after midday meal."

Darrak's voice caused me to whirl, a grin spreading over my face as he held the door open. He wore his leather armor with the King's gryphon emblazoned on his chest. His clothes were covered in dirt and grime from the road, and though earnest, his smile was weary.

"Close that door, foreigner!" Iana's voice bellowed from inside.

He winced at her sharp tone, then tipped his chin. "Care to join us, Avyanna?"

I took a deep, steadying breath before I nodded and made my way up the steps. When I entered, I flashed Iana a bright smile, which she returned while filling a mug behind the bar.

In the center of the room, two tables had been pushed together. There sat Jamlin, Tegan, Blain and Dane—Zeph was likely off with Kila somewhere.

I smiled at that thought as I strode over and took a seat. Jam passed a coin to Tegan, the two of them exchanging a smirk as Darrak and Mikhala followed.

"Wagered Rafe wouldn't tell you till tomorrow." Jam shrugged.

"He's getting soft in his old age." Tegan laughed, flicking the coin in the air and catching it before shoving it into his pouch.

I bit my lip, thinking of Rafe's actions in the field. He definitely was not going soft, but I wasn't willing to divulge those details.

"I honestly didn't expect to see you all together again," Darrak sighed, then sank into the chair next to me.

Mikhala hummed her agreement, then shoved between us to sit on the bench. I chuckled, giving her arm a playful slap as she wiggled her arse, pushing us further apart.

She pulled her elbows onto the table to rest her chin on her palms. "Didn't know who would die first."

"Such confidence, Mik," I replied dryly.

"With the Shadows advancing—oi!"

She turned a glare on Darrak when he rammed an elbow into her ribs.

"She's going to know sooner or later!" she hissed, then started again, "With their advances, and your banishment, neither of us had fate on our side."

I scoffed. "I made it over the Sands. And Leeds is hardly threatening."

"Oh, yes. Not threatening at all when someone sets your house aflame," Jamlin muttered.

Mikhala's jaw fell as she slapped her hands against the tabletop. I shot him a glare, but it didn't phase him.

"Aye, and with her in it," he added, his braids swinging with his enthusiastic nod.

"Were you trapped? Was it rogues? Wild bears?!" She spun in her seat to face me, eyes wide.

"Nothing nearly so exciting. A misunderstanding is all," I assured her. Though the idea of wild bears setting a house on fire created an entertaining image.

Blain chuckled to himself as he picked dirt out from his fingernails with a knife. "Rafe would have something to say about that."

"How is ol' one eye, by the way?" She wagged her eyebrows. "Last we saw of him, he was galloping over mountain and valley to get to you."

"Rafe is well." A blush heated my cheeks. "Our claiming ceremony was this last spring."

"I am happy for you." Her features brimmed with pride.

Iana brought over some ale for everyone, and a cup of water for me.

Mikhala raised her drink. "To newfound hearth and home."

"To peace," Darrak murmured, raising his as well.

The men chorused the toast and drank. I sipped my water without a word. When Darrak set his mug down and wiped his lips, I leaned on my elbows, staring him down.

"To who's peace?" I asked quietly.

"Can it not be everyone's?" Darrak chose his words with care, focused on the ale in his cup.

"Some have already found it," I said. "To settle peace somewhere else, they might have to be uprooted."

Darrak's gaze met mine across Mikhala's drink and he worked his jaw before replying. "You are rooted then?"

"I was banished. Of course I set down roots elsewhere."

Iana dropped a mug on the bar counter and I forced myself not to roll my eyes. Of course she was listening to the conversation.

"How are Elenor and Niehm?" I asked, changing the subject.

Darrak's shoulders relaxed a fraction with my question. "Busy. When we left, they were working on a way to evacuate the children."

I nodded, stomach tight. "Rafe told me the Shadows are marching on Northwing."

"He spoiled the surprise," Mikhala whined, leaning back. "That was my line."

"He's not wrong." Darrak ignored her. "I was sent to..." He stared at the far wall, as if the wood planks or lanterns held the word he searched for.

"Retrieve me?" I did my best to keep my tone level.

"Make sure you received the pardon," he corrected. His gaze flashed to Blain, then back to me.

"Oh, I received it. It's tucked away in a chest, under my bed, in my home."

"Avyanna, this doesn't have to be an argument." He pushed Mikhala out of the way as she reached for her mug. "Regent needs you. I understand more than anyone how being tossed out on your arse must have felt–"

"Do you, Darrak? I was left with no more than a few coins to my name. I was banished to the *Sands*. Do you know what lives there? Giant bugs the size of dragons, with more teeth than they have scales. There are monsters that fizzle into shadow, stalk you through the night. There's–"

"Yes, you went through a lot. Blame the King, blame Ruveel, but don't hold that over your friends."

"They can come here," I shot back.

Mikhala stopped looking between us and gave Jam a thoughtful look, pursing her lips.

"And give up everything they have?" Darrak scoffed.

"Isn't that what King Aldred is asking of me?" I shouted, slamming my palm against the table.

Why wasn't this easy?

Uncomfortable silence lapsed between us and Tizmet crowded my mind. Blain and Dane looked at each other as if discussing something silently, and Tegan pushed up from his seat.

"You, Caul!"

"Aye?" Mik answered him.

"Teach me some songs from your homeland!" he roared.

He threw his leg over the bench, motioning her to follow him. She hopped up so fast, she jostled our seat.

"Care for a walk?" Jam asked Blain.

I sighed, realizing they were leaving me alone with Darrak to work out our differences.

"Aye, bound to be more exciting than this reunion," Blain agreed, rising with Jam.

He slapped a hand on his twin's shoulder and Dane shifted to the side, his attention focused on Tegan and Mik in the corner. Jam and Blain headed out, and I turned back to Darrak.

"I understand. Sun above, I do, Avyanna." He pinched the bridge of his nose. "Where is Rafe?"

"This is *my* choice."

He scoffed, eyes narrowed with disbelief. "He holds no sway?"

"I'm not answering for him, but to go or to stay is my choice, not his."

"He *is* going soft."

Irritation swelled within my chest and I clenched my jaw.

He pushed out a weary sigh. "I know, and more importantly, *King Aldred* knows he made a mistake. He had to make an example out of you—and he did. But in doing so, he threw away a weapon that could turn the tides of the war." He paused and pain glittered in his eyes. "Something is brewing, Avyanna. And I have a feeling it could wipe Regent off the map."

I didn't know what to say to that. My mouth dried, as if full of gritty sand.

"If we had anyone brave enough to go behind enemy lines, we might know what it is." His laughter was bitter, setting me further on edge. "Oh, King Aldred has ordered troops on scouting missions, but they never return. We maintain the front, but they raid at night. When they do, there's something with them, some new kind of power. We've sent dragons against them, and they never return."

He paused, taking a long drink. His brows lowered into a stern glare that conveyed the depths of his sincerity. "We need a Dragon Rider who isn't afraid of them."

At that, I sneered. "Ruveel trained his Riders to flee the Shadows. You're not going to find any." I lifted my drink to my lips to clear the sensation tightening my throat.

"I already have."

With a sharp inhale, I snorted and choked on my water, then wiped my face on my sleeve. A fake grin plastered my cheeks. "I'm not a Rider anymore, remember?"

"You have your pardon, but you don't know what the King offers in recompense for your help."

"What could he offer, Darrak? His kingdom is failing."

"A home."

"I have a home."

He closed his eyes, trying for patience. "He is willing to let you live at Northwing. You and your dragon will be cared for till the end of your days."

"And Rafe?"

"Aye, him too." Darrak nodded. "And any wee ones that might be on the way." He glanced down at my belly.

"I would not be bound to Northwing, though?" I asked.

"No, you could live wherever you wish. You could return here if you wanted. With the King's favor, you could come and go as you please."

"That's not enough," I said, glaring down at my cup.

"What more could you ask for, Avyanna?"

"After what he put me through—what he put Rafe through? There's nothing King Aldred could offer me that would ever be enough."

"He did what he thought best for Regent."

"He threw me away like a soiled rag. He used Rafe until he snapped. And he would have kept using him, if not for you. I don't owe my allegiance to some King across the mountains. If anything would sway me, it would be the friends who need me." I stood, then stepped over the bench.

Darrak watched me with a look of defeat.

I softened my tone. "I need time."

"We don't have time, Avyanna."

"We have until morning." I turned my back on him. "You owe me that much, Darrak."

I stormed outside, letting the door slam behind me. Tizmet waited on the street, deterring any would-be visitors, and I threw myself at her, climbing onto her back.

'I need space,' I pleaded.

She huffed her approval and launched, flapping her wings hard. She took me high in the sky where the wind was cold and tears left icy trails down my cheeks.

Chapter 30

My voice was hoarse and my throat raw from screaming my frustration where no one could hear my rage. My anger echoed through the low clouds, but it didn't bring me any closer to a decision. When darkness enveloped the sky and the frigid high-altitude air chilled me to the core, Tizmet gracefully descended over Leeds. My eyes were dry and burned from my crying.

It wasn't fair. Life never was.

I couldn't forsake my friends, couldn't abandon them to face their deaths alone. After everything I worked through to carve out this acceptance, this happiness, I was being asked to give it up. Rafe was right, there would be no returning to Leeds after the War of Shadows. If I fought, and somehow survived, I would set down roots in Regent, abandoning everything I built here.

Kila and Durum would be without a guide or teacher. Luther would rule without challenge, Rothfuss barely keeping him in check.

Would the Tennan follow Rafe once more, or would I have to say goodbye to them as well? Tegan and Zeph made efforts to set down roots. Jamlin was a nomad by birth, having been born so close to the Sands. Blain and Dane traveled through three kingdoms at the very least, and made no motion to call Leeds their home.

Tizmet wrapped herself around my thoughts, teasing me above my sorrow and turmoil. She flew low over Rafe, and he glanced up, watching her glide above as he rode into town.

The tavern was bustling with people, the townsfolk eager to see the newcomers. He would head there and wait for me.

'A few more minutes.' I pressed my forehead against Tizmet's warm scales.

A steady rumble worked its way through her chest. *'I would fly with you all night, were you to ask.'*

My muscles ached and complained from hanging on. Even my nails hurt from clutching at her scales. She drifted through the air as gently as she could, but keeping a seat on a dragon was no easy task. I missed my saddle. It was tucked inside a storage room, behind crates of dried goods and barrels of ale and wine. It was probably rotting away in the darkness if rodents hadn't already chewed at the leather.

Part of me was ashamed I hadn't taken better care of it. It was a gift from the Healers of Regent. I never intended to strap it on Tizmet again. When I hauled it into Iana's storage addition, I buried my banishment, tucked it away, far out of sight.

Sensing my thoughts, Tizmet banked, bringing me above the inn. I took a steadying breath and straightened against her scales. My heart twisted with remorse as thoughts slid together like a puzzle. My chest ached, but I couldn't abandon my friends, not when I had a chance to help. I wouldn't let them die alone.

'Best check on it,' I said.

A dry sob racked through me, and I bit the inside of my cheek hard, using the pain to ground myself. I had till morning to voice my decision. I could only hope the last pieces would fall into place and give me some semblance of peace concerning my choice.

Tizmet landed behind the tavern, and I slipped to the side on her neck. She used her head to steady me against her shoulder as I slid down, muscles stiff and sore. I shook out my limbs, and she let out a quiet trill.

'I am well,' I assured.

'You look like a freshly hatched dragonling.' She nosed me, causing me to stumble.

'We've been in the sky over two chimes,' I said in defense. *'I'd like to see you cling to a Sky Tree for as long.'*

'I lived in the Sky Trees, little one.'

'But you didn't hang *off one,'* I huffed. The banter with her felt good after stewing in my turmoil.

Her amusement followed me as I tapped on the kitchen door. After a few breaths, the way swung open and Pachu squinted at me, blinking in confusion for a moment before throwing his arms in a wide welcome.

"Avyanna!" he bellowed.

I glanced past him and saw a small girl, Neena, peeling potatoes. She bit her lip and watched me from the corner of her eye. When I smiled at her, she offered a shy grin in return. She would grow to be a beautiful woman, and I wouldn't be here to see it. I knew her parents well. Gregor and Fiona had been some of the first townsfolk to accept me as part of Leeds.

"Avyanna?" Pachu's voice lowered, pinched with worry.

No doubt he sensed my foul mood and strained emotions. Neena tucked her blonde hair behind her ear and stared at me curiously.

"I need the key to the storage addition."

"Why? Did Iana ask you—oh."

I brought my gaze to Pachu as realization dawned on his face. He pressed his lips together and shook his head.

"Those two foreigners are taking you back?" He set his knife aside as a tight frown consumed his features. Pachu was a large man, born to wear a jovial smile, not a scowl.

"No one is taking me anywhere." I sighed and held out my hand as he fished out the key from his tunic. "If I go anywhere, it's of my own accord."

He dangled the key from its chain above my palm. "*If?*" he pressed.

I nodded and wrapped my fingers around the warm metal, but Pachu held tight. My gaze flicked to his, and my throat squeezed as tears pricked at my eyes.

"You know as well as I that by asking for this key—you've made your choice," he rasped, lips trembling.

It broke me how fast I had grown attached to the people of Leeds. I loved them—I loved Leeds. Even with its smelly bogs and gloomy fog. Even the muddy streets and stinging bugs. This place was awful, and yet, the idea of leaving tore my heart in half. I hated how much it hurt.

Pachu moved quickly for a man of his size, lunging forward to wrap me in an embrace. I let out the sob that was trying to tear itself out of my throat as he crushed me against him. My forehead pressed to his shoulder, and I ground my teeth, desperate to hold myself together.

"You come back, you hear?" His voice hitched, emotion distorting his tone. "I'll roast a whole bog lizard for you and your friends. They'll be stuffed full for a fortnight."

I nodded, breathing in his scent of spices and herbs, knowing very well if I left, I probably wouldn't return.

He pulled back, and I despised the way my heart spasmed when I saw the tear slip down his cheek. He gave me a shaky smile, then pressed the key into my hand.

"I expect you to dine at the tavern one last time tonight."

I sniffed and swiped at my wet cheeks with a nod.

Pachu's lips formed a firm line as he shooed me out. "Now, off with you. I have a chowder to add to."

My answering chuckle sounded more like a sob, and I turned away, stumbling down the steps. I tried to regain my composure and took deep, calming breaths as I walked to the storage addition.

The key slipped into the lock, and I hesitated. I was just checking on it—I still had time to turn back, to *stay*.

Clenching my jaw, I pulled the doors and propped them open, allowing the moonlight to illuminate the dingy space. I waited for my eyes to adjust, slowly weaving around crates and barrels to where my saddle was crammed against the wall.

A Dragon Rider's saddle was no small thing. Soft malleable straps and sheaths to secure my legs were folded beneath the hard, stiff leather seat. It was crafted to sit at the base of a dragon's neck, reinforced with wood and bone.

I took my time, pushing aside crates and barrels to clear a path. A soft sigh flowed out as I ran my hands along the smooth surface, frowning at the dry spots. My fingers traced the Healer's emblem painted on the flank, a blue cross over a white backing.

As I examined the straps and buckles, I was pleased to not feel any gouges or nibble marks from rodents. The only noticeable neglect was the patches of leather starting to dry out. Nothing a good oiling couldn't fix.

I immediately felt guilty for my relief. I spun on my heel to leave, though my steps faltered when I caught the shadow of a man leaning against the doorframe.

Rafe watched me, his face barren of expression, waiting for my lead. I couldn't tell if he was angry or disappointed. Maybe both. With my Rider's saddle at my back, and my heart at the door, I stood there, arms limp at my sides.

This wasn't just my life being torn from Leeds. Rafe's entire existence had been a constant battle until he came here. Here, with me, he had a hope of settling in peace. If things with Luther ever faded, we could live a quiet life. Leaving would strip that chance away from him.

"Rafe, I'm sorry–" I choked out, rubbing my arms. "I just—I haven't–"

His face didn't change as he pushed off the wall and stalked over. I craned my head back as more tears threatened to spill down my cheeks. My jaw flexed, angry that it was even possible to cry anymore. I was stronger than that.

"No regrets," he said.

I snapped my eyes up to meet his, though his expression was unreadable in the dark. He lifted my chin with a calloused hand, then pressed his lips to mine. I gripped his tunic in my fists, holding onto him for all I was worth. I let his kiss ground me, luring me into the safety of his presence.

Rafe was mine. I was his. This life was ours.

He was my home, not Leeds.

Rafe pulled away, letting cool air slip between our lips as he straightened. He wrapped his arm around me and dragged his fingertips down my spine causing me to straighten my back.

"We don't look back and wish for better things. Our choices dictate our future, and we will walk the path we made with our heads held high. We don't let the 'what-ifs' weigh on our shoulders and pull us down. We can only move forward. Remember that, Vy. You're not a Dragon Rider. You're not a little woman to be tucked away in a cottage. You are Avyanna of Gareth, and you will face your fate, staring it straight in the eyes."

I sucked in a deep staggering breath and he nodded in approval, a satisfied frown riding his lips.

"Good girl." He stepped back and lifted his gaze to the saddle behind me. "A hot meal will do us good."

We locked the storage room and returned the key to Pachu with the promise that we were heading in through the front to dine. Tizmet took to the sky and Rafe pushed open the door.

Despite my fragile state, a smile warmed my cheeks at the sight inside. Tegan played a lively tune on his lute, one boot propped on a bench as he strummed so fast he worked up a sweat. Mikhala laughed and danced on top of a table in the center of the room. Cheers and jovial singing joined Tegan's steady tenor.

"The snow was cold,
But her bosom warm.
Her mam was old,
But the broom was her warn–"

The crowd sped up the tempo and a small airy laugh of disbelief lightened my spirit as Mikhala stomped faster. With her arms locked over her chest, her feet moved with quick fancy steps, her boots throwing bits of mud with every kick. Her wild red braids thrashed about her like snakes dancing to the tune.

"Cauls," Rafe scoffed, guiding me inside.

Mik spotted me, and her smile brightened. "Avyanna! Join me!" She cried, not missing a step.

I laughed outright. "Not a chance!"

I moved to the table where the Tennan sat with Darrak, noting Zeph's presence. I scanned the crowd again as I took a seat and saw Kila weaving through with a tray of mugs, laughing easily with the townsfolk.

My relief swelled when I spotted Durum laying on the floor next to the bar. He might be the size of a cow, but he was small enough to be out of the way—mostly. He tapped the fine tip of his tail in time with the music and I shook my head at the interest the little dragonling was showing in the business of men.

I glanced between Rafe and Darrak as they muttered their greetings. Rafe settled beside me.

"Blain filled me in." He raised his voice over the crowd's heady joy.

The place was packed tonight, and as more drifted in, they took up space along the walls, forced to stand due to the lack of seats.

"So I heard," Darrak said. "I would have liked to break it to her."

"It wasn't your choice." Rafe shrugged, not bothering to meet Darrak's gaze as he spoke.

"Flaming arse."

"A sight better than yours."

"I beg to differ," Darrak sneered. "How did you earn that nasty scar?"

"Creature up in the E'or."

"What kind?"

"Does it matter?"

"Ever the conversationalist, Rafe."

He faced me, and his gaze lingered, expectant. I offered him a tight smile, then turned my back on him to watch the crowd. I wouldn't have him spoil this night for me. He'd hear my decision in the morning. He owed me that much.

Regent owed me that much.

The night deepened, and the songs got bawdier. The ale and mead flowed freely, and somehow I ended up on a table with Mik, stumbling through her dance. Iana had given up on scolding us as the townsfolk formed lines, mimicking her steps.

The chowder was warm, and the ale loosened lips, giving even the quietest folk voice to sing. Sweat beaded Tegan's skin as he kept pace with Mik and the giddy patrons. Mikhala threw her head back and laughed, and I stared down at my boots as my feet kicked wildly of their own accord. I panted with a grin on my face, missing a step, then stumbling to catch up with her.

A roar shook the tavern.

Tegan's lute stopped short with a terrible off-tune note, and Mikhala snatched the back of my tunic, catching me before I fell off the table. The crowd plunged into a tense silence, all eyes on me.

'Tizmet?!' I stared up at the rafters, as if I'd somehow see her there.

Another deafening roar shook the very timbers of the tavern, and I grimaced as dust vibrated from the beams, drifting down like snow.

I leapt off the table with Mikhala on my heels, bolting for the exit. The Tennan and Rafe fell in behind, pushing through the silent crowd. I reached over the bond shoved outside. Tizmet's fury tainted my vision red, driving me to my knees.

Veil beyond, what made her so mad?

I tempered her frenzy as Mikhala grabbed the back of my tunic again, hauling me upright. I kicked my legs, trying to get them under me.

Mik's face tipped toward the night sky. "I know that roar!" she yelled. "She's gonna eat someone!"

"No, she won't!"

I yanked free from her grasp as Rafe came between us, shoving her away. Screams erupted somewhere off in the distance.

"Sure about that?" he growled.

Without hesitation, I sprinted in the direction of the anguished cries.

'Don't eat anyone!'

I shouted through her bloodlust, trying to reach her through her fury. She slammed her outrage into me and I bared my teeth at the ire that licked my bones.

"Stars above, no," I whispered through my heaving breaths. I pumped my legs faster, throwing myself along the muddied path.

"What is it?" Rafe called, forcing his mass to keep pace with me.

"The red dragonling!"

Tizmet recognized her dragonlings were independent beings, yet she couldn't suppress her natural urge to shield and safeguard them.

Her emotions surged like wildfire, all-consuming. One of her hatchlings was hurt. By man.

We skidded down a side street, heading east. I ran until my lungs burned and screamed for air and my legs complained and stumbled. It would have been faster on horseback, but I didn't take the time to find one.

Smoke drifted above the tall wooden buildings.

I turned a corner, and hungry flames licked at the sky. My pulse sped, thumping painfully in my chest. Buildings choked with fire—shops of good townsfolk. Luther's men surrounded an overturned wagon, all of them armed with spears and bows. The rest of the street was barren, but wouldn't be for long.

My heart crashed into my rib cage, and I fell. Bracing myself with one hand, the other clutched at my chest. Gasping, I clung to consciousness as Tizmet reared, thrashing her head back with another deafening roar. Maw to the sky, she let loose a stream of fire that washed every shadow in an amber glow.

I would have screamed if I had the breath. I collapsed in on myself. Mud cradled my cheek and seeped through my clothes. Tizmet's shriek was the last thing I heard before the seizure took me.

"Avyanna, if you can hear me, we really need you." Mikhala's voice broke through my suffering.

A sharp whine whistled through my teeth, and I pushed to my side. The coppery taste of blood filled my mouth and I spit, wincing with the agony that accompanied the action.

I whimpered as my eyes fluttered open, pain causing them to roll back inside my head. Bile slid up my throat and I retched, flinging myself onto my stomach.

Strong hands hauled me from the mud. My arms trembled with the effort of keeping myself upright. I bared my teeth against the agony as I lifted my chin to take in the scene before me.

Luther's men had abandoned the wagon. They rallied beside a small cage at the far end of the street. There, Luther had his chin held high, a glare frozen to his features. Rafe stood across from him, the Tennan at his back and Tizmet looming above them. Her mouth was open, sparks skittering past her forked tongue.

Darrak and Rothfuss took up the center near the smoldering remains of the wagon—and bodies.

"No," I choked out, trying to push myself up.

Darrak's sword was drawn on Luther's men, along with half of Rothfuss' men. The other half of the enforcers were at the lawkeeper's side, weapons pointed at Rafe.

"Some intervention might be needed," Mikhala grunted, helping me to my feet.

She pulled my arm about her shoulders and took the weight off my legs. I panted. Waves of nausea rolled and burned through my stomach as we stumbled along.

Tizmet's head whipped my direction, and she lunged toward me. Her heavy paws slammed into the street as she jumped over Rafe and the Tennan, causing Rothfuss to yell and pull his men back.

People behind me screamed.

"Abyss–" I cursed as I glanced over my shoulder, seeing the large crowd. They cried out, horrified, as Tizmet charged, snapping her maw in warning.

'No, stop! You're scaring them!'

'Do not tell me to stop!*'* she hissed. She brought her head level with mine, blocking our path.

"Don't let her eat me," Mikhala whispered.

'We settled here—far from the Shadows who took my young. Here, my dragonlings are supposed to be the predators, not the prey. Here, they will live free and hunt and have a choice in what they do.' An irate roar ripped past her teeth, blowing the hair away from my face. *'Do not tell me to stop when more humans try to steal my young!'*

I leaned around her, seeing the red dragonling shoved inside the iron cage. It would be crammed in there, too big to move at all. Why wasn't it crying out?

'They have poisoned it.' Tizmet snapped her jaw, teeth clacking in sharp defiance, before she whirled to face Luther.

"Wait! Wait, Tizmet!" I rasped, trying to clear my head.

There was a way out of this—I just had to find it.

'I have waited. I have not killed them while you were ill.' Her lip curled as she snarled, *'My patience wears thin.'*

"I need to talk to Luther," I said, grimacing as I clutched Mikhala's shoulder.

She shuffled beneath me, taking my weight as her gaze bounced between the groups of men. "Aye, and who would that be?"

"The cage, Mik." I staggered with her as she walked. "The one near the cage."

Tizmet screamed in rage and I ducked my head against the force of the roar, ears ringing. She would deafen those here before the night was up.

"Avyanna!"

My name was called by both Rothfuss and Luther. One spoke in warning, the other with casual indifference.

Rothfuss threw Luther a glare, then snapped his attention to me. "Call off your dragon," he ordered.

With a shocked expression, Darrak stared over his shoulder at the lawkeeper. His wide eyes conveyed his astonishment at the man's audacious attempt to order me about.

No one would dare command a Dragon Rider in Regent.

"Avyanna, I have to second the lawkeeper. Be a dear and–"

Tizmet's roar pitched high in a shriek of fury, cutting his words short. She took three fast strides toward him, and his men cried out, shrinking back.

I could have sworn Luther flinched.

"Let it go," I called out as loudly as I dared, my body aching with the force.

I squinted, trying to peer through the bars, unable to see the state of the beast within. I hoped it was still alive—for the whole town's sake.

"On what grounds? It's naught more than game, Avyanna, a wild creature trapped by *my* men." Luther pulled on the lapels of his overcoat. "That makes it mine. The law is clear concerning that."

"Rothfuss." Surely he would back me in this. Pain shot like lightning down my spine as I twisted toward him.

"It was wild caught. There's nothing you can do." He shook his head. "Is it yours? What claim do you have on it?"

'It is MINE!'

Tizmet rose on her hind legs, blowing a pillar of fire into the sky. Globs of flaming dragon oil scattered the rooftops, setting them ablaze. She clamped her mouth down on the stream and slammed to the ground with enough force to shake a sign free from a bakery across the road.

"Tell me," I snarled, "do either of you really want *her* to take back her young?! Do you want to see what she can do?!"

Luther jerked his chin, glaring down his nose. "Is that a threat?"

"It was not hunted on your lands. It is not yours."

Rothfuss' words were like a knife to my heart. The dragonling was born in the wild and belonged in the wild.

"I'd hate to interrupt here," Darrak shouted, "but—*are you mad?*" He lowered his weapon, spinning to face Rothfuss. "That is a dragonling, a sentient being—and you are treating it like unbranded cattle. If your child stumbled away from home, does that give another family the right to take it and claim it as their own?"

"You're a foreigner. You don't know our laws," Rothfuss growled, angling his blade toward Luther in Darrak's place.

"Your laws weren't made with dragons in mind!" I screamed.

"No! They weren't!" Rothfuss seethed with a rage I'd never seen from him before. "You brought them here, and now you have to deal with the consequences! Take your dragon and *go home*, Avyanna!"

Rafe and the others slowly crept to my side, encircling me.

"This is madness!" Darrak threw his hand in the air, joining us without a care for any threat at his back.

I reached across the bond, knowing this was going nowhere. An agreement forged between me and Tizmet. She snapped her head up. Her pupil narrowed into a sharp slit, as if expecting me to take it back. I pressed my lips together, and Rafe took my weight off Mikhala.

I nodded.

"Brace yourself," I breathed.

Rafe's gaze flashed to mine at the same moment Tizmet lunged.

She cleared our small group in one bounding leap and plucked Luther off the ground. Luther's men had no chance to react, to scream, to fight. His torso disappeared between her teeth, legs whipping as she snapped her neck to the side.

A terrible squelching sound echoed over the terrified din, and his legs flew free of his body. Screams drenched the night as she jerked her head, swallowing Luther's torso in one gulp. His legs fell into the crowd below.

"Sun above–" Darrak breathed.

Chaos erupted.

Rothfuss shouted, and his men rushed us. Luther's scattered. Archers took aim while others leveled their spears. Tizmet bounded after Luther's legs, unwilling to let a single piece of him exist. Her vengeful hiss sprayed the crowd with his blood.

'My kill!'

Mikhala drew her shortsword. "Time to go!"

"Meet to the west of Leeds," Rafe rumbled, swinging my body up into his arms.

"The old mill!" I shouted against his chest.

"If I'm not there, go to the base of the mountains and wait!" he called above the screams as the Tennan crowded in around us.

"I'm not leaving without you."

Tizmet lifted her head from the thinning crowd. One of Luther's legs dangled from her bloody maw. Her eyes flashed, nostrils spewing black smoke as she tossed her chin upward, swallowing the limb. Fresh terror erupted in another wave of screams.

"Go! Fly!" Rafe threw me at Tizmet as she dropped to her belly.

I hissed in pain as he shoved me onto her shoulder and she nosed me up on her back. She reared off the ground, spreading her wings.

"I'm not leaving without you!" I screamed.

People ran, some toward the fires spreading among the shops, some seeking shelter. Every single one desperate to escape Tizmet—the man-eater.

Rafe's dark eye glittered with something similar to pride. "I know."

Chapter 31

I grimaced against the torment that accompanied each of Tizmet's wingbeats. Pain, like webs of lightning, ricocheted through my body. She flew low and fast over Leeds, easing to land behind the tavern. When I attempted to climb from her back, my strength faltered. She swept her head close, and I caught myself on her horns, breaking my fall. My legs kicked and fumbled as I tried to get my feet beneath me.

Her snarl rose to a ground-shaking bellow. The kitchen door flew open and Pachu peeked out, eyes wide. "What in all of Rinmoth, Avyanna!"

I bit my tongue, stumbling as he rushed down the stairs. Tizmet trilled low as he dropped to his knees beside me.

"The saddle!" I ground out, looking up at him through my wild, windblown hair. "I can't—I can't get it on myself."

He stilled, blinked once in understanding, then gave me a firm nod.

Another surge of agony flooded my veins. My body was rejecting my demands. Normally I had time to recoup after an episode. Still, I was lucky the seizure was so short.

I had no time.

Pachu pushed to his feet, fishing the key out of his tunic. He moved as fast as his bulk would allow, jogging to the storage shed, then fumbled at the lock.

A haze clouded my vision as I clutched my chest. I hissed in pain, and glanced back to the Inn, the building blurring through my agony.

Neena stood in the doorway, her slight frame illuminated by the light. She snatched a lantern and dashed down the stairs, hiking her dress. I groaned, forcing myself to my feet, Tizmet's head offering me much needed support. A Dragon Kind should not be seen on their knees.

I was better than that.

As Neena rushed over, Tizmet growled deep in her throat. The girl raised the lantern high, but gave Tizmet a wide berth as she walked to where Pachu had disappeared. With a few quick commands, they dragged my saddle out.

He panted as he pulled it over. "What's all the commotion?"

She huffed and lowered her head, intending to help lift it to her back. Neena shrieked and Pachu startled. He snatched the lantern and brought it closer to Tizmet's maw.

"Avyanna..." Pure horror drenched his tone.

He used a beefy hand to push Neena behind him as his terrified stare fixated on the dragon. Tizmet peeled her lips back in a silent snarl. I didn't want to know what Pachu saw embedded between her teeth.

My breaths came fast, and I pressed my palm over my racing heart. I couldn't put it on myself, especially in this state. If he wouldn't help me, I'd have to leave without it. But flying over the E'or—I needed that saddle.

"Pachu, please," I choked, taking a step. "I can't do it alone."

My legs complained and buckled. I collapsed, knees striking the ground. Cursing, I slammed my fist into the mud. Why wouldn't my body do what I told it?!

"Neena, go back to the kitchen." Pachu's voice was calm and steady, a direct opposition to his wide, panicked eyes.

The girl darted from behind him and ran toward the tavern as he settled the lantern on the ground.

"I can't help if you eat me. Remember that, you beast."

Tizmet snorted, letting her lips fall shut. I glimpsed the red streak on her muzzle and hoped that's all they saw. Neena would probably have nightmares from that alone. The last thing she needed to see was chunks of Luther stuck between Tizmet's teeth.

Tizmet nudged the saddle, then Pachu began unfastening the buckles and straps. It was a painfully slow process. He muttered off a list of different spices, keeping himself calm as he worked near a dragon who clearly just killed.

I staggered to his side, guiding him through the process as best I could. My ears played tricks on me, hearing horses and angry shouts in the distance. I kept peeking over my shoulder. I could only hope the townsfolk were too busy putting out fires to worry about me or Rafe.

Relieved tears burned my eyes as Pachu finally pulled the last belt tight over Tizmet's neck.

"Avyanna, don't leave like this," he said. "Think of Kila."

His words were a knife in my gut. I clenched my jaw as I clawed my way up Tizmet's back, nails sinking between her scales. She used her bloody nose to push me into my seat.

"That's exactly who I'm thinking of." I slipped my boots into the stirrups. "She doesn't need to raise Durum in the shadow of a man-eater."

"Stars...!" He sucked in a sharp gasp. Apparently, he hadn't realized Tizmet ate a human.

"Leeds has a chance at something. Kila can raise the next generation of Riders—*free* Dragon Riders."

I smothered the sorrow that swelled within me as he shrank away, eyes wide and hands trembling. Tizmet straightened to her full height, and he scrambled back faster.

"Thank you, Pachu." A rogue tear slipped down my cheek. "Thank you."

She launched skyward with a powerful push off the ground and a massive pump of her wings. We were in the air mere breaths later, speeding toward our cottage. Across the bond, Tizmet's emotions swirled, mixing with mine. We shared a sense of remorse, leaving our home, her nest. And yet, simmering beneath the surface, hesitant excitement stirred.

We weren't ready for the quiet life.

Dirt sprayed as she flattened a patch of wildflowers with her rough landing. I slid from her back, legs shaking as I stumbled into my home. Carefully, I pulled at the smallest drop of magic to light a candle.

Tizmet growled in warning. *'If you overextend yourself, I'll fly you away in my claws.'*

I didn't have it in me to respond. I limped through the small space, grabbing our things. It took far too long to pack our belongings and pull out our weapons. Cold sweat drenched me and I gasped for air as I dragged the items outside.

Rothfuss and his men would come for me, maybe Luther's too, in retaliation. It was interesting how that looming threat simplified what items were necessary and what weren't. Gifts from townsfolk, trades from Brandi or Saudric—those were left behind.

Emotions clogged my throat, but I held the tears at bay as I pulled my crossbow and quiver of bolts to the door. Moonlight filtered through the constant haze, illuminating the spread of belongings, and I let out a soft curse. I had to secure it all somehow. The weight of it wouldn't phase her in the slightest, but by the time I had the weapons strapped in, my feet were dragging. Tizmet snarled and hauled me up by my tunic, then dropped me in the saddle.

'We need those packs!'

Our necessities were in there. My pardon, clothes, soap, Rafe's patches.

'Sit!' she roared.

I shrunk away from her, then busied myself strapping my legs in. The weapons rattled and swung against her scales and I worried over my weak fastening, hoping they wouldn't fall off mid-flight.

She snatched the packs in her front paws and growled her frustration as she struggled to get airborne. With her immense size, she needed all four legs to launch herself into the sky. Her irritation at being packed up like a horse swept over the bond, and I shoved back with my thanks.

When she got off the ground, I panted, dizziness sweeping over me. Leaning over the edge of Tizmet's neck, the cottage shrank into the night, obscured by the fog. I expected to feel more heartache, more sorrow, but as Tizmet soared away from it, I felt nothing but emptiness.

Smoke hid us from view as Tizmet streaked through the sky on silent wings. The sight of the dying fires brought a wave of relief as we soared above Leeds. The bodies had been cleared from the streets, but the red dragonling was nowhere to be seen.

'It is safe,' Tizmet assured.

'How do you know?'

She huffed, brushing me off. *'I know.'*

We headed to the old wood mill. Long ago it served as the main site for loggers, but as Leeds spread further east, the builders' guild built another, closer to the southern forest. Now the place served as a camp where Rothfuss and his men stayed to fend off any attacks from the west.

I hoped Rafe was there. If he wasn't, I would tear Leeds apart looking for him.

'You are in no condition to tear anything apart.'

I made no comment, knowing if Rafe was truly in danger, I would do anything to rescue him. He might not be a General anymore, but I knew quite well that he could take care of himself.

Tizmet fumbled a landing in front of the dilapidated wooden structure. The beams groaned with the disturbance of her thrashing wings. She dropped the packs, disgusted.

'No more than a beast of burden,' she growled.

A head poked out of the top window, and I offered Dane a small smile. He peered into the night with his bow at the ready.

"Oi, at least you made it," Jam called.

I pulled my legs free of the straps, tossing a frown his way. "Where's Rafe?"

I slipped from the saddle, and Tizmet snarled in warning as she caught my weight. She lowered me to the ground, then flicked her tongue, testing the air. I thought about pushing to stand, but couldn't find it in me to try. I was so tired—I could sleep for days.

'You are too weak to go looking for him.'

"He was settling things with Rothfuss," Jam replied.

"Avyanna!"

Mikhala swooped in over me and dropped to a crouch. Her bright eyes searched my body for injury. Blood splattered her vest and the iron-rich stench turned my stomach. I rested my head against Tizmet's flank, forcing steady breaths in through my nose to quell the nausea.

"I'm not leaving without Rafe."

"Some of us can't just fly off," Darrak stated. He watched me with a frown, his arms crossed over his chest. "You're setting that new Rider up for failure."

"She will be–"

"You just taught them to fear dragons."

I groaned. Talking was taking too much out of me. It was too hard to stay awake. I was no good to anyone in the state I was in.

Tizmet clicked low in her throat. *'Sleep.'*

'Rafe–'

'I will wake you when he arrives.'

Mik settled against me, pulling me to her shoulder as she leaned against Tizmet's warm scales. I let their comfort and reassurance lull me into a doze. I just needed to rest my eyes...

'He comes.'

I winced as awareness crept back. Every bit of me hurt. My head throbbed and my muscles were pulled tight and sore. My tongue was swollen and tender from where I had bitten it. A groan tore itself out of my throat as I tried to stir faster than my body would allow.

"Easy." Mik's voice was soft as she held me steady.

Tizmet's shoulder shifted behind me as she craned her head. I blinked up at her, my mouth parched and eyes grimy.

'He's coming?'

'Aye. With the lawkeeper.'

Her pupil narrowed as it danced over my body, as if she was double-checking I was still in one piece. Flecks of blood still stained her lips and fangs.

The sun was high in the sky, burning through the fog behind her. Dread twisted my gut. I slept all night.

Mik offered me her support when I struggled to stand, taking my weight as I got my feet under me. Tizmet clicked and eyed me, but gave me space as I rose. My head complained with the sudden movement and I hissed in pain, ducking lower as if it could spare me.

"She's in rough shape." Mik commented to the others, then dipped her chin to meet my gaze. "What happened to you?"

"Magic." Darrak's voice was far less judgmental and more concerned as he stepped closer. "She expended too much of it when she rescued Rafe. Now, she pays the price when she overextends herself."

Blain handed me a flask, and I didn't hesitate to drink. I grimaced as my head roiled over the movement. When I handed it back, he winked at me.

"She's been coping thus far," he said.

"Ruveel will make an example of her when we return," Darrak warned.

"Let him." I tested my muscles, taking my own weight. "I couldn't care less what that dungheap thinks."

Mik nodded, face alight with pride. "I second that!"

I took in the scene through the dreary fog. The mill's tall, foreboding structure was at our back, surrounded by old moss-choked stumps, sprouting suckers and new growth. Jamlin sat on a stone, sharpening his sword. Blain reclined next to him, lounging with his face tipped toward the sky.

Zeph looked crushed.

My heart wrenched inside me, and it had nothing to do with my seizure.

His features were dull, expressionless as he stared off into the distance. He fiddled with a stone, rubbing it and turning it over in his hand as if lost in thought. His sand-colored hair was tousled, disheveled from last night's events. A muscle in his jaw twitched and his lips pressed into a thin line of irritation before settling back into the impassive mask he wore.

I knew what he thought of.

Tegan peeked up from tuning his lute and offered me a small shrug and shake of his head. There was nothing we could do for him.

I took a shuffling step toward Zeph anyway, drawing his gaze. His brows plunged into a lethal glare.

"Oi!"

Dane's voice drew our attention above to the high window. He pointed into the distance, and we all spun as Rafe came into view. He wasn't alone. Rothfuss flanked him with four of his enforcers. They rode with an air of unease, their postures rigid and their expressions filled with apprehension.

Rafe's hands were tucked against the horn of his saddle, and I squinted at them before realizing they were tied. A shiver of anger ran through me as I changed direction and headed toward the riders. Darrak followed, pressing close.

"Choose your words with care, Avyanna," he whispered. "If you plan to return, don't burn your bridge."

I didn't care about my bridge.

Tizmet straightened to her full height, her shadow enveloping me like a blanket. She let out a growl, letting Rothfuss know he had come close enough.

"Avyanna of Gareth!" Rothfuss' voice ran out clear and strong. It was not the bright tenor of my friend, but the stern cadence of a lawkeeper.

Emotions warred within. Angry that it had come to this—and saddened because this was the end. This was our goodbye. And it would not be a pleasant one. I would not cower before him. He wasn't chasing me out. I was leaving for the townsfolk's sake, for Kila's future.

I was leaving so Tizmet wouldn't eat him or one of his men.

"Rothfuss," I called, lifting my chin.

"Truce."

Nodding, I strode forward with as much dignity as I could manage. My muscles complained and I couldn't hide the slight limp in my stride as I met them halfway. Rothfuss dismounted and tossed the reins to Rafe's stallion to one of his men.

Like he was a hostage.

I held in my scoff.

Rothfuss' placid features and set jaw mirrored my sorrow. He hated this as much as I did. His sharp gaze danced to Darrak, and he gave him a brisk nod in acknowledgment.

My eyes burned as I fought to keep my lips pressed in a tight line. I wouldn't show weakness. I chose my path. Now, I had to follow it.

"You know why I'm here." His tone carried a sense of resignation as he stopped a few paces from me. He braced his feet apart and held his chin high.

"Aye." I ground my teeth together, trying not to think of our cottage—of the cottage. It wasn't mine anymore. "We won't be returning."

"If I let you have him, you are banned from Leeds." Emotion hitched his words, but his gaze held steady as he rested his hand on the pommel of his sword.

"Only me?"

He blinked, staring past me to the others. His eyes caught on a figure and he twisted his lips in thought. Staring at the person behind me, he shrugged.

"You and your dragon are one. She's committed an unforgivable crime against Leeds and its citizens. I'm not foolish enough to think that I could dispatch her–"

'Smart man,' Tizmet snarled her approval.

"Aside from Rafe and the Caul who killed my men, the rest of your friends are welcome to stay—after serving their time."

Rafe sat tall on his horse, his dark eye plastered to my face. I knew he would approve. He no longer ordered the Tennan about. We were not bound by duty, but by friendship. He wouldn't order anyone to leave, or to stay. They all had a free choice.

Some just might need a push in the right direction.

"Release Rafe and we will be on our way."

"Avyanna–" Rothfuss' expression twisted into a grimace, and his tone dropped that essence of authority. "Leeds cannot handle your dragon."

"I know." I took a deep breath, forcing my words to hold steady. "Promise me you will help the people see Durum's value. Kila is one of your own, and her dragon is malleable. They can benefit Leeds."

He gave me a mournful smile. "Durum is not Tizmet. You are not Kila. I can't say mistakes won't be made, but I can promise to give them a fair chance."

"That's all I ask."

"You've been a pleasure, Avyanna," he added.

I scoffed, and the threat of tears burned as I held them back. I would not cry. "Oh, really?" I lifted my brow in mock challenge.

"Didn't say your dragon was."

Tizmet huffed, unbothered by the jab.

"May the sun light your path." Rothfuss' gaze sparked with a mixture of fondness and grief. His eyes traced every contour of my face, as if committing it to memory. After a slow breath, his eyes pressed shut, then he spun on his heel and left.

Not only had I lost my home and my future, but a cherished friend.

One of many.

I licked my parched lips and wiped at my cheeks as Rothfuss waved for his men to release Rafe. They tossed him his reins, and even from this distance, I could see the glint of annoyance in his stare. He kicked his horse into a trot, and the beast snorted.

Plastering a bright smile on my face, I craned up at him as he rode close, blocking my view of the others. He swung his leg over the stallion's neck and dropped. Crowding me, he dipped his head, pressing a tender kiss to my lips. I closed my eyes as tears slid down my cheeks.

"No regrets," he whispered.

I sniffed and used my bandit breaker to cut the rope around his wrists. It was loose, and I knew well enough that he could have gotten out if he wanted to.

He glanced over my head, and his mouth twisted into a frown.

"Zeph–" I started.

"I know."

He strode past me and I fell into step with his horse, holding the saddle for support.

Darrak jerked his chin in greeting. "Good to see you made it."

"Wish I could say the same," he muttered.

Darrak shook his head and Mik beamed between us, as if overjoyed for us all to be reunited once again. But this wasn't over.

"Zephath of Othilies."

Zeph's blank expression dropped into a fierce frown at Rafe's use of his full name. Standing, he braced himself, holding his ground as Rafe approached like a bull and towered over him.

"Why are you here?" he demanded.

"My place is with you," Zeph replied, words slow and wary. I didn't miss the twitch of his hand as he rested a thumb on his belt loop.

"Not anymore. You've been using that head of yours since we left Regent. Try to use those brains once more."

Zeph glanced at me, and I gave him a shrug. I would be of no help to him. He had to make this choice.

"You're not banned from Leeds," Rafe said. "Why are you here?"

"I would go where you go, General."

Rafe's posture relaxed the slightest bit, and he clapped a hand on Zeph's shoulder. "You go wherever you want now."

My heart ached. The hatchlings would be left behind, the only little ones I ever thought I had the smallest right to—and Rafe was saying goodbye to the boy he saved. The one boy who rebelled against all others and followed Rafe, knowing he was safe with him.

Muscles bunched in Zeph's jaw as he stared Rafe down. Something passed between them, needing no words. With a brisk nod, he turned on his heel and Rafe's hand fell from his shoulder.

"Tegan!" he snapped.

The red-head leapt to his feet. "Aye!"

"Why are you here?"

"Not quite sure of that myself, sir."

"Leeds could use a bard."

"And I've my eye on the innkeeper." Tegan smirked, waggling his eyebrows.

"Git."

I choked on a laugh as he saluted and shouldered his lute. He hummed a tune and offered me a wink before setting off down the overgrown path back to Leeds.

Zeph hesitated in following him, turning to Rafe once more. "It's been a pleasure, sir."

Rafe nodded. "Treat that girl right."

Zeph glanced at me, as if he expected me to object to him staying behind. Once a snobby little teen, cranky and angry at the world. Hurt, and lashing out at everyone who only wanted to help him. Nose stuck in books, he refused to look at the world and what it had to offer.

Now, he had the air of a leader about him. He would be good for Kila and Leeds, and they would be good for him. He needed a place he could grow, and following in Rafe's shadow, he would be a waste.

"Someone has to teach her how to act like a Dragon Rider," I choked out.

"Aye, someone has to," he agreed.

It wouldn't be me.

He flashed me a rare smile. It transformed his severe features into that of a young man who enjoyed life. One who was ready for his next adventure. He turned down the path and rushed his steps to catch Tegan. Bittersweet grief tugged on my chest.

Tizmet lowered, nudging me with her nose. *'They will be safe, little one.'*

'How do you know?' Tears blurred my vision as Rafe made his way back to me.

'They have dragons now,' she huffed, sending warm, moist air billowing down my tunic. *'Trust the hatchlings to choose right. It is a new dawn of dragons.'*

Rafe wrapped his arms around me, pulling me tight against his chest as I sobbed. I didn't want to cry, but I hated saying goodbye. I was terrible at it.

"No regrets."

Chapter 32

Rafe said there were horrors in the E'or that were better left unspoken. Trudging across the mountains, I realized I should have trusted him.

I slipped on a wet rock as waves of rain pummeled me. The storm had Tizmet grounded, and every cave or nook we tried to seek shelter in was occupied by something far worse than raging winds and icy downpours.

Lightning flashed, and a strong hand gripped the back of my tunic, hauling me over the rock. Blain led the way, doggedly climbing in the torrential downpour as we trailed behind him, Tizmet bringing up the rear so nothing would surprise us.

That's not to say that nothing followed.

Tizmet's roar echoed over the storm, and a stab of pain skittered across the bond. I tried to turn—not that there was much I could do against something that would dare attack a dragon, but Rafe shoved me forward.

"Let her handle it!" he barked.

Streams of rainwater ran down his face. Lightning flashed again, illuminating his scarred features, making him look far more terrifying than he was. I bit my lip and pressed on, climbing over the slippery stone.

Small scaled creatures, more like bog lizards than dragons, crawled over the stones, speeding toward us. Earlier, Tizmet's bursts of fire scared them off—until the deluge started. Her flames could burn in the rain, but not for long, and Tizmet didn't have an endless supply.

Thunder boomed, rattling my teeth as I stumbled, my boots slipping on the sheer rock face.

"Ghoul!" Blain sounded the alarm.

Rafe slammed me onto the stone, hovering over me. I gasped, sucking in streams of water and choking.

What was a ghoul?

An eerie howl carried over the wind, and all sound of the storm died. Rain still pummeled us, and ran in rivulets off the stones, but the growing shriek pierced the night, swallowing all other sounds. The sharp, twisted snarl sent terror skittering down my spine.

Rafe grabbed my hands and slapped them over my ears, his eye searching the darkness, as if it held the answers.

'Don't listen to it!' Tizmet roared.

Fear clamped my eyes shut. If I wasn't already soaked to the bone, I would be drenched in nervous sweat. *'What is it?!'*

'A monster of magic!'

What that meant—I had no idea.

The path Blain led us on was a narrow slice through the mountains. It wasn't meant for a dragon of her size. Rafe rolled away, and she replaced him, descending upon me. She shoved boulders aside, and they crashed down the mountainside as she crushed me into the rock, curling around me. With her wing spread overhead, she tucked in close. Her luminescent eye flashed as the pupil narrowed. A strange emotion crept through the bond.

She was scared.

Pain jolted through me the same moment her lips pulled back with a hiss. The tiny lizards were upon her. Her scales provided fine protection, but not against teeth and claws small enough to dig underneath them.

I thought the Sands were bad, but that place was nothing compared to the E'or.

Many lessons were learned from crossing the E'or. I gained a new level of respect for Blain and his consistent trips. That Rafe crossed them alone while the Tennan struggled to catch up, had me in awe. This place made me feel insignificant and powerless. Even a dragon wasn't at the top of the food chain here.

The sight of gryphons initially took my breath away—until a flock of them unleashed a ferocious assault on Tizmet. We fought off swarms of trolls with crude knives. And goblins—squat humanoid creatures with long pointy ears who had a penchant for biting. We battled giant black spiders with awful red eyes. They were as large as our horses and twice as fast over the slick stone.

When ghouls or phantoms—ghostly apparitions that froze the very blood in your veins—attacked, Blain and Dane headed the offense while the rest of us simply tried not to die. Somehow, they were immune to their calls.

And the monsters were only half of it.

The storms were a force to be reckoned with. Tizmet could always test the air and know if she should stay grounded, or if it was safe to fly, though she rarely had a chance. We were buckled down most days due to frigid temperatures and foul weather.

These mountains were harsh and brutal. The only things that seemed to survive here were creatures befitting the cruel elements.

The kanaak, as Blain called them, were little wingless birds, the drab color of the mountain itself, with beady black eyes. Though they barely reached my knee, they were the bane of our existence. Too many times, they stalled our progress by coming at us in waves. The things took forever to die. Even after slicing one in half, its horrible white beak lined with teeth still snapped away.

By the time we descended, Mik had a slice promising to scar on her arm, bestowed by a gryphon. She refused my healing, and I didn't push her. If I had a seizure, I'd be dead weight. Jamlin had a gash on the side of his head, and I'd broken my arm from a fall—which Tizmet healed without question.

When we stumbled into Stonesmead, we all looked far worse for wear.

I relaxed in the saddle as we glided through the sky, refusing to arrive at my mother's home before Rafe. After all, she didn't even know we claimed each other. The one and only time she had seen him was at Hamsforth, right after I joined his Tennan.

A smile spread over my face as I remembered her brandishing a loaf of bread at him, ready to fend him off with a baked good. He laughed at her then, realizing where I got my attitude. My heart thumped against my chest, and I leaned over Tizmet, trying to spy the group on horseback.

'To think the mating will never end,' Tizmet grumbled, feeling my sense of longing over the bond.

'Some animals mate for life,' I said.

'And they are all the dumber for it.'

I leaned against her neck with a sigh. *'If you love someone, you won't go looking for another.'*

'If they love you, they should be willing to... impress you.'

'Will you demand Flinor prove his right to mate again?'

'Of course. I would not mate a dragon I could out-fly.'

A soft chuckle flowed out as I ducked behind the windbreak of her neck. I wondered what my mother would think of Rafe now. Though it wasn't as if she had the time to get to know him before. Would she approve?

'What does it matter?' Tizmet asked, genuinely curious.

'She's my mother. Of course I want her approval.'

'Will she mate him then?'

'No!'

'Then why do you wish for her to be impressed by him?'

How did one explain this to a dragon? Sometimes, she proved to be more a beast than a sentient creature.

'Validation, I suppose.'

'If she disapproves, will you reject him?'

'No.'

She made a choking sound deep in her throat, frustrated that she didn't understand. I smiled. She might never comprehend our ways. The relationship we shared now was a far cry from the beginning of our bond. We learned so much about one another, but there would always be things neither of us would puzzle out.

'I want to make her proud,' I said. Surely pride was something she understood.

'Is it a prideful thing to see that your young has chosen a good mate?'

'Would you be pleased if Durum took a maimed mate? One who could not fly?'

'I would eat them both.'

That was a bit harsher than I expected.

'See?' I prompted. *'You would be disappointed in him.'*

Realization dawned across the bond, and her understanding clicked into place. *'And they would be dead,'* she murmured, lost in her thoughts.

That too.

We arrived at my mother's house as the sun dipped toward the horizon. Smoke curled from Ragnath's forge, and Tizmet hummed in excitement. No matter it was the end of summer and the days were smoldering.

Flying lazy circles in the air, we watched Rafe's group approach the small house tucked away from the village. Moony, Mik's horse, took off at a run. That the horses made the trek across the mountains surprised me to no end.

I hadn't given thought of where we'd stable them, or where the rest of us would stay. Stonesmead had a small tavern that the others might cram into. The last time we visited, Mik and I slept near my mother's hearth. Rafe wouldn't leave me, and I grimaced at the internal image of both of us squished on the floor.

We drifted lower until Tizmet landed. Nerves knotted my stomach. This was my mother. She loved me, and Ragnath loved Tizmet—well, her flame anyway.

Mik dismounted and hopped up and down, waiting for me to slide from the saddle. Rafe approached with a heated glare and clenched jaw. It almost appeared as if he was nervous, too.

"Come on! I wonder if she has any of those apple things she had last time—the warm ones with that gooey filling?" Mik bounced from foot to foot. "Those were delicious. I've been dreaming about them ever since! Ugh, I'm starving. Bet I could eat everything she has!"

I laughed and shook out my legs, a familiar headache settling at my temples. My body didn't know whether it was still in the sky, or if it should be walking. The discomfort was a worthy trade for soaring over the clouds.

The door flung open as Rafe pulled up next to us.

"Girl!"

Ragnath recognized me right away. That, or he recognized Mik as she practically ran the man over. She snared him in a hug and slapped a kiss on his cheek before pushing inside. His ruddy face flushed crimson, and he pressed a palm on his jaw, clearly embarrassed over her greeting.

Darrak laughed at her actions, knowing as well as I did there was no teaching Mik decency.

"Ragnath!" I grinned, and Rafe dismounted, his feet hitting the ground with a hard thud.

My mother's mate took a double-take at Rafe, his shame at being kissed by another woman replaced by stark skepticism. Rafe adjusted his trousers and stood tall, towering over me, and my gaze darted between the two, wondering which was actually taller.

"Who're ye?"

Rafe lifted his chin, and I looped my arm in his, an attempt to avoid any intimidation tactics.

"This is Rafe. We were–"

"You're the reason she was banished!" Ragnath roared, charging at us.

My jaw fell open, and I choked as Rafe dropped his stallion's reins and braced himself.

"Avyanna?" My mother's voice tore my attention to the door just as Ragnath slammed into Rafe. I yelped, dancing aside.

"You flaming bastard son of a–" Ragnath's curse was cut off as Rafe spun behind him and looped an arm around his throat.

"Avyanna!" My mother shrieked. The pastry in her hand dripped glaze down her forearm.

"Rafe!" I screamed in outrage, propping my hands on my hips—a sign of my disbelief.

His eye snapped to mine, and he frowned as if to say this wasn't his fault. Ragnath grabbed his arm—and I had not been the only one to underestimate the smith's strength. He lifted Rafe off his feet and threw him over his shoulder to the ground.

Rafe was quick to stand, braced and ready for Ragnath's charge–

"Nath!" My mother's tone pitched high, drawing the man's attention.

"It's the blasted General! The thrice-cursed man who–"

"Banished her!" She clamped a hand to her chest, jaw falling open with her horror.

I shook my head. "Oi—no! That's not how–"

Ragnath took that moment to slam his fist into Rafe's middle.

Rafe could take a punch. He was made to fight. But Ragnath was a smith. He beat metal itself into submission. The man was a mountain of muscle and power. I grimaced as Rafe stumbled backward, sucking in a breath as he raised his fists.

"Mother!" I whirled on her. "Stop this!"

"He had you banished!"

"I'm right here!" I screamed, throwing my hands in the air.

She blinked, pausing as if she had been struck. Behind her, propped against the doorframe, Mik froze midchew and looked between us, enjoying the show.

"Avyanna!" My mother raced to me, hiking her skirts up.

I scoffed a laugh, and she squealed, crushing me in an embrace. I groaned and held my breath, trying not to let her squash my ribs as I smiled over her shoulder.

Mik's attention drifted back to the fight.

"Mother," I squeaked. "Ragnath."

"Oh!" She released me, then spun on the two.

Rafe landed a solid strike on Ragnath's chin, spinning the big man to face my mother.

I raised an eyebrow as I caught the Tennan watching the fight in good humor. Even Darrak was content to see who won the brawl, a grin riding his lips like he was a schoolboy again.

"Nath! Stop fighting like a child, and come here! Avyanna is right here!"

Mik let out a bark of laughter as the smith stumbled a step away from Rafe and blinked at me. Rafe took a step back and lowered his fists a fraction, breathing hard.

Who knew it would take a smith to give him a challenge.

Confusion distorted my mother's features. "We heard you disobeyed orders?"

"Aye–"

"To rescue a man," Ragnath spat, eyeing Rafe.

"Aye–"

"He don't look like he needs yer rescuing." Ragnath huffed, looking Rafe up and down.

"Try taking on a horde of Shadows and a turned dragon." Rafe shrugged. "I'd like to see how you fare."

"We got your letter," she whispered, tears wetting her eyes. "When we didn't receive another, we thought you were dead."

"I'm sorry." Now would not be the time to tell her I almost died. Multiple times. I offered a tentative smile. "I've been pardoned."

"You're here to stay?"

"In Regent, aye." I nodded.

"But not here."

My eyes fluttered closed at the pain in her voice. When I was little, did she entertain the idea that I would come back and join her village? Did she wish I had never chosen this path?

"No, I won't stay in Stonesmead."

A heavy silence fell, thick and suffocating.

"We will see her to Northwing, but she is free to go where she pleases," Darrak stated.

I blinked, glancing over at the men on their horses. They had all been watching with rapt attention, and I held back a laugh as their eyes danced between us all.

"Oi, mother. You know Darrak and Mik." I nodded to the group. "The twins are Blain and Dane, and that's Jamlin. They're my friends."

They examined one another and a smile stretched across my cheeks as I gestured to my mate. "And Rafe Shadowslayer."

"Former General," Ragnath scoffed.

"Had to break the King's nose to rid myself of that title," Rafe drawled. "I'm not above breaking yours."

The smith barked a laugh and some of the tension left my shoulders.

Mik snagged another pastry before trudging to Moony.

"I'll make extra for you before you leave," my mother called to her.

Her countenance completely changed, beaming like a gleeful child as she mounted.

Darrak nodded to Rafe. "We'll wait for you at the inn."

The group rode off murmuring quiet conversations among themselves.

Ragnath still watched Rafe like a hawk, and Rafe didn't take his eye off the man. My mother and I watched the two with resignation. They would have to work out their differences.

"It wouldn't be proper for ye to sleep with her." Ragnath squinted at Rafe, testing him.

I took a deep breath. "We're mated."

My mother whirled on me, gaping at my belly. Of course, she would expect a child. Tizmet's eyes flashed between us, watching with keen interest.

Ragnath bristled. "And you didn't think to seek her mother's permission?! Ye flaming–"

"We were across the E'or!" I rubbed my face. This was not how I intended for things to go.

"Mother, I claimed him and he claimed me. No, I'm not with child—I'm barren. There's to be no grandbabes unless you count the hatchlings from Tizmet's clutch."

'She's too soft to be their grandam,' Tizmet huffed, eyeing my plump mother.

'Where do you think Durum got his love for baked goods?'

Her head flew into the air with a hiss, as if it all suddenly made sense.

My mother's features washed out with her frown as she peered at my belly. To a village woman, it was the worst of curses to be barren. Without a fertile womb, there was no reason to marry. This far from King's Wall, people didn't marry for love. They married for alliances and for babes to work their land and carry on their line. I needed none of those things.

I only needed Rafe.

"It's my lot. I've accepted it," I stated, standing next to Rafe. "We are mated."

"Ye're not good enough for her," Ragnath sneered.

He met my eye as he responded, "No one is."

My heart thumped in pride and the smith recoiled from Rafe's reply, the sneer falling from his face. He glanced at my mother, who stared at us with love in her eyes. She would accept us, I knew it. Rafe was not an easy man—certainly not the type she ever thought I would end up with—and yet here I was.

He was enough.

My mother broke the quiet. "Well, come in and tell us your story."

The conversation kept us up late into the night. Tizmet curled around the forge, as happy as a hatchling with a full belly, while me and Rafe crammed on the floor.

I rolled, throwing an elbow into his ribs. He cursed and grabbed my arm, saving himself from another blow. I huffed and curled in at his side as he relaxed against the hard planks. My mother and Ragnath had the bed—Rafe had shot down the suggestion that we take it. Compared to the E'or's rough terrain, a wooden floor was practically a luxury.

"I miss our mattress," I breathed against his chest.

He remained dressed for my mother's sake. I feared her heart would fail if she saw the scars that littered his body.

"We're off to the palace next."

I propped myself upright to see him. Firelight danced across his face, casting his empty eye socket into shadow. He had offered to keep his patch on, but I knew how uncomfortable it was. My mother could handle this scar—and Ragnath could see the torture he endured and what had sent me to his aid.

"Truly?"

"Aye. Then a straight shot to Northwing."

I glanced over to be sure my mother was asleep. Her soft snores held steady.

"Darrak thinks the line will hold?" I pressed.

"Ruveel will hold it."

"I thought you didn't like him," I teased, tracing the soft edges of the scar that trailed down his cheek.

"I don't. That doesn't mean he can't fight."

"If he's so good, why was I sent for?" I mused, bringing my thumb to his lips.

"You have one of the largest dragons alive–"

'You have me? I thought I had you,' Tizmet rumbled through her doze.

"–and she's fought them. She grew up with the Shadows. She knows them. If there's something new out there, some new magic, your dragon will be the one to find it." He bit at my finger, sucking it into his mouth.

My teeth sank into my lip as his tongue swirled around my thumb in a way that sent delicious waves to my core.

I crept on top of him, glancing at the bed like a wayward child, as I straddled his thighs. "We'll be sent behind enemy lines."

"I'll be with you."

His low voice sent a shiver through me as he rocked his hips, his dark eye daring me on. His touch slid over my legs, slipping beneath my tunic.

"You're with me now." I leaned low to his chest. "Enough of the war. Tell me how we will make use of the feather bed?"

When his warm hand brushed my chest, I nipped at his jaw. He let out a muffled groan as I slid my palm between us, finding the waistband of his trousers, then–

"I'd imagine ye'd sleep on a feather bed the same as any other."

I yelped and rolled off Rafe, hiding along his side as Ragnath flopped onto his back. My mother's snores stopped short as she fought for a comfortable spot. I giggled as Rafe let out a strangled groan.

"I'll not be hearing it from you either, Rafe," the smith growled.

Smiling, I burrowed into his side, hiding from the man my mother claimed.

Chapter 33

It took over a fortnight to reach King's Wall. We pressed on as fast as the horses could travel. Tizmet took her time, flying lazy circles above them. She was still healing from her ordeal over the E'or and would sport several small scars as a permanent reminder.

When we arrived, I flew ahead of the group. There was no point in antagonizing the people or making them wonder why we were there. They would remember Tizmet as the man-eater, and me as the banished Rider.

It was only proper that I should thank the King for extending a pardon to me.

I had only met him twice and talked to him once. He had been kind and sweet—an old man who seemed quite generous at the time. I thought him balanced and fair until he signed my banishment.

Ruveel played a role, but to what extent, I didn't know. King Aldred had obviously fought against Rafe's wishes, however, and tried to keep him as a General. Yes, the war was at stake. Yes, the fight was picking up and the frontlines spreading, but it angered me that the King would try to keep us from one another.

Rafe hated King's Wall. He couldn't stand the nobles and their haughty demeanor and was liable to punch one if they got too close. He wasn't a General anymore. Now, he was a mere civilian, with the patch still inked on his shoulder. To land a blow to a noble would be a dueling offense. Not that Rafe wouldn't win, but we didn't need to stir up more trouble.

Tizmet landed stiffly in the courtyard. Soldiers ran to greet us, weapons sheathed, while others rushed inside to announce our arrival. Tizmet growled and snapped at a man that got too close—causing him to retreat a few steps.

I unfastened my legs from the stirrups, heart pounding in my chest. Without Rafe or Darrak, I felt out of place and nervous. I'd never been here without an escort.

'Calm. We are here at their request,' Tizmet assured.

My legs dangled as I peered at the ground from the saddle.

'I could fly us to Northwing instead,' she offered.

I pushed out a sigh and dropped, bracing myself against her shoulder. *'If we are to live in Regent, they need to know I'm not afraid of them.'*

'Aye, they should be afraid of us!'

I groaned, meeting her fiery gaze. I could have sworn she was smiling in her dragon-like way.

"Hail, Rider!"

I pushed off of Tizmet, straightening to find a man in a dark uniform approaching. Tizmet shook like a dog, getting the kinks out from her flight, but he paid her no mind.

"Hail. I am Avyanna of Gareth," I greeted. "I have the King's pardon."

He dipped his head in a slight bow. "Well enough, I would see it, if you please."

I sighed and glanced up at the saddle, where the pardon was secured in my pouch. Surely I didn't actually need to fetch it. The older soldier stared at me, his gaze not leaving my eyes as his hand rested on his sword.

Muttering curses under my breath, I climbed back up. Crushed inside one of the many pockets, I fished out the parchment. Returning to the ground, I handed it to him. He scanned it, lips pressed together in a firm line.

The courtyard was just as I remembered it. It was large and spacious, being designed with Dragon Riders in mind. With constant updates for the King from the warfront, Dragon Lord Ruveel was a common guest. I wasn't sure how often he traveled these days, but the soldiers didn't seem surprised to see Tizmet.

"Many thanks." The man handed the pardon back to me. "I am Segul, master of the King's Guard. We've received word that the rest of your party arrived in King's Wall. King Aldred will be briefed and will send for you tomorrow after you have rested. I trust you would be seen to your rooms?"

"Please."

I held in my groan, remembering the treatment I received here. I hadn't had a proper bath since I left Regent. Of course, I washed myself in springs and ponds. It was that, or a sponge and bucket of tepid water.

"Right this way."

I shook those thoughts out of my head. Leeds was not my home anymore. That was in my past, and did me no good now.

'You won't go tearing the palace apart this time?' I teased, following Segul.

She huffed. *'Don't give me a reason to.'*

I smiled to myself, reveling in just how far we had come. She had nothing to fear from me, besides my seizures, and I had no reason to doubt her. We trusted each other implicitly—as a bonded pair should.

Segul led me to the giant stone palace, rising above the city like some mountain of its own. The southern wing where we landed had a series of rooms with giant balconies to accommodate dragons and their Riders.

Our boots clapped along the cobblestone path, surrounded by manicured landscapes. The open space allowed dragons to move about freely. The only trees to be seen were planted along the perimeter near the iron fence.

As far as I could tell, I was the only Rider present. Tizmet would have alerted me if Ruveel and his beast were here. She hated Ge'org with a passion. He never ceased to taunt or irritate her. I thought he acted like an overgrown puppy until the day Tizmet maimed a squire by taking off his arm. He had donned the composure of Leader of the Dragon Fleet, and protected the masses while she and I fought over the bond.

Entering the palace, I nodded to the guards at the doors. They ignored my greeting and stared straight ahead as Segul turned down a hall.

"Your travels were smooth, I assume?" he asked

I deadpanned. "We crossed the E'or."

"No easy task." He clicked his tongue. "No doubt you bear some scars from your efforts. The E'or demands a tax of all who cross it." He moved to the side so that I could walk beside him. "All the same, I would say that it's safer than the route through the south at this time."

I shuddered. "I would take the Sands any day over the horrors of those mountains."

Segul came to a stop in front of a door, but hesitated. "You have been gone a long time, Dragon Rider. Things are not the same as when you left."

His eyes were intense, and his lips pressed into a harsh line before giving me a tight smile. He opened the way and motioned me inside.

Frowning at his words, I stepped into the immense room. The ceiling arched high above me, tall enough that Tizmet would have to stand on her back legs and stretch her neck to reach the top. With the furniture tucked into one corner, she had plenty of space to maneuver. Thick furs adorned the floor, both as decoration and to ward off the chill from the stone where the dragons slept.

Tizmet was already there, eyeing the unlit hearth with sorrowful eyes.

I scoffed. *'It's scorching out.'*

'Fire is always welcome.'

"Your lady's maids will be in soon to ready your bath." Segul poked his head inside, glancing about. "Will there be anything else?"

"Aye, Rafe Shadowslayer should be seen to this room." I strode over to Tizmet to remove my packs and her saddle. "He will want a bath as well upon his arrival."

"As you request, Rider."

I squinted at him. "He is my claimed," I added.

The man dipped his head. "I would expect nothing else, with the state in which he left."

A smile spread over my face, and I propped a hand on my hip. Segul was a good man, and far more friendly than half of the lady's maids I dealt with in the past.

"And just how did he leave?" I asked, curiosity piqued.

I wanted to hear it from someone other than his Tennan. How did the palace and their staff view Rafe's journey across the kingdom and E'or?

"As if not even the sun itself could keep him from you," he replied with a mischievous grin. "I daresay the maidservants have dreamed of nothing else than a love so strong as his."

Laughter bubbled up inside of me and I threw my head back, hysterical that women would think Rafe romantic.

I would have to tease him about that one.

"Is there anything else, Rider?"

"No, thank you, Segul."

"My pleasure."

Servants came while I was still working the saddle off, and I let them fill the bath while I stripped her of the leather. She'd worn it since we left Leeds, and I hated how raw her scales were beneath. A few were cracked and bloody, and she craned her head, flicking her tongue.

'You didn't tell me you were hurt.' I hadn't even felt anything over the bond.

'Do you tell me when you break a nail? Or get a pox?'

'I don't get poxes.' I sniffed, fetching a wet rag to wipe the blood away. A carved peg stuck out of the far wall, made to support a dragon's saddle. I slid it over, grumbling to myself. Clearly, it had been constructed with a man's muscles and stature in mind.

I wasn't a weakling, and my fatigue could have played a role in my struggle. Tizmet nudged it completely on, huffing in annoyance that I didn't ask for her aid. She brought her head down to my level and blinked a fiery eye at me, pupil flaring out.

'I was born wild in the Sky Trees. A few cracked scales are about as worrisome to me as a broken nail.'

She clicked in rebuke, and I rolled my eyes, walking around her to the bath.

'I am a dragon!' she added.

As if I needed the reminder.

I stripped out of my soiled, grimy clothes. The maids saw to Tizmet with reservation, but not with fear. They didn't treat her like the man-eater she was, but rather an adult dragon—worthy of their respect.

'I am worthy of their respect.'

I smiled, holding in my laugh as I slipped into the gloriously hot water. The maids left while I was bathing, save for one. When I finished, she called for the rest to empty the tub. The water's murky color was a bit mortifying to see. I was not ashamed of the dirt and grime I accrued throughout my travels, but I daresay my skin was a shade lighter than when I arrived.

Dressed in a thin robe, I fell onto the bed, reveling in the way my body sank into the feathered cushions.

'This must be what clouds feel like,' I moaned, eyelids heavy.

'Clouds are nothing more than water suspended in air,' Tizmet drawled, but amusement colored her tone.

She rested and kept watch while I drifted off to sleep.

Rafe arrived that same evening. I missed his bath and only woke when he joined me—where he made use of the bed in far more entertaining ways than sleeping.

While we dressed the next morning, he grimaced while tugging at the sleeves that covered his patch.

"You have to cover it here?" I mused as I braided my hair.

He was as independent as I, and when asked if he needed manservants to ready him to see the King, he merely slammed the door in the servant's face.

"Aye, blasted politics," he growled, tucking the tunic into his trousers.

I watched him, catching his eye in the mirror. He froze, then smirked.

"Care to call ill?"

I laughed, and a blush warmed my cheeks as I went back to my braid. "Rafe, we have a meeting with the King!"

Truth be told, I enjoyed his attention. If he knew just how much I liked it, I would have been tempted to indulge sooner.

"He can wait."

"Rafe!"

He came up behind me, batting my fingers away, and I groaned as my tight braids fell loose about my shoulders.

"Wear it down."

"It's more practical when it's up and out of the way."

His hands found my shoulders, kneading the stiff muscles. He bent in close to nip at my ear. "Planning for a battle?"

"My General taught me to always be prepared." I held his face as his lips traveled down my neck.

"Mmm. And what else did he teach you?"

Could we call off? Say we were ill from the road?

'The one with braided flame comes,' Tizmet announced, amused.

"Mik is here."

A knock sounded on the door, and Rafe cursed. We both stood, and I ran my hands through my hair, shaking it out.

He opened the door at the same time I turned. Mik held no reservations about entering and strode in.

"Avyanna, you look gorgeous." She eyed me up and down with a grin before turning to Rafe. "You look far worse."

He grunted, ignoring her. Tizmet tested the air, studying Mik as she danced about our room.

"Darrak is with the King now. The twins and Jam are free for the night. I'm going to take them out on the town."

"Gaius?" I pressed, asking after the man she loved and was willing to risk her people's wrath for.

"Perhaps we will see him," she hedged with a sly smile. "Want to join us when you're done?"

Rafe propped his boot on the edge of the bathtub and laced it up, oblivious to my inspection of his backside.

"Oh, no. I'm sure I'll be entertained by other things."

His gaze snared mine in the mirror. A small smile tugged at his lips, and he went back to lacing his boot.

"Boring," Mik huffed. "Darrak thinks we'll head out in the morning."

"So soon?"

I spun to face her. I wasn't upset that we were headed to Northwing, but with Segul's comment earlier, I wondered just how bad it was. Dread weighed me down like a stone in my belly.

Her carefree smile faltered as she met my gaze. "Aye. He told you it's not going well."

Were my friends in danger at this moment? While I spun in pretty dresses, and dined with the King? How close were the Shadows?

"Go." Rafe's voice severed my inner turmoil. "Enjoy your night."

Mik's mask slipped back in place. She was the crazy Caul once again as she skipped out our door, pulling it shut behind her.

"Rafe. What if we're too–"

He cut me off with a passionate kiss, holding the nape of my neck so I couldn't pull away. Sighing, I relinquished myself to him, relaxing into his embrace. His lips moved against mine, his tongue teasing until I opened to him.

He kissed me, demanding my attention as he pulled me toward the bed. I yelped as he fell back, pulling me with him. Sitting me on his lap, I adjusted my skirts to straddle him as he looked me in the eye.

He tucked my hair behind my ear. "We will get there in time."

"How bad is it—do you know?" I leaned into him, threading my fingers behind his neck.

"Darrak and Blain have told me a bit."

"Rafe–"

"There's nothing you can do right now." He turned, pressing a kiss to my wrist. "There is a process for everything, Vy. Trust me."

Sighing, I rested my head on his shoulder. "Tell me they're safe."

"They are safe."

"Truly?"

"I wouldn't lie to you, Vy."

We stayed like that until a servant came to fetch us. I shook out the wrinkles in my dress and looked back at Tizmet.

'Coming?'

'I will be there if you need me.'

Smiling, I joined Rafe as he followed the servant down the hall. He was the only person she completely trusted with my safety—knowing he loved me.

He loved me.

The palace was quieter than I remembered. There were fewer servants milling about, and fewer guests. During my past visits, due to Tizmet's bouts of rage, they always led me around outside. But inside, the place seemed almost... abandoned.

We traveled down brightly lit corridors painted in gaudy colors. I held in my distaste at the array. It was supposed to be bright and flashy. The King wanted everyone to know his kingdom was wealthy and strong—not losing a war.

We arrived at a pair of large oak doors, flanked by two soldiers in royal uniforms. They matched the uniform of Segul, Master of the King's Guard, but his was far more plain, as if he wore it to blend in better—which I thought was worth noting.

Inside, mirrored chandeliers hung from a tall ceiling. Candles and lanterns burned in every corner of the room, lighting it up so brightly that one might mistake it for high noon. Tables lined the room, heaped with food, which guests already fell upon. The clink of glasses reached my ears as toasts were made and servants filled wine goblets.

I clenched Rafe's hand.

"Dragon Rider Avyanna, and Rafe Shadowslayer."

I glanced at the squire, a shudder running through me. He still had both his arms, unlike the previous man.

The happy din quieted at our arrival, and Rafe gently pulled me alongside him as he strode into the room. Musicians played in the corner, strumming some soft song. The sea of nobles donned in extravagant frills and the latest fashion trends parted and moved aside as we crossed to the dais where the King sat.

He looked older—worn. His face was gaunt and his hair thin. His eyes were as sharp as ever, studying us as we approached. He donned simple clothing, though still bedecked in his usual white and gold colors, and a bright gilded crown weighed heavily on his brow.

"Ah, my Shadowslayer."

His nose was slightly askew.

Dropping into a curtsy to hide my smile, I expected Rafe to bow, but he simply dipped his chin as I rose.

"And the Wild Rider." King Aldred's voice was soft but clear. The kind of wizened tenor that hushed crowds as people strained to hear.

I bottled up the hurt this man caused and shoved it deep down in my heart. Glancing at Rafe, I expected him to lead.

Well, he led—away from the King.

I pressed my lips together as we strode away from the King, not knowing proper protocol, but feeling like that was... unseemly. Taking a deep breath, I tried to steady my nerves as the crowd grew even quieter, all eyes on us.

We stopped at a table where Rafe seated me beside Darrak.

"You are an inspiration to all the mutes in Rinmoth, Rafe," he drawled as a servant reached around us to fill our wine glasses.

I eyed it with distaste.

"Do you have water?" I asked.

The girl ducked her head. "I can fetch some, milady."

"Wine is appropriate while dining with the King, Avyanna." Darrak said quietly as another servant placed plates and cutlery in front of me and Rafe.

I traced the gold filigree on the porcelain. This plate was worth more than all the belongings in my pack.

"She's wise to know her limits," Rafe murmured, grabbing food from the center of the table. "Perhaps she could teach a few nobles a thing or two."

As the server delivered my drink, I eyed the meat and breads before me—the fruits and vegetables laden in thick gravies and sauces. I didn't even know where to start.

Rafe cursed as the sleeve of his tunic dipped in a red sauce and I laughed, snatching his arm and rolling up his sleeve. He glared across the room, daring the people that looked our way to hold his gaze. Hushed whispers broke out wherever his stare lingered.

"I do believe you're frightening them," I mused.

"Clearly, you haven't noticed this, dear. He is frightening." Darrak laughed.

He dipped his chin in greeting to someone across the table, and as I slowly filled my plate, I followed his gaze. A beautiful woman with hair the color of fresh wheat smiled back at me.

"Tis Lady Auril." Darrak leaned toward me. "She owns a port up north, where the Cauls seek harbor. She runs the trade and has the monopoly on exotic furs."

I listened as I ate, enjoying Darrak's monologue of the people around the room. He seemed to know something about everyone and made the time pass quickly.

"If it isn't the Shadowslayer returned."

The belittling voice pulled my attention away from Darrak as he explained pearl trade in the south. A nobleman slid into the seat next to him. He was an attractive man, tall and lean. His tunic clung to him like a second skin and his sand-colored hair was combed perfectly. His smile was broad and bright as he nodded at me, his icy eyes sliding to my chest before coming back up to my face.

Tizmet reached across the bond, testing the repulsion that flooded through me.

He was attractive—but there was something predatory in that gaze.

Rafe had stilled, looking straight at his food, fork and knife in hand. He chewed methodically, not giving the man a spare glance.

"I heard you were back, but I had to see it for myself. Care to introduce your little lady?" He threw a wink my way.

Back in my room, Tizmet shifted, sensing danger, and pondered whether to make an appearance. I pushed ease at her and muffled our bond. Rafe was with me. Nothing would happen.

Darrak leaned in behind me, his body warm across my back. "Please distract him before he causes a scene." His whisper tickled my ear.

Slipping my hands into my lap, I clutched my dress. Rafe was between us. I was safe.

"The scribe announced us, and as I haven't heard him announce you, clearly you were here at the time." I pasted a smile on my face, hoping it was half as charming as his.

"Ah, but it appears I was distracted."

I followed his gaze to the serving boy a few paces off. He fumbled with his wine bottle, casting a worried glance our way.

I frowned.

"Wild Rider Avyanna," I said, bringing his attention back to me. I used the title King Aldred had given me. It seemed more suitable than Dragon Rider, which indicated I belonged to the Fleets—-and Ruveel.

"Wild Rider!" He flashed a grin, showing too many teeth. "The first of many, to be sure."

Something twisted deep in my gut. His posture seemed forced, his smile didn't reach his eyes.

"I am Nothali of Jekka. I'm sure you remember my nephew, Zephath? Surely you have word of him?"

Rafe pushed to his feet, drawing Nothali's gaze. We both watched as he crossed the room toward the guards lining the walls.

"Oh dear." Nothali chuckled to himself. "He's going to do something dramatic."

I tipped my head as a guard tugged off a gauntlet and handed it to Rafe. The room fell silent as he returned to his seat, Darrak letting out a low groan. He placed the gauntlet in front of his plate. A silent threat. Aside from that, he made no attempt to acknowledge the noble.

Heaving a sigh, Nothali moved to pat Rafe's shoulder. He whirled, pulling a dagger from sun knows where, and held it a breath from Nothali's outstretched palm.

"I'll send for you, Shadowslayer." He laughed, stepping away. "We have much to discuss."

He walked off, and the room breathed a sigh of relief. Conversations picked up and clinks joined the din as people resumed their meals.

"What was all that?" I breathed.

"To throw a gauntlet is to challenge someone to a duel," Darrak murmured.

"Aye, but what was his problem?" I asked.

Rafe had been ready to issue a duel to the death at the mention of Zeph's name.

"He's a dangerous man, Avyanna. I wouldn't get caught alone with him."

Rafe leaned across the table, leveling a blank stare at Darrak as if to say I wasn't that stupid.

Chapter 34

Which I wasn't.

So while Rafe was gone the next morn, and a servant came calling from Nothali, I ignored them.

I spent my morning packing up my meager belongings. My hand stilled on my saddlebag as I checked it for the third time, my eyes drifting close. The familiar pang of loss resounded in my heart as I fought the memory of my little cottage. The chipped dishes, tiny jars of spices...

'You are here now,' Tizmet murmured, wrapping her consciousness around me.

A muscle worked in my jaw, and I blew out a steady breath. *'Aye. No point in dwelling on what could have been.'*

The door to our rooms creaked, pulling me from my thoughts. Rafe stepped inside, rubbing at his eye socket under his patch.

"Rough meeting?" I ventured, crossing the fur-covered floor to wrap my arms around his neck.

The war council requested Rafe as soon as he entered the palace. We both knew it wasn't to prepare him for heading to the warfront. They wanted information on what lay across the E'or; was it a threat or a risk worth taking one day? As Rafe would say—politics.

"They call themselves a war council," he scoffed, tucking me against his chest. "Hearsay and reports. Worse than a bunch of old ladies."

I laughed, shaking my head. "You didn't tell them about the dragonlings?"

"They'll know soon enough."

"I doubt they'd cross the E'or."

'They are their own. They go where they will,' Tizmet huffed, blowing a soft puff of smoke from where she napped.

"I'm not worried about them." He took a deep breath, his chest pressing against mine. "That flaming dungheap from last night is liable to attempt the crossing."

"Nothali?" My nose wrinkled. "He sent for me today."

Outrage flickered over his features. He clenched his jaw, gaze hard as he stared down at me.

I deadpanned. "I didn't *go*."

His stiff stance deflated a margin and he scanned the room as if he could find the words he sought etched into the walls. "He wants to know where Zephath is."

"Well, he's his uncle."

I clasped my hands behind his head, refusing to let him sneak off. He wasn't getting out of this. I waited far too long to learn about Zeph's past.

"He doesn't want to be found, Vy." His lip curled in a snarl. "Zephath's father is dead. Nothali was his guardian. The bastard has certain... tastes."

"Then he was running from him?" Nothali avoided a challenge from Rafe the previous night, he knew he couldn't take Zeph if Rafe claimed him.

"There's a reason I didn't trust the food at Northwing. Poison is the weapon of choice for nobles."

I squinted up at him. "And the food last night?"

If he wanted Rafe dead, now would be the time. What kind of man would plot to kill a General just to get his nephew back under his thumb?

"He's trying to place him. Does no good if I'm dead."

"And if he finds Zeph?"

"Zephath is a man now," he said with a jerk of his head. "He can take care of his own. Did you already forget that his girl is bonded? You think that gold would let anything happen to him?"

He was right. Zeph wasn't the scared young boy who lashed out at everyone anymore. He was a man, self-assured and confident. I pushed my worries to the back of my mind. He could hold his own in a fight, and with Kila and Durum, he had little to fear from his vile uncle.

"We will leave in the morning. Keep away from the bastard until then."

Rafe's glare promised that if Nothali came after me again, he wouldn't stay his challenge. For all that he tried to avoid politics, we were already entrenched in the King's business. A challenge to a nobleman would only complicate things further.

"I thought we were leaving today?" It was nearing midday, and I was eager to get to Northwing.

"A meeting with the King, then a walk through the city."

I pulled back with a grin. "Mik got to you, didn't she?"

He grunted. "One more night won't sway the war."

I danced on my toes and jumped up to give him a peck on the lips. Mik definitely got to him.

'You will walk the city?' Tizmet asked, rising to crane her head down at us.

'Aye. One last reprieve before Northwing.'

'I will fly,' she sighed, glancing out the balcony at the skies.

"She's going to keep an eye from the skies," I murmured to Rafe.

'I don't need his permission.'

'I wasn't asking him.' I pushed my good humor at her.

She huffed and placed her maw above me, taking in my scent. *'You don't even have your own scent anymore.'*

I frowned, tilting my head in a movement that I picked up from her, confused.

She flicked out her tongue as if she tasted something foul. *'You smell like him.'*

I laughed and pushed at her leg, urging her to the balcony. Rafe stared after her as she trotted over, her weight shaking the stone beneath our feet. With a wild thrash of her wings, she threw herself off the edge and took to the sky much faster than should've been possible.

'I thought we weren't supposed to use magic,' I drawled.

'You *aren't supposed to.'*

Rafe backed up and studied my outfit. He wore fighting leathers with his swords strapped to his shoulders. My bandit breaker was fastened to my belt, and my push dagger hung about my neck. I was dressed in a white tunic with dark green embroidery to match my Riders' skirt. Even with the trousers sewn beneath, I felt oddly feminine. I liked the way it looked.

And if Rafe's expression was anything to go by, so did he. A smile curled his lip as he approached. "You look like a force to be reckoned with," he mused.

"High praise coming from you."

He forced out a throaty sigh. "Let's get this over with."

The meeting with King Aldred was a private one. It took an unnervingly long time to traverse the palace corridors. Segul led us down luxurious halls lined with lush fabrics and vases bearing bright flowers.

As we climbed a winding staircase, I couldn't help but wonder how the elderly King made it up all these steps. Four guards stood at attention before the iron and oak door.

The room was small compared to most I'd seen, and Tizmet flew past a high window, her blazing eye flashing. A lone oblong table took up the center with the King sitting at its head. Darrak sat to his right, straight and proper. Here, he was not my friend. He was the King's bounty hunter.

I curtsied, but a sad smile graced King Aldred's face as I rose. Something told me he knew he didn't have much time.

His simple attire was like last night's, free of intricate designs or multiple layers of fine fabrics. A thin gilded crown rested atop his hair, and deep wrinkles lined his brow and framed his mouth as if he spent too many days frowning. He was a far cry from the King I had met years ago—the one who treated me with kindness and patience.

"Wild Rider Avyanna. Shadowslayer. I am thankful you've come," he greeted as we found our seats to his left. "My bounty hunter has told me of Leeds—of your home."

My heart twisted painfully. I pressed my lips together, holding in my reply as Rafe reclined in his seat, glare settled on the King.

"I see your anger, Rider. There are no nobles to play for favor here. I would have your honesty."

"I didn't come for you." The words blurted out before I could think better of it. "I came for my friends."

Darrak tilted his head, raising his eyebrows at my bluntness.

The King nodded slowly, his eyes closing for a moment as if he expected as much. "I regret your banishment."

Rafe drummed his fingers along the wooden tabletop as my frown deepened. When we offered no comment, he continued.

"I may be a King but I am still a human after all. I did what I thought was best for Regent. You were a danger to the Dragon Legion and to my citizens. Disobeying direct orders from your leader, faulty as they might have been, could have been catastrophic."

"You have a catastrophe, regardless," I said.

"Yes, I do. The decision to exile you may have been wrong, though, given the circumstances, perhaps not. Fate plays out in mysterious ways."

"You tried to keep Rafe."

"He is the one man reckless enough to lead troops behind enemy lines, the only soul who isn't afraid to stare down a Shadow. Do you believe I would willingly part with him? He could be the salvation of our people—you could be."

He took a staggering breath, his body objecting to the motion. "I have made mistakes. This is true. I wish to convey my regret for banishing you and the subsequent repercussions that have ensued. I am willing to make amends in exchange for your assistance in the War of Shadows." His eyes sharpened with keen intent. "I'm ready to end this war. It has gone on too long—taken too many lives."

"You're going to send us behind enemy lines," I accused.

"It is imperative that we acquire knowledge of their plans. And how they continue to gain significant territorial advancements despite our best efforts. They should be spread thin like we are—thinner even. Regent needs an intervention. They must be pushed back."

He pinched the bridge of his crooked nose, letting out a sigh as if his next words were a burden to speak. "Avyanna, I have no intention of driving them to the Sky Trees. I aim to force them home."

I sucked in a breath. He wanted to end the war once and for all. Darrak studied me from across the table, lost in thought. I glanced at Rafe, but he stared at the King, bored. Here the King was, asking for our lives, and Rafe was resigned to my choice. As long as he was with me, he didn't care.

"I will fight, but not for you. I will fight for my friends, my mother and her mate, for the young, weak, and elderly." My jaw clenched tight as I paused, letting my words settle in. "Remember this, King Aldred. I owe Regent *nothing*. I've paid my dues. After Rafe and I win this war, we will live however and wherever, we please. If you want me to fight for Regent's future, then you owe me mine."

After the meeting, Darrak joined us as we took our leave. He and Rafe knew the way, and I was content to take in the sights.

Rafe secured immunity from crimes beyond the common folk. He could still be called upon by the King, but he argued that if we wanted the war over, he might have to bend some laws. The price for his immunity was a permanent marking, a crown to be tattooed on top of his dragon patch when we got to Northwing.

He would be the King's Dragon.

I liked the sound of that.

'Him? A dragon?' Tizmet scoffed.

She circled in the sky, soaking up the summer rays. Her peace spread across the bond, and I smiled at her contentment. Once again, fate had plucked me up and displaced me according to its whims. But Tizmet rode the winds, adjusting her course as needed. She moved with the flow, not against it.

Perhaps there was something to learn there.

'Would you like to see the city from above, little one?'

I choked on a laugh, drawing Rafe's quizzical stare. Clearing my throat, I beamed up at him. I would lose my first meal if she shared her sight, no matter how glorious she thought it was.

'I like my food in my belly, thank you.'

Her amusement brushed against my thoughts before she pulled away, content to soar through the clouds.

As we reached an outer wall, sunlight filtered in through high windows, scattering its rays over the plush rugs.

"We will leave in the morning?" Darrak asked.

Rafe squinted at me, then focused his attention down the hall. "First light."

"I'll make sure the horses will be ready." Darrak took a deep breath, and a muscle in his jaw twitched. "You'll be going out with Mik?"

Rafe shrugged, ignoring the question.

I stepped up and nodded. "One last night before we head off to the front."

He muttered something under his breath, refusing to look at me.

This was about Gaius and the Cauls. It was surprising that they hadn't managed to navigate her people's disapproval of the bounty master, given the amount of time that had passed.

I frowned, dropping my gaze to the carpets as I followed them outside. It very well might be our last night here. If the warfront was as bad as everyone made it seem, I didn't have high hopes of ever making it back.

If I didn't make it back, would Mik?

The sunshine glared down on us as we crossed the courtyard. Servants passed without a glance, but it was... quieter. Even King's Wall beyond seemed muffled, as if the War of Shadows was pressing in on the capital.

Darrak said his goodbyes and started for the stables. As Rafe and I neared the massive iron gate, the guards nodded as we passed, and the cobblestone path melded with the city streets.

I smirked at the sleeves bunched tight over his thick arms.

"Blasted sleeves," he muttered.

The roads were wide enough for two wagons to pass with room to spare, but the structures here towered so high, they cast the streets into shadow. Though, to be honest, I was thankful for the cool reprieve. A mother pulled her child further from our path. I flashed them a smile, and Rafe glowered.

"Where are we headed?" I asked.

"Markets," he grunted.

A man dressed in fine clothes rushed by, and I pressed closer to Rafe to avoid bumping him. Still, he thrust his chin, as if our presence alone was offensive.

"You're scaring the populace," I hissed.

"You don't intimidate them enough."

I laughed. He was intimidating enough for the both of us.

Even sticking to the shade, sweat beaded my temple by the time we made it to the market district. Rafe shook off my arm to loosen the laces of his black tunic.

Children darted around, alternating between chasing each other and a ball. Dogs danced about their heels, and vendors hawked their wares, filling the square with a pleasant din. Men wore shortswords next to their hatchets. Women called after their little ones and pressed their lips into firm frowns. Every day, the warfront drew nearer, lurking beneath the busy city's surface.

"Ah, there you are!" Jam darted out from between two jewelers, his dark braids swinging as he approached.

Blain offered me a mock bow before he and Dane ducked down a nearby alley.

"Their version of the pits is found wanting," Jamlin mused.

Rafe sneered over the goods for sale. "Better than this."

This was the nicer part of the market district, filled with stalls offering fine fabrics and exotic spices. Gems and crystals caught sunlight and threw it across the street, casting rainbows.

We continued on our way and Jam fell into step beside me. "Hungry?"

"Starving!" I blurted before Rafe could object.

He shook his head with a smirk. "Food first," he agreed.

The beckoning scent of spiced meats melded with fruit and sweet baked goods lured us deeper into the district. My mouth watered at the skewers of roasted vegetables and cubed steak. Across the way, vendors sold meat and cheeses pressed between bread, heated to glorious melted goodness. Another offered fire-roasted potatoes in small paper cones drizzled with spicy sauce.

A vendor gave an earful to Jam when he dipped close to a sweet roll, taking a sniff.

I settled on a pouch of warm, fresh-baked cookies and a spiced meat pie. I temporarily regretted my decision when the heat of my first bite embraced my palate. Once I adjusted to the intense array of flavor, I devoured every bit, then licked the juices from my fingers.

Just as the aroma of hot foods lured one to the food district, the sounds of cheering and laughter drew us deeper into the city toward the entertainment district.

Living in Northwing, I hadn't seen much when it came to dancing or fighting—or any other form of entertainment. So when three women swirled their capes and skirts in tandem to a music that had my toes tapping in time, I slowed.

They wore bright shades of green that shimmered in the sun. It reminded me of some dragonlings back in Leeds. Kohl was smudged around their eyes, and their black hair draped wild and free, swishing with their cadence. A musician played a lute in the corner, his fingers living a life of their own. Two girls worked the crowd, carrying small pails that rang out with the clink of each coin.

Rafe hung back with me, glowering at everyone who passed by. Actors with painted faces sweated in their layered costumes. Jugglers performed with their dogs. A man and a bear sat at a table—the beast ate with more manners than most of the Tennan. I dug into my pouch of cookies, letting out a moan as my teeth sank into the soft warm treat.

Then I heard it.

"War! War is coming!"

The stark difference from joy to despair was jarring. Rafe stiffened, and I lifted onto my tiptoes to peer through the crowd. Jam pointed, and I followed the gesture.

A man stood on a wooden crate, lifting himself above the multitude. He wore all black but painted his face white in an eerie replica of a Shadow mask.

Unease thrummed through me. Even so, I took a step closer.

"The Shadows are coming for us all! Move to the east! Only the E'or can save us!"

The E'or? He thought a mountain range would stop the Shadows? If anything, the common folk would be killed before they even reached the summit.

Rafe gave me a knowing look when I glanced over my shoulder at him.

"We fight at the front," he said. "Not here."

The crowd's clamor faded to an odd thrum, and the cookie sat heavy in my stomach. These people were playing, laughing, making sport, all while men died on the front.

"Come now." Jam bumped into me, drawing my attention. His sad smile told me his thoughts weren't far from mine.

We left the alarmist behind and when we reached the fighting rings, I about choked on a laugh to see Mikhala wrestling with a man. Bystanders gave me a double-take, and a quick glance about the crowd proved she and I were the only females in attendance. Though her furs and trousers had her blending in far better than me. I ignored the stares and chuckled as Mik jumped on his back, wrapping an arm around his throat.

"I yield!" he choked out, dropping to his knees.

His brown hair fell over his forehead as she released him. She wiped her brow with her wrist and tossed a grin at the crowd. She pulled herself onto the fence and flexed her biceps. My laughter was swallowed by cheers and playful taunts. I leaned over the railing, rough wood digging into my chest as I tried to get a glimpse of who she showed off to.

Gaius. I should have known.

Mik scanned the commoners and squealed when her gaze met mine. I lifted the pouch of cookies and her smile split her face. She ran over while a young man enticed others to fight. Her eyes glittered with excitement, and a smudge of dirt graced her jaw.

"Avyanna! Girl! Talk ol' one eye here into fighting Gaius!" she panted, plucking out a few cookies. "The crowd would love it!"

"I didn't know he fought." I peeked around her to find the big man smiling at us.

"Oh, he doesn't. Not like this." She threw her head back, laughing. "But I'd pay a shiny coin or two just to see it."

"I can't speak for Rafe, but I'll take you on."

Mik cackled and bounced on her heels, more than eager to get back in the ring.

I shoved another cookie in my mouth, then tossed the treats to Jamlin and climbed the fence. As I threw my leg over the top rail, I met Rafe's bored gaze.

"It's *fun*," I jeered. "That's what we came here for, isn't it?"

My boots hit the hard-packed dirt. Tizmet flew low overhead, stirring a breeze that tugged at my skirts. Rafe arched a single brow and leaned his weight against the post.

The pit master strode over. "Oi, I've never had two women fight in my ring." He brushed his dark hair out of his eyes, his gaze darting down to my skirt. "A Rider as well?"

Shrugging, I propped my hands on my hips. "It would bring more coin."

"It would." He tapped his jaw, then nodded his agreement before sprinting off to yell at a boy. "Bring 'em in! Two girls! The Caul and a Rider in the ring!"

The lad ran off into the crowd bellowing, and he and a few others were swarmed by men placing wagers.

Rafe's lip curled in a smirk as he looked me over. "Fighting in that skirt?"

"Do you doubt me?" I scoffed.

He grunted, a noncommittal sound, as I tied back the fabric to reveal two loose pant legs. I fastened the panel and stretched. It would be my first time fighting in a Rider's skirt, and Mik would put it to the test.

Gaius rested against the fence, his warm brown eyes on me. I crossed the ring to speak with him as Mikhala ran around, calling wagers, urging men to bid higher. She thrived in this environment. I wondered if her boundless energy came from her personality or her heritage.

"She's excited," I mused.

He chuckled. "She lives for a challenge."

"What about you?"

"Me? I've had my fill of challenges. Running the bounty house is enough for me." His voice was deep and gruff, but his tone was gentle.

I turned to face the big man and leaned over the fence into his space. "Is Mik too much of a challenge for you?"

A surprised flush ruddied his cheeks under his dark beard. "What's between us isn't your concern, Wild Rider." His smile dropped a fraction, though he played it off.

I wasn't playing.

"She's risking everything to be with you, even for a night here and there?"

He shook his head with a low chuckle. "You don't know–"

"I don't know you—true. But I know Mik, and I know love." I stepped on the lowest rung, bringing my face to his. All mirth left his gaze. "Love wouldn't let her leave for the warfront alone. You're either scared, or you don't love her."

"I love her more than–"

"So you're scared."

He was far too easy to push around. He might be two, maybe three times my size, but the man was soft.

"Oi! Break it up!" Mik bounced to my side, throwing a grin at Gaius.

I winked at his fuming glower and leapt off the fence, turning my back on him.

"What was all that?" she asked, a pinch of worry between her brows. "He looks upset at you! How did you manage that?"

"I did nothing." I hummed, walking to the center.

The pit master stepped forward to recite the rules and start the match.

It ended far sooner than I expected.

My skirts were a liability in hand to hand combat, and Mik wasted no time revealing that. One regretful kick at her thigh, and she snatched the fabric and used it to haul me under her. She had me pinned within breaths.

Tizmet snorted across the bond. *'You should fight in your skin. Less to tangle you up.'*

'My skin is vastly more susceptible to blades than yours,' I huffed.

When I shoved Mik off me, she rolled with the movement, then jumped, whooping along with the crowd's cheers.

'And a layer of woven plant protects you?' Tizmet mocked as she soared higher in the sky, unconcerned with my defeat.

I ignored her and took Mik's hand as she yanked me to my feet. With a breathless laugh I found Rafe among the audience, his scar pulled tight with his grin. He looked happy, despite the fact I just had my arse handed to me. I braved a glance at Gaius. His hands gripped the top rung of the fence, a set look of determination on his brow. His jaw worked when he met my gaze, and I gave him a knowing smirk.

The next morning Gaius was waiting for us outside the palace gates. I smothered my smile as Mik tried and failed to hide her excitement. The bounty master would join us at the front, after all.

Chapter 35

Our journey was marked by the grim reminders of war, from the smell of smoke in the air to the sight of makeshift memorials for fallen soldiers. People flocked close to the main cities. Hamlets and villages overflowed with haggard, weary crowds. Weapons weren't rare before, but now every single man and woman sported one at their side.

We raced to Northwing, rushing toward my friends. Tizmet could have gotten me there ahead of our group, but I held her back. If I arrived before them and something happened, I would rise to action—with or without Rafe. I didn't want to be put in another situation of him trying to find me. I couldn't handle that again.

The days of travel crawled by. The sight of so many in agony was unbearable, and I couldn't shake the nagging question of what had become of my friends. Mikhala assured me that Niehm and Elenor were safe, and Darrak had seen Willhelm when he was last there.

In our journey toward Northwing, it became evident that they were making a conscious effort to keep the children at a greater distance. Fewer and fewer walked the roads and worked the farms. I wondered if the King's grounds still served as a school, or if they were successful in relocating all the little ones.

Would it ever be one again?

The day arrived when the sprawling base came into view. Longing surged through my heart as I took in the Dragon Canyon and Riders' quadrant. The Great Northern Lake glittered in the distance. Plumes of smoke swelled from campfires and forges throughout the barracks, and the dark buildings and tall spires of the school grounds rose from the plains.

Longing fell short as I noted the spiked barricades surrounding the main wall. Soldiers forced the large gate open, and a wagon squeezed through. Tizmet flew lower, and I told myself the blanket-covered load was supplies, weapons... until it hit a rut and an arm fell free of the cover. Horror consumed me, and Tizmet wheeled upward as it flooded over the bond.

'Down. I need to find my friends.'

She plummeted into a steep dive and I clenched my thighs to keep from passing out as we dropped altitude. Wind tore my hair from my braids, throwing them behind me.

She leveled out over the canyon, letting out a bugle so loud she trembled beneath me. Her cry echoed into the expanse—and petty few dragons answered that call. All of them were young, too small to fight. They shied away from the mouths of their caves, tucking out of sight as if Tizmet frightened them. Sorrow filled her, and she dropped into a rough landing on the precipice, stumbling with her emotions. Opening her maw, she forced a sharp barking call.

We waited, both of us straining to hear a familiar bellow, but none came. Where were the dragons, if not here?

Her claws dug into the stone and she roared her displeasure, snapping at the air. *'Dragons are not made to be afraid!'*

'I need to see Elenor,' I pleaded, glancing around the empty canyon.

She let out another irritated roar, disgraced by the dragons that wouldn't rise to meet her. Diving off the lip, she flew to the school grounds.

People gathered, shading their eyes from the sun's glare. When they saw Tizmet, they stared—as if surprised to see a full-sized dragon.

Fury radiated off of Tizmet as she landed. Throwing up clods of soil, she whirled on the crowd, snapping her jaws. I freed my legs and slid down her shoulder as she seethed, her outrage boiling over. She had been afraid once. It was something no dragon should ever feel.

But the people? They were... tired.

Dirt and grime marred their faces. Their clothes were torn and battered. Many were injured, bandages wrapped around their heads or arms, and a few leaned on crutches. Despair squeezed my gut as I searched for a familiar face. I was raised in Northwing. I should know these people.

They knew me.

"Where is Master Elenor?" I asked.

The crowd murmured and whispered, looking to the ground, the sky, the school—anywhere but me.

My tone lifted, loud and demanding. "Where is Master Elenor?!"

Tizmet fed off my rage, just as I fed off hers. Tipping her maw to the sky, she screamed her outrage, and they scattered like flies.

'I have to find her.'

I stormed toward the women's dorms. My unsteady legs stumbled as I ran, still adjusting to solid ground after the flight. At the doors, a pang of sorrow choked my lungs—no guards.

There were always at least two posted here at all times.

I slowed for a moment, glancing at the empty secretary desk. Papers were piled high and scattered about. It hadn't been used for quite a while.

My legs ran down the women's wing, weaving through the crowded hallways. Cots lined the halls, and I had to stop to allow others to pass through the narrow space. A man lay in a cot beside me, his eyes and head wrapped in white bandages, but his chest was bare, revealing a trail of stitches across his shoulder and sternum. Men were in the women's wing?

"You were banished."

I faltered, glancing at an old woman covered in wrinkles. She hunched over, leaning heavily on a crude cane, and squinted at me with murky blue eyes. My brain frantically tried to catch up with who this was. The hall was so silent, only the wheezing breaths of the injured broke the tension. I blinked, trying to place her–

"Meredith."

The old woman choked out a sob, and I grabbed her in an embrace. Holding her close, I couldn't help but recall the countless instances she looked after me throughout my childhood. All the times she placed wagers on me that I would make it through the ranks. She was my biggest supporter in the women's dorms.

Pulling back, I met her cloudy gaze. "I need to see Master Elenor."

"Oh, my sweet!"

She clutched my tunic and cried into the rough fabric. I glanced around at the gathered crowd, all staring in shock that I was there. Clearly, they hadn't heard about my pardon.

"Where is Master Elenor?!"

My repeated question still received no answer. Dread coiled in my belly, and unshed tears burned my eyes.

Surely not.

I pried Meredith's hands off me and tore down the hall. There was no way that Elenor, after all her years being the backbone of the school, the mother that so many needed—she couldn't be...

I wouldn't even allow myself to think the word.

Rounding a corner, I plowed into someone, my tear-hazed vision blurring their features. I blinked and wiped at my eyes, trying to clear them.

"Avyanna? Avyanna!"

The woman grabbed me and clutched me tight, driving a squeak out of me. I peered up at a halo of red frizz.

"Niehm–"

"Aye, you blasted foolish girl!" She drew back and held me at arm's length as she looked me over. She ran a thumb over my cheek. "Gracious, look at that scar!"

"Master Elenor–"

"I'll take you to her."

She didn't ask questions, but rather led down the hall at a brisk pace. She understood my urgency. I just needed to see my friends alive, to see them well. She tossed out orders to those we passed, as if she was the Master of Women.

I stuck close to her heels as she pushed through the halls and up the stairs, crowding people out of her way. The upper levels of the dorms were sweltering. I pressed my lips together, holding in my comments about the stench and the mass of bodies.

We stopped at a room as small as the one I grew up in, and she motioned me inside. I gagged when I entered, unable to prevent the involuntary reaction.

I stared at a cot, the figure motionless, not even a breath disturbing it. A heavy wool blanket concealed their features, and the essence of death overwhelmed me.

"No, no, no, no!" I clamped my hand over my mouth, panic rising within. Outside, Tizmet keened, echoing my loss.

"Sun above, that's not Elenor!" Niehm shoved past the threshold, then spun me toward another cot near the far wall. "The men just haven't hauled out that body."

A nauseating wave of relief crashed into me as I saw Elenor's face lolled to the side, her cool blue eyes staring at me. I collapsed to my knees, brushing the dark gray hair off her cheeks. She smiled up at me, as thin as a sapling. Lines and wrinkles etched her skin, age spots in abundance.

How had she deteriorated so much in just a few short years?

"It was so hard on her. She never slept. There was always more to do. I've thought about sending her away. The fresh air would do her good—but I'm afraid she won't make the trek." Niehm wrung her hands, features pinched with worry.

The stench of decay was nauseating, the blanket of death heavy. I had to get that body out of here.

"She was a thousand times better at this than I am. Northwing has become part of the frontlines. The Dragon Fleet is spread across the south and west. Soldiers come here when they're too injured to fight. We take the refugees—but send the children further inland. We can't teach them here and with the attacks we just can't–"

I rose to my feet and grabbed Niehm, holding her tight. She stiffened at first, then relaxed in my embrace.

"I'm trying, Avyanna," she rasped. Cries clogged her throat as she clutched onto me.

"I know, Niehm. I know."

It took me the better part of a chime to get the dead body to the gravedigger wagons. Repulsion gagged me the whole way, and I retched a few times. Tizmet offered to heft it into the wagon, but I feared seeing a corpse in her maw might revitalize unwelcome rumors.

After securing his body amongst the others, I traveled to the barracks, once again distraught to see the gate unguarded. People drifted through of their own accord. There was no order, no semblance of organization.

The place was crowded, chaotic. If a man was able to swing a sword, he was swinging it. I spied women handling bows, others with shortswords and shields. Whether they were just assisting the barracks or joining the fight, I didn't know.

These people were not the excited, eager soldiers I had known before, and bathing seemed to be their lowest priority. The Commanders were no longer stiff and rigid instructors. Their uniforms were dirty and torn, their boots muddy.

They were weary—worn.

I took a moment and sat on a bench. Everyone was so busy, I went unnoticed. Leaning forward, I brought my hands to my mouth and just...

Watched.

A woman hefted a basket of laundry over her shoulder, making her way to the dorms. Another stopped her, holding arrows that were missing their fletching. They headed off together—I assumed to remedy that. Two men passed by, arms full of practice swords and heavy shields, sweat and dirt lining their brows. Another woman struggled under the weight of a cart and a man stopped what he was doing to help her pull it out of a rut.

There were too many tasks and not enough people. Northwing was wounded—and despite its best efforts, it seemed in a state of hopeless disrepair.

"'Tis a sad sight."

The voice that should have brought me joy only twisted my heart more. I stared straight ahead, pulling my knees to my chest.

"I never thought I'd see it like this," he said.

My throat tightened, but I forced my words out. "What happened, Willhelm?"

"War." That single word was laden with a palpable, emotional weight. "War, Avyanna."

I turned and sought his warm brown eyes. The distant sheen in his gaze was focused on those passing by. His hair was longer than I remembered, falling into his face. His uniform was tidy, but fraying. The trousers were–

Part of me shattered. Helplessness drenched my soul.

"Willhelm." His name was a horrified plea.

"Aye, 'tis a ghastly sight, but no worse off than others."

His right leg was severed at the knee, his trousers neatly folded into a brace. A crutch lay by his side. When he looked at me, his handsome features filled with sorrow as he attempted a faint smile.

"How did it happen?" I murmured, searching his face for any sign of pain.

I was too late.

Darrak and Mik told me my friends were safe—but they were not. They were hurt, injured. And I was too busy building my happy little cottage to come help.

Willhelm lost his leg. Elenor sat at the edge of the Veil. Niehm was robbed of her peace and confidence.

They needed me, and I was too preoccupied carving out my own happiness.

"Raid in the night." He squinted off into the distance again. "I was pulled to Vinessent, the village to the south. Drafted there. General Faulkin tried to spread out our troops and had soldiers training on the front. Figured if there were more fighters in a wider area, they would think twice about attacking us.

"He was wrong. I'm fairly certain the only reason I survived was because they thought I bled out. I remember a creature—black as shadow and *wrong*."

"A Hunter."

"Aye. Took off my leg with its teeth. I woke up at Northwing."

"I'm sorry."

"As am I, but apologies won't grow it back." He sighed. "There are times I feel it—as if it's still there. Oddest thing, that."

My eyes pressed shut against the torturous beats of my heart, wishing I could do more. All the terrors of the E'or couldn't amount to the helplessness I felt here.

We sat in silence. I figured someone would look at us, order us about, tell us to do something—but no one did. Everyone was too overwhelmed, distracted by their own tasks.

I stirred when Rafe crossed the road. The smile I offered him trembled on my lips, feeling false and fake.

He frowned at Willhelm. "Sergeant."

"Ah, not anymore." Willhelm groaned as he rose, clinging to his crutch. "Commander now. Due to be sent out in the spring."

I leapt to my feet. "But your leg!"

"There are Commanders with worse injuries," he stated calmly, shrugging his shoulder. "Good day, Shadowslayer."

He hobbled off, and when Rafe met my gaze, I clenched my jaw, keeping my tears at bay.

If they sent him to the front, he wouldn't return.

Rafe gave a subtle shake of his head, then pulled me into him. I let him crush me to his chest. This is what it must have felt like for him while he served as General. He lost so many men, watched them die, be maimed, deformed for life.

I sat on my pardon for weeks before the King sent Darrak and Mik to fetch me—and my friends had paid dearly.

"Elenor's dying."

I sobbed into his tunic. I didn't care who saw me. Loss ripped my throat apart. Guilt that I somehow caused this swamped me like a swollen bog. It crashed over me and smothered me, ripping the air from my lungs.

'Be calm.' Tizmet pushed across the bond, sweeping away my shame. *'What's done is done. We can only face the consequences—good or bad.'*

Rafe held me, rubbing a calloused hand up and down my back. I pulled myself together, horrified that people were just walking by, acting like my grief was so normal that it didn't require a second glance. Was the breaking of mortal souls so common that they dismissed it?

Rafe tugged me down the road and I stumbled next to him blindly. We made our way to a tent tucked into a corner of the barracks. A grizzled man waited with a needle and ink. Time slipped by as he cleaned Rafe's arm, then added the crown to his dragon tattoo. The needle stabbed him, drawing blood, but Rafe ignored it, staring over the training fields, lost in his own thoughts.

Blain found us once, and with a glance at my puffy tear-stained face, quickly excused himself.

After Rafe was bandaged up, we headed to the dining hall.

It was packed, with no sitting or standing room to speak of. Jamlin, Mik and Gaius sat in a tight circle on the dirt floor, playing a game of knucklebones. Dane stood on one side of the building and Blain on the other. Darrak melded with the men, talking in hushed tones and moving between groups. Rafe nudged me toward the line and I shuffled along, picking up bits of conversation.

"–Rider and General–"

"–General and the girl warrior–"

"–save us?"

"–what of the south?"

"–hundred and two wounded yesterday–"

"–heard that Reyol is dead?"

"–Shamen–"

I was drowning in the voices, "Rafe, I–"

He seemed to know what I needed before I found the words. He swept me outside. We retreated to a cave that Tizmet claimed. After the long climb, we unpacked the saddle and readied our bedrolls.

We ate road rations, sparing ourselves from the chaos that was the dining hall. I wondered if the Riders' quarters were so crammed. Niehm said they spread the dragons thin. Perhaps we could seek a meal there in the morning.

"Rafe?"

"Hmm?" He pulled me into his chest, my anchor in this storm.

"How do you deal with the loss?"

Silence drowned me. Tizmet blinked a large fiery eye and stretched out. I couldn't sleep—not yet. I knew without a doubt Elenor's gaunt features and Willhelm's severed leg would haunt my dreams.

"You don't."

The air left my lungs in a rush, and I choked on a gasping sob. I curled tighter against him, as if he could shield me from the onslaught of guilt and self-loathing.

"You don't deal with it. It deals with you." His low voice vibrated against my back. "It will either strengthen you—or break you. Only you can make that choice."

Chapter 36

I chose strength.

Rafe studied me as I moved about the cavern before the sun came up. When I caught his gaze, he nodded once in approval. We packed up our belongings, then saddled Tizmet.

I wouldn't wait for the Shadows to attack. I was going to them.

We met up with our friends at first meal. Jamlin and the twins would join us across enemy lines while Darrak, Mik and somber Gaius stayed behind to help around Northwing.

The frontlines were too close for comfort, a mere three days' hard ride away.

Setting off, we traveled the same route used by the army. Tizmet grew more apprehensive as we neared. She refused to eat, too anxious that a large meal might slow her down.

Still a day's ride out, she tested the air, tilting her head up at the darkening sky. *'The red comes.'*

For the first time, I didn't feel her anger toward him. The presence of another dragon willing to fight brought her a sense of security.

"Ruveel is coming." I shoved the last bite of dried rations into my mouth. The stuff was hard to chew. I'd likely still be gnawing on it by the time Ruveel made it to our camp.

The setting sun washed out Ge'org's crimson scales to a dull, ruddy auburn. He swooped into a dive, and I caught Rafe's eye, giving him a firm nod.

We could do this.

The earth shook under Ge'org's weight as he crashed to the ground, taking a running step toward our camp. Ruveel pulled his boots from his stirrups and slid down with practiced ease. The beast huffed and dropped to his belly, flicking a tongue out curiously, but was far too exhausted to make advances on Tizmet.

Ruveel sauntered into our small camp, eyeing our packs. Soot smudged his cheeks under his eyes, and he cocked a hip to the side, lifting his chin. Despite his haughty demeanor and squared shoulders, I hadn't missed the limp in his gait.

"Well, well, well." He crossed his arms over his chest and smirked. "Come back to join the Fleet, lost girl?"

I gave him a slow, drawn out blink. "Your dragon looks a bit thin."

He made a similar comment about Tizmet once, and it stung. I hoped it did the same to him.

"And yours looks like she's been on a vacation. Living it up with ease."

"You would know. You banished us."

"I did what I had–"

"Enough." Rafe moved between us.

I bit my cheek at the way he had to step in, as if we were bickering children.

"We're on our way to the front," he said. "We will meet with Teak and Faulkin."

"Well, *commoner*. Since you seem so confident of its whereabouts, be my guest."

"A day's ride west?" Jamlin called out.

"No. It moved. Day's ride south, now." Ruveel sighed, pinching the bridge of his nose. "The line keeps moving. Do you know how hard it is to organize supply routes?"

"Is that what you and your dog are? A supply wagon?" Rafe scoffed.

"Better a supply wagon than a Shadow's puppet. Avyanna, keep your dragon high, or don't fly her at all." Ruveel glanced between me and Tizmet. "And for love of the sun—don't fly at night."

"What happens at night?"

"Dragons disappear."

Tizmet rose to sniff at the gashes littering Ge'org's hide. His wings were riddled with holes. He had patches of scales missing and deep wounds marred his underbelly. He was beaten and battered.

"A few nights ago, we risked flying over the enemy. This was our reward. Good luck to you, Avyanna."

He climbed up into the saddle and took his time strapping himself in, his gaze dancing over our small group. With an eye on the falling sun, Ge'org threw himself into the sky.

Tizmet snorted as he ascended higher. *'I will not be so easily caught.'*

'He wasn't either.' Ge'org was raised as a war machine—fighting was all he knew.

"So they're moving the lines," Blain mused.

Rafe grunted, then dropped to a crouch beside Jamlin. "Hiding something."

I paced, mulling over Ruveel's warning. If we weren't allowed to fly, or could only soar so high we couldn't see anything, what good were we except bait?

I whirled to face Rafe.

His dark gaze was already on me. "We need bait."

As we rode in, I felt the familiar buzz of excitement. This wasn't a beaten refugee camp full of men and women readying for their death. This was a mass of men living their best lives—happy to have survived another day. Tomorrow held no concern for them. Their sole focus was on reveling in their own existence.

I shared Rafe's saddle as Tizmet soared high in the sky. There were only a few dragons flying about, but I knew which one she sought.

We made our way through the camp, the soldiers' attention drawn to our party. They murmured and gathered around us, forming a crowd. I sat up straighter, my nerves skittering under my skin.

"Rafe?" a strange voice called.

I twisted in my seat as a big man pushed through the masses. He was massive. Blood splattered his face and chest. He was broad shouldered and his tunic cinched in at his waist. His dark trousers covered his long thick legs, and I grinned at his haircut. He was shaven, except for a line of hair that ran down the middle of his head.

"Teak," Rafe rumbled.

"You flaming bastard—you came back!"

Rafe pulled his stallion to a halt and dismounted. He had spoken fondly of him, though I couldn't help but wonder if him leaving for Leeds, for me, soured their friendship.

"Thank the sun I did. You're a dismal lot." Rafe slapped a heavy hand on the man's shoulder.

Teak's gray eyes flew to mine and his grin grew wider. "She'd be the reason you're back, eh?"

"Aye."

I slid off the horse and Rafe caught my waist, spinning to plop me in front of Teak. Out of all the people Rafe had ever talked about, Teak seemed to be his one friend. His equal.

"Pleased to meet you, General Teak." I spread my skirt, dropping into a shallow curtsy.

"Look at her manners! How'd a sot like you end up with a girl like her?"

"Same way you ended up with Agatha." Rafe smirked, pulling me into his side. "Fate."

A shadow of pain flickered across Teak's features before he offered me a sly grin. "Agatha has passed the Veil, but you would have liked her. Even Ru had a hard time ordering her about."

Rafe's hand tightened on my shoulder, the only sign that he was bothered by the news of Agatha's death. She had been one of the few female Riders on the front. There were others that patrolled Regent, but I wasn't sure if they had been drafted or not yet.

It would have been nice to have another woman to talk about dragons with. From the emotion that Teak smothered, he was missing her too.

"Faulkin will be pleased to see you," he jeered, slapping Rafe's bandaged arm.

Rafe grunted and moved his shoulder. "I'm sure he's waiting for me with gifts and a warm embrace."

"Oi, what's with your arm? Did the King carve your patch off?" he asked.

"Promoted me."

"Beyond General? Faulkin will love that."

"I'm the King's Dragon."

"You jest."

Rafe deadpanned. "Do I ever?"

I laughed, watching the two interact. He spoke more with Teak than anyone I've ever seen, besides myself. Even with his Tennan he was reserved and kept his guard up.

"Does Ruveel know?" Teak asked.

"No."

"That will be a joyous surprise. Make sure I'm there when you tell him."

"Headed there now," Rafe said.

Those gathered murmured amongst themselves, but cleared a path and Teak fell into step alongside us. The front moved so much that the roads through the camp were still lush with grass, only a few places worn down by wagons showed any sign of wear.

That bothered me for some reason. All those years ago, when I studied to be First Chosen, I envisioned flying my dragon through the Sky Trees, facing the Shadows on the edge of their borders. That wasn't the case anymore. The ancient, immense forest was leagues away.

We arrived at a large tent. The banner flying above it bore the insignia of a black dragon in flight.

Rafe barked out orders. "Jam, tend to the horses. Blain, stay with us. Dane, go see what you can find out."

Teak bumped into me before holding the tent flap open. "Does he order you around like that?" he teased.

"Not unless he wants to spend a night out in the cold."

Rafe smiled over his shoulder as he ducked inside.

Two others lounged in the space. Ruveel, and the other, I assumed, was General Faulkin.

First impression—he was not a kind man.

His gray hair was cut short and neatly combed, and his cold blue eyes sized me up in one blink. Scars crisscrossed his face, giving him a fearsome look. His physique was a bit more muscular than expected from an elderly man, but Rafe had told me he was the brains behind the war.

"General Faulkin," I greeted, dipping into a curtsy once again.

Ruveel scoffed. "She bows to *you*."

"You've proven you're not worth the effort," I spat.

Teak snorted, and I flashed him a smile. He and I would get along just fine.

"Faulkin, Ruveel." Rafe tossed a rolled parchment on the table, scattering figurines.

Faulkin closed his eyes, the model of patience, "Rafe. I just set those–"

"New plan."

Ruveel groaned and flopped into a chair, pinching the bridge of his nose. "Oi, you lost your rank. Why is he even here?"

"King Vasili Aldred of Regent named me his Dragon."

Rafe tore off the bandage, revealing his scabbed tattoo. Teak craned around me, beaming at the addition.

Ruveel groaned. "Why can't you just get a patch, Rafe?"

"Did the King approve your new plan?" Faulkin asked quietly.

I found it surprising that he did not harbor more resentment, given how Rafe assaulted him to be rid of his military obligations.

"He gave me permission to use my own men and a company."

Faulkin shook his head. "We're spread too thin."

"I won't need more than half a company—and a dragon."

"You want one of my dragons?" Ruveel leaned forward in his chair, his eyes flashing. "Not a chance. I wouldn't let you have one if your life depended on it."

"And if it was the life of another dragon?" Rafe taunted.

Teak watched the exchange, excitement growing in his eyes with each passing word. He knew we were up to something. "He can have the ninety-third. They're down to a half due to injuries. Might help them feel useful."

"I'm not risking a dragon for you," Ruveel repeated.

"Then bring your own." Rafe snorted, thoroughly amused. "We're finding out what the Shadows are hiding."

Chapter 37

We flew through the night.

Summer still clung to the land before it released it to the chill of autumn, and the wind was cold and muggy. I ducked against her neck. It was a terrifying thing being strapped on a dragon, flying through a starless sky. Tizmet might be able to see in the dark, but I could not. Sharing her sight while in flight was not an experience I wanted to repeat, either.

As bait, we had to trust that Rafe and his men would get to us in time.

We'd been soaring circles for chimes, trying to draw them out. According to Ruveel, every nighttime flight ended with a dead dragon, if a corpse was even discovered. Yet there was no indication of their presence, let alone them rising to capture us–

That gust of wind sounded odd.

'Did you hear–'

'We're not alone.' Tizmet pumped her wings harder, flying faster. If we could just get to the–

A high, bone-chilling screech rent the night. I flinched, tucking low against her neck. Instinct told her to dive or rise, but she snarled and arrowed straight ahead.

'What was that!?'

I scanned the darkness but saw nothing. There were giant black birds in the Sky Trees—but we were nowhere near there, and she knew their call. This was different.

The wail came again, closer this time. I twisted in the saddle, scanning the dark. Shadows moved, as if something flew just behind.

She picked up her pace, straining and stretching out beneath me. I molded myself to her neck, clinging on for all I was worth. The last thing I needed was to be plucked off her back.

Whatever it was brushed her tail, spooking her. She roared, rolling and whipping her hind feet into the sky. Holding on for dear life, we plunged upside down toward the trees, wind tearing through my hair.

In a frenzied panic, Tizmet crashed across our bond, sharing her sight with me. Righting herself out of her dive, I gagged on hot bile as I tried to make sense of what she saw. I shoved the connection away, panting as the treetops brushed her belly.

'Almost there!' she cried.

The thing of nightmares came at us again.

A foreboding depthless void, gaining with every pump of Tizmet's wings. Teeth latched onto her tail, and she thrashed. Her agony and my terror melded into a tangible vice-like fear. It jerked her upward and Tizmet curled, using whatever leverage she could, talons searching to maim.

She screamed across the bond, shoving her sight at me again. My world tilted and flipped, switching from dim dark colors to bright whites and grays. My stomach rejected the distortion, and I threw up in my mouth as the disconnect between my body and mind jarred me.

But what I saw was worth it.

"Sun above!"

Her claws found purchase, sinking in deep. The creature released her, and its shriek rent the air, raising the hairs on the nape of my neck. Unlike other dragons, she didn't attempt to engage or confront.

Tizmet fled.

We tore through the night, the hiss of its heavy wings clear now that we knew what to listen for. I felt her fear surge through me. It wasn't that she believed she couldn't fight it—the horror of the beast overshadowed all instincts.

The creature dove again, but this time, she was ready for it. Rolling, she used her claws to grab its head as it lunged. We careened toward the ground. The snap of wind drew tears from my eyes and snared all air from my lungs. Amid the chaotic spiral, she exerted every ounce of effort to ensure we stayed on top.

If I ended up on the bottom, I was dead.

The beast flailed in her lethal grip, its hind feet scoring her belly. Sharp anguish drenched her screams as we plummeted. Trees splintered and snapped as we slammed into the ground—the creature crushed beneath us. Tizmet scrambled off. Fallen trees and uprooted earth scattered in every direction, the thicket in disarray. I cursed as a branch hit the back of my head, filling my vision with bright stars.

'Your mate has to come here!' The cadence of her voice in our bond cracked with fear, her eyes never leaving the creature, even as she stumbled and faltered from the pain of her wounds.

A roar broke the silence—a blissfully familiar one.

I fumbled with my stirrups, scanning the dark forest for movement. I heard thrashing but saw nothing.

'Stay on!' Tizmet's terror surpassed anything we experienced while facing the Shaman. Her scales thrummed and trembled, her breaths heaving.

'You're bleeding!'

'Stay ON!'

'You will bleed out and be good to no one!'

Through the bond, an icy chill emanated from her, a frigidity that seeped into my bones. She was *never* cold.

Flames fell from the sky as Ge'org let loose, raining fire. Trees ignited, snapping and popping, swallowed by dragon oil. The forest burst with hot auburn light, and I shielded my face from the blast of heat. Blinking fiercely, my vision adjusted.

I almost wished it hadn't.

On the ground, a blue creature writhed in agony, its wing impaled by a tree. Bent and contorted at an unnatural angle, it thrashed again, only to tear its flesh further. Scarred, mutilated nubs took up the space where its front legs should have been. It used its wings as if they were forelegs, trying to brace itself. Remnants of some sort of saddle clung to its back. Terror gripped my heart as the firelight illuminated its face.

It was a dragon.

Ruveel swept from the sky as Rafe and his men clambered over splintered logs and mounds of dirt. Tizmet stumbled, getting weaker by the second as she watched the beast convulse. There was no logic or thought behind its panicked movements.

I reached for my buckles again, hoping to reach the mutilated creature.

'Stay on!' Tizmet whipped her head back, snapping her teeth in my face. *'It is not right! Something is wrong!'*

Ge'org landed in a wave of embers as burning debris crumbled beneath him. Teak's men scattered, following Rafe as they encircled the perimeter. My heart ached for the beast. It wasn't small—large enough to carry a Rider.

'Large enough to be my young.'

It slammed its maw into the ground. Its eyes rolled back into its skull, then it reared, sinking its teeth into its tail–

And tore off a chunk of flesh.

It spat, spraying sinew and blood into the crackling flames. We recoiled as it repeated the action over and over.

Rafe threw up a hand, halting his men. Repulsion consumed every face as the mutilated dragon let out a garbled scream, then sank its teeth into its wing, ripping the ensnared appendage free from its body.

Ge'org growled low in his throat, taking a step back.

Tipping its maw toward the sky, it keened. A sorrowful sound. A cry for help.

One I didn't know how to answer.

Then it latched onto its hind leg.

No.

Its cries were muffled through the spitting of blood as it gnawed off its toes. It was a long and painful process, one no one knew how to respond to. We stared in horror—a few losing control of their stomachs. The dragon thrashed aside, and launched its bloody digits into the air. They hit Tizmet's flank, and she flinched away from the atrocity. The beast tore itself apart, and we stood witness as it whimpered and bled out on the cold ground.

Tizmet coughed, a sound I'd never heard before. Ge'org whipped our direction as her legs gave out and she collapsed to the crimson-soaked dirt. I fumbled with my stirrups. Keeping one eye on the blue, to be sure it was dead, I slipped from my saddle as her head hit the ground.

'Thrice-curse it all!' I raged at her, feeling her recede across the bond.

Ge'org stomped over, nosing her to her side. I sucked in a breath, seeing the three long gouges under her belly. I rushed to the wounds, as wide as the length of my forearm and just as deep.

The thing's severed claws scattered the bloody dirt at my feet. They were massive, too massive for the creature's size.

"I have to," I breathed, looking up at Ruveel.

For once, I didn't see disgust or haughtiness in his gaze—instead, there was empathy.

Twisting in his seat, he glanced over his shoulder. "I would hurry before Rafe makes his way over here."

Taking a deep breath, I laid on the forest floor, shoving blood-splattered saplings out of my way. It was best that I was already on the ground when the seizure took me.

Placing my hand against Tizmet's chilled scales, I opened the door to our bond, letting the magic flood out. Guiding it, I pieced her together bit by bit, closing the wounds. Magic filled me, warming my body as if I were a long-lost friend. I pushed it at Tizmet, knitting her muscles together.

Only when I finished and I urged the magic behind its door, did it lash out. It struck at me, pushing and heaving—almost as if it sensed Tizmet wasn't there to restrain it. I struggled, wincing as I forced it back.

Then my seizure took me.

People were shouting. My head throbbed with each raised voice.

'They're talking, not yelling, little one.'

I groaned, rolling to my side.

"Catch her!"

Disoriented, I realized I was no longer on the forest floor, and I flailed, eyes shooting open as I tried to right myself. A Healer in dingy blue and white robes helped me back onto my cot. Sunshine glared down on the canvas tent, and I squinted as she brushed the hair from my face.

"I swear, you test me as a Healer."

"Rashel."

She huffed a sigh. "Not that I would trust anyone else with your constant care. You're far too reckless."

"I knew what I was doing." The words came out rough, my voice raw from disuse.

'You have my thanks,' Tizmet murmured.

To my surprise, she didn't berate me for my foolishness.

'You're not mad at me?'

'I would have bled out. I was too... fearful.'

Did my dragon just confess to being scared?

'I was distracted.' Indignation ruffled her tone. *'Wait till your young rip themselves apart and throw a limb at you. See if you are aware of your body, then.'*

Rafe sat on a cot across from us, his elbows resting on his knees as he glared at me, lost in thought. A shadow fell over me, and I frowned up at Ruveel.

"We need to talk," he stated.

"Perhaps you could wait until I get her some water?" Rashel snapped a toothy smile that said she wasn't really asking.

He waved her off, then dropped on the cot next to me. His eyes bore into mine, as if he could read my mind or pry what he needed out of my skull. I reached across the bond and felt Tizmet flying high in the sky, sorting out her own concerns.

Rashel checked my pulse and offered me a cup of water.

The cool fluid slid down my parched throat, offering a much needed respite. "How long have I been out?" I asked.

"Half a day." She took the cup and set it aside. "I'll not overstay my welcome, but I warn you, Ruveel. Dragon Lord or not, I'll not have you disturbing my patients."

Ruveel's eyelids drooped with a drawn out blink, watching her as she left the tent before he looked my way. "The blue was hers, wasn't it?" His gaze was intense—eager, not angry. "They're her young."

"I'm not sure," I hedged, reaching for Tizmet.

'Ge'org might be able to tell,' she replied to my silent question.

"There were rumors, but we never thought to look for dragons in the sky. Ours never last long under their control. They tore themselves to pieces after a few days. When the Shaman's magic wears down, so does their hold. We assumed it was because the dragons can't stand to be tainted by them."

I wanted to look at Rafe, but I held Ruveel's gaze. He was observant. He might not guess, but he would know we hid something. Rafe had used his magic on dragons a few times—and they never tore themselves apart.

Ruveel's theory had to be wrong. Unless, of course, the Shamen broke something inside them.

"How large was her clutch, Avyanna?"

Pressing my lips together, I shook my head and immediately regretted the action when throbbing ricocheted through my skull. "I'm not sure."

"That many? We need *numbers*. If they can twist Wild Dragons like that—we don't stand a chance." He rubbed the nape of his neck and closed his eyes. "We barely held our ground when we pulled our dragons back, and now they have a fleet of their own."

Tizmet rushed over the bond, feeding me her emotions.

"Those aren't dragons," I snapped. "Those are mutilated shadows that deserve to be put out of their misery."

"And how do you propose we do that?" His eyes were distant. He might have been a terrible person, but if there was one thing he cared about, it was his Dragon Fleet. "I'm open to suggestions."

"Let the dragons care for their own," Rafe murmured, drawing our attention. He tapped his fingers against his lips thoughtfully. "Keep them distracted. Take their air power like we did last night, and the men will drive the Shadows back."

"That didn't work before. Why should it work now?" Ruveel asked, propping his elbows on his knees.

"Faulkin mentioned there's been a significant decline in Hunters."

"Aye, clearly they're spending their magic on larger beasts."

"Take your dragons and set up traps like last night. With fewer Hunters, we can maintain a front on two lines. Catch them off guard and push them back."

"I think you're forgetting why Avyanna is in the medical tent right now. My average Rider cannot heal wounds like that."

"Send a Healer with them," I pitched in. "Rashel guided me through the process when I healed Rafe. They only need the basics."

"And if one loses control of the magic?" Ruveel asked. "Your handicap is blessedly confined to yourself, Avyanna. Not every magical misstep is."

"It's a risk we have to take." I winced as I tried to sit upright, then gave up. "We're losing. This isn't a fight we can win without making drastic changes. If you want to win a large bet, wager against the odds."

He sucked in a hard breath, his jaw working. "You're wagering my dragon's lives."

"I'm wagering my own as well, Ruveel." My eyes fluttered shut. "Let them watch me and Tizmet."

'I care for my own,' she agreed with a hint of sorrow.

This wasn't what she wanted, but she was the mother to some of them—if not all. These monsters were partly hers in creation. They deserved her help in putting them out of their misery.

She would do it for their sake.

Rafe and Ruveel talked about tactics as I drifted off. We had a plan—now we only needed to execute it.

Autumn Year 901

The chill that ran down my spine had everything to do with the cold, and nothing to do with the two-leg that screamed above Tizmet.

We had done this before.

I pressed myself against her scales, cursing the saddle for making me an easy target, but thankful for the security it provided as she flew through the night. She huffed, flying as straight as an arrow toward the careful trap we had laid.

'Too fast,' I said, glancing over my shoulder. I couldn't make it out in the darkness, but I could see the shadow of its wings blocking the stars.

'Too slow and we'll be its dinner.' Reluctantly, she slowed her wing beats.

So far, only one gave up on its pursuit when we flew too fast. It had obviously been young, unable to match her speed. It had a Shaman rider, and we were too nervous to start the chase again.

The Dragon Fleet rested by day, and by night, lured the creatures into traps. Tonight, we had twenty-three teams out, spanning the entirety of the warfront.

The challenge was not to be taken lightly, as there were still those who were grappling with the concept. Deil and Vinet were waiting for us to fly over the curve in the stream before they took to the air. He was to provide cover fire while Tizmet and I dispatched the beast.

She roared as something brushed her tail. Pushing herself, she flew faster, nearing the stream. I glanced at the treetops below us, hoping we could manage to drop it in the clearing we planned. Rafe was waiting and his men would–

A gold dragon shot up from the trees.

'Blast it!'

Deil moved too soon, and now the two-leg knew it was a trap. It shrieked and pulled up, banking to the right.

Tizmet let out an outraged screech. *'I'm bringing it down!'*

She twisted, flipping in a tight maneuver. Her wings slammed down, charging after its shadow. It was a trick of the light, perhaps their magic, but the beasts were near impossible to see under full dark.

She let out a burst of fire, illuminating the night in a harsh amber glow.

The green two-leg screamed and dropped into a dive to gain speed. Tizmet flew after him, jarring me with the quick strokes of her wings.

'Can you catch it!?'

'Of course I can,' she grumbled.

But I felt her strain. Her muscles shook with effort and her talons were clenched inside her claws. She hissed, and I realized we were gaining on them.

'From above?'

'Below,' she corrected.

'Don't squash me!'

I hated when they were above me—which was almost every night. But having it know that we were after it bore a greater risk.

Tizmet swooped low, then rolled, grabbing the beast's legs. An eerie scream rent from the creature's throat as she grappled with it, using her weight to pull it down.

When it snapped its wings closed, she lurched upward, teeth shredding the appendage as she frantically fought to right herself. Catching the draft, she flipped us on top–

Right before we crashed into the trees.

I screamed, throwing my hands in front of my face. Branches and debris scattered as we skidded through the woods, crushing the forest with the weight of two dragons.

Without hesitation, she snapped forward, sinking her teeth into the Shaman, severing him in half. As we slowed, she swallowed his torso whole, and the green beneath us screamed.

It was an odd sound, one I'd never heard a dragon make. Those that lost their Shaman were deranged—broken.

Tizmet jumped off the creature, backing into the path that we had scored through the forest. She brought her head low to the ground and hissed as it spun in circles. Humanoid legs sprayed blood, still strapped into the Shadow's crude mockery of a saddle.

The green threw itself onto his back, kicking its claws. A high-pitched shriek tore out of its throat as it writhed in unseen pain. Thrashing to the side, it slammed into a tree and whirled, sinking its teeth into the trunk. Tearing it from the ground, it tossed it into the forest.

Then it turned on itself.

A gold dragon landed next to us, smaller than Tizmet by a third. I didn't look at the raven-haired Rider—instead I paid the green the only respect I could.

I watched it tear itself apart.

It was the same every time. Once the Shamen died, the dragon descended upon itself. It was sickening. We were helpless to intervene. There was no reasoning with the beasts. Whether it was the mutilation or the magic—something shattered inside their minds, and they unraveled before our very eyes.

It tore a chunk out of its back, then attempted to swallow it whole. It choked and spluttered, crying out. Stumbling backward, it gagged on its flesh—before ripping off a claw. Tears burned down my cheeks. This dragon was meant for someone else. It was supposed to know the love of a Rider. If it had hatched at Northwing, it would have only known love and care.

Instead, it gutted itself.

Deil retched, but I ignored him, staring onward as the green fell to its side and bit at its belly. Its teeth sliced neatly through its scales. Within a breath, its intestines spilled over the dirt. It gnashed at them, crying out—the sounds garbled against the chomping of its maw.

After a few agonizing moments, it finally stilled.

Bile burned my throat as I slid off Tizmet's back. We always checked the bodies after they died. Not that there was ever much left, but we looked for any sign of what the Shadows were after—or anything we could use against them.

When Deil joined me on the ground, weeks of outrage and torment climaxed. I threw myself at him. He cried out, and I gripped his throat, slamming him against his dragon's flank. Above me, Tizmet roared, drawing a hiss from the gold, but it hunkered down in submission.

"What were you *thinking!?*" I screamed in his face.

He might have been taller, but with the way he shrank from me, it didn't matter.

"You were supposed to take flight after the bend!" I seethed and drew my bandit breaker, bracing it against his stomach.

"We didn't see you!" He grappled at my wrist, grasping it in a bruising grip.

I shoved off him, disgusted, and put some distance between us. Sheathing my bandit breaker, I let my rage meld with Tizmet's.

He had one task: provide cover fire. Yes, he was new at this—but it was mine and Tizmet's lives at stake, not his. If we hadn't been ready, the beast could have easily exploited our hesitation, killing us both.

"And here, people think you're the nice one."

I glanced at the heaving stallion that trotted from the woods. "Thrice-curse it, Rafe. We could have died!" My fists clenched at my sides. "I didn't ask him to attack. He was never in danger! There was no reason for him to blow his cover!"

Rafe let out a low chuckle as his horse picked its way across the disaster of the forest floor. I grumbled under my breath as we approached the steaming carcass, bile rising in my throat once again. Ruveel trained his Riders as fast as he could. We had to press our advantage while we had it—but it was hard teaching old Riders. They had been trained to run from Shamen for too long. A strategy was in place. Willing deviance from it could cost someone their lives, and hand the Shadows another dragon.

As we neared, Rafe's stallion shied and danced away, nervous. Dismounting, he stayed by my side as we came upon the body.

I had seen some horrid deaths before, but these stomach wounds were on a whole new level of severity—the worst one yet.

"Torso?" Rafe bent over the Shaman's legs, running his hand over the bloody straps holding them in place.

"Tizmet's gullet."

Someone to my left gagged, and I promptly ignored them. Rafe's team was supposed to be our backup if the trap didn't go according to plan. After the two-leg was dispatched, his team would move in, looking for anything of value.

Rafe made a thoughtful sound, picking at the remnants of the robes that managed to still cover the legs.

I brushed angry tears away and pressed my palm against bloody green scales. It would have been a magnificent dragon—one that would rival Flinor.

'Flinor is stronger,' Tizmet huffed, towering overhead. *'He would not have been so easily defeated.'*

'This dragon wasn't either,' I replied. *'If it had turned its attention on you, we would have had a fair fight on our hands.'*

She snorted, craning to peer at the remains. *'I would have won.'*

"There's nothing here." Rafe sighed, throwing the black tatters.

I walked to his side, avoiding the creature's flesh, but my boots slipped on its stomach fluids.

Pale gray skin wrapped the Shadow's legs. His blood and sheared off muscles were red—his bones white. Their insides were so similar to our own, but their outward appearance was vastly different. And their magic—a far cry from what we wielded.

I narrowed my eyes at his black boots. A series of bones carved into the shape of stars were threaded along the surface. What gods did they worship? Why did this one have carvings of the stars? Did they enjoy viewing them? Did they mean something to it?

Tizmet snarled at my thoughts. *'They are monsters.'*

'Aye. But even monsters have a beginning.'

Chapter 39

Picking a bit of fur out of my stew, I flicked it to the ground with a grimace. The camp cooks were worse than Xzanth.

A pang of remorse ran through me. Since joining the warfront, I'd only seen him once. He cast Rafe, and me in turn, such a look of disgust and affront that I had to resist the urge to chase him down. He didn't want to be near us after what had happened between Rafe and Faulkin. That he forced the older General to face a Shadow was too much for a man who lost his wife and daughter to the monsters.

I flung another bit of hair out of my stew, lip curled in disgust.

'*Picky,*' Tizmet hummed from beside me as she devoured a cow's rump.

'*I have no problem eating bland food. I draw the line at eating hair, though.*' Meat and potatoes shifted in the soup as I stirred it, searching for any other clumps. '*If I have to eat hair, I'll hunt for myself.*'

'*There's no prey within a day's flight.*'

The loud crack of a bone drew a flinch from me, but the men around the fire paid us no heed. Flinor trilled beside Tizmet, lifting his head to the sky.

"He misses the days he could hunt for himself," Dareth murmured beside me.

A frown pulled my brows down, and I set the bowl on my lap. The war leeched all joy out of the man. He used to be so cheerful and funny, but since his arrival, I found him distant and reserved.

Tizmet clicked and nudged Flinor's head, trying to bring his attention back to her. The great green male had grown in the time we'd been gone. He nearly matched her in size now, and she was one of the largest at the front. Dareth was taking good care of him, regardless of the conditions.

A soft melody drew my gaze to the fire. Jamlin hummed a tune as he poked at the embers, Blain joining in. A sad smile tugged at my features. I missed Tegan.

He would've had a bawdy song and string of jokes to ease the somber cloud that hung over the war camp.

Rafe walked past our little group, General Teak at his side. He jerked his head, motioning for me to follow him.

"Goodnight, Dareth."

He hummed an acknowledgement, and I clenched my jaw.

This had to end.

I fell into step beside Rafe. The stars were bright overhead, but the low moon was hidden behind the treetops of the forest beyond. Lanterns and firepits lit the camp well enough, and as I rested my hand on my bandit breaker, it was done out of habit rather than any sense of fear.

"I'm not saying it's the right thing, but it is the smart thing."

Teak murmured so low I could barely hear him, though he was just a few paces away.

"If it fails?" Rafe grunted.

"We're doomed either way."

My steps slowed, and I peered around Rafe to eye Teak. He caught my movement and flashed me a bright grin, winking in response to my curiosity.

"You'll find out soon enough."

"Are we headed to Faulkin?" I asked.

"Aye," Rafe said, taking a deep breath. He rolled his shoulders back, a telltale sign he was upset.

Grinding my teeth, I stepped closer to him and bumped my arm into his. It was a small movement, but it assured him I was there—I would support him. He pressed his lips into a tight smile.

We weaved through the tents, Teak calling out friendly greetings to soldiers. He was a natural leader, and the men loved him. Rafe and I had earned a sense of respect among the ranks, but they were far more leery of us.

When we arrived at Faulkin's tent, Rafe didn't bother knocking on the post before storming in. Teak grinned, holding the flap open for me, as if I were a proper lady, and I scoffed as I stepped inside.

Ruveel lounged in a chair, legs sprawled out in front of him, while Faulkin adjusted a dragon figurine on the map. To be honest, I had never seen him in a room that didn't have a map in it. The man lived and breathed strategy. He offered me a grim smile, and as Rafe collapsed into a chair, his face fell faster than a Rider tumbling off dragonback.

"Shadowslayer." He straightened and clasped his hands behind his back. "Wild Rider. Teak."

I dipped my head in acknowledgment of his status. "General Faulkin."

He waved me over. "Avyanna, I'd like you to look at this."

I narrowed my eyes, but approached the table. There were petty few reasons I could think of for him wanting my insight.

The map was a giant thing, almost as long as I was tall. It showed all the known continent and part of Caulden to the northwest. The E'or mountain range bordered the east, with the Teeth taking up space at its southern end. Below that, it depicted a chain of islands trailing into the sea. The Shadowlands lay on the southwestern edge, separated from Regent by a thin strait. The west thinned into a bottleneck that bridged our continent to the Shadowlands' borders.

Faulkin had his black figurines set up behind the line of Sky Trees, where we were camped. Pushing through the tall forests, he placed his red figurines, indicating where he wanted to move. I bit my tongue and frowned at the placement. We couldn't push that far. We didn't have enough manpower, and the longer we pressed our position at night, taking the two-legs, the more we risked losing that advantage.

"We can do it," Faulkin said in response to my silent skepticism.

My eyes flashed up to meet his.

He nodded to the table. "You doubt our abilities, but we can manage it."

The map had the skull figurines, the Shadows, gathered on the other side of the bottleneck, blocked by a red dragon.

"How?"

Faulkin sucked in a breath, as if preparing for a speech. "We push them further than we ever have—and build a wall. King Aldred already has the finest smiths and builders working on it. But for this to succeed, we need you."

Ruveel groaned. "And the Dragon Fleets."

"And the civilians," Rafe added.

My eyes darted between them all, settling back on Faulkin as he sighed.

"Civilians?" I echoed.

The Dragon Fleet was born and bred for this. We knew what we signed up for when we agreed to be Chosen. Civilians though?

"They would not be fighting on the front." Faulkin pointed to the red figurines of soldiers on his map, marching toward the bottleneck. "We have the advantage, but for how long? Ruveel could lead the Fleets and press the Shadows back." He motioned to the red dragon in front of the soldier. "There will be Shadow Men separated from the main force. The drafted ranks will deal with them–"

"You want to leave the enemy behind our lines?" I blinked in shock. "Have untrained men hunt down *Shadows*?"

We barely managed against them with experienced soldiers. To subject mere farmers and smiths to face them was... obscene.

"We have the upperhand for a few more days at most." Faulkin's eyes sharpened to a glare that he leveled on us all. "If we don't press onward, we will lose not only the ground we've gained, but the homelands."

I rocked back on my heels, staring down at the map. The skulls were spread in a long line across the continent. If we cut through their lines, it left our flanks unprotected. Faulkin wanted to call on the reserves, conscript average folk, to deal with them.

It was a death sentence.

"We get to the bottleneck. We can hold it with far fewer men than we are using now. One Fleet could hold it. Once we settle in, we can send the remaining Fleets back, as well as twenty, if not thirty, companies of men to hunt down the last of the Shadows within Regent's borders."

"Farmers can't hold off Shadow Men," I whispered, shaking my head.

"They do all the time, Wild Rider."

Faulkin's use of my formal title brought my gaze back to him.

"Where do you think our veterans come from? Where do you think they will return to when this is over? I've been fighting this war longer than you've been alive. And now, we have the chance to end it." His blue eyes glittered with restraint as he spoke, as if this was a long-lost dream finally within his grasp.

He braced against the table, pinning me with his icy stare. "Think of our future generations. I've never seen a chance like this. They're spread too thin. We can punch through."

I bit the inside of my cheek, glancing at the scar he received from a wolf-type Hunter. He wasn't wrong. This war had been going on for hundreds of years. The history books alternated between lulls and struggles, but the Shadows were always there, always pressing in.

Sighing, I pointed to the strait that protected our continent from theirs. "They won't cross the water?"

"No." There was a slight excitement in his tone, as if he sensed my acceptance. "Rumors claimed they were sailing across to attack to the south, but it was a diversion. Instead, they penetrated our line. They fear the deep. They'll wade in water, even swim, but once they reach a drop off, they refuse to cross. Even if they were to brave the shallows—they'd be easy prey. Dragonfire would sink their ships in one pass. If we build a wall, we can manage it."

"Why a wall? Why not press the advantage and take the continent?"

"Oh, how I wish we could." The sorrow in his voice validated his statement. "We just don't have the forces to stretch that far while protecting our flanks. One day, perhaps."

I hummed and tapped the table with a finger. Something unsettling skittered down my spine and I slowly turned to take in the men staring at me, waiting expectantly. Ruveel scowled, his eyes sharp and piercing. Teak offered me a crooked smile, as if he knew I was taking this all in.

Rafe was expressionless. He met my gaze, his eye steady and calm.

"There's more to this," I murmured.

Tizmet crowded my mind, interested in what had caused my spike in anxiety.

Turning to Faulkin, I crossed my arms over my chest. "How do I play into this?"

He matched my posture, leaning back with a challenging glare.

However, it was the Dragon Lord that spoke, "We need your dragon."

'They have their own,' Tizmet huffed.

"She knows the Sky Trees," he gestured vaguely, "but does she know what lies beyond?"

She scoffed. *'As if a dragon is confined by trees and forests. I own the sky. I am bound by the earth below and the stars above.'*

'You've seen the bottleneck?'

'Aye.'

I winced and clenched my eyes as images flashed through my brain, too fast and bright to comprehend. Golden sand. Green grass. Blue water. Lifting a hand to my temple, I shoved back at the flow of images, trying to slow them.

'I've seen a great many things, little one.'

"She does." Ruveel guessed, knowing how to read a Rider that conversed with their dragon.

I cracked open my eyes and glared at him. "What is it to you?"

"We require a scout."

"You need someone with the balls to go behind enemy lines," Rafe rumbled.

My confidence surged, fueled by the certainty that he had my back.

"Oh, I would go in a heartbeat, Shadowslayer," Ruveel drawled. "But Ge'org's red scales aren't exactly subtle. They would see him leagues away."

'I can find mud for him to roll in,' Tizmet suggested.

"You want me and Rafe to go beyond their lines, while they have two-legs, and scout ahead of the army?"

My mind buzzed as Tizmet shuffled through my emotions. Pleasure trickled across the bond. *'Fearless, little one.'*

She would find no fear in me.

Faulkin shook his head. "We didn't say Rafe–"

"I go where she goes." Rafe's snarl cut through whatever he was about to say.

I held back my smile at his words. It felt so good to know I wasn't alone.

'She has a dragon at her call, yet she says a human makes her feel less alone.'

I couldn't resist the small grin that lifted my lips at her comment. *'It's different.'*

She huffed in response as she retreated from my mind.

Ruveel wasn't wrong. Tizmet's mottled gray and brown scales were perfect camouflage for almost any environment. Many Riders gloated about how their dragons sparkled in the sun, how they resembled rare gems, but Tizmet's dull color was far more precious.

It made her stronger. And strength was beautiful.

"How confident are you that this will work?" I asked, turning to Faulkin.

"One can never be sure," he hedged.

Teak spoke up from behind, "We wouldn't bring it up if we believed the risk was too great, Avyanna."

I had the strongest urge to look back and ask Rafe his opinion, but knowing him, he would leave the decision to me. We were here because of me, not him.

"I need a night."

"Understandable." Faulkin dipped his head, his shoulders sagging.

Taking that as dismissal, I spun, catching Ruveel's gaze dart between me and Rafe. I resisted the urge to roll my eyes as Rafe stood, walking with me out of the tent.

"Oh, Avyanna?" Ruveel called. "Sweet dreams."

"I swear that man tests me," I huffed, yanking my tunic off.

The weak glow from the lantern barely illuminated the small tent we called home. Sorrow pricked my heart, remembering our cottage.

This was home now.

Rafe grunted, loosening his belt. "He tests everyone."

He stretched his arms above his head, and my jaw dropped in mock horror as his spine emitted several pops.

The corner of his mouth quirked up in an amused smile. "You just have to show him you're bigger than him."

I deadpanned, kicking out my hip. "Have you seen me? Exactly how am I supposed to show I'm bigger than anyone?"

His eye trailed down my body, and I tried to hide the heat it brought to my skin. He prowled toward me, all two steps, and settled his large hands on my waist, tugging me flush against him.

"People underestimate you," he murmured as his gaze dipped to my lips. "He underestimates you."

"He doesn't think I can scout?" My brows pulled into a tight frown. "Why would he say I should go into enemy territory if he doubts my ability?"

In one effortless lift, he swept me off my feet. I instinctively secured my legs around his hips, linking my arms at the nape of his neck.

"He doesn't like you, *Wild Rider*. You're a threat to his Fleets. He can get rid of you–"

"And test me at the same time."

"Aye. Now, tell me why we're talking about another man while your legs are wrapped around me?" He smirked before leaning close so his lips could explore my neck.

I sighed and relaxed against him, tipping my chin to give him access. "We were talking about him *before* you got ideas."

I moaned as his teeth grazed my skin, just hard enough to make my brain go fuzzy. Raking my nails up his back, I cradled his head, pulling him in for a kiss.

His lips met mine, eager and demanding. I smiled, plundering his mouth with just as much enthusiasm. Kissing Rafe was never a simple, gentle affair. It was a battle—one I was determined to win.

Our tongues danced and fought for dominance, and I reached between us, fumbling to shove his trousers down. He growled, lowering me to the ground. A giggle slipped out, and I stretched languidly as he kicked off his pants, eyeing me with a frown.

"You have too many clothes on."

Arching my back, I threaded my fingers into my hair. "That's your problem, not mine."

A predatory smile lit his face, brighter than the lantern light. He dropped to his knees, palms trailing from my calves to my thighs. I tugged off his patch, tossing it to the relative safety of the small cot.

We wouldn't be using it, anyway.

The last two fortnights had been uneventful. Tizmet and I flew through the night, scouting in a wide arc. We investigated any camps, noting as much as we could. We brought any information to Rafe, who made a report that was sent to Faulkin by messenger or bird.

He kept his group small. Along with Jamlin and the twins, we had Loth and Fletcher from one of Teak's companies. Both were notable warriors, but more importantly, Loth grew up caring for carrier pigeons, and Fletcher was a tracker by trade. He took great care to be sure we left no sign of our presence when we moved camp—nothing that might alarm the Shadows.

I was tired, exhausted—weary. My trousers were loose and my brain constantly felt muddled. Tizmet handled the double-duty well, as if she was made for this. After flying all night, she rested, but remained aware of any possible threat. This was nothing new to her. She lived in the Sky Trees like this for years—but it took a heavy toll on me.

Tizmet's wings were barely more than a whisper as we coasted through the night.

'How much further?' I asked, straining to make out anything in the pitch black. The mammoth trees blocked out even the smallest rays of moonlight.

'Patience, little one.'

Being behind enemy lines was more challenging than I expected. Back when I crossed the front with the Tennan to rescue Rafe, we were still relatively safe. Here, we were so far removed from the war camp, if something happened to us, we were dead.

Every movement was slow, every sound muffled. Rags were tied around bits of metal hanging off packs. Swords were strapped down and bundled in cloth. We traveled with no horses, only on foot. Horses were too big of a risk.

We passed three Shadow camps, their tents made of black oiled fabric. It was a far cry from the rough huts and shelters I saw when I rescued Rafe. With the thick canopy blocking most of the daylight, these were nearly impossible to see. Though the greater threat was the Hunters. If we were involved in a skirmish, we had to retreat. So we avoided the pieced-together abominations–

Fear flooded the bond, and a shiver ran up my spine. Sucking in a breath, I scrambled to place what had frightened Tizmet. She feared nothing.

'What is it?!'

Her mind was a jumble of frantic thoughts, and I tried to make sense of it. Her wings flapped harder, the whoosh sounding abnormally loud in the darkness. She raced through the trees, flying lower, weaving through branches as thick as buildings.

'Tizmet!'

'Do you hear it?' Her voice was tight and high. Not the low confident rasp I was accustomed to.

'No.' I strained to make anything out. *'I hear nothing!'*

My pulse thundered in my ears, feeding off her terror. She pushed across the bond, throwing her senses over mine.

I gritted my teeth against the onslaught. Frogs croaking. The flap of a darkwing in flight. A steady slurp of some animal drinking. The crunching of a creature walking over the forest floor.

A shriek of a hatchling.

Terror skittered through me as I settled deeper into my saddle. I clung to her hearing, picking out the gruff voices of the Shadow Men and the distorted grunts of their Hunters. Soft snores reached her ears, alongside the clink of metal against metal, the creak of leather and thud of wood.

A keen of a dragonling, followed by mocking laughter.

My throat closed up in a heady mixture of fear and rage. Tizmet trembled beneath me, her chest swelling with a gasp of air. If she bellowed now, we would blow our cover.

'Hold!'

Her awareness flickered, acknowledging me. I rushed over our bond, pushing calm logic at her. We couldn't face a camp on our own.

'They have a young one!'

I flinched at the stab of pain that accompanied her outburst. *'We need Rafe! We can't take them alone!'*

She recoiled from my mind in disgust and let out her breath in a soft hiss. I leaned forward, laying my forehead against her scales. Grounding myself as much as I could mid-flight, I pressed my palm to her neck and tugged at her sight. She reluctantly shared her vision with me.

My stomach revolted at the disconnect between what I was seeing and what my body was feeling. Moonlight bathed the forest in an eerie glow, where the dew settled was almost luminescent in the dark. Her gaze darted through the trees at a speed my mind could hardly comprehend. She processed so much, at such great speeds. I was tripping to catch up.

A wail rent the night, and I grimaced as Tizmet shuddered under a wave of hatred. She glided to a branch, her claws silent as they sank deep into the bark. Tucking her wings in, she craned her long neck around the tree, peering below.

Bile crept up my throat as she swung low, shuffling her feet for a better view. I swallowed against the burn, my only task to keep my seat.

'Any winged Hunters?'

'No.' Her response was curt, as if I impeded upon her concentration. Her eyes narrowed to slits as she focused below.

Dread filled me as dim silhouettes came into focus.

This was no ordinary camp quickly fashioned for war. The wooden structures were pieced together in the same haphazard way as the Hunters. Evergreen branches covered the roofs, and firelight seeped through the cracks of the planks chaotically nailed together as walls.

Figures moved with confidence, their tall and erect postures revealing their lack of concern about being observed. Stark-white masks of bones adorned every head. Tizmet's gaze shifted over the large camp quickly, trying to place the whimpering hatchling.

It was young, not having grown into the depth of calls. I would wager it was only a few days, perhaps weeks, old. My stomach roiled, struggling to comprehend how that was possible. Summer Solstice was *months* ago.

Two figures snagged her interest, and I gulped as her vision zoomed in as if singling them out. On one, the mask of bones had the unnerving similarity of a dragon's skull. The other faced away from us, its black robes bleeding into the shadows, and even Tizmet's sharp sight couldn't pick out where the garment stopped and darkness began.

On the ground, a dragonling shuffled.

Tizmet shook under me, her eyes catching the metal muzzle around its maw. Its wings were tightly bound by stifling bands, and its legs were chained, restricting its movements. Its scales were either black or too muddied to discern a color. It reached the Shaman's knees, standing docile at his feet. Its eyes caught the moonlight, gleaming in terror.

Pushing across our bond, I melded my hearing to Tizmet's, straining for their voices. They spoke in a strange, high-pitched language, a small bag passing between them. The Shaman crouched, and the hatchling shirked away, pulling its chain taut.

'Why doesn't he control it?'

The Shaman jerked the chain, dragging the dragonling toward him with far more strength than his robed figure implied.

'It drives us mad.'

I immediately thought of Rafe, how he controlled dragons before. Along with Tizmet and the Wild One that rejected me on my second Hatching Day as First Chosen, there was Elspeth, the white dragon he silenced so I wouldn't get caught attempting to force the bond. As far as I knew, none of them went mad.

'Your mate does not steal our soul, only suppresses it.'

Her words were clipped, and her gaze sharpened on the Shaman's gloved hand as he drew a finger over the dragonling's shoulder. He traced along the joint as he spoke, then grabbed the dragonling's leg, forcing it to bend, pointing out where the joint and muscle moved.

Horror soured my thoughts. *'They plan to mutilate it.'*

Would they do it tonight? Would we be able to get Rafe here in time? Could we save it?

Tizmet's claws sank deeper into the bark, drawing a low groan from the crush of wood.

The Shaman's head snapped up, the empty eye sockets of the mask darting our way. Tizmet clamped her eyes shut, cutting off our vision to prevent any light that might have been reflected.

She strained her hearing, listening as the two fell into silence. Noise was abundant in the camp. They weren't concerned about anyone this far beyond their lines. The quiet din almost overpowered the Shaman's voice as it spoke up again, quieter this time.

Moving slowly, Tizmet pulled her head behind the tree, hidden from view.

'It has to be tonight,' she said.

'Rafe and his men won't make it here by then!'

'They will butcher it.'

'They might not,' I tried. *'Let's get Rafe. We will make it here as quick as we can.'*

We both knew the hatchling would be mutilated by then.

'Avyanna.' My name was both a plea and a demand. She needed to do this now.

'They have at least one Shaman. The camp is too large. Who knows how many Shadows are down there. What if they have more hatchlings that we're not seeing? What if, by saving one, we doom others?'

Wrath and helplessness surged over the bond like a wave pulling me out to sea. I grunted under the mental strain and pressed my cheek to her scales.

'Fly.' My begging request was a drop in her storm.

She threw her head into the air, baring her teeth to the sky in a silent scream. No sound came out, not even a whisper of her rage.

Then she plummeted off the branch and glided on hushed wings back to Rafe.

The morning was still dark, the sky barely alight with the sun's first rays. I stumbled as my feet hit the ground, already running for our small tent.

"Oi!" Jamlin tumbled as Tizmet shoved him aside with her muzzle. He rolled, coming up in a crouch, and spun to face her with an offended look. "What was that for?"

'Hurry them!'

Rafe appeared at my side, catching my arm as my numb legs gave out from under me.

I whirled in his grasp. "We have to go—now!"

"Why?"

His voice was far too calm compared to my urgency. Tizmet's rage poured over the bond, and I clenched my jaw, sharing her anger.

"You have at least a day's march ahead of you. Pack to make camp."

"Sit down."

"No! There isn't time!"

Tizmet whipped our way, her claws sending up clods of dirt. She snapped her teeth at Rafe, and he ignored her, his brows dropping in a fierce frown.

"Vy, shut her out."

"Rafe, you don't–"

"Shut. Her. Out."

She threw her maw open, spewing a cloud of hot sparks. *'I will leave without them!'*

Her demand was accompanied by a wave of pain that had me staggering against Rafe. He pulled me tight, facing Tizmet in all her wrath. Even in her fury, she was careful to keep quiet.

I threw up a wall, blocking most of her rage, but left the bond open if she chose to use her words. Her claws kneaded the dirt, bringing up clumps of soil as she fumed. Jerking her head to her full height, she glared down at Rafe, lips pulled back in a snarl.

He met her glare and matched her, not moving a muscle. She snapped down, clacking her teeth so close that the force tugged at my hair. His heart beat steady under my cheek, confident in his stance.

"You done?"

Tizmet launched into the sky like an arrow, irate at his mockery. Men scattered with muttered curses and trees groaned at the gale of her wings. She pulled back from the bond, leaving me feeling empty and alone. Flying high, she disappeared into the early morning sky, and I sagged against Rafe.

"Take a breath, then tell me what happened," he growled.

Sitting on a log, he ordered the men to pack up camp with haste, and gave me a dry road ration. When his glare darted between me and it, I nibbled on the hardtack.

I relayed everything we'd seen, offering as many details as I could, worried my tired brain would forget something important.

"Did you see the Shaman leave?"

I shook my head, pinching the bridge of my nose. "We left as soon as we could. She won't let it go, Rafe. We have to move."

"We do this, and our cover is blown. They'll know a dragon is behind their line."

"It's a hatchling!" Tears burned in my dry eyes. "A few days old at most! How is that *possible?* They had it bound in iron like some—some monster. I can't stand by and let them maim it. It's a dragon."

"We have six men, Vy. Six. And a Wild Rider that can't use magic–"

"I can–"

"You can't." He held up a hand, cutting off any retort. "What you saw was not a war camp. That's a rough village. They will have trade routes going through it. Powerful Shamen could be there, supplies, weapons." His shoulder deflated with his sigh. "We don't know what's there, Vy. That's something Teak and his lot will have to face."

"She won't let me turn back." A tear burned a rebel trail through the grime covering my cheeks. "We *have* to."

Tizmet landed, shaking the earth beneath us. Placing her lips over my head, she let out a low hiss. *'We will go. Leave the coward.'*

Rafe lifted his gaze to Tizmet's teeth, which she bared for his examination.

'Tell him! We will fly to the hatchling. He may stay and piss his trousers in worry. He says he loves you, yet will not follow.'

'Tizmet, you don't understand—we're risking their lives.'

'Is the hatchling's life not in danger?'

When I tilted my head to see her, she craned down, flashing one fiery eye at me. I flinched away, feeling the ire in her glare.

'You have never been a mother—and never will be. You do not understand.'

I recoiled, both physically and mentally. Bringing my gaze down, I frowned at my hands as hurt welled within me. No, the only young I would ever know were hers. She shared her motherhood with me back in Leeds, letting me feel the need—the pride in her hatchlings. I would never have that with my own babe, my womb barren and empty.

"We travel light," Rafe said. "We should make it by sundown."

He blurred in my vision as I gave him a trembling smile. Blinking away tears, I pushed myself to my feet.

"If I say we turn back—we turn back, Vy."

I didn't even look at him as I turned to walk through the woods on foot versus taking to Tizmet's back. I needed time alone. And apparently, she was willing to give it to me.

Chapter 40

When we left, I opted to walk with the men rather than fly on dragonback—using the excuse that I needed to stretch my legs. Rafe grunted in reply, his eye darting between me and Tizmet as if he knew something had transpired between us.

She flew high above, hidden from view. The Shadows could climb, but getting to the towering heights of the trees would be a miraculous feat, and wouldn't go unnoticed. The behemoth leaves alone were larger than my room at Northwing. Even the shadow of her flight was unnoticeable.

The pounding ache in my head intensified, a result of sleep deprivation, the physical exertion of trudging through the dense thicket, and the void left by Tizmet's absence. As if aware of the pain she caused, she retreated and kept her distance.

I clawed my way over a root thicker than Tizmet was tall. Navigating the forest was a challenge because the maps we had were outdated and no longer accurate, thanks to the relentless growth. We avoided the recent army routes, fearing that the Shadows may have already infiltrated them.

Shadow Men were resourceful, using anything and everything offered to them. They recycled lumber from our outposts, used the roads carved out and packed down by our soldiers. They were a disease slowly spreading across Regent.

But we figured out their advantage.

And now we had to end it.

My grip slipped, and I yelped, sliding down the slick surface. A strong hand gripped my Riders' leathers, hauling me up. Stumbling against Rafe at the top of the root, I flashed him a weary smile.

"Call her."

Shaking my head, I tried to ignore his grumbled demand. Tizmet didn't want me right now, and I didn't want her. What hurt worse than her words was the fact that Rafe knew I needed her. I was holding the group back, slowing everyone down.

"If she wants to get there by nightfall, you're going to have to rest."

She crowded the bond at his words, and I resisted the urge to shove her out. She wouldn't come to me out of concern, but with the threat we wouldn't make it there in time—she dove like a stone. We were tired. She needed me to attack the village, and I needed Rafe. There was no reason to take my frustration out on her—even if she took hers out on me.

I glanced up as she angled for an opening between branches.

"My thanks," I drawled, glaring at Rafe.

The corner of his mouth quirked up as he adjusted the straps that secured his longsword to his back. We waited until Tizmet glided down on silent wings before Blain and the others continued down the far side of the root.

I clenched my jaw, but held my temper in check as she landed, her massive talons digging into the soft bark. I took a step toward her, but Rafe grasped my elbow and spun me to him. He dipped low, his lips meeting mine in a passionate kiss. Sighing against his mouth, I soaked up the meager comfort. He sucked my bottom lip between his teeth, cradling the back of my head as he pressed his hips into me. I clutched at his belt, drawing him closer, feeling his need.

When he pulled away, his dark eye flashed. He wouldn't tell me to be safe. We both knew that wasn't a possibility out here.

"Go."

I lifted to my toes, stretching to place a kiss against his rough cheek. "I'll see you in a few chimes."

With a nod, he stepped back. I mourned the loss of his strength as I faced Tizmet. She held her head high, staring off, as if a tree was more interesting than the scene in front of her. Her eye darted to me, then to the root beneath her claws.

Taking a deep breath, I started toward her. It would be a lonely flight.

Tizmet landed north of the village, tucked a distance away, high in the branches. We had a few moments to rest before Rafe and his men made it here—before we attempted to rescue the hatchling. Sliding down her shoulder, I chose my steps with care. The grooves of the bark were deep and rigid. I could twist an ankle at best, fall to my death at worst.

She scoffed, curling in the crook of the giant branch. *'As if I would let you fall.'*

'It's not the fall I'm worried about—it's you catching me,' I snapped before I thought better of it.

She tilted her head, then lowered to peer at me. Rushing over the bond, she pillaged through my thoughts and emotions. I held back my irritation, knowing she felt it, and didn't need me to throw it in her face.

'You're hurt.' She flicked out her tongue, tasting the air. Her eyelid blinked slowly, clear membrane trailing over her fire colored iris.

'Words cut deep,' I shot back, crossing my arms over my chest.

'Talons cut deep. Words are... words.'

'Talons hurt the body, words hurt the heart.'

She inhaled, taking a deep breath of my scent as if she couldn't place what was wrong or how to fix it. *'I hurt your heart.'*

'Aye.'

Tears pricked at my eyes, and I swiped them away. Tizmet was more than my friend, she was my bonded. She was the other half of my soul. That I couldn't have children was a fact I knew and accepted, but to have her slap me across the face with it...

It stung.

'How does one heal a heart?' she asked, tilting her head again. Her pupils narrowed and flared as she tried to puzzle it out. *'I cannot heal your seizures. How can I heal your heart after it is cut by words?'*

I smothered a choking laugh. I had no right to be angry with her. She didn't understand. Perhaps, if she had grown with me since a hatchling, she would grasp the finer details of the human heart, but she was a dragon first and foremost.

She raised her wing, and I settled in against her side.

'You could say you're sorry.'

'Sorry?' She rolled the word over in her mind, processing what it meant—and if she really was apologetic. *'Sorry,'* she agreed.

Exhaustion sapped at my strength, and my eyes slid shut, consumed by weariness. *'I'm sorry I was mad at you.'*

She rumbled a low purr, wrapping her neck around her body. Nestling me against her, the wall between us eased and lifted. Securely nestled into the side of my dragon, I let sleep take me.

Tucked into the high branches, Tizmet scanned the area for Hunters and for any sign of Rafe. The camp was oddly empty of the patchwork monsters. Rather than offering a sense of security, it only managed to make me feel more uneasy. Their confidence stemmed from the belief that they were safe from any potential attacks.

'There are none in the trees,' she assured.

We didn't come here to confront the entire village, just to rescue the hatchling. As far as I could tell, they only had the one.

'If we are not already too late.'

Anger simmered under the surface, but I was relieved to know it wasn't aimed at me this time.

'Where are the Hunters on the ground?' I asked.

I caught sight of Dane moving silently through the thick foliage, trying to circle the village. It was too large. He would never make it all the way around before we attacked.

'Scattered. There are a few of them.'

She strained to hear any sign of the hatchling. We needed to pinpoint where it was.

Dusk was falling, bringing with it the bite of autumn. As the weak light of the setting sun fought its way through the dense trees, the forest grew colder. I shivered—both from the chill and anticipation of what lay ahead.

'I cannot hear it.' She trembled, and her anxiety trickled across the bond.

I narrowed my gaze on the few skulls that I could pick out at this distance and watched as they strode through their village unconcerned. Their black robes hid their forms, concealing any discerning features, but I saw no little ones among them. They clearly weren't settled enough to bring their children this close to the war front. Still, relaxed as they were, there were far too many of them.

Two rounded the corner and stopped to talk with three more. White bones glinted in the fading light, and my nerves soured my stomach. Getting in wouldn't be the problem.

It would be getting everyone out.

A group of six more converged near a small building. The one leading the group held a bundle of something, and I squinted, trying to make it out.

'What is he holding?'

Tizmet's pupil narrowed on it, digging her claws into the tree as she craned her head for a better angle. She pushed her vision over the bond, but I could only see the Shadow's back, their bone mask obscured. The door opened and Tizmet held her gaze against the glare of lantern light, her focus slipping inside–

Where a small creature cowered in the corner, wrapped in steel bands.

'There!'

I scanned the ground once more for Rafe. While Tizmet's fire would reveal our position to him, I had no means of locating him.

'Ready yourself!'

I swallowed against the lump in my throat. Working quickly, I winched back my crossbow. Tizmet launched, and I braced against the saddle with one hand. She dove through the trees, arrowing for the building that the Shadow Men congregated around. Snapping her wings out, she caught the brisk air, and a bony mask tilted up to the darkening sky.

Shouts erupted as fire fell. Flames engulfed structures, casting everything in a haze of orange. Screams and battle cries rent the night as her inferno devoured everything in her path. Shadows called their Hunters, their howls and guttural roars scattered across the clearing.

I brought the crossbow to my chin. I didn't have a clear shot yet, and couldn't see well enough through the thick black smoke, but I would be ready when she made her second pass. Rising and banking, she swooped low over the village, and panic squeezed my throat as the Shadows ran toward the building the hatchling was in.

Pumping her wings, Tizmet raced, her claws batting as many as she could aside. I took aim at a Shadow with a large mask. I didn't dare look at his face for fear of meeting his eyes.

I loosed the bolt, and the Shadow clutched its chest and dropped, just as we flew over the shack with the hatchling. It cried out beneath us, and Tizmet snapped aside, catching a Hunter that jumped at her from a rooftop. The movement jostled me in the saddle, and I frantically winched my crossbow again.

A weight crashed into her right wing, and she roared in pain. We pitched hard, angled at the ground. I grunted and tried to bring the crossbow up in time to block the Hunter that clawed its way toward me.

'Get it off!'

The mouth of a wolf snapped at me, spit foaming as it barked and snarled. Black fur covered what looked like a man's hands, tipped with long talons. Its body rippled with muscle, and I pulled the trigger.

It let loose a bone-chilling howl.

'Avyanna!'

I was thrown to the side as Tizmet slammed into the ground, still grappling with another Hunter. My head crashed against her hard scales, and a strange ringing replaced all sound. I blinked, desperate to clear my vision as I grappled for my spear.

I jerked it free of its sheath, then twisted the blade up as the beast lunged. Impaled, black dribble spewed from its muzzle. I used its momentum, flinging it over Tizmet's side. It slid off my spear, landing against the ground with a sickening thud.

My heart raced as my hands fumbled with the buckles to the stirrups. *'Where is Rafe?!'*

'Stay on!' Tizmet roared, throwing dragonfire around us in an arc.

'We can't fight here!'

She knew that as well as I. We were vulnerable. We lost every advantage and could easily be overpowered.

'It's right there!'

She spun, whipping me in the saddle with her lurch. My head smacked against her scales again. Jumping through the burning buildings, she launched herself at the crowd of Shadows.

My heart stuttered when they didn't move.

The faint snap of wings above was the only warning I had. I threw myself, tearing my leg free of stirrups that bit at my skin.

A huge creature crashed on top of Tizmet as I tumbled to the ground.

'Away!' she shrieked, twisting her neck to snap at the massive two-leg digging into her scales.

I scrambled back, dragging my spear, fear making my limbs quake as I spun to face the Shadow Men.

They stood there—watching.

Waiting.

A scream tore from my throat as I threw myself at the wall of black robes and masks. I slashed and jabbed, moving my feet in ways I'd practiced a thousand times. Some jumped out of the way in time, while others cried out as my weapon sank into their flesh. I spun in their mass, determined to make my way to the door.

Not one of them moved to confront me.

The dragonling wailed over the sounds of battle, and I fought harder. A Hunter barreled through the Shadows. Hands grabbed at my back and I whipped around, weapon bared, creating a safe pocket for me to move.

The massive beast slammed into me, a bear-type creature. Its mass shoved me through the door as it bit down on my shoulder. I screamed and swung my spear, but it was far too close. I lost the only advantage I had.

Tizmet bellowed, and the monster tore me off my feet, tossing me aside. Air ripped from my lungs as I collided with the hard-packed earth inside the shack, my spear tumbling from my grasp. Cursing and gasping for breath, my left hand hung limp at my side as I rolled, reaching for it. The Hunter charged–

A high, sharp voice barked an order, and the beast slid to a halt.

My fingers closed around the shaft, and I struggled into a crouch, cradling my arm. The stench of blood turned my stomach, but I refused to look at the wound. Tizmet's panic warred with my mind as she fought the two-legs alone.

This Shadow wore a human skull strapped to its face. And those that surrounded us stood in stark silence as I brought my frantic gaze to its neck.

It laughed, the sound high-pitched and eerie. The hatchling lay at his feet, a front leg hacked off. The dragonling's eyes were dark as pitch, the pupil barely noticeable. Beneath the layers of blood and dirt were ebony scales—a creature of the night.

Something surged within me as it keened weakly, stretching out its neck in my direction. Its little head fell to the floor, eyes begging for help. The Shadow Man said something, clearly unconcerned about the state of his village as he rolled the hatchling onto its side with his boot.

My stomach lurched as he braced his blade against the dragonling's scales.

"No!"

He turned, his mask dipping in a slow nod, as if he understood my rage. He said something in that strange language of his and patted the hatchling's shoulder fondly.

'Avyanna!'

I launched myself at him—a weak, pathetic attempt. The Hunter threw itself between us, pinning me to the ground. Its black-furred claws dug into my shoulders. I struggled with my spear, but it batted it from my feeble grasp. Cold seeped into my bones, and my head lulled to the side.

His low chuckle raised the fine hairs on the nape of my neck, and his tone dropped to a comfortable, conversational tone, as if he expected this. Bile crept its way into my mouth as I stared in helpless horror. He pressed the serrated blade into the dragonling's shoulder, butchering it like a dispatched pig.

Tizmet's rage and fear were a dull roar in the back of my mind. Tears soaked my cheeks as the little black whimpered against the squelching that dug through its flesh. I met its eyes.

I was here. It wasn't alone.

The Hunter settled its crushing weight on me, and I gagged as the stench of death and rot filled my nostrils.

"It's—It's alright," I gasped, struggling for air.

The Shadow Man twisted the foreleg, rocking the weak creature, spinning the appendage at a terrible angle. My right hand grasped for anything at all I could use as a weapon. My bandit breaker was out of reach—my push dagger pinned between me and the massive beast.

The pain and despair in that small black gaze tugged at something in my mind. I couldn't pull magic. Not in this state.

I tore my eyes from the mutilated hatchling to the Shadow as he hefted the hunk of flesh. He reached for the mask he carried in, and horror welled within me, realizing it was a replica of a dragon's skull. His vile language competed against the sounds of battle raging outside.

He reached a gloved finger inside the hatchling's dismembered leg, separating the bloody flesh from bone. I retched as he sawed at it, prying it free. The reek of death suffocated me as he let me watch. Placing the blood-covered bone against the skull, he fit it on top as a horn.

He turned to me, and a sense of excitement devoured his strange words. With his feet spread and shoulders squared, as if to say, 'Watch what I do next.'

Terror seized my heart as my magic surged in response, like it answered his call. I grappled with it, holding tight as he tilted his head at me, as if curious. Tipping the mask, he tried to show me that the bone was now fused to its surface.

My magic thrashed and writhed against my hold. It surged and crashed again and again.

"Stop! Please!"

Shouts broke against the roar of crackling flames.

The dragonling's gaze dulled and its eyelids fluttered shut.

My magic swelled, and I screamed as if I would burst from the pressure. My back arched under the Hunter as I fought to keep it contained. It was bright behind my closed eyes, a mass of tendrils I had no hope of holding. It thrashed like an irate dragon's tail, powerful and uncontrollable. Wrapping myself around it, I vainly tried to shove it behind its door.

I barely registered the pain in my stomach, or the weight being lifted off me as I fought my internal battle.

Screams rang in my ears, my own screams, until the world went blissfully silent.

Chapter 41

Voices pulled me from my sleep, bringing me to an excruciating awareness. My breath snagged in my chest as my muscles rejected waking, screaming at me in objection. Pain radiated through every bone—every muscle and joint in my body.

Grappling with the torment, I reached across the bond, feeling for Tizmet.

'I am here, little one.'

Relief rushed through me, and I squinted against the bright sun illuminating the white canvas of a tent.

'The hatchling?'

'Disposed of.'

My heart shattered, but it was for the best. We couldn't fix what the Shadows broke, but it was the loss of a dragon—the loss of a life. My eyes burned with tears, and I blinked them away.

'Are you well?' I asked.

'Well enough.'

Scanning the space, my gaze landed on Rafe. He sat on a cot across the way, his chest bare with a bandage wrapped around his ribs. He spoke with Ruveel, who had his back to me with his arms crossed.

I raced over the bond, feeling for her injuries, but she pushed me away.

'You have enough pain.' She retreated into herself.

My eyes pressed shut as I shuffled through her emotions. Regret and sorrow drenched her.

'It's not your fault,' I assured her gently.

'I almost lost you.' There was a huff outside the tent, where she lay coiled on the ground. *'I was reckless and... acted like a hatchling.'*

A weak smile tugged at my lips. *'We tried. I can't blame you for wanting to save it.'*

She pulled away from me, wallowing in her regret. I let her go, opening my eyes once again to find Rafe's hard stare. He rose, and I didn't miss the wince from his movement. Ruveel stepped aside, letting him pass to sit beside me.

"Did we all make it out?" I rasped past dry lips.

His gaze danced over my face, mouth set in a firm line. He shook his head once and reached out to hold my cheek. His rough thumb brushed my skin as my heart stuttered.

"Who–"

"Jamlin and the twins are alive." He dipped his chin. "Jam won't be able to walk for a season, but he'll mend."

Sorrow welled within my soul, forming a hard knot in my throat. "Fletcher and Loth–"

"Gone."

Turning my head into his palm, waves of heartache crashed over me. Fletcher was close with his parents. Loth was a father. He had two little girls in Regent.

"We almost lost you," he murmured.

"And would have." Ruveel's words drew my attention. "Flayed open, much like Rafe was. There's no high hope for that kind of wound."

'Ruveel healed me?'

'The red helped,' Tizmet grumbled.

Lifting the sheet draped over my body, I looked down at the mass of scars that covered my naked torso. Ugly, raised white lines crisscrossed my abdomen, telling the tale of the beast that shredded me to ribbons. It had no semblance of beauty, like the scar Tizmet gave me along my side.

'Their care was not born out of love,' she said.

I traced the marred skin with trembling fingers, my muscles tense and complaining against the action. I tucked the sheet up to my jaw and met Ruveel's cold gaze. He lifted his chin, looking down his sharp nose. The soot smudges on his cheekbones were streaked and smeared. Dark circles stained the space below his eyes. His hair was tousled and rough stubble covered the lower half of his face.

"You healed me," I murmured.

"Wild or not, you're a Rider," he said, then blew out a long breath. "I might not like you, but I care for Dragon Kind."

"Thank you."

The coldness masking his features broke, and he sighed, shaking his head. "I'd pay gold to hear *him* say that." He gave Rafe a sour look, then turned on his heel, leaving us.

Rafe's jaw worked as he struggled with whatever thoughts held his focus, and I reached a weak hand up to cup his cheek.

"I'm fine."

He closed his eye, leaning into my touch. Pressing his lips to my palm, he gave me a chaste kiss. When he looked at me again, his wall of armor was back in place.

"We're leaving for the bottleneck in four days."

My mouth dropped open in shock as I tried, and failed, to sit up. "How long have I been out? We weren't that deep, were we?"

He nodded, face somber. "It took days to get you here. Your dragon couldn't fly and we had Shadows on our heels. We can make it through the Sky Trees if we push now."

"Ruveel is willing to risk the Fleets?"

He was silent a moment before responding, "We're risking everything."

I frowned, knowing in my heart this was our chance. We had to march now and trust that Faulkin knew what he was doing, or we would never have the upperhand again. Yet, at the same time, it was nerve-wracking—as if we were missing a crucial step.

I pressed the heels of my palms into my eyes. "They use the bones, Rafe."

"Hmm?"

"They take the hatchling's bones from their forelegs, then fuse them to their masks. Somehow, it gives them control over the little ones."

Tizmet's rage flared, but she tucked it away as quickly as it rose.

"It strengthens their magic, reinforces their hold on them," he murmured.

"Keeps them from going mad. Until the Shaman dies, then they fall victim to their mania."

The tiny beast flashed in my mind—its anguished suffering as it bled out.

"The Shaman brought the hatchling to the camp," Rafe said.

"Aye."

"Then they're hatching them out somewhere."

Dread sucked all the warmth out of me, like a dip in an icy lake. I bit my lip, trying to hold off the pain. They stole wild eggs for years, Tizmet's eggs, and raised up their own line of dragons. And now they were breeding them? Somehow they found a way to hatch clutches without the Solstice. That hatchling was a few days old. Their breeding grounds had to be close to that village.

"One war at a time, Vy."

I rolled my head to the side, giving him a weak smile. He reached over and tugged the sheet down, frowning at my stomach.

"Piss-poor job he did," Rafe grunted, tracing his fingers over the bundle of scars.

"The Hunter mauled me?"

"Nearly killed you," he sighed, covering me up. Turmoil flashed in his gaze as he took me in. "I almost lost you."

"Oi, we're even now then," I scoffed.

"Your magic–" A tight frown pulled at his lips, and his voice dropped to a rasp. "I've never seen anything like it."

"What did it do?" Instinctively, I reached for Tizmet's assurance. "Did I let it go?"

'Aye, little one. You let it run,' she hummed, unconcerned.

"It threw the Shadows and Hunters back." His dark gaze simmered with fierce protectiveness. "Somehow, whatever you released passed over us."

I leaked wild magic into the world. Despair crawled over my skin. Had it only knocked the Shadows back? Or did it slither across the earth, finding some other terrible purpose?

"It gave us an opening to get you. Your dragon handled the hatchling. We barely made it out."

"Loth and Fletcher didn't."

"No." He closed his eye and took a deep breath. "I've sent word to their families."

For all that Rafe appeared indifferent, he cared more than anyone knew. His acceptance just came more readily than others. He'd spent the majority of his life caught up in this war, witnessing countless lives ripped away.

"Small blessing, that is."

I tilted my head at his words, meeting his sorrowful gaze. How could their deaths possibly be a *blessing?*

He seemed to understand my silent question because he said, "If Ruveel knew what you did, you would be nothing more than a weapon."

"I'm a weapon now, Rafe." Reaching out, I held his large scarred hand in mine.

"Aye, but one I can follow. The bastard would risk releasing a plague into the world to use you as the first line of defense."

"He wouldn't," I scoffed.

Years ago, Ruveel warned me about the dangers of magic. He claimed women didn't have access to it because we lacked mental fortitude. Without enough focus to give it intent and purpose, even the smallest amount could produce terrible results.

"Wars make desperate men, Vy."

I nodded grimly. I doubted Ruveel would use me like Rafe suggested, but it was better that he didn't know. We could trust Jam, Blain and Dane—but Loth and Fletcher had been new to our group. They owed their Commanders, the Dragon Lord and General, more of their loyalty than the King's Dragon.

"When the Shadow pulled his magic," I stared at the sheet, clutching Rafe's hand, "it was as if my own answered. It flared and–"

I swallowed past the lump in my throat, remembering my helplessness. It rose within, refusing my will while seeking the Shaman's.

"I couldn't control it," I whispered.

Tizmet's remorse rolled over me, sorrowful that she was too busy taking on the two-leg to help me. She let me pull at her memories—glimpses of struggling to dominate the smaller beast, but it had sunk its claws deep into her scales. It managed to snap a bone in her wing before she tore it off her back. Then it scrambled off, flying into the night.

'So, they know where we were.'

I wrapped my love and understanding around her like a warm blanket. She was fretting over the past. We couldn't change what happened. We could only move forward.

'When the mutilated one left, your magic came out in a wave.' Her irritation of prey escaping her drifted over me. *'We had to escape.'*

"Worry later," Rafe grunted, pushing to his feet.

He pulled his cot next to mine and settled in alongside me. With his arms wrapped around me, I curled into him. I felt safe here, as if we weren't facing Regent's largest battle in only four days.

"It's awful. I can't believe he let Lark assist."

I stood before Rashel the next day with only my Riders' skirts on. She pressed her thin lips together as if to rein in her disgust while she ran delicate fingers over my new scars. Even I had to admit, Rafe's scar looked better than mine. The mass of tangled white welts from the Hunter overlapped the intricate design Tizmet had made.

When Rafe got us back, Ruveel saw to Tizmet's wing immediately. She had healed my belly in the same way she tended my side when we first bonded. Apparently, the Healer at hand, Lark, had been worried I was unconscious due to infection or debris still inside me. So he opened me back up. Ruveel had taken the time and effort to assist in healing, and between the two of them, I was left with the mangled scar.

"I'm just thankful to be alive." I sighed.

"You were alive before. They should have sent for me." She whirled on a Healer with an apprentice mantle. "Avyanna is my patient. No other Healers touch her."

The apprentice nodded, eyes wide with fear. I offered them an apologetic smile. The young girl swallowed audibly and dropped her gaze to the packed dirt floor.

"Lark is a fool. He can handle trauma and battle wounds. But damage like this? I'm the only one that has ever dealt with them. One would wonder what that fool of a Dragon Lord was thinking."

"I'm sure Lark was simply at hand, and–"

Rashel set her glare on me and I snapped my mouth shut.

"Aye, that's what I thought." She straightened. "If it doesn't hurt, it looks well enough. At least she didn't leave anything inside you."

She turned to the washbasin as I bound my chest. "I hear Faulkin is drafting," I said, clearing my throat.

"Aye, says it's 'the battle to end the war.'" She huffed, drying her hands. "He's pulled nearly all the Healers from Northwing and Southwing. Only King's Wall remains untouched."

"Just the Healers?"

My muscles complained as I tugged on my tunic, stiff from laying in bed for so long. I just needed to get out there and *move*. Pulling my lacing tight, I glanced up at her, waiting for her response. I found her staring at me, as if she could read my mind.

"No." Caution soaked her tone. "General Faulkin has drafted all the reserves from both barracks and King's Wall. They started arriving yesterday."

Panic thrummed through me and Tizmet crowded over the bond as if I was hurt.

"Only those able-bodied, surely."

She turned her head to watch me from the corner of her eye as if I might bolt. "If they can draw a weapon, they are able-bodied enough."

'Tizmet–'

Her low click of reassurance sounded from outside the med tent. *'None of your humans are here yet.'*

"Willhelm?"

"I am not there, Avyanna." Her shoulders drooped as if a great weight settled on them. "I cannot spare every soldier or man who I would like. If the Healers deem him fit to fight, he will be here."

I nodded, as if I understood, and tucked my tunic in. It wasn't her fault, but I needed to know. Anger and fear warred within as I remembered Willhelm hobbling on his crutches. Surely they would let him stay—they wouldn't pull him to the front to be fodder.

"Did I pass your inspection?" I asked.

She raised a single eyebrow. "As if a failed examination would hold you back." She scoffed, then waved me off.

Outside, I reached out for Tizmet. She was still curled next to our tent, resting. Flinor had joined her, and she basked in his shared heat in the brisk autumn air.

It wasn't only our advantage rushing us on—but the seasons themselves. The dragons had been pushed hard this year, and needed the rest of brumation. If they were forced through a winter onslaught we would lose many, if not all of them. Tizmet looked the healthiest of the Fleets, and she was saddle sore and had suffered a broken wing.

As I strode through the camp, seeing so many dragons grounded broke my heart. It was a far cry from Northwing, where they flew for pure joy. Here, they were tired and battle worn. They curled between the muddy streets, trying to sleep for just a few moments before they were called on again.

I rushed through the rough paths. The grass had long been trampled down and the recent rain combined with thousands of stomping boots made for a swamp of a road.

At least it wasn't the bog.

Clenching my jaw, I shrugged off the pain that came with thinking of Leeds. I was here now. I was fighting for my home, for my friends.

As I passed, soldiers ignored me as steadfastly as I ignored them. I caught the gaze of a few Riders, but they had no more than nods of acknowledgment to send my way.

Amongst the Fleets, I earned a reputation much like Rafe's. I was cold, dangerous and to be avoided. The situation with Deil wasn't the first nor the last where I'd lost my temper. And that fact did nothing to endear me to their ranks. I was an anomaly. They didn't know what to expect from me, and I didn't care about their opinions.

I was here to win a war.

Veering off the road, I wound my way through canvas tents until I came upon a group of soldiers watching the afternoon's entertainment.

Teak's feet slid in the mud, unmoving. Rafe's muscles bulged beneath his taut skin. Teak snapped a wrapped fist toward Rafe's face, avoiding his bandaged ribs, though he clearly anticipated the move. He curled a leg around Teak's and yanked, trying to pull him off balance. The man was a match for him, however, and used his weight to ground himself. In a quick movement, Teak threw Rafe into the mud.

The men cheered as he lay in there, covered in muck from head to toe. He stared up at the sky, wincing with each breath. We all dealt with stress in different ways, and Rafe needed to fight, to take out his frustration with his fists.

Teak took a step back and wiped at the sludge on his brow, smearing it. "Another round?"

The crowd whooped in encouragement, eager to watch another bout.

"I'd have a word first," I called.

Teak beamed, his smile a slash of white across his mud-covered face. "Oi, my man! She was here to see you fall!" He laughed as he offered his hand.

"Pity she didn't see the first three matches," Rafe grunted, clasping his friend's arm.

I eyed him up and down, noting how the muddied trousers clung to his thick thighs, and the cut of his thick muscles under layers of grime. He approached me, adjusting the bandages wrapped around his fists as he searched my face.

"I need to know what troops are coming from Northwing," I said, lifting my chin.

His dark gaze slid over the crowd and he frowned, shrugging his shoulders. "Those well enough to hold a sword."

"A man on crutches wouldn't be able to hold a sword."

"Depends on his determination."

"Rafe."

When his eye met mine, I didn't miss the way his jaw clenched. It made no difference to me who overheard my question. I needed to know.

"Is Willhelm coming?"

"Aye, he's due in the morn."

A wave of anger burned beneath my skin, and I closed my eyes, trying not to take it out on him. It was Faulkin's fault, not his.

"He chose to come." Rafe's words did nothing to soothe my soul. "He'll get assigned somewhere in the back."

"He shouldn't be here–"

"A man has a right to choose where they want to die."

Silence fell like a blanket over the group. When I searched for who had spoken, the others shifted on their feet, the lighthearted moment gone. I met the gaze of a young soldier. He seemed younger than me, yet his eyes were old. They told stories of the horrors he had seen. Lifting one shoulder, he shook his head, as if his statement didn't bother him at all.

Rafe's features pinched into a glower, clearly wondering if I'd push this further. This wasn't the place to fight for Willhelm to go back home.

"Later."

"Later," he rumbled in agreement.

I sucked in a breath, turning away before the men saw my frustrated tears. I made my way to our tent with my fists clenched at my sides. We left in two days—and tomorrow I would be spending it with an old friend.

It was a sad sight.

Soldiers in torn and bedraggled uniforms stumbled alongside wagons full of supplies. I sat on a hill watching as the long caravan wound through the far side of the Sky Trees and melded into the forests. The war camp had been set up on a plain, where the immense trees loomed, but we were out of their shadow.

We could only deal with so much darkness.

I leaned against Tizmet's back, her scales warm against the chill of drizzling rain. The sky itself seemed to cry at the condition of the men coming in.

'They will fight?' Tizmet asked with a sense of disgust.

'Aye. If the Healers deem them able, they will join the ranks. The numbers should help.'

As much as I hated admitting it, I understood the reasoning. It didn't make it any easier knowing Willhelm was somewhere among those trickling in.

It broke my heart remembering the one time I sparred with him—his agility and speed. Now he relied on a crutch and brace to get around. The Shadows took his leg. I refused to let them take any more.

'They will be nothing more than prey for the Hunters.'

Her words hurt, even if I knew they were true. Faulkin drafted just about every man, and based on the look of them stumbling into the war camp, half wouldn't be strong enough to wield a sword or spear.

'Men are proud. They want to be part of the last battle.'

'Humans are... dumb.' She rolled the word around as if that wasn't the one she was looking for.

I scoffed, watching a man trip, grabbing onto the side of a wagon for support. *'We have hope. These people are starved for it.'*

'Hope?' Tizmet raised her head, cold rain dripping off her maw as she flicked her tongue. *'This hope gives you strength.'* She pushed across the bond, rifling through my thoughts as she scanned the caravan.

'Aye, strength of heart.'

Her eyes narrowed on the line of wagons. *'A strong heart means nothing when your body fails you.'*

I couldn't explain emotions or the finer points of human hope to her. She was a dragon.

'He is here.'

Straightening, I pulled my hood back as if that would give me better eyesight as I scanned the soldiers.

'Where?'

She pushed her vision to me, and I braced my palms against the ground, trying to remind my stomach that my body was still planted firmly on the dirt. Her gaze narrowed to a point, bringing Willhelm's features into clear view. He sat in a wagon with his eyes pressed shut and jaw clenched. His black hair was soaked and plastered to his pale face. Something twisted inside me, realizing how painful this trek must have been for him.

'We go?' Tizmet asked as I pulled back from her sight.

'I would wait till he settles.'

I was uncomfortable with the idea of intruding upon his pain. When I was hurting, I wanted people to leave me alone and give me space. I could only offer him the same. There was nothing I could do for him, not now.

Tizmet's head snapped toward the forest, flinging water from her muzzle. She snorted and studied the gap where the caravan left the relative safety of the woods. I opened my mouth to ask her what it was—but my question was answered.

Moony tore out, a stark red and white against the dark veridian of the forest. Mud splattered his legs, but the patches on his body were bright, as if Mikhala had taken the time to comb out the dirt from his coat.

He was a running target.

She never did shy from attention.

A smile split my face as I rose to my feet, shaking the water from my oiled skirts. Tizmet stood with me, and my body complained about the lack of her warmth. If autumn was already this cold, it would be a brutal winter.

A whoop echoed across the plain, and I chuckled as Mik's braids flew behind her like a flaming banner. Tizmet arched her neck and let out a bugle in welcome. Moony veered from the wagon train and angled toward us on the hill.

I reprimanded her call. *'Ruveel wouldn't approve.'*

'The Shadows know where we are,' she replied with a mental shrug.

It wasn't as if we were hiding, but Ruveel had commanded that the Riders keep their dragons as silent as possible and out of the air.

I wrapped my cloak around me, trying to block out the worst of the damp chill as Moony charged up the knoll. I couldn't make out the shouts of encouragement that Mikhala gave her stallion as he struggled up the wet hill. He was a strong horse, but the grass was saturated and slick.

Tizmet's amusement at the beast's struggles had me shaking my head.

Clearing the crest, Mik flew off his back, tackling me to the ground. The air rushed from my lungs, and Moony skidded to a stop, spraying us with mud.

The big woman crushed me in her embrace, and I let out a wheeze as she squeezed me hard enough to break a rib. Tizmet nosed Moony away from us. He snorted and pranced a few paces, unconcerned with her size or teeth.

"Mud!" I gasped, eyes bugging out.

Mikhala sat up, bracing her arms on either side of my head. Her wild red braids hung down in my face and I tried to blow them away.

"Mud couldn't keep me from you!" She laughed, whipping her braids over her shoulder.

My mind searched for new scars or injuries almost unconsciously. Cataloging my friend's wounds. This is what it had come to. She was her jovial, happy self, but sorrow lingered in the depths of her gaze. I smiled sadly wondering if it was because of Regent's war or something else.

"I managed to make it all morning without being covered in mud," I huffed.

She sat back on my legs, crushing them. "It's my duty to remedy your state of cleanliness."

I laughed, shoving her off. She stood, then offered her hand, the flower stained to her palm beautiful, but dangerous. She pulled me up, then gave me a playful punch on the shoulder.

"Glad to see you and the beastie are still in one piece." She put her hands on her hips, gazing up through the drizzle at Tizmet.

Tizmet snorted and brought her eye down to Mikhala's level, blinking as she took the Caul in. *'Tell her she will not remain in one piece if she rides the painted horse into war.'*

"She worries over your choice of mount." I rephrased as Mik patted the dragon's cheek. "You're joining the fight?"

"To the bottleneck, aye. It's all anyone at King's Wall is talking about." She raised a brow. "That's not all they're talking about. There are rumors about a Wild Rider on the front as well."

"Oh?" I shrugged. "Do they talk of all her glorious victories?"

"Her glorious recklessness is more like it." She grabbed me in a hug once more. "I'll make a Caul out of you yet!"

Chapter 42

As we sat around the fire, I could almost pretend we weren't all headed to our deaths.

Jamlin played dice with Blain and Darrak on a fresh-cut log. Mikhala had talked Dane and Gaius into arm wrestling. It was amusing to see the lean man give the behemoth a challenge amid the laughs and jeers of our small group. Willhelm sat next to me, his half-leg stretched out in front of him. Rafe was on my far side, talking to Teak about some tactic involving the sea at the bottleneck.

We had only managed a wild soup tonight. Mushrooms, herbs and potatoes in a thin broth. Game was getting scarcer and what little we found was reserved for the dragons.

"It's almost like we could be back at Northwing," I muttered, gaze trailing to the flickering flames.

"As it once was," Willhelm agreed.

I flashed him a sad smile, and he offered me one in reply—one that didn't quite reach his eyes.

"I never would have thought I would come this far."

"Everything has an end."

I clasped my hands, then curled over to press my head against them. "I just wonder if it's the end of the war or the end of us."

"Time will tell." He rubbed at the lower half of his leg. "General Faulkin is confident we have a chance."

"A chance?" I scoffed. "That isn't enough."

Jamlin let out a groan as Blain laughed and pulled the pile of coins to his side of the stump.

"When that's all you have, it's enough." Willhelm gestured toward the two. "Look, your friend just lost his bet, yet he still places down coin. Hope and chance make for a heady draft."

Wrinkles creased at the corners of his eyes, and a new wrinkle had formed between his dark brows. His face was thinner than what I remembered, though I recalled the old Willhelm in my mind—the one with both legs.

"Tell me you'll remain at the back," I begged.

He laughed, but it was a dry, bitter thing. "This old cripple can still hold a shield."

"Just how effective would you be?" I snapped, angry at his determination.

"Doubting my battle prowess?"

"You'd be more useful in the rear, at camp. You can help here with the wounded."

My attempt at persuasion was a futile effort. Willhelm was just as stubborn as Rafe, both men bound by their warped principles.

"There will be enough men helping at the war camp. Every soldier with half a brain will seek orders to stay back."

"You obviously don't have half a brain," I spat.

How could I focus on the Shadows if I worried about Willhelm? Not to mention Darrak, Mikhala, Gaius, Blain, Dane and Jamlin. I was only one Rider. What ever happened to the girl that had no friends? Now I had too many to protect.

He shrugged and sat back. "Perhaps not, but I still have two arms and a leg to offer."

I turned to Rafe, disgusted. Willhelm always seemed too level-headed—wise beyond his years. Yet, here he was, a cripple, charging into war.

"-wade through the shallows." Rafe finished his statement and twisted to face me, feeling my attention on him.

I ground my teeth together, trying to contain my frustration. His dark gaze flitted to Willhelm, and a frown pulled at his lips.

"Oi, so if we get spearmen to hold the shallows–" Teak started.

"Aye." Rafe cut him off, not taking his eye off mine.

I bit the inside of my cheek as he searched my face, knowing full well he could read me like a book.

He stood. "Discuss it with Faulkin. I have a tent to pack."

A look of disbelief pinched Teak's features. "As if you have much to pack."

My answering smile was weary as I rose. Heads turned our direction and Mikhala glowered, throwing her fists onto her hips.

"The night is young!" she cried in feigned dismay.

Gaius startled and glanced at Mik. Dane took that opportunity to fling his arm to the wood stump they used as a table.

Her gaze snapped back to them so fast her braids slapped her cheeks. "Cheat!"

A smirk rode the quiet man's face as he lifted a shoulder in a weak shrug.

"I'll see you in the morn," I called, following Rafe.

We were stationed in the officer's quarters, a luxurious title for the simple canvas tents gathered in the center of the camp. It was quite the walk from where Willhelm and my friends stayed.

"He will fight," Rafe said. He stated it like a fact.

There was nothing I could do about it.

"It's foolhardy."

"Aye, only a man with an addled brain would fight at the front."

I glared up at him and his mocking tone. "It's different, Rafe," I shot back. "We are able-bodied. I have a dragon, and you are—well, you at least still have full use of your arms and legs!"

"Mm-hmm. It's not as if you can't use magic or overextend yourself without seizing. Your dragon is a known man-eater–"

"Hush!"

"And I'm missing an eye," he went on. "Perfectly able-bodied."

I shoved his shoulder and shook my head as a smile tugged at my lips. We all had our handicaps—some perhaps more limiting than others. I sighed and tugged aside the canvas flap to our tent. We already put together our packs, neatly stacked beside our cots, our weapons propped within reach.

We were ready to move out.

"He's a grown man, Vy."

I jerked off my cloak and threw it over my pack, holding in my comment.

"Let him make his own choices," he said.

"He gets to choose where he dies—is that it?" I collapsed on my cot, tearing my Riding skirts off. "It's all about *pride*."

Tizmet rummaged around the bond, groggily searching for the source of my irritation.

"That's all a man has in battle. Pride and survival. It's what separates the cowards from the heroes." He came to stand in front of me, lifting my chin to face him. "Don't force him to be a coward."

I snapped, catching his finger between my teeth. He let me bite down once in warning before he pulled away and hauled his tunic over his head.

"Better a coward that's living than a hero that's dead," I snarled, tugging at my laces.

Rafe stilled. The judgment in his eye had me regretting my words. Somehow, they triggered him, and I wish I could pull them back into my mouth.

"Your ignorance of battle is astounding."

My regret morphed into something dark and angry. "So you say, yet I've faced the Shadows more than once."

"Facing them with a dragon at your back is one thing." His tone was cold and distant.

Even in my anger, I knew I had hurt him.

"Facing a horde of Hunters with nothing but a piece of steel in your hand is not foolhardy." His lip curled in a snarl. "Don't rob the dead of their pride."

"I didn't mean–"

"No, you didn't." He ripped off his belt, tossing it to his pack. "You didn't think."

I snapped my mouth shut, studying his form as he disrobed and climbed into the cot next to mine. He yanked off his patch and rolled his back to me.

My shoulders sagged as I deflated. His words were bitter, but accurate. He witnessed countless men die in combat, leading them to that fate. If they were all cowards, more interested in survival than fighting for the greater good, he would have no one to lead.

Willhelm was trying to do the honorable thing by helping the soldiers, helping *us*, win the war. And here I was, calling him addle-brained as a mule, robbing him of that dignity.

Muttering a curse under my breath, I rolled and cuddled against Rafe's back. I snuck under his blanket and stole his warmth. He grunted in acknowledgment, but didn't turn to me as I wrapped my arms around him.

There was so much about battle and war that I didn't know. I could only hope I would live through the next few days so he could teach me.

Men milled about in the cold quiet morning, seeing to the minor tasks that packed up a camp. Horses neighed and donkeys brayed. I caught a few women in the mix, helping where they could. When I joined the ranks, the idea of a woman wanting to fight at the front was absurd. Now that we had committed to a path of victory or demise, they were granted acceptance. The outcome of this battle was not influenced by gender. It would either end for everyone or be everyone's end.

I saddled Tizmet, fussing over the buckles as she craned her head to watch other Riders do the same with their dragons. There would be little rest after this, and a blanket of quiet tension hung over the camp.

A dragon let out a trill in the distance, its call filled with anxiety. I paused my task, following Tizmet's gaze. A young blue, no more than four winters, whipped its head around nervously. The female Rider stroked its shoulder, speaking over its calls, trying to comfort it.

Tizmet huffed and clicked over the din, and the blue's sapphire eyes latched onto her. She snorted and bared her teeth in rebuke before snapping at the air.

'Dragons do not fear,' she said in disgust.

'They are young.'

I strapped down my weapons and checked the buckles one last time. Running my hands over the Healer's cross painted into my saddle, I tried to assure myself that it would be fine.

'My young did not fear.' She said, referring to the dragonlings across the E'or.

'Your young had no predators. The Shadows would like nothing less than to capture that blue and rip off its forelegs.'

Tizmet snarled, clacking her teeth together next to my shoulder. *'Do not presume to remind me of what we face.'*

'And here you said men were proud,' I teased, gently pushing her scaled head away from me.

Rafe stalked over, finished securing our packed tent into a wagon. His packs were missing, and I assumed he tacked up his stallion as well.

Nerves knotted in my stomach. This wasn't just a scouting trip, nor just another battle. We were pressing toward the bottleneck, where we would either push the Shadows back—

Or die trying.

If we failed, Regent would fall. Niehm, Elenor, my mother and Ragnath. Apprehension chilled me to the bone, a pressure so vast, as if the world was crumbling down around me.

Rafe crushed me against his chest, pressing his cheek against my ear. "Steady."

Pulling away to meet his gaze, a shaky smile warmed my cheeks. "Steady yourself. Embracing a woman in public," I scoffed. "It's as if we're heading to our deaths."

His eyebrow raised in challenge. "I can do a lot more than embracing."

I laughed, pushing him away, catching the glare of a soldier. Joy was not welcome on this ominous morning when the clouds hung so low to the earth and we marched into the unknown.

Rafe smirked, then double checked the belts on my saddle. Tizmet snarled, but he steadfastly ignored her.

"Is everything in order?" I asked .

"Aye, Ruveel will spearhead the army, and Teak will man the northern flank."

"Faulkin?"

"Safe in the center, giving the orders."

"And you?"

His eye found mine, and the corner of his mouth lifted in a taunting smile. "To the southern flank."

With me.

"The others?"

I bit the inside of my cheek, trying to quell my nerves. I hadn't asked him to get them in the southern Fleet. It was selfish of me to ask that my friends remain where I could see them when so many others would be separated.

"I sent Blain under Teak," he started. He would want to know right away if anything happened in the north, not relying on Faulkin's missives. "Dane will be with me. Darrak fights where he wants, and Mikhala and the big man follow."

I stared at him, letting the unspoken question fall between us.

He scoffed at my refusal to voice it. "Aye, your Sergeant has been placed in the southern flank."

A relieved breath rushed out, and I braced my hands against Tizmet as she sniffed at my hair.

'They will be safe,' she assured me. *'We will protect them.'*

I refrained from mentioning the extent of our protection when she was ambushed by a two-leg.

Rafe nodded at the saddle. "Mount up."

Taking a deep breath, I climbed up, situating myself in the seat. I maneuvered my riding skirts and buckled my boots into the stirrups, Rafe's eye on every movement. He frowned, watching me tighten the straps, and I held in any parting words I might say.

We would see each other that night.

And many nights after.

The land changed beneath us as we traveled west over the stretch of plains. The war had not only ravaged Regent, but every patch of soil that the Shadows crossed.

Weeks blurred together in endless skirmishes, leaving me and Tizmet tired and bloody. The southern Fleet flew above the sparse forests that peppered the land, setting fire to the trees, pushing out any Shadows that sought shelter.

We fought the two-legs that rose to meet us, holding the advantage of our larger dragons. They might have had Shamen guiding their actions, but they were smaller, easier to dominate in the air.

The Shamen adjusted to our advance and took their poisonous darts to the sky. More than one Rider was hit with cloudflower poison, saved only by the straps that held them in place.

Tizmet and I led the Fleet, spearheading the dragons, even if we didn't give the orders. We led because we weren't afraid.

At least that's what I told myself.

Our first casualty came three days into the march. It was the first death I had seen on the battlefield and one that I would remember for the rest of my days.

The twelve two-legs shouldn't have been a match for our twenty-three dragons, but they were. Inexperience played out before my very eyes and I finally understood the reason Ruveel pulled the Fleet off the front whenever a Shaman made themselves known.

The creatures concealed themselves among a wall of trees, shooting into the sky behind Tizmet. They were large—larger than most. Their size only validated the fact that some of them were Tizmet's from past clutches, stolen away and mutilated.

We battled a dirty, mud-covered two-leg, fighting for our lives when a horn sounded.

'What was that?!' I screamed.

I clutched the saddle as Tizmet rolled, narrowly avoiding sharp talons. The beast screeched and wheeled to meet her, but she'd been flying longer than it had been alive. Banking, she snapped out, sinking her teeth through skin and bone, crushing its neck in her massive jaw.

The horn blared again, and I hefted my crossbow as the two-leg keened and tumbled. Tizmet panted, blood dripping from her maw as she watched the creature spiral toward the ground. I took the breather to scan below, searching for the cause of the horn blast.

A silver dragon was down, its Rider a broken body beside it. A two-leg landed nearby, and the Shaman slid from its makeshift saddle, approaching the silver as it roared.

'They're taking the dragon!'

Tizmet responded to my urging and plummeted into a steep dive to intercept, wings pinned to her sides. I pressed flat against her neck, crossbow tucked between my body and hers.

'If you get between them, can you block the magic?!' I asked.

'I'm not–'

Something bit down on Tizmet's tail, yanking her to the side. She let out a deafening screech and whirled in the air, flinging me so hard I almost lost the grip on my crossbow. My hands trembled as I grappled to steady myself.

It flew at her neck and extended its claws toward the saddle's straps.

'The saddle!' I screamed.

Tizmet used her foreleg to shove away its open maw and whipped her head to bite into its leg. It let out a blood chilling shriek as she hauled on it, trying to tear it from its body. The movement tossed me like a rag doll, and I clenched my jaw from biting down on my tongue.

It lunged at her neck, latching on. Its teeth were small, but still sharp. Tizmet screamed around the leg, but refused to let go. We staggered through the sky on frantic wingbeats.

I met the eye of the reddish beast. It was far closer than I ever wanted to be to the mutilated creature. I fumbled my crossbow, bringing it up.

Take down the two-leg, and the Shaman would fall too.

Its pupil narrowed to a sliver, locked on me. A keen bubbled out from the blood that gushed down Tizmet's neck. Bile crept up my throat as Tizmet shuddered beneath me. I stared down the length and squeezed the trigger.

The bolt sank into its eye, and the creature *screamed*. Tizmet used that moment to shove it off. It fell, struggling to paw at the bolt with forelegs that weren't there. Tizmet pulled up and steadied. The two-leg thrashed, unable to even out. It crashed to the ground, throwing debris, neck twisted at an impossible angle.

'The silver!'

She banked at my words, and dread sank like a stone in my belly. The giant beast marched toward the line of foot soldiers. I scanned the skies–far too many dragons struggling. They wouldn't get there in time.

'They're still using their blasted fire!' I raged, frustrated.

Throwing a flammable oil was not only a terrible strategy up here, it wasted their stores that could be used for flushing out Shadows. Unless they were on top of a Shaman, using it was foolish.

'To the skies or ground?!' Tizmet demanded, her gasping breaths heaving her chest.

I glanced down once more, seeing the Shaman tucked in front of the two-leg that protected him from above. A darkness thrashed inside me at the wrongness of it.

'Ground!'

Tizmet roared, dropping into a dive. I twisted in the saddle, my hair tugging loose of its braid, whipping my cheeks. Blood flew from her tail, but it wasn't a mortal injury. I glanced around to be sure that no other two-legs were converging on us before turning back to Tizmet's neck.

She threw her head down, adjusting her angle. I checked my spear, wondering if I should take the Shaman on foot, but decided against it. It was safer to fight at a distance.

On the ground, Hunters tore through the lines, Shadows tucked in the tall grass and behind trees. They had been ready to ambush us.

Hunting them down was a gruesome and bloody affair—one that took time.

Something we didn't have.

A man on horseback charged through the line, straight at the silver dragon—a man I recognized.

"No!" I screamed.

He would never hear me.

Darrak streaked across the plains, lance tucked under his arm.

A roar beneath us was the only warning Tizmet had before the two-leg shot a burst of fire in her path. She twisted, throwing herself to the ground. My teeth clacked together with the landing and blood filled my mouth.

I spit it to the side as the creature maneuvered around the Shaman. It balanced on the crook of its wings, pitching forward at an obscene angle. It let out an awful screech before spewing fire again, setting the plains ablaze.

I spun just as the silver batted Darrak's horse. He leapt from its back, then darted for its belly, slashing his sword at its legs.

Tizmet shook with the force of her roar as she reared, fanning the blaze toward our enemy. Gripping my crossbow, I fumbled for another bolt as she sucked in a breath. She came down with enough force to shake the earth as she threw a stream of white hot flames.

The two-leg squealed and drove its wing in front of the Shaman, protecting it from Tizmet's attack. The controlled silver was more valuable to him than the creature it was bonded to.

Rage flooded me. *'Get me a clear shot!'*

I winched my crossbow back as fast as I could, pushing my emotions aside to be dealt with later. I had a Shaman to kill.

Tizmet's scream melded with a roar as she threw another bout of dragonfire at the pair and ran behind it. It shifted to clear the flames, twisting to face us. My hips rolled with Tizmet's movement as I readied my aim, waiting for the two-leg's wing to come up as it adjusted itself around the Shaman.

I sucked in a breath, pulled the trigger, and by the time I let it out, the wing had come back down.

'Did I–'

The creature opened its maw, white teeth flashing in the sunlight as it thrashed. A terrible sound ripped from its throat as it slammed its head down next to the Shaman.

'The dragon!'

Tizmet shifted so I could see the silver clearly. She recoiled in the wrongness of it as Darrak pulled his sword free from its belly. The world spun as intestines spilled to the dirt. A flood of blood and organs silhouetted him as the silver tried to step away, revealing the tiny mortal that had brought down a giant dragon.

My gaze was torn between them and the two-leg that thrashed. The latter won my attention as its body contorted, but its head lay absurdly still next to the kneeling Shaman.

Disgust warred with hatred as the Shaman clutched the crossbow bolt embedded in his chest, then rested his gloved hand on the two-legs brow.

"No!"

Tears blurred my vision as I frantically loaded another bolt. It would not desecrate the creature as it died. A sob choked me, and I blinked away tears, sighting down the stock. A sound drifted over the distance, a mournful cry of comfort from the two-leg. My finger tightened against the trigger, hovering on the arm that lay between the mask of a dragon and the mutilated creature. A gurgling cry tore from its throat as its back leg twisted up to slice its own neck with a talon.

I readjusted the crossbow against my shoulder as Tizmet shifted. Her gaze locked on something above. A sob wrenched through me as the Shaman crumpled forward—dead.

The two-leg tipped its head skyward, its scream of loss garbled by the blood that spurted out of its throat.

Darrak walked up behind it, studying the exchange as well. His hard gray eyes met mine over the distance. Blood splattered his armor.

His sword fell, beheading the two-leg as Tizmet threw herself into the sky.

There would be time to mourn later.

Chapter 44

War is brutal.

It is a bloody and gruesome affair.

Regent's army left a trail of death in its wake. Skeletons littered the plains, evidence that the Shadows had occupied the land for too long. Their corpses and those of their Hunters were burned, ours were gathered and buried.

Except the dragons.

They fell at a rate that was unsustainable. When the push started, there were over a hundred to Regent's name. Every night, less and less returned. Ruveel pulled his Fleets tighter, bringing them to the front of the army as the numbers dwindled. Their fallen bodies were burned with dragonfire, their kind sending them beyond the Veil in a manner they deemed appropriate.

Tizmet was a cold beast at times. She was reserved and hard, but when another of hers fell, her soul answered its last plea for help. She kept a tight leash on her sorrow, trying to keep it from spilling across the bond. I had only pressed once, and she snapped at me, her rage meeting me instead. She was not ready to share her grief—if she ever would be.

All sense of time blurred as we advanced. The Shadows were just as powerful in the light of day as they were at night. They moved more freely in the dark, but we faced them no matter the hour.

I saw little of Rafe between my rounds. When I was off duty, I found the nearest cot and collapsed. Tizmet barely ate enough to replenish her dragonfire. She had been healthy and fat when we flew here, but in the weeks of marching and flying, she thinned to a worrisome state.

All the dragons were skinny.

At night, they fell from the sky like stones, eating in a rush and crumpling to rest. Even Ge'org was thin and tired.

We pushed on as fast as we could. The foot soldiers struggled to keep up with the Fleets. Skirmishes slowed us only until the army flanked and dispatched the Shadows.

They were retreating, and we soon found out why.

Tizmet and I flew alongside Ge'org when we crested a hill to the bottleneck. The Dragon Lord and Wild Rider, leading the Dragon Fleets to war.

It was there we met the Army of Shadows.

Tizmet produced a startled bugle, and Ge'org huffed, pulling short.

Below us, the Sea of Protection, as the men came to call it, stretched out to the south. It went on, twinkling in the bright midday sun, an endless stretch of water. To the north was the Melting Ocean, its teal waters so different from the deep blue of the southern sea. Between them lay a stretch of land, visible from shore to shore, peppered with darkness. Black buildings towered over the moving specks—Shadows and their Hunters. I was a poor judge of their numbers, but it seemed far more than our own army.

The Fleet halted behind, the only sound being the leathery beat of their wings. Ruveel's hand shot into the air, drawing every Rider's attention, waiting for instructions. He signed for us to land, and we descended. Tizmet snarled a warning when an older dragon dove a little too close to her.

Ge'org hovered above, while Ruveel faced the Shadows with a spyglass in hand. It winked in the sunlight, giving away our location, but by the way the massive black shapes in the distance swarmed, they already knew we were here.

Ge'org tucked into a dive and landed, sending up puffs of dirt from the plains. Tizmet bared her teeth, but remained still as we waited.

"Dareth, you and Jyra fly north. Make sure they're not cutting us off," he ordered. Flinor and a light blue dragon launched skyward. "Leor, take Sycur and head south."

Tizmet craned to watch as the two dragons flew off before arching her neck and snorting.

'He won't order us,' I assured her.

"Avyanna, you and Kyt come with me. We're scouting."

'He won't order us?' she mocked.

"The rest of you, stay here. Kyt, Avyanna—follow my lead." With that, Ruveel took to the sky, his large crimson dragon glittering in the sun.

Tizmet huffed at my admiration and leapt behind him. *'Red is naught but a brighter target.'*

I smiled against the unease that spiraled in my belly as I leaned forward in the saddle. If they sent two-legs after us, it would be a mad flight back to the others.

I hadn't said goodbye to Rafe.

Tizmet clicked beneath me. *'We will not die this day.'*

If only I could believe her.

Kyt was a large rider with black hair he kept pinned in a bun. He rode a deep emerald green. With the exception of the dragons that flew north and south, we had the largest of the Fleet.

Not that there were many of us left.

Behind Ge'org, Tizmet's gaze locked on the red dragon as I stared at Ruveel's hands, waiting for him to signal. We coasted along, using height to our advantage. The Shadow's scrambling slowed, as if they knew only three dragons would not attack an entire fortress.

The black structures spread across the middle of the bottleneck into the Shadow's territory like a disease, growing with the distance from Regent.

If they would only stay on that side of the continent.

Ge'org coasted in slow, lazy circles, Kyt and I flanking him. Kyt's green, Kagen, caught the midday sun, gleaming bright despite his scales being dulled by stress. Tizmet glided on exhausted wings, alternating her gaze between Ge'org and the black specks below that swarmed like bugs. As we drifted lower, I could see the stark-white of their skeletal masks. It still unnerved me that I had never seen one without them. Only Dragon Kind could use magic, yet somehow, every single Shadow learned to twist it, abuse it for their purposes.

Shadows crowded around five two-legs, and Ruveel halted his descent as they scrambled up to their odd pieced-together saddles. Ge'org banked back toward Regent and Tizmet raced to keep pace with him. Glancing back, the Shadows stayed grounded, their two-legs lifting their heads as we flew a hasty retreat.

They weren't interested in a battle today either.

"We have to lead with the Fleet."

"I'm telling you, we can't man the skies and the ground!" Ruveel leaned over a wide table made of hastily cut logs and spans of wood. A map sprawled over the length with Faulkin's figurines set atop.

"I need you to."

Faulkin's eyes were cold and hard, but he didn't look up at the Dragon Lord, instead he shifted a dragon piece, shook his head and returned it to its previous position.

"It's not a matter of what I want, but of what is possible," Ruveel snapped, pacing.

Tizmet refused to leave me, resting on the cold ground as I watched the two argue.

"If we move the archers here," Teak murmured, pointing north, "we can make way for the horsemen."

"Archers stay in the center," Faulkin replied without looking at the bow figurines. "If we need air support, they are the only ones who can give it to us."

"Fire," Rafe rumbled.

Faulkin looked up with a bored expression. "We are between two seas. Setting the plains ablaze wouldn't fix anything."

Rafe shrugged, his shoulder jostling me. "Fire would distract them on both ends. Let them fight flames behind their line and a battle at their front."

"We have far less to lose if they use that tactic against us." Ruveel braced against the table, staring at the map.

"Who would be flaming mad enough to get past their line?" Teak scoffed.

Faulkin fingered the skulls littered along the bottleneck. "You reported thirteen two-legs?"

"Aye, but those buildings could house more." Ruveel pursed his lips. "They're almost as large as Northwing's barracks. We don't know what's inside."

"Burn them down," Rafe said. "If we got there fast enough–"

Teak arched a brow at the map. "Who's your quickest flier, Ru?"

'Tell me it's not you,' I grumbled.

Tizmet snorted, and everyone turned to me.

Ruveel dipped his chin. "The Wild Rider."

"Tizmet is hardly the fastest," I shot back, not liking the way they all stared. "The blue is the youngest here. They would be the swiftest."

Ruveel kept his gaze leveled on me as he spoke. "Aye, but he's a nervous wreck, has limited dragonfire, and can't fly in formation, let alone evade a two-leg if he needed to."

"Tizmet is a larger target."

"Ah yes. With her dull scales and vast experience avoiding the Shamen's gaze? Do go on about how she would not be the perfect candidate," Ruveel drawled.

Faulkin rearranged a few figures. "She can do it," he muttered.

I bristled. "Just because she can–"

"We need something to pull their forces away, and lure any two-legs to the sky." Faulkin locked his cold stare on Rafe.

Fear coiled in my belly, and I sat up straight against Tizmet. "You're not using Rafe."

It was the same ploy they used after my banishment. Where the Shadows knew he was, they converged—like he was special. The one who got away. A half-breed. The bastard son of a Shadow Man.

"You don't get to make the call, Vy."

I snapped my gaze to meet Rafe's. He studied my face, and I despised the look I saw in his features. It wasn't hard or cold. It was love.

"Don't you dare," I breathed. "You are not bait."

"If we use Rafe as bait," Faulkin continued as if I said nothing, "we need to get him into position without them knowing. Spread them out thin and have them surround him."

This wasn't getting better.

Faulkin rearranged more pieces, nodding as if his plan held all the answers. "Smuggle him in with the troops, then pull back. It will make him a more appealing target. She can fly in with the Fleet, and in the chaos, get behind their line and rain fire."

Teak nodded along. "And when they're pinned between us and the flames, we can take them."

"You have a lot of faith in their ability to be distracted," I growled, refusing to tear my gaze away from Rafe.

He held my stare with an unnerving amount of determination and patience.

Faulkin waved off the sarcasm in my tone. "Between our forces and their base on fire, walled in by seas they won't cross, I think it would cause any army to panic."

The corner of Rafe's mouth twitched and his gaze told me he was resigned to this plan.

"We can do it," he murmured so low his voice caught.

"I don't want to." My eyes filled with traitorous tears. "I don't want to leave you—my friends. You can't ask that of me."

"I'll be in plain sight."

"Perfect," I hissed. "I can watch with the rest of the Fleet as you get butchered." Angry, I pulled away from him, trying to resist the urge to run. I wasn't a child. I didn't flee from my problems.

"Do you have such little faith in me?"

"Don't, Rafe. Don't ask this of me." I shook my head and glared off into the distance, unable to meet his unwavering gaze.

"I'm not asking, Vy."

It was the harsh wind, not the torment welling within, that caused tears to leave frozen trails down my cheeks.

Tizmet flew behind Ruveel in formation with the remaining forty-three dragons. The army marched long ago, taking far more time to cross the plain.

I refused to think about the previous night and the things Rafe whispered in my ear. How he held me, cherished me, protected me as only he could.

Gritting my teeth, I brushed the tears from my eyes and resisted the urge to glance down at the army below. I didn't want to see the soldiers smuggling Rafe to the frontlines, didn't want to bear witness to them pulling back, abandoning him like bait for a game trap.

Tizmet flooded over the bond, tearing my anxiety away, leaving me numb. I ducked and pressed my forehead to her scales, taking a deep breath of cold air while she flew along the southern coast.

'Calm, little one.'

My grip on my crossbow ached. Still, my fingers clenched as I held it closer. We were at the very edge of the wing, and when the Fleet took on the two-legs, we would go our separate way.

It was as if Rinmoth herself knew our need and lowered the clouds for us. We soared just high enough to disturb the lowest layer of mist, the damp soaking into my clothes. I shivered against the wind, tucking in close.

The Shadows below swung inland, swarming to the center.

Despair, frigid and unyielding, paralyzed me, gripping my heart like a vise.

They had revealed Rafe.

Bellows and roars filled the air. To the north, dragons dove to meet the massive flock of two-legs. There were far more than thirteen.

'It is time.'

Tizmet huffed in response to my worry and rose into the clouds, flying higher into the dense moisture. She would be nearly invisible in the gray cover, and once again, I counted her dull coloring a blessing.

She was the most beautiful dragon I had ever seen.

'Such praise,' she mused.

Her wings beat harder, bringing us above the thick cloud layer. My breath caught in my throat and I clung to the saddle, fingers frozen. The sun was so bright, its glaring rays soaking into my cold bones. It flamed in a clear blue sky, the clouds a carpet of gray below.

It was as if we were in another world, where Shadows and wars didn't exist.

Here it was peaceful, the roars of Dragon Kind distant and fading. Cradling my crossbow in my lap, I threw my arms wide, tipping my face up to the sun, soaking up the warmth and meager comfort it offered. Tizmet hummed her approval as she coasted, granting me this moment of peace.

'Ready?'

I took a deep breath. *'Ready.'*

I barely secured my crossbow and gripped the handle of the saddle when she dropped into a dive. My thighs squeezed as she plummeted with unbelievable speed. Her wings plastered against her sides, covering my calves. The force of the wind shook them against my legs and I clenched my jaw as my ears popped with the quick change of altitude.

We broke through nearly right on top of the Shadows' fortress. Buildings that mimicked ours spread out below, fading into the distance. These were far more put together than the war camps in Regent.

If I could have taken a breath, I would have only managed one before Tizmet snapped out her wings, jarring me against her hard scales. She opened her maw, spewing dragonfire at anything and everything.

'The roofs!' I called, noting the tarred thatch.

She bit off the stream of flame, pivoting for the rooftops. Two structures succumbed to her blaze before Shadows poured out of nearby buildings.

These wore human skulls for masks.

'Fly!' I urged.

Tizmet hefted her weight, pumping hard. Flying north, she moved fast, casting plumes of dragonfire as she streaked through the air. I hefted my crossbow, scanning the eastern skies behind enemy lines. There was nothing. No danger to her, aside from the archers below taking aim. It was clear that they never expected to take up arms themselves.

Glancing west, my heart faltered. *'To the west!'*

In response to my panic, Tizmet bit off her flame with a cry. *'Trust him! We are to rain dragonfire–'*

'TO THE WEST!'

She snarled, whipping her head westward where a two-leg blocked our view of the army. The behemoth was easily twice as big as Tizmet, if not three times. The giant spread its immense wings, casting the troops in darkness.

Where Rafe was being used as bait.

Tizmet pushed hard as the first volley of pitiful arrows clacked against her scales. She ignored the one that tore a hole in her wing and launched toward the giant.

The brown-mottled monster was so large, each flap of its wings sent men staggering against its gale. Nothing that big could remain in the sky for long. Tizmet strained under me, pitching herself as far forward as she could with each pump.

A sapphire, the size of a hatchling compared to it, charged. The monster let out a burst of dragonfire in a barking cough that echoed over the din of battle. The sapphire's scorched remains tumbled, its Rider falling free. A black dragon banked hard, lining up for attack. Two-legs swarmed, and within a breath, ripped off its wings and sent it plummeting to its death.

We were too far away.

'We won't make it!'

Helplessness tore at my soul. Magic rose to my plea, and I shoved it off. I couldn't use it now. The risk to me and Tizmet was too great.

The beast landed with enough force to send shockwaves through the very earth. Men and Hunters alike staggered with the impact. Its gnarled, dirt-colored back blocked my view of Rafe and the soldiers. Dragons fought two-legs in the sky. Though it was clear with the distraction, the enemy was winning. The Shadows were converging, their Hunters a black speeding line flanking our troops.

"No!" I screamed, but the wind snatched the word from my throat.

Tizmet angled toward the Shaman on top of the beast, attempting to attack the more vulnerable of the two. This Shadow was different somehow. He didn't have just a mask of bones, but a crown of them atop his hooded head.

As we neared, it twisted with unnerving speed. Terror skittered and writhed in my stomach as my magic flared. Tizmet pulled up with a screech, launching upward as the Shaman zeroed in. Whatever power he wielded, my power answered its call.

Tizmet roared her frustration as we evened out far above. I swallowed my horror as the Shaman's unholy mask tracked us through the sky. Something snagged his attention and his focus lowered toward the ground.

Toward Rafe.

My heart lodged in my throat at the sight of him. Tizmet banked as he faced the Shaman and two-leg alone. Blain and Dane were a distance behind him, holding off the Hunter's mass of teeth and claws. To the south, Mikhala's red hair flashed while she and Gaius fought back to back with Darrak. Gaius swung a heavy war hammer through the wall of Hunters separating them from Rafe's group.

Willhelm was somewhere in that sea of death and bloodshed.

My friends were going to die.

Rafe was going to die.

Tizmet flew overhead, circling back to Rafe. The monster of a two-leg dwarfed him. He was a speck, a flea to its size.

Yet, it didn't move to attack.

Rafe staggered to his knees and panic tore through me when I realized what had drawn the Shaman's attention.

'Down! I need down!' I yanked at the straps of my stirrups, frantically trying to unfasten them.

'We will lose our advantage!' Tizmet roared.

'Ground!'

I clawed at my other stirrup, tearing the leather when it didn't come free. Tizmet snarled, and angled downward, knowing full well I would throw myself from her back if she didn't land. She let loose a roar, crashing to the grass. She threw dragonfire in an arc, separating us from everyone as I slid off her shoulder. When my feet collided with the hard-packed earth, I clutched my crossbow and ran.

Rafe knelt, one knee pressed to the blood-soaked ground. A vein bulged along his temple and down his neck. Sweat dripped from his jaw.

Here, the Shaman was tucked out of sight behind a formidable wall of scales. I'd never get a shot. The monster's breath rolled over me, its golden eye locked on Rafe, pupil narrowed to a fine slit. I flung myself to him, knees skidding through mud. A sob tore from my throat as I searched his face.

Silver swirled in the depths of his iris.

He stole control of the monster. His will was stronger than that of a Shadow King.

I spun, taking aim, intent on killing it while I had the chance.

'Don't!' Tizmet roared, spewing flame to keep the Hunters at bay. *'This is not one of the monsters we know! What if their souls are entwined?!'*

My breath snagged, and my crossbow dipped. When a Hunter fell, it didn't kill the Shadow controlling it. The memory of the Shaman reaching out to the two-leg flashed in my mind. Rafe was different, but how much?

I couldn't risk it.

Blood trickled from his nose, and he grunted, lurching forward to brace against the ground, refusing to take his gaze off the monster. He shook under unseen pressure, the weight too great for him.

'What should I do?!'

'I am out of dragonfire!' Tizmet roared, clicking and throwing sparks in fury.

A sob tore through me, and tears scoured my cheeks. I dropped my crossbow and shuffled behind him. With my cheek pressed to his back, I wrapped my arms around his middle, holding him tight against me.

He wasn't supposed to do this. I was the Dragon Rider. It was my duty, not his.

'No!' Tizmet snarled.

But her warning came too late.

I opened the door to our magic.

It flooded over me in a wave, crashing about my mind like an angry storm. Closing my eyes, the mass of glowing threads thrashed and writhed like a living thing—and I guided them. Wrapping them around me and Rafe, I tied our bodies together just as I had when I rescued him. The glowing web answered my call, eager to please. It wound about us as if it already knew what I would ask of it.

Rafe drew in a staggering breath, his body shuddering under my wet cheek.

If he was using magic to ground the beast, I would lend him mine.

Tizmet cried, feeling millions of miles away. Here, encircled in magic, I was tucked far from the world. Nothing could touch us here. We were safe. She curled around us, pressing us against her scales. Her emotions mauled through our bond, angry and enraged. Her power joined mine, a steel armor of protection, and I smiled.

I was here for him.

She was here for me.

Magic flared, its glow becoming a blinding light before it faded and flickered. I gasped with the pressure and agony that cascaded through my chest.

'He tests us,' she murmured, a note of mourning in her tone.

'We are stronger than him,' I said. *'Together we are more.'*

She didn't reply, but her sorrow was a tangible thing as the magic flared again and again. Pain radiated, ripping a gasp from my lungs. Rafe's staggered breaths joined my own. I was pulling too much. Not a glimpse of darkness showed between the threads.

My tethers to Rafe trembled and shook, pulled taut, ready to snap. It flared again, this time a crescendo of blaring light as if the Shaman called on his magic.

There was no coming back from this.

There'd be no happy ending for me and Rafe.

'I love you.' Tizmet's words were drenched with regret, spilling over with grief, heartache—and permission.

Shaking with a sob, I pushed over the bond. *'I'm so thankful I was able to share my life with you.'*

'And I you, little one.'

With a strained, shaky breath, I tore open the door to my magic. The writhing gold threads hesitated, as if shocked by my acceptance. I smiled against my tears and reached out to them, coaxing them through.

Power rushed over me in a wave, snatching all air from my lungs, ripping all strength from my limbs. I collapsed, crushed between Rafe and Tizmet. A stabbing ache smothered me, like a boulder pressing down on my chest. I couldn't move, couldn't breathe.

And still the magic came.

Searing heat scorched a trail from my temple to my spine. Golden light surged within, spilling out in a giant wave, crashing over anything and everything.

I had no thought of the troops, of my friends, of the Shadows.

There was only pain.

Then it all *exploded*, as if every bone in my body shattered, every joint ripped from its socket. The pressure built, my eyes bursting from the strain. My blood boiled, my skin peeling and flaying.

The ringing in my ears succumbed to vacant, death-like silence. Everything went white. I could almost see my father in the blinding light, a welcoming smile on his blurry face.

And somewhere far out of reach was Tizmet's cry—the keen of a dragon losing their Rider.

Rafe

Agony pitched me forward, and I caught myself with trembling hands. Control the beast. Give Vy a chance to bring it down. That's all I could hope for.

The power I robbed from the Shadows still lived in me. My very blood was tainted by them. I battled for dominance over the Shaman's hold, the pressure behind my eye building. I clenched my jaw in a vain attempt to keep my head intact.

Something wrapped around me, embracing me. Warmth trickled down my nose, over my lips, and I grunted as the Shaman pushed against my will.

Mine.

The creature was mine.

My snarl came out more of a gurgle as I shoved at the force crushing my brain.

A warm touch pressed against my back, and my hope shattered. Vy was the only one who would come to me—the only one foolish enough to hold me until I crumbled under the Shaman's magic.

Light flared in my mind, a bright, uplifting thing. I inhaled a tight breath as the pressure faded the slightest bit, as if someone shared the burden with me. I seized the marginal relief and pushed back at the power holding the monster.

We battled for what felt like an eternity. I challenged the golden eye, Vy pressed at my back. Her dragon curled around us, sheltering us without obscuring my view.

So this was how we would die.

My mind snapped, recoiling at the sudden renewed vigor of the Shaman. My body jerked with the pressure, and Vy's tiny hands clutched at me, as if saying goodbye in her own silent way.

I wished I could say it back.

The pain swelled with the wave that would finally take me under. The golden eye trained on me blurred and wavered.

Everything went silent.

The pressure vanished.

The battlefield was thrown into hues of sunshine, a flood of gold saturating the world. I blinked, bringing my gaze from the beast to the odd, luminescent glow that overtook Rinmoth. The Shadows, the giant two-leg, the Hunters—everything was bathed in the unearthly radiance–

Then it shattered.

Vy's dragon *screamed*, and reality snapped into place. Shadows and Hunters collapsed. The behemoth towering above us emitted no sound as it struck the ground, shaking the earth.

I stumbled forward, rolling to my shoulder as I crumbled. Vy toppled beside me, her body limp. I sucked in a breath, ignoring the carnage, not sparing a thought to see if her friends had made it.

She was pale.

Far too pale.

I struggled to shove myself upright, my weakened state slow to obey my demands. I rolled her onto her back, brushing her white hair from her colorless face. The seizure hit fast and hard. I clutched her in my arms as she thrashed. Blood trickled from her eyes, nose and mouth.

Her dragon tilted her head skyward and a bone-chilling wail rent the air—the soul-wrenching sound only a dragon losing their Rider could make.

She gave up too easily.

"Curse you!" I snarled, voice strained.

Her seizure faded almost as quickly as it started, her body going limp in my arms. Still—her lashes fluttered once, splattering blood across her snowy cheeks. And her life breath slipped past her lips.

I stared at her fragile form tucked against mine, unwilling to accept what every inch of my being knew to be true.

My lungs heaved in rapid bursts, the world slipping from my control. I wouldn't lose her. I couldn't lose her. Not after all we'd gone through.

Panic spiraled, waking a darkness deep inside. The slippery black thing felt all too familiar as it struggled to tear free of my grasp. My head fell back with the force of my scream. All my rage, all my anger ripped from me. It wasn't fair.

I was done being pushed around by *fate*.

Just as Vy had once done with me, I poured the darkness into her, entangling her drifting soul with mine. My magic was a shadowy thing, bleak and colorless. I felt my way along the tendrils of shadow, scrambling for the fleeting sensation of life evading my grasp. It shied away, trying to escape this world.

My jaw shut with a click. A pained smile spread over my lips as I choked on my own blood.

She wouldn't cross the Veil without me.

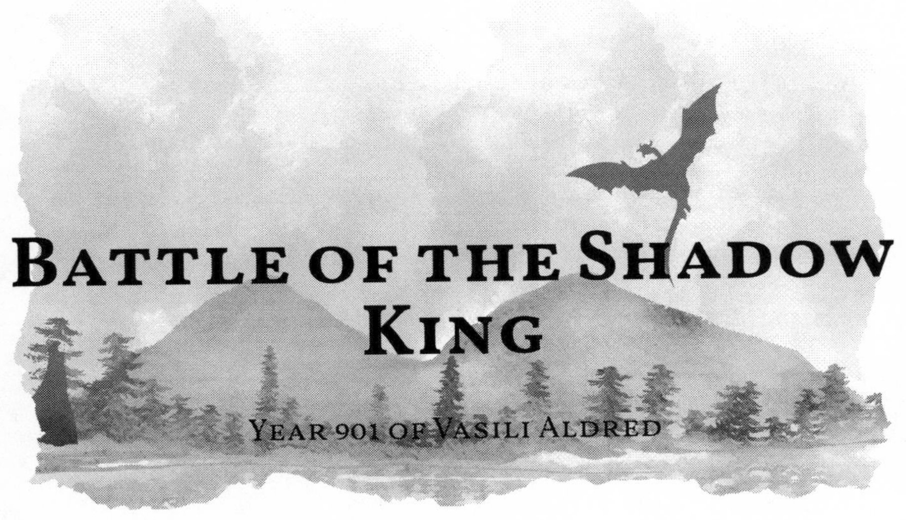

Battle of the Shadow King

Year 901 of Vasili Aldred

Blain plunged his sword into a vicious Hunter, yanking it back as quickly as the thrust. Whirling, he kept his back to his twin's as he attacked another, this one with the form of a bear. Dane moved in sync with his brother, knowing where he was without looking back. He searched each writhing body, picking out the stark-white skull masks—bringing them down one by one.

Rafe threw his cloak aside, baring his face and tattoo'd shoulder. The enemy turned on him immediately, clawing their way through Regent's soldiers. He was the one who got away. The mad General—a magnet for darkness.

The twins fought at his back, a compliment to the longsword the King's Dragon wielded with both hands. A shadow moved in the low-hanging clouds, darkening the weak light.

'Gods above—what is that?!' Blain shouted down the bond to his twin.

A vision flashed in Dane's mind, dissipating in a blink. The two were accustomed to sharing sight from the other.

'A two-leg?' He drew his bow, loosing an arrow with confidence.

'It's too far away—too big. Abyss, it's huge!'

Blain spun with Dane, taking on a Hunter that hurtled toward them at alarming speed, long black talons digging into the blood-soaked grass. Fangs flashed and claws gleamed as it slashed at the twins.

Dane glanced at the Shadow that flew closer, every wingbeat sending a gale rippling through the mass of soldiers. Pressing his lips together, he lowered his bow, searching the press of bodies once again.

'It's too far. I can't bring it down.'

'I hope Avyanna starts that fire soon!'

Blain staggered against Dane's back as two Hunters attacked at once. They turned as a team, facing them without hesitation. The ground was slick with blood and death. The onslaught of Hunters pushed them further from Rafe, the one they were trying to protect.

Dane grunted in agreement, then slipped on a mess of intestines and sinew. He threw his hand wide to regain balance, and a creature with the face of a wild cat snatched his bow in its strong jaw, snapping it in two. He spun, putting Blain between him and the beast, drawing the shortsword from his waist.

'No chance of taking it down now,' he muttered, keeping his footing as a black fur-covered snake tried to coil up his leg. *'The girl will have to take it down.'*

'Will she turn back?' Blain fought off the wild cat, wiping at the ebony blood that splattered his face, smearing it across his cheek.

Dane slashed at the matted snake at his feet. *'She will see it.'*

As the Hunters forced the twins further from Rafe, Darrak and Mikhala fought with Gaius. The giant bounty master swung a warhammer through the blackness that threatened to engulf them. Hunters flew through the air, and those that pressed in between his swings, Mikhala dispatched with her shortswords.

With Darrak at their side, together they killed everything that closed in. The few soldiers stationed with them had already fallen. Gaius carved a path toward Rafe, and Darrak kept his eyes on the sky as the Dragon Fleets attempted to take on the massive creature.

Undeterred, the beast flew straight at Rafe, shooting a sapphire blue dragon down in a stream of fire. The charred body careened toward them, and Darrak called out shoving at Mik. She shouted, grabbing Gaius, swinging the big man out of its path with her momentum.

The earth trembled as the behemoth two-leg landed, and the crash of the blue's body followed. Mik fell, and Darrak snatched the back of her tunic, hauling her up as Gaius swung his warhammer in a mighty arc. Covered in blood and dirt, the Caul flashed a nervous smile of thanks before launching herself at a wolf-type Hunter.

There was no backup.

There would be no retreat.

They were alone on this battlefield.

Away from the frontline, Willhelm stared, horrified. The thing was massive. A mountain compared to the flies that were Regent's dragons. How something that large could even take flight was a wonder. He staggered on his good leg, bracing himself against the soldier to his right.

"Sun above..." the man breathed, horror lacing his voice.

It was a distance off, but even without making out details, he knew there was no chance Rafe could take down such a monster.

It lowered its giant head, pitching forward on wing tips instead of forelegs. The mutilated beast met the King's Dragon and stilled.

Willhelm staggered, limping through the ranks.

"Where are you going?" someone called out.

"We have to help him." The words fell from Willhelm's mouth, uncaring that he was ordered to remain at the back.

He'd seen his fill of battle these past weeks, but to leave a man to his death in the name of *bait*—he refused. He gripped his sword, dragging his brace through the lines.

"There she is!"

The hushed words nearby halted his shuffle. They were spoken with hope and awe, and he scanned the gloomy skies. Cripple or no, his eyes were still sharp, and he could make out the silhouette of a dragon in a steep dive.

A dragon the color of stone.

The one-legged Commander abandoned his men, running as only a cripple could. Limping through the stunned ranks waiting to be ordered to their deaths, he caught himself on their shoulders, pulling and throwing himself closer.

He couldn't let Avyanna face that monstrosity on her own. He wouldn't stand by as fodder for the war while she braved the enemy.

Darrak threw himself at the wall of black writhing creatures, but the more his small team cut down, the more took their place. It was an endless sea of mutilated beasts.

Mikhala slashed and stabbed, but where one Hunter fell, another lunged. She tried to carve a path to Avyanna, her teeth bared and a battle cry clinging to her lips, but it was no use.

Gaius swung his warhammer in a protective arc, the only space they had against the press of teeth and claws and rotten flesh. Their boots slid in a soup of gore and mud and Darrak slipped. Mikhala jumped over him, protecting his flank, but lost her footing in the sludge. Crashing to her back, a Hunter with the face of a deer but the teeth of a wolf dove on her. She screamed fumbling, with her weapon–

The creature snarled and the sick life left its eyes as it slid off Darrak's sword. There was no time for words of thanks as he pulled her up.

Gaius stumbled to a knee, and the fangs of a Hunter sank into the space between neck and shoulder, shredding and ripping. The Caul's scream was swallowed by the sounds of war as the bounty master's warhammer fell to the muck. Unable to stop, unable to breathe a cry, claws and teeth swarmed them. Darrak stumbled over to Mikhala as a Hunter bit his calf.

Dane and Blain had Rafe in their sight, but Tizmet threw a wall of fire, encasing him and Avyanna in her protection. She pounced like an enraged cat into the river of blackness that thrashed around the twins. There were petty few pockets of soldiers left, the Hunters a wave of death crashing over the battlefield. They faced terrible odds before, but nothing like this.

'Thank the sun she's landed!' Blain said, moving in sync with his brother.

'She can't take it. Tizmet's too small.' Dane's inner voice was calm even as his breaths came in gasps and his back trembled against his twin's.

'She won't use Tizmet.'

Blain's words sent alarm through his brother and ringing across their bond. Dane spun, facing the fires that consumed the Hunters, belching smoke into the hazy sky. He cared far more for the white-haired Rider than he ever let on, and in his experience, magic was not something to be trifled with.

The amount of power that would have to be used to take down that creature—it would be too much to ask of one soul.

Tizmet roared, but the Hunters dismissed her, unafraid. They pressed in at her legs and tail, biting and clawing as she thrashed. She screamed her frustration and released a burst of flame, cutting it off short with a bellow of fury.

Her head whipped toward Avyanna, and her eyes flared, pupils thinning to a needle-like point. She scrambled for her Rider. Through the break in flames, Dane glimpsed Avyanna holding Rafe upright from behind. She clutched him to her as Tizmet threw her body around the couple, spewing one last plume of fire that died in her throat.

'She's out of flame.' Dane would have shaken his head if he weren't fighting off a bear with the talons of an eagle.

'We've not lost yet!' Blain shot back.

'She shouldn't use–'

'She will.'

The enemy swelled with renewed passion, as if they sensed the stakes were raised. They pressed in, and the twins finally felt fear—true terror.

The wave of darkness crashed over the soldiers, the masks of Shadows lost in the flood of death. Willhelm never made it to Avyanna. Hunters cut through his path, and he drew his sword to meet them. He fought hard, but with only one leg he was no match for the black patched-together creatures fueled by sick, twisted magic.

He fell beneath the mass, the soldiers of Regent joining him on the hard-packed earth that grew soft with their blood.

The Army of Regent, the Dragon Fleet, the last defense against the Shadows, was swallowed. Darkness swept over horses, soldiers, war hounds. It flew over men and women alike, warriors and farmers. The vile creatures only knew to consume, deal death and obliterate life.

Yet even as carnage passed over the bottleneck, spreading toward Regent like some plague—a spark flared. A light that refused to go out, one that wouldn't let her friends die.

A guardian to the Veil.

In that sea of black, a single ray cascaded. It was not from the sun, still hidden by low-hanging clouds, but rather a spark of magic. It flickered, then rushed out in a rippling wave, casting everything in a golden sheen. Shadows and Hunters flinched, their lives forfeit as that light enveloped them.

Avyanna gave everything to spare her friends. And it was her life force that flooded the battlefield, rushing over the blanket of darkness—banishing it.

Light surged, ripping life from the Shadows and their beasts. Soldiers froze in awe, holding out swords that grew flowers, or wincing from vines that burst from the ground, biting at their skin. That wave of pure magic flooded the bottleneck, crashing into the sea where it fizzled and popped, turning the waters green and orange.

Tizmet lifted her head to the clouds, bearing a cry so drenched with loss it shattered the hearts of all that heard it.

Blain and Dane shook off the golden glow, hurtling over corpses as they ran. The behemoth monstrosity that stood in front of them shuddered and crashed to the earth, sending the very ground trembling.

Blain threw out a hand to halt his twin as Rafe let out a guttural scream. The air itself shuddered with his torment, yet the small body in his arms didn't move. The black magic that had been released with the death of the Shadow Men came rushing back to one person.

Dane jerked under his brother's grasp, but they stood still and watched as the King's Dragon funneled that dark essence into Avyanna, tethering her soul to his. Blain cast his brother a knowing look and shook his head, eyes dark and glittering.

It was over in seconds; the world snapping back into normal hues under an overcast sky.

Rafe collapsed over the woman, and the twins closed the distance as Tizmet huffed and skittered back from her Rider. Her wild gaze flashed to the brothers, as if she wanted them to explain this. Her talons dug into the earth, a sign of her confusion.

Dane slid to his knees in the muck, helping his twin pull the big General off the woman. Blain placed his hand on Avyanna's tattered chest, and Dane pressed blood-covered fingers to Rafe's neck.

'They're gone.' Sorrow consumed Blain's words. His shoulders slumped with defeat.

Dane gritted his teeth, pressing harder into the big man's throat. *'It worked.'*

'It didn't, Dane. It's over.' His brother's words were soft in his mind, yet they cut him deep.

A pulse whispered under his touch.

Sucking in a breath, Dane stared at Rafe—waiting in agonizing suspense for another pulse, anything to assure him he hadn't imagined it.

A flicker of pressure.

The twin's eyes snapped to meet, and a smile teased the corner of Dane's mouth.

Blain's words were the only assurance he needed. *'Her heart beats!'*

Rafe

Following the Battle of the Shadow King

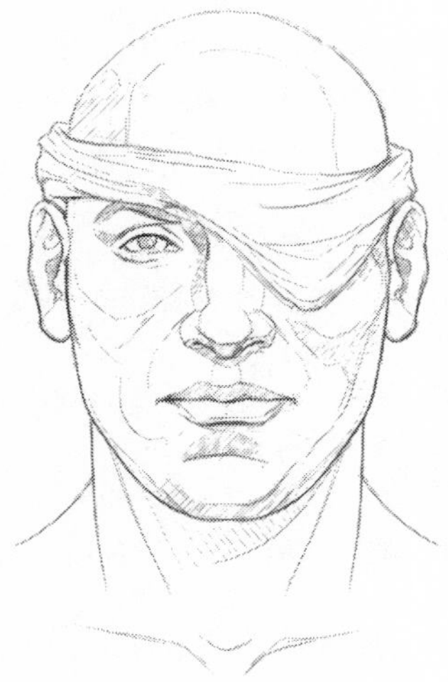

Voices nagged at me. They pulled relentlessly, never giving me a moment's peace. They were like those blasted gnats in Leeds, always buzzing and droning on. I wanted nothing more than to drift back into the blissful dark that eluded me now.

Something slithered through my mind, snapping me to awareness. I barely caught myself before I opened my eye. Everything came crashing back to me; the Shadow King, the last battle, Vy's limp and bloody body in my arms.

Harnessing all that power.

The shadow's caress was soft like a lost lover. It curled around me, comforting and warm, muffling the voices. I grabbed it and shoved it into the cage in my soul. It seemed bigger, harder to wrangle. It fought against my hold and I locked it in, suppressing a shiver.

"He'd want the fortress." Jam's voice came from my left, and I relaxed—trying to pretend I was still sleeping.

"He should bunk with the Generals." And that was the reason I kept my eye closed. Ruveel was here, and if my remaining eye had turned just as my left—he would gut me without a word to my defense.

"He claimed Vy." Blain's voice came from further away. "Besides the fact that he's claimed, he doesn't belong to Regent. What's to say he won't return to Leeds or find a home elsewhere?"

"The more you talk, the more I wonder if *you* belong to Regent," Ruveel replied in a dangerous tone.

"Five years. After that, our lives are our own," Blain replied in an unconcerned tone.

There was a rustle of fabric and a feminine snort of amusement. "He still hasn't woken?"

My fingers twitched in barely restrained relief. Vy. She was up, awake—and from the sound of her voice, well.

Proud satisfaction bubbled up in me. I brought her back. I didn't yet know the price, but I had forced the shadows to pull her back. It was worth whatever the cost.

"Not yet, we were discussing where to put you two," Jam offered.

"Where to put us?" she scoffed. "I am the--"

"Yes, yes. The Wild Rider and he's the King's Dragon. We know," Ruveel snapped.

"And you know the King offered us our choice of where to go. I want him moved to the old lookout on the Great Northern Lake."

"Called it," Jam laughed.

"It's best that you're both away from the men, with you deserting and him foolhardy--" The whisper of steel slipping from a sheath interrupted him. "I'm going," Ruveel spat.

"All of you, out." That was the woman I loved. Confident and assured. She had fought enough Shadows and lived through enough battles to earn the tone in her voice.

The sounds of shuffling feet filled the tent, and a groan was pulled from Jam as Blain grunted. It seemed he was still unable to stand on his leg, so I hadn't been out too long. The bed dipped under a slight weight and my thumb twitched with the urge to reach out to her.

"I know you're there," she whispered as the tent flap fluttered one last time. Something tugged *inside* my chest and the shadow in my mind writhed, trying to escape the confines of its cage. I waited a breath more, straining to hear anyone else in the tent.

She tugged on our bond again, the sensation akin to someone grabbing my heart and trying to tug it out of my body. My eye snapped open and I hissed, lifting a hand to shade the blinding light.

"I knew it!" Her exclamation was accompanied by a smothering embrace, crushing my arm between us. She pulled back and I squinted against the halo of white that blurred her features. The sun had to be directly overhead. It was excruciating. Pain stabbed at my brain as I gritted my teeth, trying to make out the details of her small face.

"I felt you wake," she murmured, tracing a thumb over the scars beneath my empty eye socket.

"I felt you trying to tear my heart out," I rasped as my eye slowly adjusted to the light. She grabbed a cup from a table near my bed and helped prop me up to sip. I stared at her face the whole time, studying those bright green eyes for any disturbance. A small smile quirked at the corner of her lips as her gaze darted to mine.

"Still dark," she assured me.

My eye drifted closed at the relief that crashed through me. Still dark. Not silver. I kept my eye. Only half of me was Shadow. I was completely tainted but managed to keep my human eye.

"Small miracle," I grunted, trying to push myself upright.

"I assure you, what you did wasn't small."

My gaze sped along her pale arms and clean tunic, down her riding skirts, and back to her face. "What was the cost?"

Her smile faltered a breath and she stared at the floor. I sat up and held her jaw, tugging her attention back to me. "What was the cost?" I repeated.

My gaze flickered down her neck, and I frowned at the whisp of black ink that peeked behind the laces of her tunic. I dropped my hand to peel her collar from her neck and dread sank like a stone in my gut.

"We match." Her voice was high and uncertain. She flashed me a tight smile and stood as I lifted her tunic revealing a mass of black webs spreading over her skin. She yanked it over her head and tossed it to the bed. The black threads that marred her skin spread and webbed out over her stomach and shoulders.

As if my shadows had shattered her soul.

My heart stuttered as rage and horror filled me. I had harnessed the shadows to pull her back. There was so much power after she snuffed out the Shadow Men, and it was there for the taking. I didn't pause to think of the consequences and didn't regret it one bit.

But fear skittered through me at the black veins that spread down her belly.

What had I done?

"I feel no different." She tried to assure me, looking down at the mass of dark lines that congregated under her chest binding. Over her heart. "Tizmet feels nothing different in me."

A snarl echoed outside the tent as the shadow of a dragon blocked out the glare of the sun. Vy looked up with a mischievous smile. "She says thank you."

"She said no such thing," I accused, looking down at my own chest, bared by the blanket that fell to my waist. The veins along my skin were mirrors of Vy's but—they were golden.

Bile rose in my throat and I bared my teeth, pulling the sheet down further to see the mass of golden web. Mimicking hers, they congregated over my heart, spreading down my abdomen, and across my hips. The new markings were flush with my skin, not raised like my scar from her. They reached to my chest and up to my neck where they disappeared out of my sight.

I jerked my gaze back to hers "If Ruveel finds--"

"He knows."

I cursed and threw my legs over the side of the bed. "How much does he know? Waiting till I wake to kill me?" I stood, throwing out curses as my knees buckled and Vy shoved me back onto the bed, grabbing my face.

"Rafe, stop."

My nostrils flared as I searched those forest green eyes that sparked with life. Her brows furrowed and she tilted her head and leveled a stern look.

"He knows. There was no hiding them when we were both in the Healer's tent. He's seen both of them and has questions, which is why he was waiting for you to wake. I told him it was the magic."

"Not a lie," I snarled. My magic was naught but Shadow. Her's was pure and bright. It would only damn me further.

"My thoughts exactly. And who knows why magic does what it does," she murmured, taking a seat next to me. "We were lucky it only took the Shadows when I released it."

I let out a resigned sigh. My eye hadn't turned, so I could play off Vy's story. The magic did what it did. When it was loosed, it was a wild and chaotic thing. "You knew what you were doing," I said, sensing her doubt.

"I gave it intent," she scoffed. "but had no idea if it would work. It listened to my heart and brought down the Shadows well into the bottleneck." She sat down next to me and wrapped her arms over her chest. Worry rolled over her face and she slumped her shoulders. I glared at the movement as if I could single-handedly save her from her worry.

"It didn't get them all." She sniffed. "Riders saw some retreating from their settlement, deeper into their lands."

"Let them rot there," I growled, pulling her against my chest. A sigh escaped her, and the corner of my lips quirked. I was her home. She had that blasted dragon looming above us, but I was the one to push aside her fears.

"It's been quiet. We've flown over the Shadow Lands." She placed a hand over my heart when I stiffened. "We've not seen anything. Tizmet and the others refuse to fly too deep into the land, claiming it's *wrong*, but we're holding the bottleneck with no lives lost. We're building a wall to keep them at bay."

"We don't have enough to press the advantage," I muttered in thought. We were stuck holding our land, but we couldn't eradicate the vile creatures.

"Not with the dragons refusing to go further," Vy said. Her beast of a dragon rumbled its agreement above the tent. She sat back and a trembling smile graced her lips. Her eyes searched mine. "Rafe, we won."

The weight of her words crashed into me and I blinked.

We won? They were still out there. "It's not over."

"It is for us." She breathed, her small hand tracing the stubble on my jaw. "We fought our war. We're done."

"And when they come back?" I hissed. They were still out there; they would come back.

"Faulkin says--" She glared at the growl his name drew from me. "The *scouts* have reported the bottleneck is clear. We can hold the land. Regent is safe. We don't need to fight anymore."

I ground my teeth together, looking down at my hands. This was where I fought. I followed Vy back to these war fronts, and it was so easy to fall back into the role of General.

But I wasn't General Shadowslayer anymore.

"I want..." she trailed off and I met her gaze once more, trying to relax my jaw. Turmoil stormed in those green depths. "Well, the old fortress is abandoned."

"Northwing?"

"If you don't want to stay there, we could--"

"Better start picking out furs." My lips quirked at her look of confusion. "It's blasted cold in the winter."

She grabbed my face and yanked me in for a kiss. With a hiss, she pulled back and glared at my chin. "You're far too prickly."

"I don't think you've ever seen how fast I can shave."

With a laugh, she grabbed me in a hug and I wrapped my arms around her, tucking her against me. Her heart beat against my chest, echoing my own. Her scent—whatever those blasted yellow spring flowers were—filled my nostrils.

The dragon above us huffed in disgust and I scoffed, glancing up at the shadow over our tent.

Home.

Vy was my home. It didn't matter where we settled as long as she was there.

Avyanna

The horse under me nickered, lifting its hooves in prancing steps as the gates of Northwing came into view.

"Warhorse," Rafe scoffed next to me. He rode with reins in one hand, his other laying idly against his thigh as his stallion plodded along. The horse had its ears pricked forward, the only outward sign of excitement for the coming grooming and grain.

'They eat grain like the prey they are, and I eat--'

'You're not eating the horses.' I cut Tizmet off. She banked through the sky, flying lazy circles that twined with Flinor and Dareth. I opted to ride with Rafe, enjoying his company, and she was thankful for the relief of flying without a saddle.

'They are prey,' she shot back. *'They are meant to be eaten. Though the stallion is getting old. Tough meat. Just like your mate.'*

'He's tough meat?' I choked and Rafe raised a brow at the noise.

'He is meant to be eaten.'

I laughed outright and he shook his head pressing his lips together. She wouldn't leave him alone, and he would never stop antagonizing her.

Grinning, we rode into Northwing's southern gate, packed in the middle of the military parade. Faulkin and Teak were at the front and Ruveel had flown ahead, heading to King's Wall. I was glad to be rid of his scrutiny. He hadn't left Rafe alone and Ge'org had become increasingly more volatile toward him. It was almost like he could sense something inside him despite Tizmet's assurances that there was nothing different with me nor the way Rafe smelled or felt.

She slipped over the bond, caressing my thoughts then retreating as Flinor passed her in a spiral. I shaded my eyes against the glare of the sun as she rolled in graceful acrobatics and flanked him, harrying his flight playfully.

Peace settled deep in my bones. This was *right*. This was where we were supposed to be. We would take the old fortress, and Rafe would oversee training special forces while I taught with the Masters in the Rider's quarters.

Tizmet was only the beginning. There were more dragons out there, wild but vulnerable to the bond just as she was. There would be more unsuspecting Riders out there. They needed a teacher who hadn't been crammed into a mold and would teach them to explore the bond in a safe place.

I would be their teacher. They would be my students. My heritage.

Flinor dove and grabbed for Tizmet. She spun away and left him, arrowing toward the sun.

'Tease.' I accused and amusement trickled from her. She goaded him and led him on but wasn't ready to mate again. She would be a difficult dragon to mate. She knew her worth and didn't need a male. She would only mate again when she wanted hatchlings, and I didn't know if she would even lay here in Northwing among Dragon Riders.

The gate's shadow fell over us, and Rafe gripped the reins with both hands, the only sign of his discomfort. A crowd lined the roads, peering at the parade. As we rode into view, cheers went up and the horse under me tensed and lowered its head. I offered a tight smile.

We were flanked by wounded soldiers bound in rags and dirty clothes. Women who were haggard and thin. Children in their teen years whooped and pumped their firsts, a dark maturity in their eyes. Their souls were too old for their bodies.

War was brutal.

But it was over.

A bellow shook the air and I ducked my head before grinning up at Tizmet as she flapped hard over the crowd, sending a gale that pulled at loose clothes. She flew low over the buildings, pivoting and aiming back at me.

'Don't scare the horse.'

A rumbling laugh boomed from her as she threw sparks over the crowd, maw open revealing row after row of sharp teeth. The crowd ate it up, and the horse under me was not alone as it shied away from her before she pulled up and flew at the sun once again.

"Nuisance," Rafe muttered, pulling his stallion clear of the horses that pranced nervously. Military stock or not, they weren't used to a dragon throwing sparks straight at them.

We settled into the fortress, the remnants of the Tennan sitting on the floor as we ate a hot meal of soup and bread. It wasn't much, but the land needed to heal and the farmers to return to their work before we could expect better rations.

The cold of the stone bit into my backside even through my riding skirts. Jam sat across from me, wounded leg stretched out in front of him. He had a brace of wood around it and I had given up attempting to heal it. Rafe and Tizmet found common ground in keeping me from using my magic.

If I thought they were bad when antagonizing each other, they were far worse when teamed up.

"How much excitement do you want?" Jam asked Blain with a laugh of disbelief.

Dane sat against the wall, eyes closed. His dark hair had grown out and flopped over his forehead. His arms were wrapped around his chest, his legs stretched out and crossed at the ankle. If it wasn't for the wrinkle between his brows, I would think he was asleep.

"More than you have," Blain beamed, sitting with his bodycurled around his bowl of soup like he could leech the warmth out of it.

"You almost died crossing the E'or," I pitched in.

"Ah, but I didn't die!" he chuckled, lifting the spoon to his lips and slurping down the broth.

"Where will you go?" I asked, shaking my head and leaning against Rafe's shoulder, trying to steal the warmth that still burned through his bare arm.

"Who knows. South?" He paused and tilted his head like he was thinking about it. "Southwing perhaps. They suffered when the Shadows hit them hard. Perhaps we'll see what's down there."

'They're running,' Tizmet commented. She had left, retreating to the caverns to bask in the warmth of the springs, but nosed about my thoughts.

'From what?'

'Their fate.'

The conversation drifted to sending word to Zeph and when the twins would leave. It hurt that they were leaving, but Blain and Dane were wild spirits. They couldn't be penned in. Perhaps when they were older and travel took more of a toll, they would settle.

Tizmet's words lingered in my mind.
What did fate have in store for them?

Epilogue

Four Years Later

Rafe

Cheers and shouting bombarded my ears. A bard nearby sang a terrible tune, and I tried to block out his clanging chords. People jostled my arms, and I reined in my irritation. Taking a steadying breath, I closed my eye.

"It's not that bad, Rafe."

The annoyance at the crowd faded at the sound of my name on those lips. Wisps of her white hair drifted around her small face, teased by the subtle breeze. She could braid it all she wanted, and still strays rebelled and escaped. Even her hair was a reflection of her. Freckles dusted her pale skin, congregating over her nose. A scar marred her cheek, but did nothing to dampen the sheer joy and life in her forest green gaze. Those eyes—so full of adventure and challenge.

Her lips quirked up in a smile as she tilted her head, much like her dragon would do.

"What is it?" she asked, scooting a little closer.

The heat in the amphitheater was stifling, but I couldn't push her away. I offered her a frown and dipped my chin. She didn't need to waste her worry on me, especially on the Summer Solstice.

"Rather be stabbing something with that sword of his," a fiery red-head called, her arched brow daring me to respond.

"Leave the man alone, Niehm."

Elenor patted Niehm's thigh, her cold gaze meeting mine—a silent order not to rise to the woman's antics. She might have walked slow and needed Niehm's help, and carried a blanket against the constant chill in her bones, but she had been the Master of Women once, and despite her age, still acted like it.

Next to Elenor, Willhelm gave our little group a stern look as he directed our attention to the amphitheater's center. A blanket of silence fell over the crowd, and Vy's hand pressed into my thigh as she leaned forward in her seat, craning for a better view. A snort of amusement came from one of the dragons perched near the roof, and from the smile that teased Vy's lips, I knew it was hers.

There, in the middle of the sand, sat a cluster of seven eggs. Encircling them, sitting cross-legged and still as stone, were seven young Chosen. Behind them, another fourteen more. The next generation of Dragon Riders.

The air stilled, not a breeze to mar the sound that echoed across Regent.

Crack!

The End

Thank-You

"So you see, you can't do everything alone." – Rosemary Clooney
I've done it. I published my first Trilogy. It's done. The End.

But I couldn't have done it without you.

Writing is one of those things that everyone can do. Anyone can put pen to paper, fingers to keyboard or voice to text—but no one can *make* anyone read. You joined my characters, and stayed by my side while I wrote this story—you took this adventure with me—and for that I am more thankful than you could ever comprehend.

Being an Indie Author is no simple task. It's overwhelming. It's like jumping into the ocean as a hurricane is blowing overhead and not knowing how to swim. I would have given up long ago if not for my husband who pushed me and Sarah Emmer who pulled me along and gave me the confidence. The Fate Unraveled Trilogy would still be a dream if not for Erynn Snell who took the time to take this confused writer, and taught me how to *let* my works be edited. She took the mess of my manuscripts and polished them to the gleam they are. She took my self-doubt and turned it into confidence. I want to thank Jennie—who pushed through my 20-some-odd first draft that was still raw—and read it, demanding more. You were my first "stranger" reader; your comments and enthusiasm helped push me to where I am today. Mariva—my dear Mariva. You are stronger than you know. Thank you so much for proofreading my books and pointing out all the things that didn't make sense. You are truly a Godsend!

I want to take the time to thank my school teacher. No matter how many times I went to her and said "I can't!", she taught me to persevere. Keep going. Never stop. Never give up.

Every single person in my life has a part in these books. This is not my success alone. This is ours.

The End of an Era

No more cliffhangers. No more reaching for the next book. No more Rafe and Avyanna. Their story has been told. They got their "Happily Ever After".

This has been a long journey, quite fast for you, dear reader—but for me it has been four years in the making. Back in 2020 during the pandemic that swept the world, I wrote the book I wanted to read. One turned into two, and two turned into three. What was a hobby turned into a part-time job, then a full time, then an overtime job. In three years of writing, and seven months of publishing—I have a trilogy out in the world.

Yes, you still have questions. What about Mik? The rest of the Tennan? Breathe easy, dear reader. We have not seen the last of Rinmoth.

"There will come a time when you believe everything is finished. That will be the beginning." – Louis L'Amour

"...even monsters have a beginning..."

M.A. Frick

M.A. Frick is a mere peasant.

Once upon a time, she read to escape the world. Now she writes to create worlds.

Not only the mother of worlds, but the mother of three children—she is joined by her husband who supports every adventure, no matter how absurd it may be.

The Password is: Po-ta-toes.